Celtic Witches Series

THE CONNELLY BOYS

CELTIC WITCHES, BOOK 1

LILY VELEZ

The Connelly Boys (Celtic Witches, Book 1)

Copyright © 2018 by Lily Velez

www.lilyvelezbooks.com

All rights reserved. No part of this book may be used or reproduced in any manner whatsoever without written permission from the author.

This book is a work of fiction. The names, characters, places, or events used in this book are the product of the author's imagination or are used fictitiously. Any semblance of characters or names to actual people, alive or deceased, is completely coincidental.

The verses used in the circle casting ritual featured in Chapter 41 are an adaptation of The Witches' Rune by Doreen Valiente and Gerald Gardner. No copyright infringement is intended.

Cover Art by Covers by Juan, www.coversbyjuan.com

ISBN 13: 978-0-692-18387-8

ISBN 10: 0-692-18387-6

1

Massive heart failure shouldn't have been possible at seventeen.

And yet here I was, navigating the hair-thin line between a normal heart rate and cardiac arrest.

Over two dozen boys stared at me, their intent gazes impaling me like enemy spears. My eyes slid to the only escape in the room, which was the very door I'd willingly walked through only seconds ago. I guessed that meant I only had myself to blame.

I shifted my weight from one foot to the other and bracketed my hands onto the straps of my backpack, knuckles white. Beside me, Professor Foley droned on to his pre-calculus class. Preoccupied as I was with ensuring my heart didn't burst from my chest, I only caught fragments.

"Remember what the headmaster said…

"…is to be treated with the utmost respect…"

"…will not tolerate…"

"…father is a much loved member of our faculty…"

Father. Right. The reason I was here at all. St. Andrew's Prep was a traditional all-boys Catholic boarding school in Ireland, the elite kind where students came from old money and were vying for spots at places like Oxford, Cambridge, Harvard, and Yale. The only other school in this God-forsaken town had closed years ago for lack of funding. So every year, in a show of charity, St. Andrew's opened its doors to a handful of locals, boys and girls alike, who wished to take advantage of its world-class education. This school year's scholarship students had already been selected, but lucky for me (and I used the word 'lucky' with no shortage of sarcasm), my dad, hotshot professor that he was here, had been able to pull some strings on my behalf.

"Miss Monroe, if you would…" Professor Foley cleared his throat. "Scarlet?"

I snapped out of my thoughts. The man was gesturing for me to assume a seat. I took a hesitant step forward.

As I did, a trident of lightning split the charcoal sky in two in an ear-splitting *crack*, the classroom windows momentarily glowing white. The sound sent my heart somersaulting. While the fluorescent lights above flickered, I quickly gathered my bearings. *Breathe*. Though I couldn't deny the raging storm outside was the perfect backdrop for my present state of misery.

Once the power righted itself, I surveyed the classroom to see what seats were vacant. Now that I was actually looking at them full-on, I saw there were all kinds of boys before me. Boys with wiry frames and boys built like oxen. Boys with flawless skin, boys with acne scars, boys with ruddy cheeks, boys with handsome, dark tans. And like me, they were all wearing the school's signature navy blue blazer with the crimson and gold insignia over the heart, which featured a lion over a shield and the school motto: *fiat lux*, let there be light.

Each desk sat two students, and I noticed more than one boy elbow his neighbor with a smirk and then glance in the direction of a desk at the room's dead center. I read the message loud and clear. Apparently this was the desk they'd all betted on me picking.

I could see why. Its single occupant was movie-star gorgeous. The only problem was he knew it. He knew it all too well. You could spot that kind of arrogance from a mile away. It was any wonder he sat alone at all, though maybe he'd forced his neighbor to sit elsewhere on today of all days, just for this opportunity.

I schooled my expression to keep the grimace off my face. *No thanks.* A guy like that would feel like he'd won something if a girl sat next to him, would view her choice like an invitation. While some girls might've counted it a fantasy to be one of only a few females at an all-boys school—and I'll admit, once upon a time, I would've counted myself among them—I'd made the decision long before arriving on Irish soil that I wouldn't give any amorous attentions the time of day. Because as soon as I finished my prison sentence here and graduated, I was heading straight back to the United States.

There were only two other vacant seats in the classroom. One was beside a red-faced boy who was sweating so much dark stains were developing at his armpits. I looked toward my last hope. It was a desk by the window, and its sole occupant was the only boy who wasn't paying me an iota of attention. Instead, with the side of his face at rest against a loose fist, he stared boredly at the wretched grayness outside. It seemed he couldn't care less whether the new student at school was a boy, a girl, or a polka-dotted extraterrestrial.

As such, and with great relief, I made my way toward him. There were snickers as I walked right past Mr. Movie Star, who tried to appear unfazed by the rejection and shot venomous looks at his classmates. I feigned obliviousness and continued on.

I pulled out my chosen chair, the slightly rusted feet scraping against the tile, and it was only then that my new neighbor finally regarded me.

My heart stalled. I was momentarily stunned by the look of him. There was a loveliness about his face, the kind you saw in paintings of angels. His brown hair was still wet, presumably from that morning's shower, and was styled in disarray as if mussed by the storm winds outside. But it was his eyes that most gave me pause. They were the lightest blue eyes I'd ever seen, like two clear lakes on a summer day.

He was clearly taken aback by my company, as if I'd yanked him out of a daydream. I offered him a tight but somewhat friendly and mildly apologetic smile as I sat. He stared back, his face completely devoid of expression. Then, without a single word, he went right back to looking out the window.

I blinked, feeling as if I'd come right up against a wall. *Okay...* So much for a warm reception. Maybe he preferred having a table all to himself, but would it have killed him to be slightly less rude? Whatever. I'd survive. I decided to ignore him right back and faced forward as Professor Foley began today's lecture.

Soft clicking filled the room, and I was surprised to find several boys recording notes on netbooks or tablets. As far as technology went, my laptop back at my dad's house was the same one I'd been using for the past six years. My mom and I hadn't been poor by any means back in Colorado, but annually upgrading to the latest gadgets hadn't exactly been in the budget either.

Mom...

A spark of pain stabbed my heart like a thorn, and all at once the flashes of memory came: the pink, paisley scarf wrapped around my mom's head, the incessant beep of hospital machines, the seemingly endless tables of bouquets and sympathy cards.

I pushed it all down immediately. *Not here.*

Desperate for distraction, I went old-school and pulled a

spiral-bound notebook out of my backpack to copy down the equations Professor Foley was writing on the dry-erase board up front, his marker squeaking against the white surface. He was teaching from a particular chapter in the class textbook, but he'd clearly forgotten he hadn't issued me a textbook of my own, and I wasn't about to raise my hand to request one. I'd just look off my neighbor's book for the time being.

Except that when I bothered to look, I realized his textbook remained unopened in front of him. Even now, he still stared out the window. Either he was having a killer of a bad day, or I was sitting beside the class slacker, who couldn't care less about impeccable grades.

I studied him more closely. He had pale, almost milky white skin. Nearly every square inch of him was covered in freckles, which gave him an especially boyish look. The backs of his hands, his neck, his jawline, his cheeks—freckles everywhere. I also realized his hair was more so a reddish-brown, closer to auburn. I tried to place his cologne. Strangely, he smelled like petrichor, that sweet, earthy fragrance that filled the air after a rainfall.

He was so engrossed in whatever he was looking at that I followed his line of sight. The storm was growing angrier still, lightning whipping across the dark skies. Rosalyn Bay had only three weather conditions: rainy, rainier, and rainiest. I couldn't even remember the last time I'd seen the sun since arriving here a few days ago.

Rivulets of water streaked across the windowpanes, miniature comets with long, crooked tails. In the shrieking wind, a tree's sinewy branch continuously tapped against the window beside us. It sounded like Morse code. Maybe I could send an S.O.S signal back.

A thick vine was wrapped around the branch. St. Andrew's was covered in ivy, so I didn't think much of it and was about to return my attention back to the lecture. And then it happened. I blinked, certain it was a trick of the lightning flashes, but no. As sure as I was sitting in a classroom filled with Catholic schoolboys, my eyes weren't deceiving me. The vine was *moving*.

Like a serpent slithering along its way, the vine inched across the length of the tree branch. My jaw unhinged as I gawked at the sight. *What on earth...?* The vine's leaves, already beginning to take on the rich gold and pumpkin hues of October, were moving too, but not in a way that was congruent with the wind speeds outside. As the other leaves in the tree canopy rattled violently from the assault of rain, the vine's leaves moved in a sort of floating way, like a fish's fins in water.

My eyes swung to my neighbor. Was he seeing this? I wasn't losing my mind, was I? Judging by the direction of his gaze, I wasn't. He was also focused on the vine. The only difference was he didn't look alarmed. On the contrary, he was as cool and composed as ever. Bored even, as if vines moving of their own volition was hardly a blip on his radar for strange and unlikely occurrences.

His left hand, the one closest to the window, was flat against the desk. Except for his index finger, which he'd lifted ever so slightly, eyes still trained on the vine like he was following its course. His finger drifted higher still, almost reaching a forty-five degree angle, and like a snake dancing for its charmer, the vine stopped at a fork in the branch and slowly began to rise, rearing back as if preparing to strike an unseen enemy.

"Oh my God." The words flew right out of my mouth.

When they did, the vine suddenly became inanimate, collapsing onto the branch as if the life had been instantly sucked out of it, and my neighbor, startled, quickly looked my way. As did two dozen other boys, whose heads snapped in my direction in a move that made me think of dogs coming to attention at the crackling sound of a bag of treats opening.

"Miss Monroe," said Professor Foley. "Is everything all right?"

My face burned. "Yes," I managed, nodding. "Sorry."

After a few, awkward moments, the lecture resumed and the other students slowly faced forward again. My neighbor, however, was still looking at me, but his expression had gone from startled to shuttered, revealing none of his thoughts.

I opened my mouth to whisper something, something to the effect of: *Did you see that? How on earth did that happen? Is there something in the water here?* But before I could, he reached for his textbook, flipping to the page written on the board up front, and buried himself in pre-calculus. Clearly the subject of the vine wasn't on the table for discussion.

I couldn't so easily dismiss what I'd witnessed, though. After all, I knew a thing or two about plants. Back home, I'd helped to start a community garden as part of a service project. I'd enjoyed it so much I'd pursued all things botanical in the years that followed: making terrariums, pressing flowers, decorating the windowsills of my home with potted perennials, and more. All that to say I'd never met a vine that behaved the way the one outside had. There was just no rational explanation for it.

For the rest of the class period, my neighbor didn't engage me in the least bit. He didn't even share his textbook. He simply proceeded to act as if I weren't there beside him. So when Professor Foley distributed quizzes for the final fifteen minutes of class (he excused me from taking one), I rehearsed how I would broach the subject.

From watching the boy write his name on his quiz in small script, I gathered his first name was Rory. It was all I gathered because, perhaps feeling watched, he threw a quick glance in my direction and I had to feign sudden interest in the composition of my gel pen.

I flipped to the last page in my notebook and started

doodling to let my mind wander, trying not to get distracted by the raindrops pummeling the roof and how they sounded more like paintball pellets. I risked a glance toward that unruly vine, but it still hung limp across the branch, as if it'd done so all along. I hadn't imagined the entire ordeal, had I?

Finally, the bell signaling the end of class sang out. It wasn't the electronic bell over an intercom like at my previous school. It was a traditional, round, silver bell with a small hammer beside it. It was loud and shrill and startled me out of my thoughts.

All around me, binders snapped close and boys zipped up backpacks as they prepared to head to their next class. Beside me, Rory completed his own quiz and slowly stood as he reviewed his answers. Perfect. Now I could ask him about the vine. I angled my body toward him. The movement caught his attention, and his gaze casually drifted my way, landing on my open notebook. Except when he saw my doodles, his entire body went rigid.

At his reaction, I looked down at them. There were a few simple daisies here and there with fat bumblebees and big-winged butterflies, but the majority of the page was taken up by a design I'd been drawing for as long as I could remember. It featured three spirals which sprouted from a shared center. I'd always liked it because it reminded me a little of a flower head.

For some reason, it was that very design that made Rory look stricken.

I started to ask him what was wrong, but before I could even get a word out, he yanked his backpack from the floor, handed in his quiz, and rushed out of the room, as if he couldn't get away from me fast enough.

2

"How has your first day been so far?"

When lunch time came, I opted to take my meal in my dad's empty classroom, preferring the awkwardness of his company over braving the gawking of hundreds of boys. Back at my old school, I hadn't exactly been completely invisible, but I definitely had spent most days flying under the radar, largely unknown by the majority of my peers. Here at St. Andrew's, the simple fact that I was of the fairer sex made me about as rare as a four-leaf clover.

As such, the attention around campus had been inescapable thus far. As I'd walked from class to class amidst all the locker slamming, horsing around, and cacophonous chatter, everyone would look up from what they were doing at some point or another to watch me. It was, needless to say, unsettling.

Especially when I'd learned there were probably less than a dozen girls currently attending the school, none of whom were in any of my classes so far. Apparently, most students had gone the online learning route after their school had closed. It was an option I would've loved to pursue myself, but my dad didn't feel comfortable leaving me home alone for eight hours a day, so that was that.

"Do they serve food like this every day?" I asked, deciding it best to avoid his question. Because the truth was my first day here had only magnified my homesickness. I moved around the Bolognese sauce covering my pasta. It looked like something a Michelin-starred chef might've prepared.

"Do you not like it? If you'd prefer to bring a packed lunch from now on, we can make a stop at the grocer's later today. I know we haven't gotten around to fully stocking up just yet, have we? Perhaps some deli meats for sandwiches? Is that something you'd like?"

It was something a parent wouldn't normally have to ask their child, but there was hardly anything normal about our situation. The truth was, though we were unmistakably related given our matching brown hair and eyes and similar facial features, we were practically strangers to each other. My dad had visited Colorado two or three times when I was little, and he'd sent me a birthday card with money and a kind, handwritten message inside every year, but I still barely knew anything about him, the type of things you'd know from living with a person all your life. Like what their favorite foods were.

Still, he was trying. I had to give him that. I forced a smile. "Yeah, that sounds good."

His shoulders relaxed, his face brightening. He felt he'd made headway, the gestures said, and he was happy about it, which only made me feel guilty. He obviously wanted me to be as comfortable as possible here. I hadn't told him of my plan to return to Colorado eventually, but for the time being, I could at least make a better effort at trying to build a relationship with him. Or at least the semblance of one.

"I nearly forgot to mention it," my dad said. "I'm afraid I have a faculty meeting this afternoon. You're welcome to wait for me in here if you'd like, but the meeting may potentially run long. You might have a better time enjoying today's rugby game instead. St. Andrew's will be playing one of its heated rivals: Xavier."

"Is it true you used to play rugby in college?" I suddenly remembered my mom telling me something of the sort years ago.

My dad's face slightly reddened. "Not at the collegiate level. It was a simple, recreational team, one a friend of mine insisted I join. I didn't last very long either. I sprained my ankle in our very first game. It was the beginning and end of any athletic hopes I might've entertained. I'm far more at home with my books."

This time, my smile, though faint, was genuine. That was one thing we had in common at least.

The classroom door swung open, and a curly-haired boy stepped inside. "Professor Monroe?" His accent was distinctly English, clipped and posh. Almost half the students at St. Andrew's were from outside of Ireland, hailing from all parts of the world.

"Ah, Thomas. Thank you for coming. Scarlet, this is Thomas Mooney. He's a student ambassador for St. Andrew's as well as a senior warden for one of our dorms. I've asked him to show you around the campus."

"Miss Monroe." Thomas strode over to where I sat and shook my hand in greeting as if we were closing on a business deal. "Shall we begin?"

I cast a final look at my pasta, which was already turning cold. "Sure," I said. "Lead the way."

It had stopped raining about half an hour ago, but the trees and awnings of St. Andrew's were still dripping. Despite it being the site of my captivity, even I had to confess the school was breathtaking to behold. It had the majestic façade of a medieval church with flying buttresses and stained glass windows, its gray stones masked with ivy. At every topmost corner, gargoyles were stationed, their fanged mouths gaping and their eyes trained skyward, as if awaiting a signal from heaven, and heavily ornamented spires punctured the sky like the lances wielded by brave knights. Arches towered above each doorway and passage, boasting decorative moldings covered with sculptures of angels and saints.

"St. Andrew's used to be a monastery," Thomas explained. "Most classes are still held in the Gothic-styled buildings. In the early twentieth century, when the school opened, new buildings were added to accommodate boarders and meet other needs."

We eventually made our way to a second-story balcony, where the entire campus unfolded before us. The neatly manicured, emerald lawns were separated into quads. The grass was still damp, glistening with beads of rain so that each quad looked like a field of pearls, but the wet grounds didn't stop any boys from enjoying their break from class.

Some used their blazers as blankets and sat on the grass with loosened ties to quietly eat their lunch and catch up on homework. Some played Frisbee, the ends of their striped scarves trailing behind them as they ran. Others talked and joked around in small groups under the canopies of oak trees that looked tall and wide enough to hold up the slate-gray sky, their dripping leaves as bright as peaches. Overall, the scene was something you'd expect to see in a school's full-color catalogue. Happy, rich students luxuriating in their happy, rich lives.

Thomas continued to intone a speech about campus history and which classes were where and so on and so forth. I could tell he'd given this tour probably a million times before because he recited everything as easily as breathing. Unfortunately, his delivery was in complete monotone. He was efficient, no doubt, but he wasn't exactly a storyteller. I found myself hoping this was the final stop in the welcome tour.

As Thomas segued into a lengthy monologue about faculty members, I spotted a boy coming down one of the walkways that weaved between the quads, a priest beside him. The priest was perhaps in his sixties, red-faced, round, and bespectacled. The perfect candidate to play the town Santa come December. But I didn't focus too much on him. It was the boy who stole my attention.

Because he was unbelievably, breathtakingly, heart-wrenchingly beautiful. Leave-you-speechless beautiful. Momentarily-forget-your-name beautiful. He was tall, easily over six feet, and he was athletically built, with short, dark brown hair done up in a messy quiff and a long, masterfully carved face that could've graced the posters of cologne ads.

I'd seen the St. Andrew's uniform on countless boys today, but on *this* boy, it was like the blazer and pants and crimson-and-gold-striped tie had been tailored just for him. It made him look elegant and stately, and he radiated power. I watched as those gathered on the quads immediately quieted down at the sight of him, turning to watch him pass and then whispering amongst themselves once he did. The boy, however, engaged only with the priest, nodding along with something the older man was saying, one hand at rest against the messenger bag slung over his shoulder, its brown leather well-worn.

I couldn't take my eyes off him. He was quite possibly the most stunning boy I'd ever seen. If Rory had looked like an angel, then this boy most assuredly looked like a god.

But there was something else, something I couldn't quite place until he was nearly beneath the balcony. There were dark patches under his eyes, as if he hadn't slept for days. Though he spoke with the priest, he was also somewhere else, his thoughts faraway. He almost looked haunted. Beautiful and broken all at once.

Beside me, Thomas dragged a sigh out of his lungs. "Of course. Why am I not surprised?" Disapproval sat on his face, though I didn't know if it was because I'd gotten distracted or because of whom I'd gotten distracted by.

"His name's Jack Connelly." I guessed it was the latter. "St. Andrew's royalty. It seems the prince has finally returned to the plebeians."

"He's a prince?"

"God, no. But he might as well be with the way these mindless sycophants flock around him."

As he said it, the priest gave Jack a comforting pat on the shoulder before leaving. Almost immediately, those on the quads drifted over to Jack to greet him.

"You don't seem too thrilled about his return."

Thomas shrugged. "It's nothing personal really. We simply don't swim in the same circles. Jack is captain of the varsity rugby team, which I suspect he'll lead to finals once again this year. He's the quintessential boarding school student. Smart, athletic, richer than God, and all but worshipped by those who want to be just like him."

The way he said that last bit, it was like the words left a bitter taste in his mouth.

"He and his brothers have got virtually all of St. Andrew's wrapped around their fingers," he went on. "It's a disgrace, if you ask me. In my opinion, most of the tossers here could stand to muster up a bit more dignity."

I didn't respond. I didn't like it when people put others down, especially behind their backs. Besides, Thomas's acerbic tone seemed to stem from nothing but envy.

"Why are so many people coming up to comfort him?" Several of the boys below were putting a consoling hand to

Jack's shoulder or arm just as the priest had done, their faces sympathetic, and though some had been boisterous just minutes ago, in Jack's presence, they were muted versions of themselves.

"Jack's been out of class for some two or three weeks now," Thomas explained. "There was a tragedy in the family."

My heart grew sore at the words. "What kind of tragedy? Do you know?"

"Oh, yes. Everyone in Rosalyn Bay does. Maurice Connelly, the family patriarch and Jack's grandfather, was found dead at the rocky bottom of one of our famous coastal cliffs."

I whipped my head in his direction, my stomach flipping as if I'd missed a step on a staircase. "What happened?"

Thomas shrugged. "All evidence seems to point to it being a deliberate act on Maurice's part. It certainly is the explanation that makes the most sense. At least where the Connellys are concerned."

Deliberate. Now my stomach twisted. Good thing I hadn't eaten. "What do you mean it's what makes the most sense?"

"There's a train of whispers about the Connellys that has traveled throughout Rosalyn Bay for years. In short, people say they're cursed."

I stared at him. "Cursed."

"It sounds positively primeval, I know, but Rosalyn Bay has always been a bit behind the times when it comes to superstitions. Nonetheless, it's hard to ignore the stories."

"And what are the stories exactly?"

"The more popular ones? That madness runs in their blood, that trouble follows them wherever they go, that they're all doomed to meet an early end."

I almost laughed. Was he serious, or was he just trying to scare me? I'd known people who held superstitions before, of course. People who didn't like the number thirteen or opening umbrellas indoors or being anywhere near a black cat. This, however, seemed a bit excessive. Hyperbolic even. A little too doomsday for me. Besides, I didn't believe in curses, just bad luck.

"Why would anyone say things like that?"

"Let's just say the matter of Maurice is far from being the first tragedy to come their way."

"If people legitimately think they're cursed," I challenged, "then why are so many boys expressing their sympathies?" Even now, boys continued to swarm around Jack and offer their condolences as opposed to outright avoiding him like the plague.

Thomas continued watching the scene below, the set of his mouth clearly indicating he found the sight repugnant. "The students here rarely commune with the locals, so most haven't fallen privy to the stories. Instead, they run to the Connellys like obedient spaniels. How very much like the moth drawn to the flame, wouldn't you agree? But a word of warning if I may, Miss Monroe. Steer clear of the Connelly boys, yes? It can only end badly for you if you don't."

3

I'd never seen a rugby game before, so I was far from prepared for what I witnessed. First of all, I hadn't anticipated the zealous displays of team pride. The bleachers across the way, which had to be forty or fifty feet high, overflowed with St. Andrew's students, and now out of class and out of their proper gentleman jackets, they looked every bit the part of boisterous and rambunctious teen boys.

They hollered at the top of their lungs whenever St. Andrew's scored a point, booed whenever Xavier did, laughed, name-called, made gestures unbecoming of Catholic schoolboys, and more or less made a circus of their spectating. Some of them had even painted their faces in the school colors: one half crimson, one half gold.

A student band taking up the first few center rows merrily belted out popular songs throughout the game, but during tense moments of play, they filled the air with what was unmistakably traditional Irish fighting music, spirited and dynamic and filled with enough explosive energy to probably fuel an atomic bomb. And then the boys in the bleachers would really lose it, jumping to their feet and roaring as a lion mascot with sharp fangs and a regal mane ran up and down the side of the field, waving its paws to hype them up even further. With faces painted as they were, and with the pounding drumbeat from the band, which I could feel pulsating around my heart, I might've thought I was watching a battle between Viking warriors.

The chaos was part of the reason I elected to watch the game from the away team side, which was empty save for a few Xavier coaches and benched players. That, and I'd crossed paths with Mr. Movie Star from pre-calculus when I'd arrived at the rugby field. He clearly hadn't gotten the message this morning because he'd smirked at me and started to close the distance between us in an overconfident saunter, his eyes combing over the tights I wore under my plaid skirt. A real class act, that one. I'd turned around and headed straight for enemy lines before I had to endure whatever pickup line he'd prepared for me.

But what most surprised me about rugby? That calling it a contact sport was clearly an understatement. These boys were out for blood. I cringed with every *smack* as the boys recklessly threw themselves against each other. Some players donned mouth guards, but with the exception of light padding on the shoulders of each shirt, there was nothing to protect the players from injuries. No one even wore a helmet.

Oddly enough, no one seemed to care either. Back in the United States, it wasn't unusual to see athletes feign the extent of their injuries during televised games. Here, it was more about pretending you *weren't* hurt, as boys would insist on continuing to play the game in spite of blood, cuts, and bruises.

Nevermind the trash-talk. The referees constantly had to pull boys apart in the midst of burgeoning, foul-mouthed arguments. The guiltiest among them was Number 22, a boy with short, dirty blond hair and fire in his veins. His rough-around-the-edges attitude clearly warned in red flashing lights that you'd better not cross him if you knew what was good for you.

My best friend Natalie back in Colorado would've called his bad-boy vibe "hot as hell."

If it was true what they said about Irish tempers, he was clearly the poster child for them. When an Xavier player tackled him down at one point, Number 22, practically baring his teeth, shot up to his feet, balled a fist in his opponent's shirt to yank him up, and then shoved him so hard the Xavier boy tripped over himself and fell. Number 22, not even done, not even having begun, went for him again.

"Connor!" Jack yelled, roughly grabbing the crook of Number 22's elbow to firmly turn him around.

It didn't take very many words from Jack to get Connor's head back in the game, who stormed away from his victim muttering something under his breath. Probably a string of obscenities. Jack pinched the bridge of his nose as if to keep an incoming migraine at bay before offering a hand to help the Xavier boy to his feet.

It was clearly a familiar dance between Jack and Connor, as was the way they played on the field. Connor was almost always at Jack's side, ready for a pass, ready to defend his captain. More than once, they'd exchange a look, and one would nod, knowing exactly what his teammate was communicating.

Jack was definitely in his element on the field. He was faster than any of the other boys, dodging his opponents with flawless grace. The movement of the muscles in his well-toned thighs was like poetry in motion, like gears in an impeccably designed machine turning and shifting in perfect harmony. He looked so different out of his school uniform. In the rugby team's crimson jersey, black shorts, and black, knee-high socks, he'd gone from looking like a prince to now looking like a soldier. And still with that commanding presence about him.

More than once, my heart leapt as if jumping hurdles. I mentally chided myself but ultimately excused my heart its betrayal. It wasn't the poor thing's fault Jack was devastatingly attractive.

In the second half of the game, with St. Andrew's in the lead, Xavier apparently decided to turn up the heat, ramming into their opponents with both anger and relish whenever possible. Three of their players went for Connor during one play, slamming into him like wrecking balls. I winced at the impact. It would've been enough to have me seeing stars for days. I didn't expect Connor to rise as quickly as he did, lip bleeding and all.

"Ah, hard luck, mate," one of the Xavier boys called out, grinning.

Connor leapt for him, but a referee intervened right on time, awarding the guilty parties a foul and St. Andrew's a penalty kick.

By the next play, Connor had reined in his anger, a decision clearly made in his dark eyes. Xavier had the ball now, and one of the boys who'd charged into Connor earlier was breaking for the goal line. Connor was on him like a fuming bull after a red flag.

At the speeds they were going, they abandoned all their teammates and the referees behind. It seemed to be a part of Connor's strategy, as did the way he gradually coaxed the Xavier boy toward my side of the field, completely isolating him from not just his teammates but pretty much everyone else. When they were just about to zip right past me, the Xavier player still a few feet out of Connor's reach, Connor brought his hand low in front of him, palm facing down, and did a strange flicking motion with two of his fingers. Immediately, the Xavier boy cried out and dropped to the grass fast like a boneless doll.

Connor stepped back as referees, having finally caught up, rushed to the fallen player and tried to make sense of what had happened. One toed at a shallow depression in the ground, which the Xavier boy had apparently stepped into, causing his injury and fall. I hadn't noticed it there before.

Connor kept his blasé expression in check as the player was carried off the field by two teammates, but there was a dangerous gleam in his eyes. Jack materialized beside him, and the two exchanged a look. Jack's was disapproving. Connor's was along the lines of something else entirely, as if to say, *Does it look like I give a damn?*

I didn't have much time to think about it because the game was already underway again. The tension between the teams was electric now, and when the new play began, the field became complete and utter chaos as many things happened at once. Xavier kept passing the ball from player to player in a dizzying round of keep away that was trying their opponent's patience. As this was going on, several Xavier boys went for rivals they'd had bad blood with since the game first started, picking them off one-by-one until there were numerous different arguments exploding like firecrackers all around the field. But all of this was just a distraction, because the team's true motive became apparent when half a dozen boys in Xavier's blue and silver jerseys suddenly beelined for Jack.

Jack, who'd stolen possession of the ball seconds earlier, only had enough time to register their approach before they smashed into him like a moving concrete wall. A referee peeled the boys off Jack one by one and checked him for injuries. The hit had to have been bone-breaking. There was no way Jack would walk away from it without at least a concussion.

The boys in the bleachers were in an uproar, outraged that Xavier would have the audacity to bring down their captain. Connor was already in the guilty parties' faces, and though I couldn't hear the words leaving his mouth over the cacophony of his classmates, I'm pretty sure his colorful phrases would've made all the school mothers clutch their pearls.

The referee helped Jack to his feet, securing an arm around him as he led him toward the St. Andrew's benches, Jack slightly limping the whole way. Before they cleared the field, though, absolute pandemonium broke out. I didn't know who threw the first punch (my bet was on Connor), but the scene before me quickly devolved into a mess of right hooks, shoves, and insults. All the adults on duty rushed headlong into the mayhem, disentangling blue jerseys from crimson ones or staunching the flow of St. Andrew's students to the field.

Jack, meanwhile, was clearly in too much pain to help quell the revolt. He continued limping toward the bench, and then he continued on right past it, straying to the side of the bleachers. Once there, he leaned down and pressed his fingertips to his ankle, massaging it slightly, a grimace on his face. He stayed like that for a few seconds. When he straightened, he rotated his foot in circles and then tested his weight on it. There was still discomfort on his face, but at least he could stand on the foot now.

For a moment, he leaned back against the side of the bleachers and closed his eyes. The tired look hadn't left his eyes, nor had the dark patches under them. It looked like he had the weight of the world on his shoulders. I couldn't imagine what it'd felt like for him to receive the news about his grandfather, especially if they were close. Add to that whatever gossip his family had to endure thanks to Rosalyn's Bay affair with superstitions.

How small-minded and ridiculous to call a family cursed just because fate had dealt them a bad hand of cards a few times. Based on that logic, I guessed I was practically cursed too. Losing your mother, being uprooted from the only life you knew, moving thousands of miles away from friends to live with a father who was completely foreign to you. Yeah, that definitely checked a few boxes. Really, though, who didn't have misfortunes in life?

Jack detached from the side of the bleachers and disappeared behind the structure. He probably needed a few moments to himself before rejoining his teammates, who were still going at it on the field. I started to turn to make my way back inside the school, figuring my dad's faculty meeting had to be over by now.

But then one of the benched Xavier players, who I was pretty sure hadn't been there a moment ago and who for whatever reasons hadn't joined the big fight, rose and strode in Jack's direction, the set of his shoulders filled with purpose. As he rounded the edge of the bleachers to follow after Jack, he slid something out from an inside pocket of his team jacket. I only caught what it was because of the brief glint of light off silver.

A knife.

4

I never ran so fast in my life.

I was on the other side of the field in seconds. While I'd thought to recruit a referee or coach or teacher for help, one glimpse at the commotion on the field told me it'd be a challenge. For one, they probably wouldn't hear me over the roaring din of arguing boys. More importantly, it would waste too much time. Jack needed help *now*. Arriving even a second late could undoubtedly end badly.

I obviously wouldn't be able to physically stop the rogue Xavier player myself, but I was hoping my presence would be enough to deter him. With a witness on the scene, maybe he'd lose his nerve and back down from his demented plan.

Seriously, all this over a rugby game?

"Spare me the pleasantries," the rogue player was saying when I finally stepped behind the bleachers. "There's a price on your head, and I intend on collecting it."

It was like a whole new world back here. All the central beams and cross bars made it seem like I was traipsing through the skeletons of uncompleted skyscrapers. I quietly crept over discarded bags of potato chips (or 'crisps,' as they called them here), a scattering of cigarette butts, and broken wooden pallets, wrinkling my nose against the stench emanating from a row of portable toilets to my right. I could still hear the clamor from the rugby field, but it wasn't as overpowering, as if someone had lowered the volume on the entire scene.

"I'm not going anywhere until the situation with my grandfather is resolved." Jack. His voice was melodic. He spoke in a faint but beautiful lilt, the words gracefully sliding up and down like boats riding the ocean waves.

I was only a few yards away from them now. I drew closer and hid behind a beam to continue listening.

"There's nothing you can do for Maurice."

"You know I don't believe that."

"I couldn't care less what you believe," Rogue said, tightening his grip on the knife. The blade was saw-toothed, and the handle was fashioned out of a carnivorous animal's jawbone. "Your time's up whether you like it or not. Surely you've made peace with your fate by now, as have your brothers. Unless..." He tilted his head in an animalistic way, studying Jack for a moment. Then a sneer split across his face. "That's it, isn't it? They don't know. You haven't told them what you've done. Oh, this is delicious."

Jack's eyes hardened, a shadow passing over his face.

"I wonder, Jack. Who will be their keeper when you're Underneath? I suppose there's only one way to find out." He rushed forward in a blur of movement, quicker than a king cobra's strike, the knife coming down fast in an arc of silver. Jack shot out his arms and caught the boy's wrist. The point of the knife was no more than an inch or two from his face.

I wasn't sure what got into me. Before I'd even made up my mind to do something, my body was already springing into action. I charged at Rogue and threw my weight into his side to knock him off balance. The impact jolted my skeleton. Every bone in my body felt like a Xylophone bar that had just been struck hard by a mallet. It probably would've hurt less to ram into a statue made of stone.

"What's this?" Rogue turned my way, upper lip curling as he made a sound like a quick growl. For the briefest moment, I could've sworn his eyes were as red as rubies, but it had to be a trick of the light. He paused to study me. The way his gaze raked my body put frost in my veins. "Well, now, you look like a tasty thing."

"Step back, or I'll call the police!" I yanked my phone from my pocket and shoved it in his direction lest he think I was bluffing. Granted, given Rosalyn Bay's notoriously spotty cell signals, it would probably take me half a dozen attempts to actually connect with the police, but I was counting on him not considering that.

Jack used the distraction to tackle the boy from behind. They both crashed to the ground in a loud thud and struggled against each other for possession of the knife. One of the sharp canines of the jawbone handle dug into Jack's palm, drawing blood. Grinning like a maniac, Rogue applied more pressure and the tooth sank deeper into Jack's skin. Jack cried out in pain, and Rogue seized the opportunity to shove Jack onto his back and come on top of him.

My eyes darted around me, looking for a weapon. I ran to the discarded wooden pallets and pulled at one of the slats to break it off. It took a few tries, but the board finally cracked at the middle and came free. I shot back to the boys, angled the board over my shoulder like a batter preparing for the pitch, and then I swung at Rogue's head with all my might.

My weapon shattered on impact into dozens of splintery shards, as if I'd hit a brick wall. I stared dumbfoundedly at the remaining piece in my grip. It was no bigger than a stake.

"You're going to regret that," Rogue snarled. Forgetting Jack, he leapt to his feet and lunged for me with the knife.

Just as his hands were about to fall on me, the stake flew out of my grip as if an invisible force had yanked it free. It drove its point into the boy's neck. He roared, rearing back to yank the stake free. I looked wide-eyed between my now empty hand and the stake, flabbergasted. How had *that* happened?

I wasn't about to stick around to find out. I raced past Rogue to get to Jack, whose hand was upraised toward us as if he'd been trying to reach for something. There was what looked to be a burn scar peeking out from under his black, terry cloth wristband, but I didn't see it for long because his hand fell flat to the earth as I approached.

He was still on the ground, one arm curled protectively around his midsection. I sank to my knees beside him. He was covered in dirt and cuts, some of which were mildly deep lashes.

"Jack, are you all right?" It felt strangely intimate to use his name when we hadn't as of yet been properly introduced. I touched his shoulder, and a peculiar, warm buzz filled my fingertips.

His eyes skated right past me, though, and grew in size. "Watch out!"

I twisted around just in time to see Rogue storming for us, his knife at the ready. He was too close. There was no time to get to my feet and stop him. With only seconds left, I threw up an arm to block my face.

And then a blinding white light exploded in front of me.

I flinched, thinking at first a shotgun had gone off. My palm was scorching hot for a string of seconds, but the sensation quickly abated. I looked at my palm, but there was no injury to explain the heat I'd felt. When I lowered my arm, Jack and I were alone. Rogue had completely vanished. In his wake, plumes of quickly fading smoke as black as ink drifted in the air.

What...?

"Where did he go?" I leapt to my feet and spun in wild circles, trying to spot him. There was no way he could've disappeared that quickly. My heart rattled in my rib cage like a trapped bird flapping its wings in a riot. He had to be hiding behind one of the beams, waiting for the perfect moment to strike. But as much as my eyes darted around to catch him, he was nowhere to be found. It was as if he'd just evaporated.

There was a moan behind me. I startled, and then I realized it was only Jack. He was sitting up, wincing at his injuries. I returned to him, kneeling in the dirt.

With immediate danger out of the way, I couldn't help but take in this close-up view of him. His eyes were the color of fine cognac hit by sunlight. He had a light sprinkle of freckles on his face, two of which were under his left eye in an almost perfectly vertical line like dots on a domino. There was also a very masculine smell about him, a combination of wood, forests, and newly turned earth. I kept going back to those eyes, though. Framed by long, dark lashes, they were deep and soulful, like the eyes of someone who'd lived many lives, who'd seen far too much. It was easy to see how someone could get lost in them, could drown in the hypnotic velvetiness of them.

It wasn't until he spoke that I snapped out of my thoughts.

"How did you do that?" he asked. His tone was one of awe, and he looked utterly confused.

That made two of us. I shook my head. "How did I do what?"

His eyes searched my face, as if trying to place me. "Who are you?"

I guessed he hadn't heard about me yet. Thomas had said Jack had been out of school for some weeks, so it was likely he'd missed the memo. "I'm Professor Monroe's daughter. Scarlet. I go here now."

His eyes were calculating as he registered my response. Then it was like his thoughts snagged on something. "Wait. Your name is *Scarlet*?"

"Uhm, yeah." Maybe he had heard of me then.

Except the look he now fixed on me was one of total disbelief. In fact, he outright gawked at me, which only made me feel ridiculously self-conscious. Maybe I hadn't been what he was expecting. My face grew hot at the thought.

Jack, meanwhile, had seemingly forgotten how to speak. His gaze was fastened to me with no signs of giving way. I could tell his mind was somewhere far away, trying to make sense of something. What, I didn't know. He looked dazed, though, and I started to worry he'd won himself a concussion during that last play after all.

"Jack? Jack!" A coach nudged me out of the way, his eyes growing large at the blood on Jack's hand. "What are you doing back here? We need to have your injuries looked at."

I rose and backed away. "There was another boy—"

"It was nothing," Jack cut me off, apparently not wanting anyone to know about the attack.

The coach looked me over, finally realizing who I was. "Another boy? Where?"

Jack caught my gaze and gave a quick shake of his head. He didn't want me to share what had happened. The question was why? That Xavier boy could've killed him. And me. He needed to be apprehended.

Even so, I hesitated. Jack clearly had his reasons for remaining tight-lipped. Rationally, it didn't make any sense, and I was nothing if not a rational person. But a well of feeling deep in my gut told me to trust his judgment nonetheless, crazy as it was.

"On the field, I mean," I told the coach after a few brief seconds. "There were some other boys who were injured too, I think."

The man frowned, probably thinking I was a bit soft in the head. "Right." He turned his back on me to help his star player to his feet. "Come on, Jack. The medic's waiting."

As the coach led him away, Jack glanced over his shoulder at me. His eyes remained stuck on me the whole way, and they were still looking for answers.

5

The next morning, I crossed the asphalt to the charter bus idling in the St. Andrew's parking lot. Professor Byrne, who taught history, was whisking his students away to the countryside this morning for a hands-on lesson. As I waited in line to board the bus, my eyes strayed to one of the school's colossal oak trees. Beneath its amber canopy, two boys loitered.

My heart missed a beat. The taller boy was Jack. He was stuffing a textbook into the messenger bag at his side while he spoke to his companion. At first, I thought it was Connor. They had the same dirty blond hair. Then, when the boy happened to glance to the side, I realized it couldn't be him. This boy's hair was longer, reaching the tops of his ears in a shaggy style befitting a surfer.

How did you do that?

Jack's question had stayed with me long after the rugby game. How had I done *what* exactly? And what was with the way he'd acted once I'd told him my name? Though honestly, the answers to those questions were the least of my worries. I'd hardly gotten any sleep last night, my evening instead fraught with nightmares about red-eyed boys approaching me with strange-looking knives. How had the rogue Xavier player disappeared so quickly? And why had he wanted to hurt Jack in the first place? Nevermind his feral behavior or that strange light and exploding noise. It was enough to make my head spin.

I was so lost in my thoughts I didn't realize I was staring. Until Jack's friend turned and met my eyes full on, as if he'd felt the weight of my gaze. Jack was now looking my way too.

"Are you getting on?" a voice behind me asked.

I faced forward. I was next in line and there was a gap of a few yards between me and the bus. Wonderful. How long had I been standing there like an idiot with my eyes trained on Jack? Cheeks burning, I hurried onto the bus.

I didn't want to spend too long deciding on a seat. The sooner I picked one, the sooner I could escape all the attentive gazes aimed at me. Hopefully, it'd only take a few more days for the novelty of a new female student to wear off.

A boy with hair as black and shiny as polished obsidian watched me with an open, friendly face. He was sitting by himself.

I approached him. "Is this seat taken?"

He threw a quick glimpse out his window, presumably to check if whatever friend he was saving the seat for was in the dwindling line outside. Then he gestured to the empty space, as if to say, *It's all yours.*

"Thanks." I sank down, heaving a long breath I didn't realize I'd been holding. "I'm Scarlet, by the way."

"I know," he said, smiling. "Liam Collins Misaki." He offered his hand.

I shook it. "Does everyone here introduce themselves so properly?"

He laughed softly at that. His dark eyes were warm and

expressive, crinkling at the corners. "You know, I never really noticed that, but you're right. I suppose it's instilled in us from a young age. How are you enjoying St. Andrew's so far?" His was a sing-song accent with stretched vowels and slightly rolled *R*'s.

I groaned in response to his question.

"Extraordinarily well, I see," he said, laughing again. "We haven't entirely put you off, though, have we?"

His laughter tugged the edges of my mouth into a soft smile. "I just haven't fully processed it yet, I don't think. It's been an eventful twenty-four hours. I may have to get back to you on that."

"Take all the time you need," he said. "You're from the States, aren't you? I've heard that's where some of the oldest trees in the world are located. Is it true?"

My smile lengthened. Impressive. "As a matter of fact, yes. They're in the White Mountains of California. Thousands of years old. One of them was actually alive around the time Stonehenge was being built."

"Is that right? How remarkable."

"Are you a fellow nemophilist?"

"A what?"

Now it was my turn to laugh. "I guess not. It's just a person who loves forests."

"You could say I've been developing a fondness for them as of late. I have a friend who loves nature. Particularly ancient trees. Hence my earlier question. Though I have to say, we have some breathtaking forests and groves right here in Ireland. This isn't your first time in the country, is it?"

"Actually, it is. My parents met at Trinity College in Dublin as students. My mom had been studying abroad for a year as an undergrad. When she found out she was pregnant with me, moving to Ireland wasn't really an option for her, and since my dad was in the middle of his graduate studies, she didn't want to pressure him into relocating to the United States. So they amicably went their separate ways, and my mom raised me on her own in Colorado."

I didn't normally bare my life story to people like this, but something about Liam made me feel comfortable, like I was speaking with a friend I'd known for years and not just for a few minutes.

"Speaking of which, I'm very sorry for your loss," Liam said. "About two weeks ago, they gathered us all for a special assembly to explain the situation since we typically don't get new students transferring in mid-term. Were you and your mother close?"

An invisible fist squeezed my heart. "Very," I said softly. "Between you and me, I was surprised to learn she wanted me to live with my dad once she was gone. It's not that he was ever entirely out of the picture, but my best friend's family would've been more than happy to take me in for my last two years of high school. With my dad's blessing, I stayed with them for close to four months after my mom's passing while arrangements were being made for the funeral, the sale of the house, and my move abroad. I don't have any other close family, so they've always been like relatives to me. As for my dad, our relationship is pretty much non-existent."

"Maybe your mother hoped to change that."

"Maybe."

The last of our group filed onto the bus, among them the priest I had spotted yesterday with Jack, whose name I learned to be Father Nolan. I was disappointed to discover Jack himself wouldn't be joining us, but the boy he'd been conversing with under the oak tree currently made his way down the aisle.

His eyes were a striking electric blue, bright and lively and filled with mischief. His hair fell slightly over them, and he casually jerked his head to the side to get the fringe out of his lashes. He had impossibly flawless looks the likes of a teen heartthrob, but there was something roguish about him too that I couldn't quite place. Maybe it was the smirk tucked into the corner of his mouth, hinting at a rascally nature.

He winked at me in passing as if we were in on a secret. I couldn't help my cheeks from pooling red, still embarrassed he and Jack had caught me staring earlier.

"Lukifer!" some boys cheered at his arrival. He slapped hands with them and sat a few rows behind me.

"His name's *Lukifer*?" I asked Liam.

Liam smiled. "No, that's only a friendly moniker. His actual name is Lucas, though most call him Luke."

The last person to board was none other than Rory from my pre-calculus class. His auburn hair was as disheveled as it'd been yesterday, and judging by how quickly his chest rose and fell, my guess was he'd woken up mere minutes ago and had raced across campus to catch the bus. He ambled down the corridor, eyes flitting from one classmate to the next as if looking for someone in particular.

When he neared where Liam and I were sitting, he paused for the slightest moment. His gaze switched from Liam to me. His face was perfectly blank, totally unreadable, but as he continued past us, I caught the slightest ember of something in those sapphire eyes as a muscle feathered in his jaw.

He was bothered by the sight of me. It was like a stab to the heart. No one wanted to be disliked. What had I done to offend him? Maybe he was still peeved I'd sat next to him in class yesterday. Or maybe he was still weirded out by my drawings for whatever reason.

I'd still intended on asking him about that, not to mention

the vine, but now I was getting the vibe I should simply drop the matter and leave him be. It'd probably be best if I sat somewhere else in class tomorrow too.

And here I'd thought today would be an improvement from yesterday. Clearly I'd been very, very wrong.

6

The drive to our destination didn't take more than half an hour. I hadn't yet seen much of Rosalyn Bay, but I wasn't surprised to discover just how remote the town's outer bands really were. We cruised by pastures framed by sagging, wooden fences where sheep silently grazed. We passed crumbling, stone houses topped with thatch roofs and abandoned lots overflowing with rusting car and ship parts. Miles unfolded between one cottage and the next so that I wasn't even sure the term 'neighbor' was appropriate. It was definitely a far cry from suburbia.

There were almost no traffic lights and very few road signs, and of the signs that stood, none of them were in English.

"Irish Gaelic," Liam explained. "Rosalyn Bay is part of the Gaeltacht, regions in Ireland where Irish Gaelic's still spoken as a first language. Although here inside the country, it's simply called Irish."

Once we reached our destination, Professor Byrne and Father Nolan led us on a trek across the sloping greens of a cemetery. The mist-covered grounds were expansive, seeming to unroll for eternity toward the horizon. I crossed my arms to incubate warmth against the whistling winds, though the chill more so came from our surroundings: above-ground tombs, mausoleums covered in lichen and moss, and Celtic crosses and towering stone angels standing guard over their dead. It wasn't really my scene. Especially given how eerily silent the place was, the only sound the crunch of dry autumn leaves under our footsteps.

After a while, I picked up on a trend. Every resting place had a metal cup beside it, into which was set a white flower with six points like a star. I recognized it immediately.

"What's with all the asphodels?" I wondered aloud.

Since Liam and I were near the front of the group, Father Nolan overheard me and answered with a gentle, grandfatherly smile. "The locals believe it helps guide the spirits of the deceased into the afterlife."

"You'll also notice the occasional wreath made of blackberry, ivy, and rowan hung on some headstones," added Professor Byrne.

"What do they do?"

"They're believed to drive away demons."

The red eyes from my nightmares came to mind, and my heart leapt. I pushed the image away immediately.

We crossed the vastness of the cemetery and surmounted one last hill, and then the sight waiting for us on the other side took my breath away. There were rows upon rows of towering, free-standing stones waiting for us like giant soldiers frozen mid-invasion.

"As we're currently studying the Neolithic period in class," Professor Byrne said, guiding us to the stretch of land below, "it's only proper we pay homage to perhaps the most well-known artifacts from that time in history: menhirs. The word comes from the Welsh for 'long stone.'"

The stones reached more than four times my height. For some reason, I found them unnerving, a chill sliding down my back. It didn't help that the way the stones were arranged created long alleys, allowing the biting, cold winds to better course through. My hair whipped all about my face until I eventually pulled it back into a ponytail.

"Menhirs are located all across Europe and Britain," Professor Byrne went on. "They can be found standing solitarily, as part of stone circles, or in clusters such as these here. Though the purpose they served remains unknown, there's an abundance of theories: memorial monuments, territorial markers, sacrificial altars."

Sacrificial altars? Gooseflesh covered my arms, and I nearly shivered.

"Of course, these particular menhirs are unfortunately tainted with a dark history. As monotheistic religion spread, many Celts retreated to Ireland and Britain to avoid persecution. Rosalyn Bay was one of their last strongholds, a sanctuary where they could practice their nature-based way of life in peace.

"But the conquerors eventually caught up with them and slew an entire village of Celts on this very land. They were particularly brutal toward the druids, who held a high place in Celtic society as priests. Then, as recently as a few centuries ago, tragedy struck again when witches believed to be the very descendants of those druids were burned at stakes erected in front of the largest stones. As such, these menhirs have borne witness to some truly heinous acts."

My stomach churned. So much death, so much bloodshed. And to what end? We'd studied the Salem Witch Trials back at my old school, and it was an accepted fact that persecutions like that had been fueled by nothing more than irrational fear and mass hysteria, with the accused typically being people who were outliers of society. Besides, everyone knew magic-wielding witches only existed in fairytales.

"Mr. Gallagher, is there a problem?"

Mr. Gallagher was none other than Mr. Movie Star from yesterday. He was standing close to one of the stones, snickering with two friends. "We were just wondering about the whole burning-at-the-stake matter."

"Oh? Do share."

"It had to have taken a while to burn to death, right? So how long exactly did they barbecue their witches for? Did they cook them until they were well-done and crispy?" His friends snorted with laughter.

Ugh. I rolled my eyes. Seriously?

The winds surging up and down the lanes between the stones picked up. The boys' ties took flight like kite tails, and lecture notes Professor Byrne had been holding shot up and away in a whirlwind of white paper and leaves. A particularly powerful gust stormed through, and Gallagher somehow lost his balance, tripped on the leaves and twigs at his feet, and fell forward against the menhir, his face smacking right into the stone.

He cursed loudly, blood streaming from his nose. Several of his classmates guffawed at the impeccable timing, perhaps deeming it just deserts for the boy's tasteless remarks. Among them was Lucas, who looked the most amused out of everyone. His eyes were dancing with delight as he wore a devilish smirk. When he caught my gaze, he raised his hands with a shrug, as if to say, *What's one to do?*

Professor Byrne allowed the group some time to disperse among the menhirs, and I drifted to one of the largest stones in the cluster. While examining it, I noticed something that made my pulse pick up in a rapid staccato. I stepped closer, not believing my own eyes.

Carved into the menhir was the triple spiral I'd drawn my whole life, the very design that had seemed to spook Rory yesterday morning. I had seen variations of it growing up, of course, but they were never quite like my own triple spiral. This one, however, was a dead ringer. The same amount of loops within each spiral and everything. I could've etched it into the stone myself.

"What's this symbol?" I asked as Father Nolan was passing by.

The priest adjusted his glasses, leaning forward. "Ah, yes. You'll find many of the stones decorated with it. It's called a triskele. It's an ancient Celtic symbol representative of many things, not the least of which is Brigid, The Triple Goddess of inspiration, healing, and smithcraft. Three was a sacred number to the druids, you see. The witches who once made their home here also incorporated the triskele into their rituals and art."

"You mean the people *accused* of witchcraft, right? They weren't actually witches."

"That seems to be the general consensus, yes." He smiled and continued drifting around to answer others' questions.

I remained before the menhir, feeling unmoored. How strange that I should draw something like this, something that had been such a staple in an age-old culture unknown to me. I pressed my fingertips to the engraving, a sensation like static meeting my skin.

And then suddenly, a swift reel of images flashed through my mind, inexplicable sensations overcoming me.

The metallic clash of weapons as men astride horses rushed into battle. Smoke that gagged me and drew tears from my eyes. Huts burning like pyres, and women and children wailing as they fled into the pitch-black night, trying to hide behind massive stones. And then a woman striding through all the chaos and carnage. War paint on her face, a necklace of canines clattering against her breastplate, feathers tied to the ends of her hair. The hilt of a sword peeked out from behind her shoulder.

An orb of white light glowed in her cupped palm. Screaming, she flung it forward, cancelling everything out in a deafening burst of brightness like an exploding star.

I yanked my hand away, gasping. My heart cartwheeled, and I stumbled back, feeling as if the ground were tilting.

How had that just happened? Better yet, *what* had just happened? I tried to steady my breaths to control my racing heart. I felt like I was going to be sick. I moved further away from the menhir, deciding distance was for the best, and quickly wiped the tears from my cheeks. As I did, I had the sense of someone watching me and swiveled around.

It was Rory, and judging by the wariness in his eyes, he'd witnessed the whole thing. I got the sense he somehow knew exactly what I'd seen in my mind too.

"Scarlet, are you all right?" Liam gently touched my elbow. "You look faint. Do you want to return to the bus? Professor Byrne has already started going around to let people know it's time to head back."

"Yeah, let's go," I said, trying to hide the tremor in my voice. I wanted to get as far away from this place as possible.

7

When we returned to school, lunch was already in session. Liam invited me to join him and his friends in the refectory, but I politely declined, telling him I was still feeling ill and would instead spend the period in my dad's classroom.

"Is it a pressure headache, do you think?"

"Maybe." Indeed, the air was thick with the promise of rain, an endless gunmetal sky above us. But I knew it had nothing to do with the weather.

Inside St. Andrew's, I headed to one of the restrooms set aside for female students. I splashed cold water onto my face and stared at my reflection. Was I losing my mind? Maybe my mom's passing was finally sinking deep into my bones, causing my sanity to fracture little by little. I needed to get a grip before I had a nervous breakdown.

Minutes later, I made my way to my dad's classroom. I rounded one last corner and then stopped short. Up ahead, Lucas was leaning against the wall beside the classroom door. He had a deck of playing cards and was springing them from one hand to another in a smooth, clicking flourish.

"There she is," he said upon noticing me, eyes glimmering as he straightened. "Pick a card, any card." He fanned them out for me.

I didn't really feel like being social right now, but I didn't want to be rude either. I'd humor him for a few minutes and then excuse myself.

I looked over the cards, which had forest green backs. White plaits trailed along their borders and each center bore an elaborate, interlaced knot similar to ones I'd seen on the Celtic crosses at the cemetery. I pulled one, and at Lucas's direction, I glimpsed its face. The queen of spades, represented by a stout, raven-haired woman with a spear in hand and what looked to be a bull at her side. Once prompted, I tucked the card back into the deck.

Then Lucas shuffled the deck in a number of fancy ways I supposed were meant to impress me. Admittedly, I was impressed, though I tried to keep my face neutral.

"And now for the reveal." He whipped a card from the deck and showed it to me. "Is this your card?"

It was the three of hearts. "No."

"What?" He looked at the card's face. "Are you positive?"

"Pretty positive, yeah."

"What about this one?"

"Unfortunately, no."

"This one?"

"No again. Sorry."

Lucas scoffed at the deck as if it were the one to blame. "Ah, bollocks. I suppose we'll have to continue workshopping that one, won't we?" He winked at me as he tucked the cards into an inside pocket of his St. Andrew's blazer. "But enough chit-chat. I'm here on official business. Jack Connelly has requested the honor of your presence." He bowed like a footman who was about to present me to the lord of the manor.

I hated that I couldn't keep my heart from fluttering at the sound of Jack's name, but maybe it was more so the fact that he'd asked for me. When he'd spotted me this morning, he and Lucas must've talked about me. What had he said?

"Did he happen to mention why?" Surely it had to do with what had happened behind the bleachers yesterday, and explanations were exactly what I needed right now.

"It's anyone's guess," said Lucas, eyes glowing merrily. "But wouldn't you like to find out?"

As Lucas led me through the hallways of St. Andrew's, he greeted friends with high fives, tossed jokes back and forth, whistled to himself during the quieter parts of the journey, and then eventually pulled out his deck of cards and started doing flourishes with them again.

Finally, we came to a section of the building that was more or less abandoned. Half the overhead lights were either altogether out or were flickering, casting the corridor in constantly shifting shadows. The majority of the doors were marked as custodial or storage closets.

Lucas opened one door and slipped through. My feet remained riveted to the ground. The door had a red plaque on it that clearly read, 'Staff Only.'

"Are you sure we're supposed to be here?" I asked the gap of darkness the door had formed.

Lucas's face appeared in the gap. "Of course we are. Come on."

The room beyond overflowed with old, industrial mop buckets, tangled volleyball nets, and a graveyard of broken classrooms supplies that included dusty projectors, chairs with missing legs, and a skeleton in a lab coat with safety goggles on.

"Up here."

Lucas was halfway up a flight of grated, metal stairs attached to a far wall. The stairs ascended three levels, bringing us to another door. When Lucas opened this one, we were not only outside but also on the roof of the building. The students below looked like miniature pieces in a diorama, and the ashen skies were close enough to touch, engorged clouds drifting by in no particular hurry.

The only problem was Jack wasn't here. Besides Lucas, my only other company was a cluster of industrial generators humming in unison and rows of exhaust pipes venting out white air. Just when I thought I'd been duped, Lucas made his way around a high wall behind us covered in electric meters and valves topped with cast iron handwheels, disappearing once more.

I followed, kicking through a thin carpet of dead leaves, and once I cleared the barrier, I came to a halt and stared.

Up ahead, hidden at the very center of the roof, was an idyllic, white greenhouse overrun with ivy and flowering climbers. It was nestled in a sanctuary of green. Saplings in planter boxes made of reclaimed wood stood guard at every corner. Terracotta pots overflowing with plants swarmed around the greenhouse on crates, step ladders, small tables—pretty much on any available real estate. It looked like nothing short of a tucked-away paradise.

"I didn't know the school had this up here," I said. The machines on every side of the roof effectively kept it out of view.

"And with good reason," Lucas said, smiling. "It doesn't belong to the school."

"Who does it belong to then?"

"You'll see."

He opened the door of the greenhouse and gestured for me

to enter. It was like stepping into a forest, into another world altogether, and for the first time in a long while, I instantly felt at home. I could've teared up at the sensation that overcame me in the presence of all these living things, the rich perfume of soil filling my lungs.

Prior to moving to Rosalyn Bay, I had spent the past year and a half working at a used bookstore to save up money. What was I saving up for? It all went back to my sixteenth birthday, when my mom and I had gone to Olympic National Park, where we'd spent the morning hiking through and exploring gorgeous rainforests. It had birthed in me a desire to see all the national parks, rainforests, and botanical gardens in the United States.

The Everglades, Yellowstone, Yosemite, Kings Canyon…I wanted to visit them all. There was just something about nature that soothed me, that spoke to me. Even when I was simply picking flowers to later use in resin jewelry or raking my fingers through potting soil, it was nothing short of therapeutic. So the plan was to embark on a cross-country road trip once I'd saved enough money. It was one of the few dreams from my old life I hadn't let go of. Not yet at least.

I furthered into the greenhouse. Plants of every possible shape and size were arranged under fluorescent bulbs which mimicked the sunlight that never seemed to grace Rosalyn Bay. White labels stuck out from the soil in neat rows, small cursive written along their lengths to identify each plant. Some of the seedling names I recognized. Indeed, they were varieties I had worked with during my community garden project. Rosemary, sage, lemon balm, basil. Others I wasn't overly familiar with. Mugwort, henbane, feverfew, catmint.

Continuing on, Lucas a step behind me, I came upon a scarred, wooden worktable with burn marks. Upon it sat mortars filled with a variety of ingredients: spices, seeds, herbs, flower petals. Beside them, a leather journal was left open, its crème, papyrus pages filled with the same penmanship that had catalogued the plants. In the middle of one page, the journalist had sketched a seedling and diagrammed its anatomy, writing at length about the uses of each part of the plant. The words 'good for second sight' pointed to the roots, whatever that meant. Beyond the journal, primitive-looking, gold coins sat atop a constellation wheel along with loose pages covered in drawings of moon phases.

"What is all this stuff?" I asked.

"All in due time," Lucas said.

We made our way to the back of the greenhouse, pushing past plants and trees. From overhead faucets, a gentle mist showered down on us in a quiet *shhh*. In some places, vines covered the walls and ceilings so completely you might've thought they were claiming the greenhouse as their own, transforming it into a part of nature.

We passed the final plants and stepped into a clearing, where three very familiar boys were waiting, Jack among them. He'd been pacing with arms crossed, but at my arrival, he stopped, straightened, and let his arms fall to his side. He wasn't wearing his St. Andrew's blazer, and the sleeves of his white dress shirt were rolled up to his elbows, his tie loose. I tried not to think about how he wore the relaxed look so magnificently well. I focused instead on the fancy watch he donned in lieu of his rugby wristband, which made me wonder about that burn scar of his I'd glimpsed yesterday.

"Scarlet," he said, "thank you for coming."

I couldn't help the slight somersault my heart performed at the sound of my name in his mouth.

"What the hell is she doing here?"

I glanced in the direction of the hostile voice. It belonged to none other than Jack's teammate Connor, who happened to be glaring intensely at me. He seemed different than he had on the rugby field. His school uniform gave him a more distinguished appearance, but it was more than that. Today, he wore glasses, the two-toned kind that were black on the top half and clear on the bottom. It was almost obnoxious how glorious he looked. More so when I realized his scowl only enhanced it.

Jack held up a hand. "I'll get to that in just a moment. But first, some brief introductions are in order. We're already somewhat acquainted ourselves, of course, but for formality's sake, I'm Jack Connelly. These are my brothers. You've met Lucas obviously."

I turned to my escort, who winked at me, eyes still twinkling.

"This is Connor." The brooding blond only glared at me further.

"And that's Rory over there." The aloof, auburn-haired boy from my pre-calculus class watched me warily with his hands in his pockets. He stood closer to the surrounding plants than he did any of us, as if he preferred their company.

So these were the legendary Connelly boys. Was I surprised? I wasn't sure. I'd briefly considered the likelihood of Jack and Connor being related while watching their interactions during the rugby game. I'd guessed at the possibility of Lucas being another brother this morning while he'd spoken with Jack. Rory was perhaps the only true surprise, but then again, maybe he shouldn't have been. Assembled together as they were, one glance was all it took to know the same blood ran in their veins. Even if their hair and eye colors varied, they had the same face shape, the same bone structure, the same eyebrows. In fact, the similarities were striking the longer I studied them.

Jack stepped forward. "There really isn't any tactful way to prelude this, so I'm just going to get right to it." He paused and raked his fingers through his hair. Whatever he needed to say, he obviously wished he didn't have to say it. "Scarlet, I'm not sure if you're aware, but we recently lost our grandfather. The authorities ruled it a suicide, but I don't believe he took his life. I believe he was attacked."

His eyes held mine firmly before he continued. "And I believe the five of us are next."

8

"Well, that's certainly one way to kill the mood," Lucas cheerfully supplied after a moment, right before he resumed with his card flourishes.

Meanwhile, I tried to form words of my own, but Jack's announcement had wiped my brain completely clear of any intelligible response. My first thought was that this was some kind of prank, a twisted form of hazing the brothers regularly performed on newbies like me. Except no one was laughing, so either the Connellys had mastered their poker faces, or this wasn't a joke at all.

"Attacked," I repeated. It was the best I could do given the circumstances.

"It *was* hunters then," Connor said. There was a fierce blaze in his eyes.

"What would anyone be hunting on a cliff?" I asked.

Connor rolled his eyes so far up I thought they'd fall back into his skull.

"Not hunters," Jack answered.

"I'm really sorry about your grandfather," I said, "but why on earth would his attacker target me?"

"Because of your bloodline, of course."

"I always knew there was a reason I carried on so well with Professor Monroe," Lucas said. "Which clan do you hail from, love?"

"*Clan*?" Images of Highlanders in kilts came to mind. "I have absolutely no idea what you're talking about."

"What about this symbol?" Jack asked. He motioned to Rory, who slipped a piece of paper from his pocket and handed it to his brother. Jack unfolded it and showed it to me. It was a sketch of a triskele, the design from my doodles and the symbol that had marked that menhir.

A trap door in my stomach gave way. "What about it?"

"What significance does it hold for you?"

"None," I replied. "I didn't even know what it was called until today. It's just something I've always drawn."

"We should send her away," Connor said, his dark eyes full of poison, like I'd committed some kind of treason against him. "We don't know who she is or where she comes from. This could be nothing more than a trap."

"I find that highly unlikely," Jack said, "considering the fact she banished a demon yesterday."

Rory's head whipped in my direction, Lucas's cards flew out of his hands, and Connor's eyes grew larger.

But my attention was on Jack. "Wait, what? A *demon*?"

"Yes, the one under the guise of the Xavier student."

I laughed. A short, breathy laugh that held no merriment whatsoever. "You can't be serious." But in the back of my mind, I remembered those red eyes I thought I'd seen, the boy's animalistic tics, how he'd been so fast and so strong.

But...no. What was I thinking? Demons weren't real. Just the stuff of horror stories.

"Look, I don't know if this is some kind of joke—"

"It's not a joke," Jack said. "I need your help, Scarlet. I don't understand the extent of it just yet, but you're clearly integral to what's happening right now in Rosalyn Bay and beyond. And in light of what you were able to do yesterday, it's safe to say you're one of us as well."

"What does that even mean?"

Lucas had gathered his cards and was reorganizing the deck in hand. "That's easy to answer. We're wi—"

"Lucas," Connor snapped. Then to Jack: "Are you mad? She shouldn't be here, and we shouldn't be discussing any of this in front of her either. This doesn't involve her. What makes you so certain it does?"

Jack passed a hand through his hair again as he sat on the answer. I could see in his eyes he was trying to decide whether or not to share it with us. Finally, he heaved a long sigh. "Shortly after we lost Grandda, I visited a Seer. I'd been having nightmares about him, of his soul not being able to find rest. I needed answers. I needed to know if there was any way I was supposed to help him. The Seer imparted a simple message. She said, 'a bird of rare feather will arrive and lead the way.' I didn't know where to begin deciphering something like that, but I continued my search for answers. I found some, including more information about the force behind the attack, but nothing that could seemingly help Grandda overall.

"I decided it was time to return to St. Andrew's to bring you all up to speed so that we could decide our next steps. It hadn't been my initial intention to resume with classes as well, given everything on my mind, but Father Nolan encouraged it. So I visited each of my professors to apologize for my absence and to collect any missed assignments. Professor O'Dwyer from American Lit had a particularly hefty pile of books for me."

"O'Dwyer's brutal, isn't he?" Lucas chimed in. "I had him last year for 'Intro to something or other.' Does he really expect us to read all those bloody short stories and novels in so short a time? It's as if he doesn't think we have lives outside of class."

"Once back in my dorm room at the end of the day," Jack went on, "I dumped the contents of my bag onto my bed to sort through it all. And what stared right up at me but this?" He crossed over to a wooden draft table and slipped a thin book out from the messenger bag I'd seen him with around campus.

The book was probably only a few dozen pages long. He extended it to me, and I took it, the glossy white cover smooth under my fingertips and glowing under the greenhouse lights. There was a bird on the cover with a long, down-curved bill and brilliantly red plumage. At first, I thought it was a flamingo, but then I saw the book's title: *The Scarlet Ibis*.

"Almost at once, the Seer's words came back to me. 'A bird of rare feather will arrive and lead the way.' Unfortunately, I didn't have much time to reflect on this newest piece of the puzzle. Word of my return had quickly spread across campus, meaning Coach Stewart was knocking at my door not a minute later, insisting I put on my rugby jersey and report to the field immediately. So I did. And imagine my surprise when a girl not only contends with a demon on my behalf at the game but also tells me her name is Scarlet."

That explained his shock after I'd told him who I was, why he'd looked at me with such disbelief.

The rest of us fell into a silence as Jack's story settled into our minds.

"It's you," Jack said then. "You're the one from the Seer's message. You're the one I've been waiting for."

My face flushed. I couldn't find the words to respond. This was crazy. Bizarre. And just a touch unsettling.

Restless souls? Enigmatic messages? Demons? It was well beyond my pay grade.

"I'm sorry, but I don't know anything about what happened to your grandfather. I wish I had answers for you, but I don't. I have no idea how I'd 'lead the way' or help in this search of yours."

"Maybe a message has come to you in your dreams?"

Apart from last night's nightmares about the rogue Xavier player, my dreams had been nothing short of normal since moving to Rosalyn Bay. Nothing prophetic about them in the least. I shook my head. "Not really."

"What about any strange visions? Rory mentioned you having some sort of experience among the menhirs this morning."

Goosebumps puckered along my arms, and a chill worked its way through my bloodstream. "I did see some kind of attack, but it was from another time. The people wore tunics and animal skins. To be honest, I'm pretty sure it was only my imagination. I was probably trying to picture the things Professor Byrne had spoken about in his lecture." The words didn't land quite right in my gut, but what else could the vision have been? There was a reasonable explanation for everything, wasn't there?

Connor gave another dramatic eye roll. "She clearly knows nothing. Let's cut her loose and drop it. We've already said too much."

"Wait," I said. "What about your grandfather's attacker? How would he know me? I'm new to town. With exception to the students here, no one in Rosalyn Bay even knows I exist. You mentioned it had to do with my bloodline. Does that mean my dad's caught up in some kind of trouble? Am I in danger?"

Even as I said it, it was hard to picture. A mild-mannered professor owing some kind of debt to underground crime lords? Then again, I hardly knew the man. Who's to say he didn't have a shady past he'd hidden from me and my mom all these years?

Jack shared a look with Connor for a long moment, an entire

conversation passing between them. Finally, he breathed out a long sigh and shook his head. "I think this has all been one big mix-up on my part."

I was taken aback by his sudden backpedaling. "What are you saying then? You brought me here and told me about attacks and demons and Seers, and now you're saying it was all a mistake?"

"I should..." Connor trailed off and tapped the side of his head with two fingers. What did *that* mean?

"No," said Jack.

"No? Jack—"

"I said no." Jack's tone was firm and final. Then he fixed his rich cognac eyes on me. "Yes, I was mistaken. I thought you might know something about my grandfather, but by your own admission, you don't. In which case, it seems you won't be able to help us unfortunately. We shouldn't have troubled you to begin with. I apologize if we've upset you in any way. Please don't let us keep you any longer."

His tone was kind and gentle, but I knew exactly what the words were. A dismissal. The worst part was I actually did start to feel like I was imposing. I wanted to stay. I wanted to ask more questions. But what else was there to say? I had told Jack he was mistaken, and he respected that. Now I was going to be offended by it?

"Right," I said. I awkwardly stepped back, trying to keep my pride intact even as I wished to continue speaking with Jack. Any appropriate parting words were hard to come by, especially when my head was starting to hurt with all the things now buzzing between my temples. I settled for something simple. "Well, in any case, I honestly do hope you manage to find the answers you're looking for."

Jack bowed his head in a nearly imperceptible nod of gratitude. Those world-weary eyes of his, though—God, how they swam in sadness.

It occurred to me maybe he didn't believe he'd ever find those answers.

9

"Liam, do you know the Connellys very well?"

I'd spent the remainder of the week avoiding the Connellys, which wasn't saying much considering they'd avoided me right back, but by Friday, my curiosity was hemorrhaging, and I knew I'd go crazy if I didn't make an attempt at getting answers. Though it was lunch time, I found myself in the school library sitting opposite Liam, who was diligently finishing up a homework assignment for chemistry.

"Not all of them," he replied, scratching out an error in the chemical equation he'd written. He furrowed his brow, staring the equation down. Somehow, the strategy worked. The correct answer came to him a moment later and he scribbled it upon the page. "I was lab partners with Rory last fall for biology, though. He's the youngest brother."

"What was he like?" Was he as standoffish with others as he'd been with me?

Liam smiled, looking up from his homework in reflection. "He was sweet."

Sweet? Definitely not the word I had in mind. My thoughts must've been written all over my face because Liam laughed.

"He's hard for most people to get to know. He's not very open. But I was able to spend some time with him outside of St. Andrew's earlier this year. It was during a school trip to Japan over our Easter holiday."

I lifted my eyebrows at that. My previous school had never organized a spring break trip before, but if it had, it would've probably been to a neighboring city, not another country, and even that was wishful thinking.

"It all started at the beginning of biology class one day," Liam said. "A folder of his dropped to the floor, and sketches came sliding out. He rushed to gather them back up, but I'd already seen them. They were done in an anime style, with the characters in beautifully drawn samurai kimonos. Many of them had Japanese words written down the sides as well.

"He was mortified, even though he had no reason to be. I told him the drawings were incredible, but that seemed to only embarrass him further. I let a few days pass and then asked him if he intended on going on the school trip to Japan, given his obvious appreciation for certain aspects of Japanese culture. He wasn't, but I kept insisting on it in the weeks that followed."

"And he eventually caved?"

"I suppose I wore him down. Most people write him off because of his withdrawn nature, assuming he's pretentious I'd imagine, but he's just a naturally quiet person. A little shy too."

Guilt flooded my chest. I'd done the same thing, hadn't I? Written him off. Which was pretty hypocritical of me. Among my best friends, people I felt comfortable around, I was as outgoing as they came. But drop me in a classroom with people I didn't know very well, and I instantly clammed up and talked very little.

"What about the others?" I asked quietly, eyeing a group of boys who were perusing book stacks not too far from us. I didn't want it to get back to the Connellys that I was digging into their personal business.

"Jack's the eldest at eighteen and a year above us. He's very well liked among the students and faculty. And then Connor and Lucas are both seventeen and in our year."

"Are they fraternal twins or something?"

"Tandem twins actually. They were born within nine months of each other. You'll typically find Connor wherever Jack is. They're very close. And then Lucas...well, he has a reputation for being a bit of a class clown at St. Andrew's. He always pulls a big, colorful prank at the end of each term, which most students have come to look forward to."

"You said Rory is the youngest brother. How did he have a class with you last year then? And he's in my pre-calculus class now."

"He turned sixteen at the beginning of the month, but he skipped a grade when he first started here. He's incredibly brilliant. Then again, they all are. Top marks in all their classes." Liam finished up another equation and then looked up at me. "Oh, before I forget, are you doing anything tomorrow? You said you hadn't had a chance to properly take in Rosalyn Bay, and I thought I could give you a tour of the main square in town. I think you'd really enjoy it."

I hadn't anticipated the change in subject. There were still things I wanted to know about the Connellys. But hanging out with Liam tomorrow would undoubtedly give me a chance to follow up on my inquiry. Plus, it would be nice to get out of the house and spend time with a new friend. I smiled and nodded. "Count me in. That sounds great."

I spent my Saturday morning unpacking the last of my moving

boxes as I whiled away the hours until my meetup with Liam. The only other plan on my social calendar was a catch-up date with Natalie via video chat later tonight. It wasn't too much of a far cry from what I'd normally be doing on the weekends.

Saturdays back in Colorado were usually reserved for sleeping in, doing something garden-related, and working on a few new pieces of resin jewelry. In the evenings, I'd watch a black-and-white movie or other classic with my mom, given her love for the Golden Age of Hollywood. I was even named after Scarlett O'Hara from *Gone with the Wind*, what had been my mom's all-time favorite novel and movie. Then on Sundays, we'd enjoy a nice, big breakfast as we leafed through the Sunday paper and cut out comics (my mom had been a big fan of the *Peanuts* strip, adoring all things Snoopy), and later, I'd get all my homework done while chatting online with my friends. Low-key weekends were the best in my opinion.

I smiled at the thought, standing before a bureau upon which I'd set out an array of framed pictures cataloguing my most cherished memories from that life. I picked one picture up. In it, my mom and I were beaming at the camera, dressed in poodle skirts. She'd thrown a 1950s-themed birthday party that year. People had later remarked it'd been one of the funnest parties they'd ever attended.

She'd always been like that, full of life and able to get even the most reserved people laughing and enjoying themselves. It'd been one of my favorite things about her. My throat tightened as I stared at the picture, and I promptly returned it to the bureau, my heart growing heavy. I took a deep breath and slowly let it out.

One day at a time, I reminded myself. It was the only way I knew how to move forward.

Downstairs, my dad was engaged in his typical morning routine: reading the newspaper as he drank tea and ate two slices of toast spread with apricot jam. This was his preferred method for catching up on world news. He explained it was easier to read about events than to see the hard images that sometimes aired on news channels. In fact, he rarely watched TV at all. I was more likely to find him reading a book in his study or listening to educational radio. And he was also never dressed down. Even now, he was dressed as if he planned to speak in front of an audience of his peers at some esteemed university, not a hair out of place. According to my mom, he used to lecture at such places all the time, but he'd eventually taken a sabbatical to write an academic book, assuming a teaching job at St. Andrew's to supplement his income. That had been years ago. I guessed the peace and quiet of Rosalyn Bay had grown on him.

"Good morning," he greeted. His voice was coarse. I noticed the cold medicine beside the tea. It was a minor thing, but my heart missed a beat anyway. I'd seen my fair share of pill bottles and prescription labels this year, and it'd never meant anything good.

"Are you all right?" I asked.

"Just a cold," he said, waving a hand. "The tea's been a massive help, though. Here, why don't you pour yourself a cup?"

"That's all right. I'm not really a tea person."

"I insist," he said, already fetching a cup from the cabinets. "I'd hate for you to catch my bug. A student of mine gave me this blend and swears by it. He says it's the reason he's never had a single sick day at St. Andrew's."

I obliged him, joining him at the table. The drink had a sweet, blackberry taste that was hard not to love. I downed the rest of the cup with ease, letting it warm my throat and chest.

"Good, isn't it?"

"It is, yeah."

There was an awkward pause of silence, during which I repeatedly rubbed my thumb across the tea cup's porcelain handle while my dad fidgeted with his newspaper. Yeah, this was definitely going to take some getting used to. I was about to excuse myself to spare us both from the overbearing discomfort of trying to make small talk, but my dad spoke up again before I could.

"I had something for you. It's...I thought...well, I...here, let me get it."

He returned a minute later, carrying a gift box, which he set before me on the table. I hesitated. It always made me uncomfortable to open presents in front of people. Mostly because I was a horrible actress, and I didn't like making people feel bad for picking out something that wasn't really my style. But my dad was already waiting on me, so I drew the box closer, rehearsing appropriate facial expressions in my mind.

I lifted the lid. Inside, set upon a bed of tissue paper, was a book. No, not a book, I realized as I took it in my hands. A photo album. The blush-colored covers were made of book cloth, giving them a soft and elegant look. I opened the album, and the first picture that greeted me made my throat swell up.

It was from the day I was born. My mom sat up in her hospital bed, cradling a tiny infant in pink swaddling blankets. She wore one of the biggest smiles I'd ever seen on her face. As I turned the pages, images from my first years of life beamed up at me. Birthday parties, outings to the zoo, trips to the park, swimming lessons. Some of the pictures I recognized from my mom's own collection, but most were completely new to me. My heart overflowed with emotion as I took them in for the first time.

"You didn't seem to have very many pictures of you and your mother from your early childhood," my dad gently said. "So I thought you might like to have these. I hope I haven't overstepped in any way."

I shook my head, momentarily at a loss for words. "No, I...it's beautiful." I turned another page. In one picture, a three-year-old me was sitting on my dad's shoulders, my mom beside us. Behind us in the distance was a field of giraffes, a shot most likely taken at Cheyenne Mountain Zoo in Colorado Springs. I didn't remember the day, but I was surprised by how happy I looked, how at ease I was with my dad.

"What's this?" There was a folded piece of paper behind the picture. I tugged on the edge and pulled it out. I opened it, revealing a child's drawing of stick figures, giraffes shaped like rectangles, and a smiling sun. I tried to ignore the fact that the sun only had three rays, and that each one was done up in a spiral, making it look more like a triskele than I cared to admit. Had I drawn the mysterious symbol even at this young an age?

My dad chuckled softly. "Your mother said you wouldn't stop talking about the giraffes for weeks after that visit. That was a drawing you sent me in the mail."

My chest cracked like thawing ice. "You kept it all this time?"

"Of course," he said. "I kept everything your mother ever sent that had to do with you. Pictures, drawings, copies of your honor roll certificates. I was only happy to be included in it all."

I didn't know why I was so taken aback. My mom had never had a single bad thing to say about my dad. Indeed, she'd named him as one of the kindest men she'd ever met. He'd even visited her in the hospital in those final months and had attended her funeral as well. I guessed I'd just never thought *my* existence played that much of a factor in his life once I got older, once I stopped sending those drawings, once my attentions turned elsewhere. Yet here he was, sounding every bit the part of a proud father still.

I took my time going through the rest of the album, treasuring every snapshot of a time in my life I couldn't recall but that clearly had been filled with the utmost love and happiness.

My dad had taken the time out to put this together, and he'd done it all for me.

It looked like I wouldn't have to put my acting prowess to the test after all. I closed the book and smiled at him. My heart felt warm, and I knew it wasn't just because of the tea. "Thank you," I said. The words didn't seem enough to express that it was one of the best gifts I'd ever received in my life, but he nodded with a smile of his own, and for a moment, we felt a little less like strangers.

10

Rosalyn Bay boasted a grand population of 1,602 and was located on a western tip of Ireland shaped like a crab's claw. Today, despite it being a weekend, the place was a ghost town. Along the uneven, cobblestone streets, shiny from last night's rain storm, tired, stone buildings leaned against each other as if huddling against the chilly October winds. Awnings still dripped water, a steady *plop, plop, plop* resounding from puddle to puddle as I made my way through, pumpkins of every size proudly sitting upon many a windowsill.

The smell of fish and seawater was in every breeze. Even from here, you could hear the Atlantic Ocean's unrelenting crash against the cliffs along the coast. I continued past rundown sandwich boards advertising everyone's special of the day: clam chowder, crab cakes, or halibut. But the one thing that everyone had? Oysters.

My dad had told me Rosalyn Bay's coastal sandbanks were home to a natural oyster bed that produced some of the finest oysters in the world. So fine in fact they apparently were highly sought after by restaurants in New York, Paris, and London, as well as being prominently featured in oyster festivals throughout Ireland. He'd said it all with a matter of pride (I guessed every small town needed a claim to fame), so I couldn't bring myself to admit I'd never tried an oyster before and probably never would if I could avoid it.

I met Liam at a simple eatery, where we ordered steaming bowls of lobster bisque and baskets of fried cod. His hair was plastered to his forehead, beads of water still clinging to some locks. He donned a black and blue wetsuit, his surfboard leaning against the wall in a corner of the establishment.

I couldn't believe he'd gone surfing in this weather, but apparently September to May was the best time of year for it here. I wasn't a stranger to the cold, but blissfully sunny Colorado was landlocked, so I wasn't used to arctic-like, coastal winds in the least or to nonstop rain. Add being submerged in the icy ocean on top of that, and surfing was an automatic no for me.

We enjoyed our food as we talked about everything and anything. Eventually, I guided Liam into a conversation about our classmates at St. Andrew's, asking him who was worth befriending. It was the perfect way to segue into the topic I really wanted to discuss. "What about Thomas Mooney?" I asked.

"Mooney's a year above us, so I don't know him personally. Come to think of it, I've never really seen him with a group of friends. I think he prefers to be a lone wolf."

"I kind of got that impression too," I said, telling Liam about the tour Thomas had given me. "Actually, he mentioned a few things I'm still not sure what to make of. It was about the Connellys. Have you heard any of the stories people tell about them?" I couldn't believe I was repeating anything that had left Thomas's mouth, but I just couldn't stop thinking about the things the Connellys had said in the greenhouse. The words had played on an endless loop in my mind.

Liam shrugged. "Everyone's heard at least one rumor, but that's all they are. Rumors. Of course, the matter with Maurice Connelly hasn't helped to quell them."

"Why were people so quick to say he'd taken his life? Isn't it possible he could've just accidentally fallen?" *Or been attacked?*

"Anything's possible, of course. But because there are guard rails on the cliff edge to prevent accidents, everyone's mind was already made up the moment he was found. It's an unfortunate aspect of human behavior. When you're at the top of any kind of social hierarchy like the Connellys are, there will always be those who relish bringing you down, who live to see the mighty fall. But in my opinion, I think there are enough people in this world who discriminate against others just because they're different. Why add to it?"

"Are the Connellys really all that different, though?"

"According to the townspeople here, they are. It bothers me really. I've seen mothers who pull their children closer and make the sign of the cross when a Connelly boy passes them by in town, and more than one storefront owner has turned his sign from 'Opened' to 'Closed' when spotting the Connellys out in the main square."

The images were bewildering. It's not what I'd expected to hear at all. I furrowed my brow. "Why would they act like that?"

"Do you remember Professor Byrne's lecture about the menhirs? Particularly what he said about the things that had happened there?"

"Of course. The slaughtering of the Celts and then later, the witch trials."

"Apparently there was a woman burnt at the stake all those centuries ago of the surname Connelly."

My jaw slackened. "Was she...?"

"Related to the Connelly boys? So they say. The Connelly family has been a staple of Rosalyn Bay for centuries, so it's not unreasonable. The woman accused of witchcraft was simply someone who practiced folk medicine, though. Even so, the townspeople frowned upon her trade, believing she consorted with the devil to craft her cures. But here's where it gets interesting. According to local legend, as the woman's pyre was lit, she began to curse the entire town."

"What did she say?"

"She warned them that one day, her descendants would rise up against the people of Rosalyn Bay and ensure the town was devoured in fire just as the townspeople had used fire against her."

"And that's why the townspeople fear the Connellys so much?"

Liam nodded. "That's the long and short of it. They believe the Connelly boys mean to exact vengeance against the citizens of Rosalyn Bay and that they continue their ancestor's practice of regularly communing with demons."

Demons. There was that word again. My heart shuddered. "Actual demons?"

"In all their glory."

"Is that a word that gets thrown around a lot here?"

"I'd say so. The people of Rosalyn Bay are a superstitious bunch. There are a number of shops here that sell special wreaths and charms to stave off curses from all sorts of creatures: banshees, kelpies, and other malevolent spirits. I remember seeing one vendor hawk a candle in the square a few months back, claiming its light would protect your loved ones from Carman, the Celtic goddess of evil magic."

"Wow." I hadn't expected the superstitions to run so deep.

Liam shrugged again. "I suppose everyone needs something to believe in, and I'd like to think the myths serve a purpose. After all, if there's great evil in the world, then that means there's great good as well, a force that will protect us and keep us safe. I just wish the Connellys hadn't ended up as the villains in the story."

Liam eventually had to return to St. Andrew's to meet up with classmates for a study group. Not ready to head back home just yet, I continued exploring on my own. I found my way to the beach, where the harbor was crowded with deep sea fishing boats unloading their nets and fresh catches of the day. At neighboring docks, smaller vessels bobbed excitedly in the dark, choppy waters. Their bells pealed a nostalgic tune.

Up ahead was the red-and-white-striped lighthouse Liam had told me about earlier today. It sat solemnly atop a bluff and apparently afforded the perfect view for whale watching as humpbacks made their way further north. When I reached its observation deck, though, I could only see the few brave souls still surfing the powerful ocean waves.

Inside the light house, at the center of a circular room, sat a large block of stone. A plaque was embedded into its exterior, affording a brief summary of the lighthouse's history. The block of stone itself was said to be a broken off part of a larger menhir. There was even a triskele carved into its face. I pressed my hand against the symbol, wondering if another vision would visit me, still unsure over what I'd seen during Professor Byrne's field trip.

I waited. Five seconds, ten, fifteen.

Nothing happened.

Disappointment washed over me. Maybe I really had just imagined those images in my head. They had seemed so real, though, so vivid. I was about to pull my hand away when a rush of heat covered my palm, as if I held it above a hot stove. Almost instantly, there was a strange pulsing sensation at the center of my hand, as if a second heart beat there. Something pulled at me, tugging at the innermost parts of me. Gasping, I yanked my hand back. The heat vanished at once, as did the strange pulse. What had just happened?

Before I could reflect on it further, the ominous sound of thunder rumbled throughout the darkening skies. I sighed. Wonderful. It looked like I'd have to begin the long trek back home sooner than later after all.

Forty minutes later, I wasn't even close to halfway home. Worse still, the rain was coming down in sheets.

I mentally chided myself for not taking my dad up on his offer to let me borrow his car, but the point still stood that I didn't feel comfortable driving on the left side of the road yet. I crossed my arms to stay warm, thankful at least for the little protection my rain coat provided, even as my sneakers trudged through a practical swamp on the side of the road. Their material let out a squishing noise with every step, and my socked feet were already mostly submerged in water. I didn't know why I'd decided to try my luck wearing them instead of donning proper rain boots. Or why I hadn't thought to bring an umbrella with me today. Maybe I'd hoped Rosalyn Bay would cut me a break from its miserable weather for one afternoon. So much for that. I was definitely going to soak in a nice hot bath once I got home.

Suddenly, a pair of high beams striped the road before me.

Startled, I spun around.

A shiny, black SUV was slowly crawling toward me.

I faced forward and picked up my pace. Ever since Jack had unceremoniously informed me I was being targeted in some senseless attack, I couldn't help myself from looking over my shoulder at least a dozen times a day. Even though he'd later retracted the comment, paranoia wasn't an easy thing to shake off.

The SUV was drawing closer. So close in fact I could hear the pop of gravel under its tires even over the clamor of rain. The vehicle was a new model, probably from this very year. Which meant it belonged to someone with plenty of disposable income, the type of income that could easily come from illegal activities. If my dad really had somehow gotten entangled with the wrong people, this was definitely the type of car they'd be driving.

The SUV pulled up right beside me then and stopped.

My heart instantly went double-time. They were going to try to snatch me right off the road!

I wouldn't give them the chance. I bolted off at full speed, and when the SUV's driver accelerated to pursue me, I pushed myself even harder, pumping my legs like pistons. Jack had been right. Someone was indeed targeting me. And now they'd gotten me all alone on some God-forsaken stretch of road where I'd be an easy casualty.

My only chance at surviving was to lose them altogether. I cut hard to the right, crossing into a pasture. Except I misjudged a step and went down before I could take another.

Behind me, the SUV was idling. A door opened and closed. Purpose-filled footsteps trekked across the grass.

They were coming for me.

I clawed at the slick grass, hoping to find a stick, anything with which to defend myself. My fingers closed in around a rock.

They might have caught up with me, but I wasn't going down without a fight.

Armed, I whirled around to face my attacker.

11

Jack Connelly came to a halt.

One hand held an umbrella and the other floated upward in a gesture of surrender.

"Jack?"

Behind him, someone powered down one of the SUV's rear windows. Lucas's face appeared, and he was grinning from ear to ear. "Don't stop on our account," he called out over the rain. He popped a strip of fried clam into his mouth and munched away, enthralled by my aggressive posture.

I let the rock tumble out of my grip and fall to the ground, and Jack immediately closed the distance between us, holding the umbrella over me and offering a hand to help me to my feet. His skin was soft, warm, and despite the circumstances, my chest heated at the touch.

"How did you know I was here?" Above us, the rain drummed against the umbrella, fast and loud.

"I didn't. My brothers and I were returning from an errand. This road leads back to St. Andrew's."

Oh. Right.

"I thought..." I trailed off, thinking it best not to finish that sentence. Jack would probably think I was mental for believing I was under attack even when he'd told me otherwise.

"Will you let us give you a lift home?"

Only a fool would turn down the invitation in weather like this. I followed Jack back to the waiting car.

It took only minutes for the toasty interior of the SUV to wrap around me like a warm blanket and ease my discomfort. The heated front seats had helped with that, though I could still feel Connor's glare boring holes into the back of my skull at having to give up riding shotgun.

My clothes were still soaked, of course, and I was embarrassed to be dripping water all over my leather seat. It was, without a doubt, the fanciest car I'd ever ridden in. I wouldn't have expected anything less from a Mercedes-Benz, though.

"Do you want some?" Lucas shoved a Styrofoam takeaway box through the space between the front seats. There were a few clam strips left, along with thick, wavy 'chips' (the name for fries here) drenched in ketchup.

"Oh. No, thank you. I actually already ate."

"You were in town then?" Jack asked, eyes trained on the road. The car's wipers scrubbed the windshield at full speed, but even then, it was nearly impossible to see more than a few feet in front of us.

"I didn't want to be cooped up all day. My dad's stuck grading papers for the weekend, and besides that, he's not in any condition to be out in this weather. He's nursing a cold."

"Is he all right?" Jack asked. "Does he need anything? I think we might actually have some tea that tends to help with that sort of thing." He started to lean toward the car's glove department.

His concern touched me. I was also slightly amused by how much people here were devoted to their teas. "Actually, he has all the tea he needs. A student was kind enough to give him some, and it looks like it's already helping to fight off his bug, so I think he'll be fine." But I'd already decided that if my dad was still under the weather tomorrow, I'd go into town and buy the necessary ingredients to make him a nice chicken noodle soup, the way my mom had always done for me. In light of the album he'd given me this morning, it was the least I could do to show my appreciation and pay him back in kind. It still warmed my heart that he'd put together such a thoughtful gift for me.

"And did you have some tea yourself, Scarlet Ibis?" Lucas asked. "We can't have you catching a bad dose too, now can we? Then both Monroes would be out for the count."

"Don't worry, I did." In fact, I thought I might have another cup once I got home. It would certainly put some warmth back into my bones. Especially in light of the slight chill that coursed through me at what Lucas had called me. I pushed thoughts of Seers and cryptic messages out of my mind.

We settled into a comfortable silence after that, the only sound in the car the music from the radio. It was set at a low volume, but I was pretty sure every single song was straight out of the fifties. I smiled as Bill Haley started singing "Rock Around the Clock."

At one point, I risked a glance at the rearview mirror to check on Jack's brothers. Lucas was working on a second take-away box. Connor sat beside him, wearing earbuds that were connected to his phone. Rory was in the row behind them, back pressed against a window and knees drawn up to create a makeshift desk for his sketchpad. Maybe he was working on one of those samurai drawings Liam had mentioned. Being that it was the weekend, they were all out of their St. Andrew's uniforms and in 'civilian' clothes. It didn't stop them from looking like models, though, like A-list celebrities who'd been dropped in the middle of nowhere for a film shoot. Jack looked especially striking, donning a black pea-coat with the collar popped up to protect his neck.

I thought about what the townspeople believed where it concerned the Connellys. Riding in a car with them like this, it was hard to picture them as the wrathful descendants of a persecuted, would-be witch who were now hell-bent on burning Rosalyn Bay to the ground.

And yet there were things from the past week I still didn't have explanations for, things for which at least one Connelly had always been present.

What are you getting at, Scarlet? That doesn't necessarily mean anything.

Maybe. But then again...what if it did?

"Thanks again for the lift," I told Jack once he'd pulled up to my dad's house. It was a weary-looking cottage that had seen better years, vines and roots climbing across its stone face. True to Rosalyn Bay fashion, there were also no neighbors for miles around, as if the cottage had simply dropped out of the sky one day and had landed in no-man's land.

"No thanks necessary. Stay warm, and give your father our regards."

Jack waited until I was safely inside before he started to pull away. I closed the umbrella he'd lent me and dropped it into a tall vase by the door. Then I braced myself for whatever fashion of parenting my dad was prepared to dole out. It's not like he'd given me a curfew or anything, but he had to have worried once the storm had moved in, and since cell phone signals in this town were basically non-existent, he wouldn't have been able to check in on me.

Oddly, though, the house was virtually soundless.

Was he asleep? Maybe his cold medicine and tea had knocked him out. I quietly tiptoed through the house in my wet socks, wincing every time a floorboard whined. This house was definitely on its last legs. Everything from a strong wind to the gentlest step made its tired bones ache.

I entered the hallway where my dad's bedroom was located and nearly screamed at the girl who appeared on the far side.

I sagged against a wall, pressing a hand to my palpitating heart. It was only my reflection. I'd forgotten about the mirror that hung on the back of my dad's bedroom door. While I waited for my pulse to relax, I noticed the line of light underneath the closed door to my dad's office down the same hall. Strange, as he wasn't in the habit of closing the door when he worked, so accustomed was he to having the house to himself.

I knocked. "Dad?"

I waited, listening for any sound coming from the other side. Nothing.

I knocked again. "Dad?" I called for him louder this time.

When he failed to answer again, I slowly opened the door, the hinges whining, and leaned in.

And then my heart shot up my throat.

The office was in complete disarray. Across the way, a shattered window gaped open like a mouth filled with pointy teeth, matching glass shards glistening from the floor like fallen puzzle pieces. The curtains billowed wildly in the storm breeze. Everywhere I looked, there was nothing but chaos. The desk was overturned, as were two book cases with broken shelves. There were graded papers littering the floor, some scattering to the far corners of the office with every gust of wind.

I furthered into the room, trying to make sense of it all. It was only when I made my way around the desk that I saw him.

It was my dad, lying face-down on the ground, absolutely motionless.

12

My dad wasn't dead.

I could still detect a pulse lightly tapping against the warm skin of his neck. It was barely there, but it was there. I tried to maintain a grip on my phone as I pulled it out to call for an ambulance, but the tingling in my fingers made it near impossible. I dropped the phone twice.

Breathe, Scarlet!

With trembling hands, I unlocked the screen and started to dial.

"Scarlet?"

I yelped at the intrusion and dropped the phone again, but the sight of Jack calmed my rattled nerves. A little. "I don't know what's wrong with him," I said, my throat pinching around the words. "I've tried waking him up, but he won't come to."

Jack rushed over, taking my dad's wrist despite my telling him I'd already found a pulse. Maybe he wanted confirmation. I hadn't imagined it, had I? But no, he felt the pulse too. Even so, the tension in my shoulders and upper back was still coiled tight. My hands were still shaking as well.

Jack's brothers filled the doorway to the office then, their eyes stuck on my dad's unmoving body.

"How did you...?" I couldn't find the words to complete the question.

"Something felt off as I was pulling away," Jack answered. "I wanted to check in and make sure you were all right."

"Was this done by the man who attacked your grandfather?"

Jack strode to the broken office window, the scattered shards of glass crunching under his footfalls. The curtains still swelled out in the storm breeze. Jack leaned out the window and looked skyward. When he turned back around, his face was grim.

"A western window," he told his brothers.

"What does the position of the window have to do with anything?" I asked. "And you haven't answered my other question. Do you know who's behind this? What's wrong with my dad? Why isn't he waking up?"

"That's more than one question," Connor said, his tone impatient.

"I think I'm entitled to ask however many questions I want, considering it's my dad who's unconscious on the floor. If you guys know something, then you'd better be ready to tell the police. I'm calling them right now."

Connor scoffed. "They aren't going to be able to help you."

I ignored him and dialed. The call immediately failed. Gritting my teeth, I tried again.

"Scarlet," Jack said, his gentle voice placating. "You'll have to trust us on this. I'll give you all the answers you want, but right now—"

A thunderous flurry of beating wings came from outside, as if a flock of birds were rushing past. Jack's spine went ramrod straight. If he were an animal, the hair down his back would be standing tall.

"They're still here." His face momentarily paled. Then his features hardened into a look of utter determination, and he charged out the office, his brothers on his heels. I hurried after them, reluctant as I was to leave my dad behind, and found them gathered at the sitting room window.

"They've surrounded the car," Connor was saying.

Surrounded? Were we outnumbered? I pushed my way between Connor and Jack, but what I saw outside completely baffled me. Under the torrent of rain, a horde of ravens encircled the Connellys' SUV in a storm of menacing black. I knew birds tended to fly closer to the ground during bad weather to escape the uncomfortable air pressure, but the behavior I observed now was bizarre.

"What are they doing?"

"Catching a scent," Jack answered.

"I thought birds hunted by sight."

"Most do," he said. "But those aren't birds."

I cut another look toward the raging mass. "I'm pretty sure they are."

"Oh, Scarlet Ibis," Lucas said then. "You are quite behind on your Irish folklore, aren't you? What you see before you, love, are the sluagh."

"The sluagh?"

"Otherwise known as The Host of the Unforgiven Dead. They're the restless spirits of people who were so evil in life the Celtic deities rejected them in death. With no home to call their own, they're forced to roam the skies aimlessly for eternity."

I blinked. Was he out of his mind?

Was I, for not immediately objecting to the idea?

"Is there an attic here?" Jack asked, ripping me from my thoughts.

"Y-yes. But—"

"Get her upstairs," Jack told Connor. "We have only seconds before they strike again. Barricade yourselves inside the attic and don't come out no matter what you hear. I'll try to fend them off."

Before I could process his words, Connor was already dragging me up the stairs, an iron grip on my upper arm. I struggled against him, but he was immovable.

"Let me go!"

"We're trying to bloody help you," he shot back, pulling me along the second level of the cottage, eyes fixed on the ceiling to locate the attic.

He yanked on the chain to the attic's hatch door and quickly unfolded its ladder. "Climb."

I hesitated. "What about my dad? He's unprotected."

"The sluagh aren't going to attack your father again."

"*They're* the ones who attacked him? A bunch of birds?"

Connor bracketed his hands on my arms and pushed me into the ladder. "Climb!"

I would've argued further except the front door below suddenly burst open, a whoosh of wind racing into the house along with the deafening wing-beating of what had to be dozens upon dozens of birds.

I raced up the ladder.

Once inside the attic, I patted down the walls to find a light switch. A single overhead bulb flickered for a few seconds before fully illuminating the space, critters scrambling back to their dark crevices at the first sign of light. It smelled like decaying wood and old clothes up here. It was also freezing, a fact made no better by the reality that I was still in wet clothes, the fabric like ice against my skin.

As Connor ascended the ladder, I rummaged through the few boxes scattered about the attic. I'd hoped to find something I could wield as a weapon. Ideally a baseball bat. Unfortunately, it seemed my dad really was as unathletic as they came. I'd have to make due with a heavy, old-fashioned lamp.

There was a crash from the ground level, and the fluttering of wings grew louder, closer.

Connor hauled himself over the edge of the hatch door and then turned around to pull the staircase back up.

It was too late.

A rush of black surged through the doorway, throwing Connor onto his back. The birds rocketed upwards, forming a terrifying cyclone of shadows that kept getting bigger and bigger. It was as if a nightmare were materializing before my very eyes. Feathers flew in every direction as the cyclone grew taller, reaching the attic's ceiling.

Then, like bullets fired from a rifle, the ravens shot toward me one by one. I swung the lamp at the first bird, barely dodged the second, and recovered in hardly enough time to strike a third. No sooner had I righted myself, a dozen more had taken the place of their fallen brethren and clawed at my hair or snapped at my skin, drawing blood. I swatted at them, but they kept coming at me in an unrelenting assault.

It was like being in the middle of a funnel of talons, beaks, and feathers. One bird flew right up to my face, lunging at my eyes with a snap. I backhanded it before it could get any closer. Its own eyes had been red. Unmistakably red.

Connor finally managed to fend off his own gang of ravens. "Get out of here!" he yelled over the cacophony surrounding us.

The problem was the legion of birds was blocking my escape. Then I spotted a window on the opposite end of the attic and ran for it. I heaved it up on whining hinges and climbed out, my heart faltering when my foot nearly slipped on a wet roof shingle. After slamming the window shut, I slowly stood and cautiously made my way across the roof. There was a trellis on one side of the cottage that I could use to descend.

The wind shrieked as it soared past me. I focused on putting one foot in front of the other, my arms held out on either side of me for stability. From this height, out the corner of my eye, I saw Jack contending with birds by the SUV. How many of them were there?

Glass shattered. I carefully rotated my body to see the source.

I wish I hadn't.

Behind me, ravens were bleeding out the attic window like plumes of toxic vapor and coming right for me.

I quickened my steps, wobbling as I tried to strike a balance between speed and safety. The roof shingles were slick, and rain streaked down my face, getting into my eyes. When I was just steps away from the trellis, my foot slid out from under me. I landed hard on the roof and skidded down its slope. Fast. There wasn't even breath in my lungs for a proper scream. I tried clawing at the roof, but I only managed to scrape my palms as I continued to fall. Seconds later, I cleared the edge and was in the air. The ground was coming at me at breakneck speeds. I closed my eyes tight and braced for impact.

And then I wasn't falling anymore. Some kind of force like a burst of wind blew up against me and stopped my descent.

I opened my eyes. The merciless ground was still waiting for me, but I wasn't getting any closer to it. Then I realized why. *I was suspended in midair*!

And Jack Connelly, now only yards away, had his palm stretched out toward me as if he were the reason why.

He *was* the reason why, I realized with wide-eyed disbelief.

At Jack's hand movement, the force of air gradually lowered me to the ground feet first. My knees almost gave out. No sooner had the moment passed, the ravens from the attic sped toward me like torpedoes.

Jack made a sweeping motion with his arms, like a baseball

umpire calling 'safe.' The instant his hands shot outward, every last bird around us exploded into feathers and black smoke.

"Scarlet," he called out, "run!"

He didn't have to tell me twice. I bolted into the nearby woods and took cover behind a tree, my heart pounding so hard I thought it'd give out any second. I needed to catch my breath. I leaned over, planting my hands on my knees, and tried to steady my breathing.

Letty-Bean, you don't have to be afraid.

Letty-Bean. It was my mom's nickname for me, created from the second syllable of my name: *let*. My mom had called me that for as long as I could remember, back when I still played with tea sets and stuffed animals.

The words brought me back to a hospital room, my mom before me frail, pale, and shriveled up. Medical machines surrounded us, beeping nonstop.

"Oh, Letty-Bean," my mom had said that day, when the doctors had given their final prognosis. Nothing was working, they'd said. The cancer was too aggressive; they'd done all they could. My mom had weakly reached for my hand, hers ice cold. There were small tubes coming out of its veins. An orange band dwarfed her wrist, smelling like something between baby powder and antiseptic. "You don't have to be afraid." She'd meant the words to be comforting, but they'd only made me cry despite how hard I'd tried to be strong for her.

Now I heard those words again. *You don't have to be afraid.* Back then, my mom's voice had been soft and coarse. Now the voice that spoke was strong, crystal-clear, soothing. And...real.

It wasn't coming from inside my head. It was coming from behind me, spoken aloud.

I spun around.

And then I scrambled back against the tree in shock.

Before me stood my mom. But not as the woman I had

last seen. This rendition of my mom was radiant. Strong, healthy. Her hair—her hair had grown back!—was its typical cinnamon brown. Thick, lush, and cascading just past her shoulders, where it slightly curled at the ends. There was blush on her cheeks and a vibrant light in her eyes.

"M-mom?" I stared at her, my throat suddenly parched as if lined with sandpaper.

"It's me," she said. Her voice was musical, loving. Her smile was like sunshine.

"But how? How is this happening?"

She held out a hand to me. "Come with me, baby. It's okay. I can help you. I can protect you. Let me take you away from here."

There was a blinding light all around her. At the hospital chapel, there'd been little prayer cards available with saints on one side, an aura of gold surrounding them. My mom looked like one of those saints now.

I looked down to her outstretched hand. It had been months. Nearly four, to be exact. Four grueling, painful, heart-rending months. Though I had my pictures and my videos, which I turned to on nights when the heartache was particularly unbearable, it was nothing like my mom's actual physical presence. Nothing would ever be like that.

I wasn't sure what was happening right now. I didn't know how it was happening either. But I reached my hand forward, reached for my mom's fingertips, simply wanting to touch her skin again.

As I did, ribbons of black cloud started to surround me like mist. They filled my nose with a heady fragrance. At once, I felt light and airy, as if all my worries had been washed away, as if nothing else in the world mattered. My eyelids grew heavy. I was so tired...

Five deafening gunshots blasted into the air. My mom's form vanished like a snuffed out candle.

"No!" The scream that left my mouth was the sound of a tortured soul. I stared in horror and then faced the culprit. It was Jack, striding in my direction, eyes still fixed on the point where my mom had been standing, gun still aimed if she chose to reappear. In his black coat, he looked like a specter of darkness.

"Are you insane?" I yelled at him over the rain.

"Whatever you saw, it was only an illusion."

"No," I said, shaking my head. It couldn't have been. It was real. It had to be. I needed it to be. "My mom was right there."

"That wasn't your mother."

"I think I'd know my own mother if I saw her."

"He's lying, Scarlet. Of course I'm real."

I whirled around. My mom had reappeared. She extended her hand toward me, still wanting to help me.

"Mom!" I moved toward her, but the gunshots came again, and just when I was about to turn on Jack in a rage, my mom's image suddenly devolved into a shrieking, horrifying, demonic thing. In her place stood an emaciated creature with desiccated skin, razor-sharp fangs, and eyes as red as blood.

This thing, this thing that had been wearing my mom's face, snarled and lunged for me, teeth bared, but Jack sent one more bullet into its face, and it exploded into shadows and dust and feathers.

I sank to my knees, lightheaded, drained, out of breath.

Jack knelt beside me, a gentle hand to my back.

Feathers still floated in the air. We were surrounded by them. They stuck to our arms, to our faces. Shaking all over, I rushed to brush them off me, not wanting anything to do with whatever that *thing* had been.

"Scarlet, are you all right?"

No, I was far from all right. My head was spinning. I couldn't keep my eyes open. Something was happening to me, I knew, but I couldn't get the words past my tongue.

"Scarlet?"

The last thing I remembered was slumping against Jack's body. Then my eyes were filled with nothing but black.

13

When I finally awoke, it was to the sound of birdsong. My eyes reluctantly peeled open. Pillars of sunlight slanted through the window, lace curtains ballooning out in the breeze.

I blinked once, twice. When my vision focused, I stared at the sight opposite me. An unfamiliar, antique dresser with a three-panel mirror on top displayed my reflection. I lounged on the white sheets of a large canopy bed, sheer fabric tied back to each of its four posts.

I bolted upright. Then immediately regretted it as my head swam dizzily. Once the spell passed, I swung my bare feet over the edge of the mattress and stood. The freezing floorboards creaked in protest.

Beyond the window, there was nothing but rolling green fields topped by mist. I was at least three levels high, and there was not a soul in sight across the property. Where was I? How had I gotten here?

As if in answer, a deluge of memories overcame me like a tsunami. My dad motionless on the office floor, the Connellys materializing, the mob of ravens Lucas had called the sluagh, my mom...

My heart sank at that last one. She'd looked so *real*. It had been the realest experience I'd had of her since her death, far more affecting than a simple photograph or a ten-second clip on my phone of her blowing out birthday candles.

And it had been devastating to discover I'd only been interacting with...with what exactly? Red eyes glowed in my mind. Gunshots exploded between my ears. The flashes of memory came to me in a muddled haze. The last thing I could vividly recall was overwhelming dizziness. After that, nothing.

Unfortunately, my surroundings didn't offer much in the way of clues. I was in the same clothes I'd been wearing when the sluagh had attacked, though they were miraculously dry now, but I definitely wasn't in the same house.

I cracked open the bedroom door, frowning at the bandages on my palms, and looked up and down the hallway. I was completely alone. The corridor was long, seemingly unending, and dimly lit. The top half of its walls was covered in old-fashioned wallpaper. The bottom half boasted gleaming, cherry oak paneling.

At the end of the hall was a grand spiral staircase, the kind with two, curved arms branching off the center. Above, a giant chandelier dripped from a towering ceiling. This wasn't just any ordinary home. It was an estate.

I descended the stairs. The ground level was decorated tastefully with furniture from another era and rugs so thick your feet sank into them with each step. There were portraits in gilded frames on the wall, some of landscapes and some of people, the latter a bit unsettling if only because it felt like the subject's eyes were following you as you passed. A fireplace was lit in a quiet nook, the flames snapping and popping, but I couldn't shake the sense that the estate had a feeling of emptiness about it, as if it wasn't quite lived in. As if it were a tomb.

As I furthered along, light conversation leaked out of a

nearby room. I followed the voices but stopped short of actually entering the space. Instead, I peeked through the crack between the open door and the wall.

The Connelly boys were there, speaking with a man who sat behind a large, claw-foot desk. The room was a library, two-levels high with rolling ladders and balconies. I'd never seen so many books in a person's home library. The spines made up a multi-colored tapestry that wove all around the room.

"You know the rules about bringing outsiders here," the man behind the desk said.

"We couldn't just leave her in Rosalyn Bay," Jack replied.

"Yes, we could've." Connor. I narrowed my eyes at his backside.

"Your brother's right," the man said. "We know nothing about the girl. I'm sorry to hear of her circumstances, but you should've never gotten yourselves involved. In doing so, you've only endangered yourselves."

"A risk I was willing to take," Jack said. "She plays a part in all this. I know it. Even if she knows nothing about our world, she isn't Sightless. How else would she have been able to banish that demon?"

"I still don't understand why a demon approached you in the first place," Connor said. "What did it want? What did it say to you?"

"Nothing of consequence," Jack replied easily.

I drew up short at that. The demon—God, was I actually using that word?—had definitely said plenty of things of consequence.

That's it, isn't it? They don't know. You haven't told them what you've done.

Jack was lying. The question was why...and about what exactly?

"Scarlet was attacked last night same as all the others," Jack went on, addressing the man again. "She's clearly one of us, and now she's directly involved in what's been happening to our people. The Seer's message is coming true."

The man let out a heavy sigh. "Jack, we've been through this enough times, haven't we? You're making connections where there are none to be made. How can you truly believe this girl is the missing element in your quest to help Maurice? There's no reason why she would be, especially when, by your own account, she knows nothing of our world. Who is this Seer into whom you've put so much trust? I have half a mind to speak with them myself."

"Does it matter? The signs are clear. Somehow, Scarlet is instrumental in helping us. I know she is."

I switched my weight from one foot to the other to get more comfortable, but when I did, a floorboard creaked. Oops. The man and the brothers whipped their heads in my direction.

Seeing no point in continuing to hide, I stepped out from behind the door to reveal myself.

The man frowned at me, clearly unhappy by my eavesdropping. "Jack," he said, "see to your guest, please."

"Where's my dad?"

Jack and I had just exited the estate—he offered me a spare pair of rain boots on our way out—and we were now walking toward a wet grove of moss-covered trees, twigs snapping underfoot upon the squishy ground. There was a feeling of oldness about the trees, as if their leaves, which dripped rainwater at a languid pace, held timeless secrets. Overhead, birds tossed chirps back and forth in riveting dialogue, but other than that, the place was entirely still.

"We brought him to a hospital on the outskirts of Rosalyn Bay. He's stable, and he's being monitored around the clock."

"Stable? Does that mean he's woken up?"

"The situation's a bit more complicated than that."

I took a deep breath, willing the tightness in my chest to go away. "Meaning?"

"As you now know, your father was attacked by the sluagh last night. If they hadn't shown up themselves, we could've guessed it from the west-facing window in his office. The sluagh only ever enter a home from the west. They're also the ones who attacked my grandfather, and they're responsible for a number of other similar incidents throughout Ireland over the past four weeks. Your father's case, however, is unique in that he's the only known survivor of their attacks."

It should've bolstered my spirits, but it only made me feel queasy. "Why did they spare him?"

"Trust me, it wasn't their intention. The sluagh are soul thieves. When they attack, it generally means certain death for their victims, as a body can't exist without its soul. Not unless certain measures are taken."

"What kind of measures?"

He weighed his words before answering. "Did your father ever mention which student had given him that tea for his cold?"

I missed a breath. "It was you?"

"Lucas actually. He has a class with your father. When he informed me your father had fallen ill, I knew it was the perfect opportunity for us to intervene. Rory prepared the mixture at my request and then Lucas presented it to your father, insisting he share it with you as well lest you catch your father's bug."

I thought back to the tea I'd enjoyed yesterday, how I'd marveled at all the different ingredients in the sachet: flower buds, leaves, pieces of bark, berries. "Are you telling me a *tea* is the reason my dad's still alive?" It wasn't necessarily the craziest thing I'd heard so far, but I still struggled to find a holding in the revelation.

"In short, yes. It's not an ordinary tea. It's spelled."

I was sure I'd misheard him. "Excuse me?"

"It's preserving his body in a way, holding him in a fixed state until his soul can be returned to him, at which point he'll awaken again."

The specific word he'd used—*spelled*—was still in the back of my mind, but I had more pressing questions. "What happens if his soul isn't returned? Does he stay asleep forever?" Guilt needled my heart. I hadn't made much of an effort to connect with my dad ever since moving here, and now he was going to be taken away from me too? I couldn't accept that. We had just begun to make some progress in getting to know each other.

"Not exactly," Jack said, though he didn't look inclined to elaborate.

"What is it?"

"Scarlet, the tea is only so potent. It can only stave off the inevitable for so long. And because it must be ingested while a person is still conscious, there's no way to replenish the supply once someone has fallen asleep."

"What are you saying?"

"Your father's body has little more than one or two weeks in this fixed state. If his soul hasn't been returned to him by then..."

My stomach roiled. No, this couldn't be happening. I stared at Jack, shell-shocked. "Then I'll lose him?" I thought I was going to be sick simply saying the words.

Jack's face was pained, as if the loss was his own. "I'm so sorry."

"But at the greenhouse, you said there'd been a mix-up, that you'd been wrong about me. You said my dad and I weren't in any danger."

"It was clear you knew absolutely nothing about our world, and I didn't know what to make of that. If I was severely mistaken about you, then sharing too much could potentially be to my family's detriment. I had to rein myself in until I was absolutely sure about the role you played in this. Even then, I did what I could to protect you and your father should the sluagh target you both next."

"I don't understand. Why were we targeted at all? Why are the sluagh doing this?"

"That's what we haven't quite figured out yet, their motive. This is typical behavior for the sluagh, but no one has ever seen an attack on this scale in so short a window of time. Something big must be happening, and the sooner we can stop it, the sooner we can save your father before it's too late and the sooner we can allow the sluagh's other victims to find peace."

"Your nightmares about your grandfather," I said, thinking back to what Jack had shared in the greenhouse. "This is the reason for his soul's unrest, isn't it?"

Jack nodded. "The sluagh have no interest in releasing their victims to the afterlife. That's part of the fun for them. The kidnapped souls are tethered to their assailants. Eventually, they lose all sense of self and devolve into demon-like creatures, following the flock for all eternity, not even remembering they once had families of their own."

Yeah, I was definitely going to be sick. I swallowed back the bile rising in my throat. Then I thought about the thing that had pretended to be my mom. "That's how they ensnare people in the first place. By wearing the face of family members or friends, people that you love."

"It's their cruelest trick. Once you take your loved one's hand, you're doomed. Of course, by that point, you don't even see it coming. The mist that surrounds them is something of a poison, leaving you transfixed. It doesn't matter how nonsensical the illusion is. You'll believe it, and you'll want it more than anything else."

That I could verify firsthand. I rubbed my chest as if to soothe my bruised heart. What had my dad seen in his office? What had Maurice seen that had led him over those guard rails and straight off the cliff edge?

"Is that why I lost consciousness? Was I poisoned by them? Am I still poisoned?"

"You were affected, yes, but I fortunately got to you in time. You were able to sleep off the toxin overnight since it wasn't a substantial amount. And if your memory of the incident has been foggy in any way, it should clear up by this evening."

I supposed I had him to thank for that. Truthfully, I had him to thank for a lot. The only reason my dad was still clinging to life was because of Jack. The only reason I was able to have this conversation right now was because of Jack.

"So how do we stop them then?" I asked, only a little surprised by the iron in my voice. My dad was the only family I had now. I thought back to the album he'd given me just yesterday morning, the kindness and love he'd conveyed in so simple a gesture. He didn't deserve this. He needed me to help him, and so I'd get his soul back no matter what. This couldn't be the way our story ended. Not when it'd only just begun.

"That's what we're here to figure out."

"And where is here exactly?"

"We're just outside of Galway, about two hours southeast of Rosalyn Bay. And this is Crowmarsh. It's been in my family for generations. My uncle Seamus, the man you saw earlier, is the current proprietor."

"He didn't seem too thrilled about my being here."

"He's only being cautious," Jack explained. He took a moment to weigh out his next words. "People have always feared what they don't understand, and unfortunately, fear can sometimes result in terrible acts. As such, he isn't very keen on offering room and board to the Sightless."

There was that word again. "What do you mean when you say 'Sightless?'"

Jack didn't answer at first. He glanced toward the estate, as if he feared the repercussions that might follow if he answered my question. Ultimately, for whatever reason, he decided to continue. He let go of a sigh.

"It comes from the Irish words *gan léargas*. They literally mean 'without visibility.' We use them to describe someone who's Sightless. They're unable to see the world as we do."

"And how exactly do you see the world?"

He met my eyes full on and searched for something in them. Maybe assurance that I could handle whatever he was about to say next. Then he spoke again.

"My family is descended from a unique lineage, Scarlet." A brief pause, and then, "You could say it's rather...magical in nature."

14

A unique lineage. Magical. I instantly thought back to Liam's story. "It's true then. You're related to that woman who was persecuted in Rosalyn Bay centuries ago."

Jack looked both surprised and pleased that I knew the history. "We are. Her name was Elizabeth Connelly."

Elizabeth Connelly, who'd been accused of witchcraft.

Suddenly, a memory from last night surfaced, one I supposed had been suppressed by the sluagh toxin until now. I'd been on the roof of the cottage at one point, hadn't I? I'd fallen. I stared down at the bandages on my palms, remembering the way the shingles had scraped against my skin. I'd slipped right past the edge, seconds away from a landing that would've surely killed me. Or at least broken several of my bones.

But Jack had kept me in the air simply by holding out his hand.

I stared at him, the words right on my tongue but my deep sense of rational thinking incapable of pushing them out. But could I really deny it any longer? The evidence was as clear as day.

I thought about Rory unfazed by the moving vine in class

that first day, the way his finger had seemed to follow its path. I thought about Connor's strange hand gesture during the rugby game and how well-timed it was with that Xavier boy's fall, how a referee had found a depression in the ground I was sure hadn't been there before. And what about the wind picking up to punish Gallagher when he'd made those offensive comments at the menhirs and how Lucas had looked so entertained?

Nevermind, I now recalled, the way Jack had utterly destroyed the ravens surrounding us once he'd guided me back to my feet from my fall last night.

"You're witches," I whispered, shock and awe coloring my tone. Real-life witches with the ability to do impossible, unexplainable things. Things that defied the very laws of nature. Things that no ordinary human being could do.

I continued gawking at him, at a loss for words. The ground became uneven, and I braced a hand against an oak, trying to control my hiccupping heart. "Is there any truth to what the townspeople say then? Do you and your brothers mean to avenge Elizabeth?"

Jack sighed, tucking his hands into the pockets of his black coat. "I see no shortage of rumors have found their way to you. But no, whatever 'fire and brimstone' stories you've heard, it's not our intention to harm anyone, as much as Connor might wish otherwise."

"The things you're able to do, though? How...?" I shook my head, losing my place, still trying to gather my bearings. "Were you born with those abilities?"

"Like I said, ours is a unique lineage, one that can be traced back to the druids of ancient Celtic societies. We are, in fact, among their last remaining descendants."

"The druids were witches?" I couldn't recall Professor Byrne making any mention of the sort in his lecture.

"They were judges, healers, philosophers, priests, lore keepers, and more. They taught others how to cultivate love and respect for nature. They even served as advisors to legendary kings. Some were kings themselves. But they're most known, at least by us, for the magic they practiced and their mystical abilities. Some could see the future. Some could know a man's thoughts just by looking at him. Some could even take on the appearance of any man or animal."

I tried to swallow, but my throat was too dry. My mind was spinning now. "Do you have those abilities too?"

He smiled a little. "Every Celtic witch has the ability to call upon the four Quarters, or what you might be more familiar with as the four elements."

"Earth, air, fire, water." That explained some of the phenomena I'd witnessed thus far.

"Apart from that, we're also each born with something called a Mastery. It's an innate gift that fully manifests once a witch comes of age. Usually around sixteen, though there are no hard rules. There are all kinds of Masteries, and sometimes a witch may have more than one."

He didn't mention what his Mastery was, and I couldn't bring myself to ask. Maybe a part of me preferred not to know just yet. I was having a hard enough time processing what he was already revealing.

"So are you and your brothers the only remaining descendants of the druids, or are there others?"

"Our lineage is one of only seven remaining druidic lines. Although we believe it may very well be six these days, as one hasn't been heard from in decades."

"What happened to them?"

"Like I said before, people have always feared what they don't understand."

He led me to an area marked off by a black, iron fence. It was a cemetery, and as we weaved between its tired oaks, my stomach twisted unpredictably. Jack stopped at a headstone against which was set a small teddy bear and a bouquet of flowers. The name Bree Ó Broin was engraved into the marker. The occupant of this resting place had died last year. She'd been three years old. My heart sank.

"My uncle's daughter," Jack said. "My cousin. And beside her, my uncle's wife."

The second headstone read Neala Ó Broin.

"What happened?"

"Neala had gone to France to visit family. Bree was with her. They were targeted by long-time enemies of our people."

"In the greenhouse, Connor had mentioned hunters." At the time, I'd been thinking about a hunter of a completely different type.

Jack nodded. "When the Celts were conquered throughout Europe, their beliefs were demonized. Your typical, run-of-the-mill fear-mongering and ignorance. They accused us of devil worship, of performing sadistic rituals. A sect began to emerge, a band of hunters called The Black Hand. Its members wanted to purge their newly conquered territories of any and all pagan influence. They believed the time for gods and magic and reverence for nature had come to an end and that it was their solemn duty to wash the lands clean of sin. So they hunted down known druids and their descendants and slaughtered them like animals. And so began a very long history of persecution that reached its peak during The Burning Times."

"The Burning Times?"

"You're probably more familiar with the American incident in Salem, Massachusetts. Most people don't know there were countless other witch trials all over the world: the North Berwick Trials in Scotland, the Torsaker Trials in Sweden, and, of course, the largest witch trial in European history: The Witch Trials of Trier. Which was, by all accounts, a massacre.

"More druidic bloodlines than we can count were killed off during these mass executions, leaving us with just the seven. And even among those clans, there are those who haven't passed down the traditions to their children, fearing persecution. That said, there are people all over the world at this very moment with druidic blood in their veins, and they're none the wiser. The magic is dormant in them."

"I don't understand. Why does the persecution persist to this day? This is the twenty-first century."

"The Black Hand is filled with fanatics, zealots. Because of our abilities, they believe we're the offspring of our ancestors' alleged liaisons with the devil. To them, we're abominations to the natural order of things and therefore a threat to their corrupted dogmas. Exterminating us has become their holy mission."

There were so many headstones marking so many graves. "Are all of these people...?"

"Victims of hunters? No. Many of them are, but the great numbers here are simply due to the fact that every Connelly has been buried in Crowmarsh for generations. Including extended family, which is why Neala and Bree are here. I think that's part of the reason Seamus accepted my grandfather's invitation to oversee Crowmarsh after he lost them, so that he could be closer to them. Plus, the upkeep would give him something to do to take his mind off the grief inasmuch as possible. And then further down that way is my grandfather's resting place, though his marker hasn't arrived yet from the stonecutter."

"What about Elizabeth? Is she here as well?"

"The Connellys alive at the time weren't able to recover her remains, unfortunately. Doing so would've been punishable by death. But there's still a headstone here by which we remember her."

I was quiet for a moment as I turned something over in my

head. "Inside, you were trying to convince your uncle that I was one of you. Did you mean a witch?"

"We don't know why the sluagh have been attacking on such a large scale, but we do know they've been uncharacteristically particular about their victims these past weeks. They've only been targeting witches from one of the remaining clans. It stands to reason that if you and your father were attacked..."

Then it had to mean we were witches. And it was highly likely that my dad, who definitely didn't practice any kind of magic, wasn't even aware. After all, Jack had said the secret had been withheld from many descendants over the years to protect them from persecution.

But the very notion was absurd. I shook my head. "But I can't do what you and your brothers do."

"You haven't been raised in the ways of a Celtic witch, and so your magic's dormant. Neglecting it has stunted the natural emergence of your Mastery. With the right training, guidance, and instruction, there's no telling what you'll be able to do. You're already powerful as it stands. Look at what you were able to do to that demon. I've never seen any witch banish one like that, not without sigils or spellcraft."

"Demons. Right. Those apparently exist too." My head was starting to throb. "Where do they come from? Hell?"

"They come from a forsaken land in the Otherworld, which is where they return when they're banished. They generally don't interact with the Sightless. Witches are another matter."

"I think I need to sit down." Everything was tilting at a steeper angle now.

Jack placed a hand to my lower back and guided me to a stone bench. As we sat, I tried to ignore the gathering warmth in my stomach at his touch.

"I know it's a lot to absorb, but it's true, Scarlet. There's far more to the world than most people ever see in their lifetime."

I was finding I liked the sound of my name in his mouth. I liked the way the *R* curled against his tongue. Unfortunately, not even the musical cadence of his words lessened their gravity. The fact still stood that the sluagh were targeting witches for unknown reasons, and I had almost been one of their victims. But Jack had intervened before I'd fallen prey to them, and he'd protected my dad as well with the 'spelled' tea. I realized I still hadn't thanked him for that.

I angled toward him, looking deep into those striking, dark amber eyes. The dark circles under them only added to the air of sorrow about him. He released whatever thought he'd been reflecting on and switched his eyes to me, holding my gaze steadily. My pulse stuttered, and just like that, I missed a breath. I hadn't noticed how close we were sitting, our knees almost touching. It was a typical, fall afternoon, but I could barely feel the chill in the air anymore.

I parted my lips to say something, something that would no doubt inadequately encompass the gratitude I felt toward him in that moment.

A throat cleared from behind us, and the spell broke in an instant. I twisted around, hoping my cheeks weren't too red. It was Connor. Why wasn't I surprised?

Arms crossed and lips set in a straight line, his eyes practically branded me. I wondered if there was ever a moment when Connor wasn't angry about something.

"Seamus wants to see her," Connor said, speaking to Jack but keeping his blazing eyes on me.

"It's all right," Jack said softly to me.

I hadn't realized I'd tensed at Connor's words, as if my turn had come to stand before a firing squad. It certainly felt that way.

15

When we returned to the library where I'd first spotted Jack and the others, Seamus was paging through a large, leather book with yellow pages that made a sound like crunching leaves as he turned them. Sitting on his desk was a framed picture of a woman in a valley of wildflowers, holding a little girl on her hip who clung to her affectionately. The woman had smooth, radiant skin the color of caramel and curly, black hair. The girl was the spitting image of her mother. Neala and Bree.

As for Seamus, he looked to be in his mid to late forties. He had salt and pepper hair and medium-length stubble. He brought to mind the type of guy who wore flannel shirts, lived in a cabin in the woods, and cut his own firewood.

"Scarlet, is it? We haven't as of yet been properly introduced. I'm Seamus Ó Broin. Jack has told me a great deal about you."

His voice was a deep baritone, rich and smooth like cake batter, but his features were guarded. After losing his wife and daughter to hunters, he was clearly on high alert against any threats to his family, which meant I was more foe than friend to him right now. I swallowed the lump in my throat.

"Tell me," he went on. "What possessed you to come to my

nephew's aid when that demon confronted him? Jack was a complete stranger to you. You owed him nothing. And yet, by his account, you did everything in your power to protect him."

My cheeks burned. It was awkward enough to answer the question with Jack standing right there beside me. But his brothers surrounded us too, hanging on my every word. I cleared my throat, feeling like it was lined with cobwebs all of a sudden. "To be honest, I don't know. I just felt compelled to help him, I guess. It all happened so quickly. I didn't really have the time to second-guess myself, only to act."

Seamus's eyes remained fastened on me for a few long moments, as if he were sifting through my thoughts, trying to unearth the truth. "And your ability to banish the demon—what do you make of that?"

I shook my head. "I couldn't tell you. I've never done anything like that before. I'm still not convinced I did anything at all. I've only ever lived an ordinary life up until now. I doubt I'd be able to do it a second time if I had to."

"You've never witnessed strange, inexplicable occurrences before then? Perhaps you once noticed something peculiar about your father or another family member in his bloodline but were quick to rationalize it?"

"I've never met my dad's side of the family, and trust me, there's nothing 'witchy' about him. He's just an every-day guy."

Seamus's eyes switched to Jack, and he frowned slightly before looking back to me. "I see my nephew has shared more than I imagined with you. Now you know the truth of what we are, and possibly of what you are as well."

"He was only trying to help me understand," I said. "I promise you I'm not interested in putting your family in any kind of danger. Right now, the only thing I care about is getting my dad's soul back before it's too late."

The man held my gaze, seeming to weigh my words. Finally,

he nodded. "You must forgive us if our welcome hasn't been quite as warm as you might've hoped. These are dangerous times for our people. We must exercise caution when interacting with those we know nothing about. Though I would've preferred my nephews to avoid becoming entangled with an outsider, there's little I can do about it now. We can only move forward, and we must do so hastily. For I believe we have to consider the possibility at this point that the sluagh aren't acting of their own volition."

"What do you mean?" Jack asked. "You think someone's controlling them? Who?"

Seamus rubbed his forehead, a deeper frown pulling at his mouth. "Hunters."

My nerves jumped. It wasn't the answer I'd been expecting. According to Jack, The Black Hand was ruthless, merciless. Its members had to be if they'd go so far as to take the life of an innocent toddler like Bree.

A flurry of thoughts passed behind Jack's eyes. "We initially suspected hunters when Grandda was first found. I ruled them out once I learned it was the sluagh. But if the sluagh are actually working for The Black Hand, that would explain why they've specifically targeted witches these past weeks."

Seamus nodded. "Of course, if the sluagh are indeed being directed, then we have to accept that the hunters are working with a witch as well, as only a witch can summon and control supernatural creatures such as the sluagh."

"Wait," I said. "Why would a witch work with hunters? Doesn't that go against their own self-interests?"

"Unfortunately," Seamus said, "there have been witches known to betray their own kind over the years. It's happened more often than any of us would care to admit. Working in tandem with hunters, they travel all over the world and ingratiate themselves with established communities of witches, doing whatever they can to gain their trust. Then they turn on them."

I guessed it made sense then why Seamus cautioned his nephews against befriending outsiders. Even if someone appeared to have the best intentions—in the form of banishing a demon, for instance—who was to say they didn't intend on selling you out later down the road? Had it not been for the fact that the sluagh had targeted me last night, there'd be no way for the Connellys to prove I wasn't their enemy.

Maybe that was what had spooked Rory on my first day of class. I'd drawn a symbol long associated with the witches in Rosalyn Bay, but I was an unknown, and therefore I could've easily been bad news. It also explained why Connor wanted to turn me away at the greenhouse, insisting my presence could be nothing more than a trap.

"This isn't a rival we can confront on our own," Seamus continued. "We'll need to reach out to the other clans and unite as one body if we hope to stand a chance. I think it'd be best to request an audience with The Council of Elders. They'll know how we might be able to defeat the hunters and the sluagh, and more importantly, free the souls of our people."

The words kindled a spark of hope in me. If this Council knew how to rescue the kidnapped souls, that meant I was one step closer to helping my dad. "Where is The Council located? Will it take us long to get there?"

"I'm afraid I must seek out The Council on my own. Your presence would present far too great a risk."

I blinked, taken aback. "What? How?"

"The sluagh have already caught your scent, which makes you a walking homing beacon wherever you go. Because they assisted you last night, the same holds true for my nephews. Now the sluagh, tireless predators that they are, will stop at nothing to claim your souls. Even if I were to cloak you with magic, they would still smell you."

Another reason why he would've preferred his nephews to not get involved with me, I realized. I really had endangered them. "Isn't there a way to kill them?" I asked, turning to Jack. "Last night, you shot at them, didn't you?"

"Those bullets didn't kill or banish the sluagh; neither did my magic against them. Both just forced the sluagh to briefly dematerialize so I could buy us time."

"That said," Seamus continued, "for your safety, the five of you will remain here in Crowmarsh, which I've already spelled to ward off any attacks. The sluagh won't be able to get to you so long as you remain within the estate."

"No way," I said. "I'm not going to sit here under lock and key while my dad's body wastes away in the hospital."

"This is the surest way to help your father."

"No, I need to *do* something."

"Stubborn little thing, isn't she?" Lucas draped an arm over my shoulders. "Scarlet Ibis, you've got some fire in you. Uncle, can we keep her?"

I shrugged him off, rolling my eyes. "If this is really about whether or not you can fully trust me, isn't there some kind of spell you can do to determine that?"

"She's talking about spellcraft now?" Lucas wiped at nonexistent tears. "They grow up so quickly, don't they?"

"Trust me," Connor said, "I'd love nothing more than to file through your memories to see who you've been colluding with recently, but you could've easily altered them in anticipation of an interrogation. Or blocked them altogether."

"And unfortunately," Lucas added, "we don't exactly have a spare Hallowstone casually lying around Crowmarsh."

"What's a Hallowstone?"

"It was one of witch-kind's most cherished relics," Jack

answered. "It came from a time when the Celts lived in peace in present-day Rosalyn Bay. Back then, there was a king named Fionn, who was very loved by his people. He was loved by the Celtic deities as well. So loved, in fact, that The Triple Goddess, Brigid, daughter of the All-Father, became his consort. In a symbolic sense, of course. Brigid could only walk among men on her feast day, Oimlec, which modern witches now call Imbolc. It marks the beginning of spring. So when Fionn and his people came under attack one summer night, she was unable to rush to their aid in her full power. Instead, she selected a single young woman from the clan, coming to her as an apparition and imbuing her with the strength and courage of the gods so that she could act on Brigid's behalf."

"Like a proxy?" I asked.

"In a way, yes. Brigid armed the young woman with two weapons. First, the legendary Sword of Light, which belonged to Nuada, the Celtic god of divine justice and truth. Forged in the Otherworld, it always struck true, and its blow was always fatal. The second weapon had been plucked right out of the night skies: the Allhallow, the brightest star in a constellation venerated by the local Celts.

"With these two weapons, Brigid's heroine was able to fend off an entire army of conquerors while the last of her clan escaped to safety. She and the other women Brigid selected over the centuries to protect her people became known as the god-touched, the Daughters of Brigid, a revered class of warrior witches entrusted with the sole purpose of protecting their clans. The last of their kind lived during The Burning Times, but every witch learns about them from a young age."

My chest tightened. "The vision I had at the menhirs—I saw a female warrior with light glowing from her palm, as if she were holding a star. There was a sword strapped to her back too. Could that have been...?" *The first Daughter?*

"What you saw was an Echo," Jack said. "It's a pulse of energy from witches who've come before us. It's meant to show truth or provide guidance."

"Have you seen the same vision too?"

"No, Echoes are selective when it comes to revealing themselves. A hundred witches might've touched that menhir after you, and not a single one would've seen anything. In your case, it's clear the Echo appeared to you to reveal the truth of your heritage, that you're a Celtic witch like us. And yes, it sounds like you witnessed the legend herself.

"As for her weapons, the Sword of Light was eventually returned to the Otherworld, where the gods dwell. The Allhallow, however, remained in the hands of the god-touched, passed from one Daughter to the next over the ages. During The Burning Times, The Council of Elders, which was newly formed then, insisted the Allhallow be broken into seven, smaller pieces called Hallowstones, each for the remaining druidic lines. It was meant to protect them against their enemies, so that persecutions would never happen on that scale again. But it was also meant to help them discern truth in times of darkness, as in the hands of a Celtic witch with an honorable heart, the stones were said to glow like the original star from which they came. Unfortunately, no one knows what ever became of the Hallowstones. A powerful witch stole them from the clans generations ago, but there's never any mention of them after that, leaving most to assume they were lost to time. In recent years, some have even suggested they were never more than a legend to begin with, a metaphor at best."

"Which is why our focus right now," Seamus said, "must be on The Council of Elders. They're our only hope at obtaining the answers we seek in this crisis we face."

"Although that might not necessarily be true," Jack said, coming to a realization. "What about The Wise Ones? We could always consult them. And it wouldn't take nearly as long as it would with The Council."

Seamus shook his head with a sigh. "I doubt they'll be much help at all, Jack. You know no one's had a proper audience with them in some time."

"But Grandda—"

"—was a dreamer," his uncle finished. "He was a man who liked to tell stories. And can you blame him? Your grandfather had such a difficult childhood. Poverty, tragedy, and then, of course, the war once he was a young man. He found comfort in the stories he told you. He enjoyed living in them because they consoled his broken soul. But you must know that's all they were. Stories. Folklore, legends, myths. There's no stock in most of them, I'm afraid."

I glanced to Jack, and the crestfallen look on his face pained me.

"Let me seek the wisdom of The Council," Seamus continued. "In the interim, I urge the five of you to remain here. My request has little to do with trust and everything to do with wanting to ensure your safety. We have endured enough losses, have we not?"

I had to remind myself of Neala and Bree, of how Seamus had to feel about facing off against the very ones who'd taken away his wife and daughter. It sobered me slightly, and the fight slowly left my body. I sighed. "How long will you be gone?"

"A few days at most."

It was too long when I already had so little time to recover my dad's soul. But I nodded nonetheless and kept my lips sealed. Seamus may have wanted me to stay put, and I'd pretend to oblige him for now.

But the fact of the matter was I was going to leave Crowmarsh the first chance I got.

16

In the predawn darkness, I crept through Crowmarsh on cat's feet, my heart thumping wildly at every moan of wood. Seamus had already left for The Council of Elders not half an hour ago. Jack and his brothers, however, were still asleep. This was my chance to escape. It was now or never.

Every shadow had a more sinister edge as I moved through the estate. Three times already, I'd stilled in my tracks, lungs clenching at what I thought was one of the Connellys watching me. It turned out to be a suit of armor in one case, a crowded coat rack in another, and billowing curtains on the third occasion. Nonetheless, I continued to strain to hear the telltale sounds of someone stirring from their sleep.

Even when I finally reached the ground level, my muscles were still tight, like springs coiling up and preparing to launch me into flight should the need arise. I moved quickly now, spurred on by my proximity to freedom.

The plan was to call Liam once I'd put enough distance between me and the estate and ask if he could wrangle up transportation and collect me. Of course, this all depended on my being able to catch a cell signal in this remote stretch of land.

Yesterday, I'd received a delayed text from Natalie asking why I'd missed our video chat date...about twenty hours after she'd sent it. I'd tried to text her back several times, but the delivery kept failing.

Finally, there it was: the entrance, marked by two, mammoth front doors with arched tops. Like most of the house, they looked to be from another era.

Almost there...

Before I knew it, my hand was on one of the doorknobs. Then I was unlocking the door and easing it open ever so slowly, relieved its hinges were well-greased.

Only when I glimpsed the property beyond did I allow myself to let go of a breath. The estate grounds were misty and indigo blue under the lightening skies. The last of the stars were dimming, and birds were beginning to awaken, calling out to their companions in quick, shrill notes.

I put one foot in front of the other to quickly pass through, but just as I was about to cross the threshold, I slammed into something that felt like a sheet of glass.

I reared back, my forehead throbbing from the impact. *What on earth?* Had I overlooked an exterior door, one of those glass-paneled types? I reached out a hand to test the doorway, and my palm came against something somewhat solid but also strange. When I applied more pressure against it, it felt like the repelling force sometimes created by magnets that refused to stick together.

There wasn't a second door at all. No hinges, no lock, no handle. My view of the estate's front lawn was as clear as ever. So then what *was* that?

"It's the ward."

I whirled around, breathless, the shock of the voice giving my heart a painful squeeze.

With the flip of a switch, stark light bathed the foyer. My

eyes winced at the sudden brightness. Connor was only a few steps away from me, arms crossed and shoulder leaning against the wall. Even dressed down in a simple shirt and lounge pants, that blistering look of his was still daunting. He looked like a wrathful deity.

How long had he been standing there? It couldn't have been more than a minute or two. I must've been so preoccupied with the mysterious non-door that I hadn't heard him approach.

He arched an eyebrow. "Going somewhere?"

I steeled myself. Maybe Connor was used to successfully intimidating rugby rivals and whatever St. Andrew's classmates grated on his nerves, but I wasn't going to cower away from him.

"I need to leave," I said, practically speaking through my teeth.

"That's not going to happen."

"You can't just keep me here. I'll call the police if I have to."

He shrugged. "Have at it. You think they want to come anywhere near this place? Not that they'd be able to anyway. No one in, no one out. That's sort of how a double ward works."

So much for Seamus offering me sanctuary. This was more like a prison sentence. Heat filled my chest. "What part of 'my dad could die' don't you understand? I'm not going to sit here, twiddling my thumbs, while your uncle talks to whoever these Council people are."

"Don't you get it? You're a danger to anyone you're around right now because of the sluagh. Jack's blind faith in you is reckless. Believe me, I want nothing more than to cut ties with you, but Jack would only go after you. And you'd definitely get him killed."

"Except, as you can see, I'm alone right now. It was never my intention to drag Jack along."

"And how exactly did you picture that working out for you? You don't know the first thing about how to help your father."

"You're right. I don't. Having your family's help would be ideal. Unfortunately, it doesn't look like I'll be getting that any time soon so long as your uncle has his way, so I'll have to figure things out for myself. If that means dealing with the sluagh on my own, then so be it."

Connor scoffed. "You mean the way you dealt with them back at your father's house? You practically served your own soul to them on a silver plate."

It would've hurt less had he slapped me. Anger simmered in my veins. What a jerk. If only he'd known how the sluagh had lured me in, how they'd played my grief against me.

"What's going on?" Jack strayed into the foyer then, his hair slightly disheveled and those black patches under his eyes more pronounced than usual despite a full night's rest. Assuming, of course, he'd slept at all.

When he saw one of the front doors open and realized I was dressed for the day, he instantly came to alert. "Where are you going?"

"Nowhere, apparently," I said, shooting a skewering look Connor's way.

"You know Seamus has always seen us like sons," Connor explained at Jack's questioning look, though the bite in his tone had dropped. Apparently it was only reserved for people he didn't like. Like me. "We're the only family he has now, and he'd do anything to protect us. This is him watching out for us, Jack, same as he's always done. The double ward—"

"*Double* ward? The ward was only meant to keep the sluagh out. Seamus made it so that we aren't able to leave either?" Jack strode to the front door to test the force field. Sure enough, it wouldn't budge for him.

"It'll only be in place until his return."

"You knew about this beforehand? And you said nothing?"

"I knew you'd object to it. And I happen to agree with him. In fact, I helped him cast the spell. I'm the totem upholding it."

"The totem?" I asked.

"Spells of this nature require on-site totems to uphold them," Jack explained. "They serve as a sort of conduit for the magic. If Connor's volunteered himself for the role, then he's the only one who can say the unlocking words that will reverse the spell and cause the wards to drop. If he doesn't, they stay in place."

"It's for the best," Connor said. "We neither know what we're up against, nor what we've invited in." He cut a searing glance in my direction at that.

"We already know Scarlet is not the enemy here, Connor. The Seer—"

"To bloody hell with the Seer, Jack! I swear to the gods, would you listen to yourself? You have demons approaching you in broad daylight. Don't tell me that doesn't faze you. Or have you stopped caring? Have you become like this one here, who'll run straight into the arms of demons at the first chance?"

"That's enough."

"No, I don't think it is. Maybe it's time you confess to Scarlet why Seamus and the rest of us are so insistent you sit this little demon-ridden escapade out."

My eyes ping-ponged between them in the tense silence that followed. "What is he talking about?"

Connor shook his head. "As I suspected. You've told her nothing about it, have you? You've gone on about our histories. You've told her a fair share of our witching secrets. But you've withheld this one truth from her. You knew it would send her running in the opposite direction faster than anything else."

"You know," I said, "you can stop talking about me as if I'm not standing right here."

Their eyes remained locked on each other, though, as if I

hadn't spoken. Jack's jaw was clenched tight, a single muscle pulsing at his cheek. Connor met him measure for measure, the hardness in his own gaze like stone.

"Go on, Jack," he said. "Tell her."

I couldn't imagine what more could be hiding beyond the smoke and mirrors. I shook my head. "Jack, whatever it is—"

"I'm cursed," Jack said flatly. He finally pulled his eyes away from the gravitational force of Connor's unbreakable stare and set them on me. There was a storm in them, fragments of both anger and despair. Perhaps a portion of worry too, as if he thought he might scare me away just as Connor had said.

"You know I've already heard all the stories."

"Not this one." Unceremoniously, he unfastened his watch and then showed me the inside of his wrist, where I'd first seen that burn scar.

But it wasn't a burn at all.

It was more than that.

It was a *brand*.

And the pink, raised skin formed a strange design. Within a circle was a stylized *X*. The *X* was intersected by a vertical line. And to the right of the top half of the line were two dots like a semicolon. Together, the symbols looked foreign, otherworldly.

"It's a demon's mark," Jack explained. "My mother and father had spent years trying to conceive children early on in their marriage. Just when they were about to lose hope, they became pregnant with me. They called it one of the happiest times of their lives.

"But when my mother went into labor with me, it was the start of a very difficult childbirth. At one point, the midwife didn't believe either of us would survive. My father couldn't stand to lose us, so he fled into the night and petitioned a crossroads demon for a favor. Spare our lives, and he would give the demon anything in return.

"The demon granted my father his request. My mother survived childbirth, and I came into the world healthy and strong...and Marked. Because, as with all such bargains, there was a catch. My father had offered anything, and so the demon's price was the very son my parents had spent years longing for.

"The demon didn't take me away right then and there, of course. A baby was of no use to him. He wanted me to be raised in the witching ways and allowed to come into my power. Then, on the Old Moon during my eighteenth year, he'd finally come to collect the debt owed him."

My pulse stuttered as dread pooled in my stomach. *Cursed.* The unbelievable stories Thomas and Liam had shared did, in fact, hold some truth. But in a frightening way none of the townspeople would've ever expected. In a way *I* would've never expected.

I groped for words, my mind whirling. All I could do was stare at the brand on Jack's wrist. Then I remembered something. Jack was already eighteen, wasn't he? So...

"When is the Old Moon?" I asked, my voice barely above a whisper.

"It's what we call January's full moon."

My stomach lurched. That was only three months from now. That had to be why the demon had come for him at the rugby game. He and his kind were apparently getting an early start. Jack's time was slipping away from him fast like sand between his fingers.

My throat dried. "And what exactly happens then? Do you...*die*?"

Jack was already fastening his watch back into place to cover the mark. "In a sense. I'll take up permanent residence in the Otherworld. Demons are rarely wasteful creatures, so I imagine they'll find some sort of use for me there. A witch as their puppet would be a powerful weapon to wield."

He answered so casually, as if discussing nothing more than a summer trip from which he planned to return. Then again, he'd been living with this for eighteen years. He'd probably come to terms with it by now.

"Couldn't you hide from them somehow?" Was it possible to hide from demons? I had no idea.

"If I renege on the bargain, then the demon will come for one of my brothers instead."

And naturally he wouldn't let that happen. *My brother's keeper.* The saying fit Jack to a tee. He really was a protector in every possible way.

"Connor's right. I should've been more forthright about my circumstances from the very beginning. There are certain risks involved in keeping company with me where demons are concerned. But my grandfather believed we could break the curse. We were getting closer to unearthing a way to free me from the demon's bargain. The night of his death, he'd found something he'd intended on sharing with me, something relative to the curse. It's one of the reasons I knew he hadn't taken his life."

"What are you talking about?" Connor asked him, furrowing his brow. "You've never mentioned anything like that."

"I didn't want to get anyone's hopes up in the likely case that we failed. And now with Grandda gone…" He shook his head, his eyes unreadable. Whatever he was feeling, though, he easily shook it off before addressing me.

"I'll understand if you want to part ways from this point on," he said. "But I do think we're better together, the five of us. I still believe you're the one from the Seer's message, and as much as you might waver on the idea, no one can deny you're one of us as well. I can help you come into your magic, Scarlet. More importantly, I can help you save your father. Seamus has turned to The Council, but I believe The Wise Ones can give us the guidance we need right now too, and I'm willing to bring you to them. And inasmuch as I'm able, I won't let any harm come to you if you agree to take this path."

His words sent a flutter through my chest, unwound some of the knots in my stomach. I wasn't going to lie. A part of me was scared. Jack's confession had increased the severity of the situation by a hundredfold. But even so, crazy as it was, much as it didn't make sense, I still trusted him. The same way, I realized, I'd been trusting him ever since the demon attack at the rugby game.

I still didn't understand this world or my place in it—if I had a place at all—but I knew it was far from Jack's fault that a demon had Marked him as its own. And beyond that, I knew continuing this journey with Jack by my side would be a lot easier than trying to help my dad on my own.

I pushed a long breath out of my lungs. There was no way of knowing whether or not I was making the right decision, but a decision had to be made nonetheless. "All right then," I said. "Let's go see The Wise Ones."

17

"So who are The Wise Ones anyway?"

It was a three-hour drive to our destination, but thanks to a monsoon of a rainstorm, we weren't making any considerable progress on the road. I'd asked earlier if the brothers couldn't simply dispel the rain but was told such an exertion of magic, sustained for the length of our journey, would only attract demons. I didn't press the matter further, given the tension already ballooning in the car between Jack and Connor, the latter having not spoken once since reluctantly saying the unlocking words that brought down the double ward on Crowmarsh.

In all honesty, I was surprised Connor had eventually given in to Jack, though I also got the feeling it wasn't the first time he'd relented to one of Jack's absurd ideas. Maybe learning Jack and Maurice had been trying to break the curse had something to do with his change of heart.

"And what about The Council of Elders that your uncle went to see?"

Jack lowered the music as The Four Aces began crooning "Mr. Sandman." Yet another selection from a by-gone era. I was surprised his brothers hadn't protested it or tried to change the station. Either they were also fans, or they followed the rule that the driver got to select the music, no questions asked.

"The Council of Elders consists of the seven eldest witches among druidic descendants—or six now rather—who each hail from one of the remaining bloodlines. As I mentioned before, The Council was assembled during The Burning Times. In the beginning, they mainly existed to inspire hope during what was nothing short of a dark era. Over time, they started to take on the role of disputing legal matters: territory lines, inheritances, intermarriage with the Sightless or with witches outside of the druidic clans. They also have the power to excommunicate a witch if he's believed to be traitorous. In that case, they would take away his powers."

The words sent a shiver through me. I pulled my cardigan closer. I'd been able to wash my clothes last night while outfitted in borrowed pajamas, and this morning before leaving, Jack had let me forage through a cousin's closet for additional clothes. They were folded in a backpack and stored in the trunk, joining a few duffel bags the brothers had packed which were filled with an assortment of weapons and other strange tools I didn't want to think about.

"What constitutes as treason?"

"If a witch loses himself to dark magic, the study of forbidden spellcraft, it's grounds for excommunication. At that point, he'd be too much of a threat to himself, to his clan, and to the other bloodlines as a whole."

"Have witches been excommunicated before?"

Jack's face turned grim. "It's happened a handful of times over the centuries. Generally, people who practice dark magic have an insatiable lust for power. They seek to upset the natural orders of the world, to tip the sacred balance in their favor. They tend to be so far gone they won't let anyone stand in their way of acquiring more power, even if it requires lethal means. That's why The Council removes their powers.

"But it's been at least a hundred years since anything like that has happened. These days, The Council is more so ceremonial in nature, a formality. Once in a while, they'll convene to deliberate a question that will restore balance to the clans. Otherwise, they tend to only be consulted by pilgrims who wish to receive their blessing and pursue more advanced studies under their tutelage. My uncle studied under them for a time after his loss, once managing Crowmarsh put him back on his feet."

"And the Elders live here in Ireland?"

"Yes and no," Jack said. "They live Elsewhere. It's a dimension of sorts. Think of the world as you know it as one large room in a house. At any time, you can open a door to step into another room—that's Elsewhere. There are countless rooms all over the globe a witch can access. It's only a matter of knowing where a door is and how to pass through it."

"And the door to see The Council?"

"Tucked away on a mountain peak."

"If The Council might have the answers we're looking for concerning the sluagh, then why are we going to see The Wise Ones?"

"At the end of the day, The Council, though I respect them immensely, can only lean on their own acquired knowledge, intuition, and magic. You might put it this way: The Council has a drop of insight whereas The Wise Ones will most certainly have the entire ocean."

"Then why didn't your uncle go see the latter?"

"Because my uncle is a pragmatist, and the more practical solution would be to seek the wisdom of The Council. The truth of the matter is The Wise Ones don't offer counsel to just anyone. They only grant an audience to one whose heart is pure, and they've been silent for so long. Of course, no one wants to believe themselves unworthy of an audience, so anyone who petitioned The Wise Ones only to be turned away without an answer decided The Wise Ones no longer held any significance in our lives and should be written off as a remnant of days long past. The last witch who spoke with them did so decades ago, though most don't believe the incident ever occurred."

"And who was that person?"

He smiled sadly. "My grandfather."

The storm worsened, forcing us off the road to take shelter in a shadowy tavern that smelled like nicotine and dirty toilets. I sat in a booth with Lucas and Rory, yellow foam poking out of the torn upholstery. The laminated menus were sticky and sparse, listing a handful of greasy foods that couldn't tempt even my hungry stomach.

Jack had disappeared for a short period earlier, but now he stood in a far-off corner, his phone pressed against his ear. I realized after a few moments that he wasn't speaking with anyone, only checking voicemail messages. Now that we'd left Rosalyn Bay and Crowmarsh behind, our cell signals had thankfully improved. Somewhat. I had called the hospital where my dad was staying earlier but had only caught thirty seconds' worth of updates from the nurse before the call had dropped.

In another corner, Connor was taking his frustration out on a dart board. I wasn't sure what to make of him at the moment. I had the distinct impression he would've preferred to toss me into a ditch along some back road and never have to deal with me again. Admittedly, I couldn't exactly blame him. I was the reason the sluagh had caught his and his brothers' scents after all.

I shifted, wincing slightly at the soreness in my muscles. Though I'd removed all my bandages, my body was still recuperating from my confrontation with the sluagh. Jack had offered me another spelled tea this morning before we'd set out, this one meant to rejuvenate my strength, but our current predicament had me wired and antsy. With every passing hour, the window to save my dad was growing smaller and smaller. Sitting around until a storm passed had me feeling like contents under pressure.

I switched my attention to Lucas's fifth game of solitaire before I worked myself up. With every flick of his finger, a new card from the stock pile flipped over without his touching it. With another flick, he'd send any usable card to a waiting tableau. If no one had noticed Lucas's hand movements, they'd think a ghost was playing the game. Fortunately, the only other patrons in the tavern were busy nursing their drinks or playing pool.

"Tell me more about the magic," I said.

Lucas's eyes glimmered, that mischievous smirk tugging at his lips. "What would you like to know, Scarlet Ibis?"

"For starters, how do you cast?"

"My, my. You're a quick learner." He flipped through a few more cards in his stock pile before apparently growing bored with his game. With a twist of his wrist, the cards levitated off the table and made lazy loops and spins as they shuffled themselves into a single deck. Then the deck rested neatly back onto the table. As before, the other patrons were oblivious.

"I guess my real question is how do you get started with waking up dormant magic?"

"Is this you coming to terms with your witchiness, love?" He tugged on my hair playfully. "I think you and I could have a lot of fun raising hell at St. Andrew's with our magic. We'd drive Jack mad, of course. Stickler that he is."

"Lucas."

He reclined into the booth, draping an arm over its back, and smiled at me. "It's a process. Most of us begin our witching journey straight out the crib. While Sightless children are learning nursery rhymes, we're learning verses of protection. We're surrounded by magic at all times. It's as much a part of us as the air in our lungs."

My shoulders wilted. If I'd missed such formative years, what hope did I have of awakening the magic in me so late in the game? Assuming there was any magic in me at all.

"The way they teach it is like this. All witches have kindling in their hearts that has to be ignited before they can come into their magic. So from a young age, we're encouraged to spend time in nature to get the first sparks going."

"Nature?"

"Sure. Witches recognize every living thing as inherently magical. The leaves on a tree, the petals of a single flower, the deer that drinks from a forest stream—all of it contains magic. When we tap into any of those things and feel the connection that binds all life, it rouses the magic in us. What's wrong?"

My eyes had gone distant, my attention drifting. "I'm thinking about how I started to spend more and more time outdoors as of a few years ago, how working with plants has always felt restorative to me."

"Ah, see? That's the witch in you craving communion with nature. Now once we've got that connection going, which is typically enough to summon the four Quarters and move things with our mind, the fun really takes off as we begin our studies in sigils and spellcraft. Most of what we learn during this time hails from the grimoires in our own family libraries."

"Those are spell books, right?"

"They contain more than just spellcraft. The books are typically hundreds of years old, passed down from generation to generation. Their pages are filled with our bloodline's history, Sabbat rituals, and the family deities—written right alongside crystal uses, incantations, and the medicinal and metaphysical properties of herbs and plants. Every family has their own grimoire, but each witch is encouraged to create their own book eventually, since spellcraft can be highly personal."

"Do you and your brothers have your own books?"

"We do, though Jack's is the most involved. He's always been the more studious among us, always reading and learning as much as he can. Me? Not so much. I rely mostly on the abilities we all have. And on my Mastery as well."

Right. Masteries. I'd almost completely forgotten about that part. "And what is your Mastery?"

He put his hand to his heart. "I'm scandalized, Scarlet Ibis. It's considered rather uncouth to ask a witch what their Mastery is, you know."

"Oh. Sorry."

He winked at me, his eyes sparkling. "Ah, I'm only slagging you. I've never been one to follow the rules. I'm a Wayfarer. I can cast myself to any destination I please, provided I've been there before."

"Like teleportation?"

"A handy trick to have in your back pocket should you ever find yourself between a rock and a hard place."

Considering Lucas's penchant for playing pranks at St. Andrew's, I could see how such a Mastery worked to his benefit. It was hard to get caught red-handed when you could simply vanish into thin air and appear somewhere else.

"Rory here," he said, nodding to the youngest Connelly, who hadn't spoken a single word to me yet and was presently sketching away on a napkin, "is a Binder. He can bind himself to someone's or some*thing*'s life force. It's a rare Mastery but an extremely helpful one. Binders in the past have typically worked with Healers. They could hold onto a person's or animal's life force to keep them alive while the Healer worked, letting the injured party borrow some of their energy, so to speak."

"What about Connor?"

"Connor's both a Reader and a Revisionist. He can read a person's memories and revise them as he sees fit. Or steal them straight out of your mind altogether."

"That's horrible."

Lucas laughed. "And yet it makes me think of all the things I could get away with if I were a Revisionist. Mastery envy: it's a real thing." He smiled, gathering the deck of cards and tucking them into a pocket of his jacket. "Don't even get me started on my uncle's Mastery. He's a Shapeshifter. He can assume any man or woman's likeness just by thinking it. The fun I'd have with an ability like that."

With all his talk about family in the past few minutes alone, Lucas had made no mention of his mother or father once. At Crowmarsh, I hadn't seen any pictures of the boys with their parents either, though I'd happened upon an oil painting with the name Maurice engraved on a gold plate at the bottom of the frame. The painting had rendered him as a tall, slender, and dignified elderly man. But what had become of Mr. and Mrs. Connelly? Had tragedy struck them, giving the rumor mill more coal for its fire?

"And Jack?" I asked.

The light in Lucas's eyes dimmed the slightest bit. "Jack has more than one Mastery actually. A lot more."

"Is that common?"

Lucas shrugged. "It's not uncommon. Sometimes a witch might stumble upon a second or third Mastery later on in life. But Jack has more Masteries than anyone living or dead has ever had, making him the most powerful witch to ever be born into one of the seven clans of Ireland.

"Of course, it's helped he's been nurturing his magic since he was yea high." He brought his palm to a height of about two or three feet. "He and Maurice were two peas in a pod. They'd spend hours talking magic together. It's one of the reasons Maurice's death has hit him so hard. When the rest of us returned to St. Andrew's after our leave of bereavement, Jack couldn't bring himself to do the same. He was still a bit of a mess. We offered to hang back with him—I certainly wasn't going to object to getting to bunk off school a few more days—but it was clear he wanted to process everything on his own."

I watched Jack, imagining the relationship he must've had with his grandfather, how much he'd still had left to learn about magic from the man. Unfortunately, he hadn't been able to protect Maurice with a spelled tea the way he had for my dad. He'd known nothing about the sluagh attacks until he'd begun looking further into his grandfather's death. I was sure that had to weigh on him.

"Nonetheless," Lucas continued, "Jack isn't overly fond of discussing his Masteries, so I'd better stop while I'm ahead."

"Why does he feel that way?"

"Shame, I suppose."

My forehead wrinkled. "He's ashamed of being so powerful?"

"Ironic, isn't it? You'd think someone as powerful as Jack would have admirers far and wide among witch-kind. Unfortunately, he's experienced quite the opposite. For Jack, the world couldn't be any more of a lonely place."

It was nearly dusk as we hiked through a forest twenty minutes outside of Killarney. From the moment I'd stepped out of the car, the unmistakable odor of burning wood invaded my nostrils. Because we were flanked on either side by soaring trees, I couldn't see any actual smoke.

"Where's that smell coming from?"

"There's a lumber mill a few miles from here," Jack had explained. "It must be them."

As we continued our trek, the mesquite-like smell stayed with us, hanging heavily in the air. The surrounding nature was mostly quiet, save for the occasional chirping of insects or the distant call of an owl. Now and then, something stirred in the underbrush as we passed, and I found myself staring at the duffel bag Connor carried, hoping the boys had packed something with which to fend off predators.

We followed a stream that curved this way and that between the trees like a string of blue thread. The deeper into the forest we journeyed, the darker and cooler it became. I pulled my cardigan closer, shivering. The smell was even more pervasive now. I guessed we were getting closer to the lumber mill. I coughed once, twice. I couldn't imagine how The Wise Ones made this place their home.

"How much farther away is the...temple, is it?" I couldn't imagine what else would be tucked away so deep in a forest like this.

Jack and Connor exchanged a look.

My heart stalled. "What is it?"

"The Wise Ones aren't going to be what you're expecting," Jack said. "They don't live in a brick-and-mortar temple. They live in what we refer to as a sacred grove. In ancient times, it was a place in the forest where druids could perform holy ceremonies and rituals."

So The Wise Ones were basically off-the-grid holy people who lived off the land. It didn't sound too crazy. I imagined what their non-temple might look like. A giant treehouse perhaps? A cave?

We finally cleared a thick wall of trees and stepped into a clearing.

And then we froze.

Up ahead, there was smoke everywhere, its long, dark fingers curling around trees as if to strangle them. Just beyond the smoke was a glimmer of red, yellow, and orange.

Fire.

Jack broke off at a run, the others right on his heels. I did my best to keep pace with them, covering my nose and mouth to guard against the smoke.

Finally, we reached another clearing, this one much bigger than the one before. A circle of trees took up the majority of the space, an outer band of massive stones similar to the menhirs encircling them. At the center of the ring of trees was a giant oak that had to be over a thousand years old. Something about it gave you the distinct impression it had quietly observed more history than anyone could ever know. As had the trees surrounding it, each ancient looking and otherworldly in their own way.

And that's when I realized it.

These were the The Wise Ones.

And they were on fire.

18

Jack and his brothers tried to control the fire, but it wouldn't heed their demands. Then they summoned water from the neighboring stream and cast it upon the trees in a rushing tidal wave, but the flames were impossibly unresponsive. Again and again, Jack sent one crash of water after another, and every time, the fire hissed but refused to be extinguished.

There was nothing we could do but watch in horror as the fire raged on. Its flames were blinding, brilliant, and scorching hot as they rose skyward like so many yellow tongues, devouring the trees completely with an insatiable appetite. The smoke was thickest here, and I choked on its fumes, coughs sputtering out of me.

I was about to tell the boys we needed to flee before the fire spread, but then I noticed the flames were contained within the ring of stones and touched nothing else in the forest, as if they'd been intended for The Wise Ones alone. Seconds later, the flames abated, steadily shrinking back until they disappeared altogether as if snuffed out by an invisible force. The remaining embers glowed brightly, and then dimmed, and then went black. The smoke cleared. All around us, the forest stilled.

The Wise Ones.

Jack had spoken of them with such reverence. Now they were nothing but charred fragments reaching deep into a scorched earth. They had the look of trees that had been struck by lightning. Black and dead. It was like staring at a forest of charcoal.

Jack staggered forward a few steps and then fell to his knees, unable to take his eyes off The Wise Ones. The sight pinched my heart. This fire, to Jack and his brothers, was the equivalent of someone burning down a place of worship, a most holy temple.

There was a deep sadness in the air that was inescapable. It was heavy and thick, like moving through molasses. I strayed to the remains of an ash tree, pressing my palm to its blackened, still-warm bark. Then I closed my eyes, trying to focus on connecting with the tree the way Lucas had talked about in the tavern.

I wanted to provide it with some kind of solace. I wanted it to know it wasn't alone in these final moments, that while we'd come in search of truth, we'd now be paying our respects. I furrowed my brow, focusing harder and harder until I gave myself a headache. I thought there was a prickle along my fingers, a faint buzz, but I could've just as easily imagined it.

Sighing, I studied the other blackened trees, reaching out to them with my heart. There was a willow tree across the way. Beside it, a birch. A rowan tree, an alder tree, a hawthorn tree.

My lips must've been silently counting the trees because from beside me, a light and satiny voice said, "Thirteen."

My shoulders jumped. Rory. I hadn't heard him speak once since first meeting him in pre-calculus. "What?"

"The Wise Ones. There were thirteen of them. The Celtic year is broken into thirteen months. A month for each tree."

Even though he was mere steps away, I had to strain to hear him, so softly did he speak. His words were like a whisper in the wind. "Can you still feel them?" I asked. If Rory could bind his life force to that of another living thing's, perhaps he could yet sense something from the trees.

Rory's eyes were distant, his face vacuumed of any and all emotion. The face of numbness. I knew it well. I'd seen it plenty of times in the mirror in the wake of my mom's death.

"They're already fading," he said, so gently that I wasn't sure if he was only speaking to himself. His eyes stared at nothing in particular, blank and unfocused. "There wasn't enough for me to hold on to."

"I found something!" Lucas called out then. He was a few yards west of the sacred grove.

When we gathered around him and looked down at the spot in the ground he was pointing to, my heart seized up as a chill touched every bone in my body from head to toe. Someone had burned a symbol into the earth. Six feet long and four feet wide, the last of its embers were still glimmering like sinister eyes.

"A demon's mark," I said, unable to hide the tremor in my voice. The symbol was similar to the one on Jack's wrist, though within this one's circle, there was an inverted triangle with a Greek cross drawn over it.

"Someone summoned a demon to burn down The Wise Ones," Connor said.

"Why wouldn't they just do it themselves?" I asked.

"The grove is filled with immense supernatural power. Only a supernatural creature with an equal amount of power would be able to overcome it."

"This had to be done by order of The Black Hand," Jack said.

"But how would the hunters know about this place?" As soon as the words left my lips, though, the answer came to me. Back in Crowmarsh, Seamus had mentioned only a witch could summon and control supernatural creatures. "The witch who's working with them. But why remove The Wise Ones from the equation?"

"They must've known someone would eventually come here or go to The Council for answers. They want to leave us in the dark so that we're not able to recover the stolen souls in time or stop them from hunting down more witches."

"So what do we do now?"

All eyes switched to Jack, but Jack looked every bit as helpless and lost as the rest of us. After a moment, he opened his mouth to respond, but before he could get a word out, there came a moan from somewhere in the forest, from the mouth of a creature that seemed to be in pain.

I stilled, scanning the nearby trees and underbrush. The last remaining daylight had faded quickly. It wouldn't be long before we could barely see a few feet in front of us.

"We should head back to the car," I suggested.

The moan came again, this time louder.

Then a body zipped past me at the same time Connor called out, "Jack, wait!"

Jack, of course, didn't wait. We charged after him, following his flight across the cold stream, a series of splashes filling the air one after another, and then through hanging vines that got tangled in my hair and thickets that scratched my arms and face until we cleared a wall of shrubs and stumbled upon a most peculiar sight.

The pale moonlight illuminated a haggard and disheveled old man sitting against a tree in a threadbare, brown cloak. He was pale, almost ashen, with hollow cheeks, sunken eyes, and a gaping, toothless mouth. He looked like a walking corpse, his skin spotted with signs of age. I wasn't even entirely sure he was human. He had matted and thinning white hair and a coarse beard that fell to his bare chest, the skin there pulled as taut as violin strings against his exposed ribs. His fingernails were so long they curved in on themselves. They were yellow and caked with dust.

Jack moved quickly, striding to Connor to relieve him of the duffel bag. He rummaged through its contents frantically before finally pulling out a leather pouch that clinked in his hands. He poured a handful of ancient-looking, gold coins onto his palm. Then he knelt in front of the old man as if genuflecting before royalty and transferred the coins into a rusty tin cup the man was holding. Jack was paying him alms.

At first, nothing happened. I looked between Jack's brothers, but their gazes were steady on the beggar in anticipation. The old man closed his eyes then, and I was sure he'd fallen asleep.

Except he hadn't. He was murmuring something. And when he finished, he stretched out a trembling arm and touched the top of Jack's bowed head, like a king granting favor to a newly dubbed knight. Then he brought his hand to the mouth of the tin cup, murmuring again in a language I couldn't place.

As he slowly raised that hand, the coins within the cup levitated as if he were pulling them upward on invisible strings. Though the skies above were darkening, the coins shone brilliantly, pirouetting in the air in dazzling sparks. The old man rotated his hand so that his palm was facing up, and the coins gathered above it in a mini cyclone of gold until they merged into a radiant ball of light. The light intensified and became so bright I had to momentarily shield my eyes as it flared like a sunburst.

Then the light vanished, and I uncovered my eyes. The coins were gone, and in their place was a seed. The old man shoveled away some dirt in the ground and buried the seed deep within the earth. He cupped his hands around the newly turned soil and whispered, as if speaking directly to the seed, coaxing it. As he did this, a vein of blue slid across the earth, heading straight for the seed. It was a branch off the main stream, seemingly summoned by the old man, who sat back against his tree, saying no more.

Not that he had to. Because what happened next left me stunned.

The seed began to *germinate*. What should've taken weeks, months, years...it was all occurring right before my very eyes. It burst from the earth, fastly becoming a sprout with one leaf, then two, then half a dozen. It transformed into a seedling, its soft, green stem hardening to become bark. It grew taller and taller, its limbs stretching wider and wider, until it was waist high, and then neck high. And then it was a sapling, getting stronger, reaching taller. With every life stage, we took steps back, craning our necks as the cycle unfolded. Within minutes, a fully mature yew tree stood regally before us, wearing a crown of leaves in striking colors of apricot and gold.

"Thank you," Jack said to the old man, bowing with hands clasped. Then he rushed to the yew tree with the duffel bag.

I moved to follow him, but Lucas grabbed my elbow. "Careful," he said, motioning to patches of dead grass that dotted the clearing here and there. "Don't step on those parts. They're cursed."

"What happens if someone steps on them?"

"They'll develop a lifelong hunger that can never be sated."

Hunger. The old man had looked as if he hadn't eaten a bread crumb in ages. I glanced to the place where he'd been perched, but he'd disappeared. I swiveled around, trying to catch sight of him, but he was nowhere to be found.

"They tend to do that," Lucas said. "Rascally things, aren't they?"

"What was he?"

"That was the fear gorta. Man of Famine. He's a spirit that travels the land. He'll often materialize before someone who's in great need of a miracle, taking on the appearance of a beggar to test them. Those who take pity on him and give generously are rewarded with the desires of their heart. Those who are selfish and give nothing are cursed until the end of their days with poverty and bad luck."

"So what was Jack's desire?"

"Jack wished to seek the counsel of The Wise Ones to find out how we could stop the sluagh. While having an audience with them is no longer possible, the fear gorta gave him the next best thing: a seed from one of The Wise Ones, from the yew tree in particular, the wood of which we're fond of using in certain spellcraft."

Jack was hammering a gold coin onto the yew tree's trunk. When finished, he stepped back and waited. An offering, a request for permission. The tree must've granted it because he set to work cracking off one of its branches.

Then, with branch in hand, he took a long knife Connor extended, situated himself upon a small boulder, and set to work cutting up the branch into smaller pieces the likes of thick poker chips. After making a certain number of chips, he took them one by one and carved a symbol onto each of their faces. The symbols were made up of sharp, straight lines. There was a main artery like a stem and then strokes coming off it in branches that were sometimes horizontal and other times diagonal.

"Runes," Lucas explained. "Ogham runes, to be more precise."

"What are they used for?"

"For divination, of course. That's why witches come to The Wise Ones. They provide the wood for divining spellcraft. You hold a question in your heart, cast the runes, and they provide the answer."

"Why have people accused them of being silent for so long then?" I didn't know anything about casting runes, but the practice sounded similar to drawing Tarot cards, which I'd seen plenty of times in TV shows or movies, and it always seemed like people just interpreted their results to their liking. I figured once the runes fell, a witch could divine whatever answer they pleased.

"The Wise Ones make their response very clear." He winked at me. "You'll see what I mean soon enough."

Jack finally stood, dusting off the wood shavings from his palms. He collected the runes he'd crafted, and he looked to his brothers with a nod. "All right. Let's say the blessing."

He went from Connor to Lucas to Rory, pouring the chips into each sibling's cupped palms, each brother bringing the runes to their lips to whisper Irish over them, as if beckoning to the magical essence within each piece, as if summoning it to arise for this sacred purpose.

I was surprised when Jack stopped in front of me to give me a moment with the runes as well. I tried to keep my hands from shaking as I cupped them together to receive the runes. The wooden chips were warm against my skin. And they felt...*alive*. As if they were buzzing with some kind of energy.

I didn't know Irish obviously, nor had I known what the brothers had asked of the runes. So I simply spoke my own prayer in my head. *Please give us the answers we seek.*

I returned the runes to Jack, my palms suddenly cold in their absence. He stepped back, his brothers doing the same so that they formed a wide circle. I wondered if I should excuse myself, if this ritual shouldn't include me, but Jack caught my eyes and nodded, assuring me it was all right for me to stay.

My stomach tightened and my heart started striking a fast-paced beat against my ribs. The stars were out now. Dozens of them. Maybe hundreds. Under their watch, and in the pearly light of the moon, whatever was about to happen felt so mystical, so otherworldly. Nevermind the fear gorta's yew tree, a silent giant in our midst trapping us within its black shadow.

Jack's eyes fell shut as he murmured something in Irish. He closed his palms over the runes, caging them. Within moments, soft, sapphire light seeped through the cracks between his fingers. The light grew brighter and brighter, until it was as if he were holding a swarm of blue lightning bugs.

Gradually, he parted his hands, and the runes began to float in the air between them. He widened his palms further and further, giving the runes more room to drift and slowly spin as that blue light emanated from each one, growing brighter still.

"*An fhírinne a fhoilsiú,*" he said to the runes. He repeated it over and over again, his voice getting louder, more emphatic. "*An fhírinne a fhoilsiú, an fhírinne a fhoilsiú.*"

A fierce gust of wind charged through the forest, rattling the leaves on nearby trees, whipping my hair in every which direction. Overhead, lightning speared the sky in a deafening crack that jolted my nerves. It was followed by another bolt, and then another right after.

"*An fhírinne a fhoilsiú!*" Jack called out, throwing out his hands. When he did, the runes flew through the air as if launched from a cannon, spreading out far and wide in the center of the circle we formed. Sizzling energy shot out from the runes, enclosing us in a globe of beautiful, blue light that snapped and crackled as if charged with electricity.

Bolts of lightning started taking aim at the ground near us, stabbing at the earth, sparks flying as small fires roared to life. Inside the blue globe, a whirlwind raged, making it nearly impossible for us to stay upright. And then came the deluge of rain, which the globe did nothing to shield us from. Within seconds, I was soaking wet, my hair plastered to the sides of my face and my clothes heavy with water.

"Jack!" Connor yelled, but you could barely hear him over the howling wind.

Jack was so engrossed in his casting he didn't notice the power he was exuding, couldn't see the endless flashes of lightning all around him nor hear the angry bellows of thunder from above. In that moment, he wasn't just a boarding school student or a brother or even a witch. I saw him the way others like him had no doubt seen him.

The most powerful witch to ever be born into one of the seven clans of Ireland.

The earth began to tremble, and I lost my balance, crashing to my hands and knees.

"Jack!" Connor yelled again. "Control it!" He ducked his head, trying to push against the raging winds to make it to his brother, but the winds knocked him back, seeming to pin him in place. Lucas and Rory exchanged a look of alarm.

I watched breathlessly as Jack seemed to summon the very forces of heaven and hell in a frightening, spellbinding display of authority. The entire sky lit up in a show of flashing white, and then Jack reached one hand upward as if calling down the lightning. It obeyed without question, and in one massive beacon of light, it surged down, racing straight for us.

I screamed.

The lightning smacked into the top of the blue globe in an ear-splitting crash, sending a violent tremor down its curved walls. But the globe withstood the impact, absorbing the energy and shooting it out toward the runes in glowing arcs like shooting stars. The runes, soaking up the magic, spun in place rapidly.

"*An fhírinne a fhoilsiú!*" Jack yelled one final time. There was one last monstrous snap of lightning, and then all at once, the rain ceased, the winds withdrew, the thunder retreated. Even the fires outside the globe ebbed away into nothingness.

And immediately, all but a few runes dropped lifelessly to the earth as if the magic had been sucked out of them.

But Jack didn't pay any attention to those. His eyes stayed affixed on the remaining runes still floating in the air. He approached the center of the circle to meet them as they lowered to his eye-level and started to arrange themselves into a straight line like a row of Scrabble play pieces.

Jack, rainwater still dripping from his hair, slowly read the symbols, piecing together whatever message they spelled out, whatever answer The Wise Ones were giving him. He blinked, then furrowed his brow and read again.

"What does it say?" I asked as I climbed to my feet, doing my best to appear unfazed by what I'd just witnessed. Failing miserably, I was sure.

"It's a name," he replied, his tone wonderstruck.

"Whose name?" Connor asked.

There was a long pause. Jack swallowed and met his brother's eyes. "Our mother's."

19

"It doesn't make sense that her name would come up," Connor said for the umpteenth time.

We were in the parking lot of the first inn we could find, where we'd decided to stop for the night to gather our bearings.

"What about the past few days has made any sense whatsoever?" Lucas quipped.

Connor ignored him. "You should've cast again," he told Jack. "Or better yet, you should've let one of us have a go." Indeed, Connor had made the suggestion multiple times back in the forest, convinced there'd been some sort of mistake, that perhaps Jack had influenced the runes somehow to give us such an answer as they had.

"The Wise Ones are never wrong," Jack said.

A street lamp flickered above us, illuminating half a dozen puddles, yellow orbs glowing on their inky black surfaces. I wrinkled my nose against the stench of car exhaust and asphalt and gripped the straps of my borrowed backpack. In the back of my mind, I longed for a steaming hot shower and dry clothes, but right now, I was too caught up in what The Wise Ones had revealed. The boys' *mother*? What part did she play in all this?

"I couldn't care less about their supposed track record," Connor said. "They're definitely wrong about this. Maybe there's a reason no one's sought their counsel in decades. For all we know, Maurice's account of doing so could be nothing more than one of his stories."

A muscle feathered in Jack's jaw. "He never lied about The Wise Ones."

"We should wait to see what information Seamus brings from The Council."

"We don't know how long that's going to take. She's the one The Wise Ones recommended we see, so that's what we're going to do."

"What could she possibly know about all this?" Connor countered. "When's the last time we even saw her?"

A pause, and then Jack said, "I visit her at least twice a month actually."

His brothers stared at him, at a loss for words.

Connor seethed at this. "Since when? And why would you go by yourself?"

"Why do you think? Every time you've seen her in the past, you've been fuming. Do you really think she can't feel the energy rolling off you in waves?"

"I hope she does."

Lucas tutted. "Well, he's certainly not in the running for favorite son this year."

"Are you starting?" Connor challenged, stepping toward him.

Jack dragged a hand down his face. "Can we not do this right now?"

"I think it's the perfect time to do it actually. Of course, Lucas, as always, is all bark and no bite."

Lucas rolled his eyes. "Come off it already, Connor. There's no need to get all out of sorts just because Mam and Da didn't give you enough hugs and kisses growing up."

Something blazed in Connor's eyes. In the next moment, he lunged for Lucas, shoving his brother up against the side of the SUV. Beside me, Rory boredly checked the time on his phone with a sigh. Lucas and Connor continued to scuffle, but it didn't last long. Jack forced his way between them, fisting the front of each brother's shirt to yank them apart.

"That's enough!"

The street lamp above us exploded in a shower of sparks at the words…as did every single street lamp down the winding length of the road. The brothers stilled. Lucas watched the glistening shards of glass fall to the street, but Connor's attention was on Jack, as if trying to gauge something.

Control it! It's what he'd yelled at Jack back in the forest.

Jack, remembering himself, released his brothers and took a step back, glass crunching under his shoes. He took in the now darkened road and rubbed his forehead, his lips forming a straight line.

"Jack," Connor said, his tone almost pacifying, "we're in over our heads. We should go back to Crowmarsh. Paying her a visit won't be good for anyone."

"Why do you always act like this whenever she comes up in conversation, as if what happened is her fault?"

"It is her fault. She was the most powerful Seer of her generation, and she couldn't see her own husband's death? Do you really swallow that pill so easily?"

"Connor, we can't blame her for Da's decision."

"Maybe you can't," Connor said. "But I can. And I will."

An hour later, freshly showered and outfitted in a cozy cardigan and flannel pajama pants, I ventured out of my room with a few weathered euros to hunt down a vending machine. I hadn't taken half a dozen steps before I stopped suddenly, espying Jack up ahead.

Our rooms were on the second level, and Jack leaned his forearms against the outdoor railing, staring absently at the mist of rain descending. His cell was in his hands, playing voicemails on speakerphone. Every time the automated message prompted Jack to either save or delete the message, he always selected the former option.

The voicemails were from an elderly-sounding man. Maurice no doubt. They were simple, every-day messages. In one, Maurice congratulated Jack on being named rugby captain. In another, he asked Jack if he'd be up for lunch at a local 'chipper' after school.

Though Crowmarsh had been Maurice's permanent residence, I'd learned from Lucas he'd spent significant amounts of time in Rosalyn Bay to be closer to his grandsons, Jack especially. I supposed it had to do with him helping Jack find a way to break the demon's curse. Indeed, a few of the voicemails hinted at that, with Maurice mentioning a grimoire he'd found or a relevant anecdote from a long-forgotten myth.

Guilt pestered me the longer I stood there eavesdropping, so before Jack could move on to the next voicemail in his queue, I cleared my throat to announce my presence.

"Scarlet." He promptly ended the call and pocketed the phone.

I offered a tight smile. "Couldn't sleep?"

"I can't remember the last time I could."

I joined him at the railing. Was it my imagination, or were those dark circles under his eyes blacker than usual? "Does your grandfather say anything to you in the nightmares you have?"

"He might call out my name, but it's always a chaotic scene, as if the world's bleeding away all around him. I'm running out of time. I can practically feel the essence of his spirit fading."

My chest constricted, and I swallowed thickly. I knew my dad hadn't been a prisoner of the sluagh for as long as Maurice had, but the fate that awaited him was still hard to shake. I couldn't imagine how Jack managed to keep his wits about him, especially given how close he and his grandfather had clearly been. My heart swelled with sympathy.

"I'm sorry you had to hear all that before."

At first I thought he meant the voicemails, and my pulse spiked. Then I realized he was referring to the disagreement with Connor. "You don't have to apologize."

"Connor's almost certain The Wise Ones made a mistake. He thinks we should return to the forest first thing in the morning to cast the runes again."

"What do you think?"

"In the forest, you heard me speak in Irish. 'An fhírinne a fhoilsiú,' I said. It means 'reveal the truth.' Unfortunately, the truth isn't always something we want to hear. In my heart, I'd asked The Wise Ones how we could defeat our enemies and save the souls of our people. For whatever reason, seeing our mother was the answer they gave."

I bracketed my hands onto the railing. It was like touching ice. "What did Connor mean about your mom not being able to see your dad's death?" If I hadn't been standing so close to him, I wouldn't have noticed the way his muscles slightly tensed. I instantly regretted asking the question. "I'm sorry. That's none of my business. You don't have to answer that."

"No," he said. "You're a part of this now." He massaged the palm of one hand as a commotion of thoughts darted by behind those somber eyes. "My mother—Alison is her name—was a particularly strong witch, as firstborns tend to be in her bloodline. Throughout childhood and adolescence, she'd had premonitions of the future. At first, small things: what she might score on a school exam to the exact number. Later on, bigger things:

when someone would die. That kind of knowledge made people fear her, as if she were a plague.

"The day she met my father, she began to have visions of her own future. In them, she was warned that falling in love with Redmond Connelly would only end in tragedy, though she wasn't shown exactly how. The visions haunted her regularly. But she was young, and my father didn't view her the way other witches did. He was kind to her. Much as she tried to resist it, she couldn't help but give her heart to him. She chose to believe in a person's ability to change their own destiny, so she ignored the visions, and they eloped."

It sounded like any other tale of forbidden love. How many times every day did young, star-crossed lovers refuse to let even fate tear them apart?

"You have to know they were incredibly happy in those early years. If you were to look at pictures of them during that time, it'd be easy to see. But eventually came their struggles with starting a family, and after that, a difficult childbirth. What my father had done to save us drove a wedge between them from that moment on. He was crushed by the weight of his shame and guilt. My mother, meanwhile, was heartbroken, thinking herself selfish for pursuing happiness despite what her premonitions had warned.

"They were relieved when Connor, Lucas, and Rory were all born without a mark. But having one cursed son was enough to damper any hope of full happiness. For the most part, they tried to give us as normal a home life as they could, but there were times I could tell they were haunted by the inevitability of my fate. It was the guilt, I think, that ultimately drove my father to take his life. I was only twelve at the time."

An invisible fist squeezed my throat. I tightened my grip on the railing, winded. To have lost a parent at so young an age and in such a way. It was heartbreaking.

"After that, my mother became a ghost of herself, retreating inward. She hardly spoke, hardly even looked at us, as if we weren't there at all. She was in every way an absent parent. Connor never really forgave her for it. He felt she should've been able to foresee our father's death and stop it, but her visions aren't always so specific. His anger only grew the more inattentive she became. It was my grandfather, along with Seamus and Neala, who stepped in and parented us in those years. That's when my brothers and I moved into Crowmarsh with our grandfather. It became our permanent home up until we each started classes at St. Andrew's."

I turned to him and placed my fingers upon the back of his hand. His skin was smooth, warm. A slight buzz of energy radiated off him. Magic. "Jack, I'm so sorry." The words were weak, I knew. I knew because I'd heard them time and again after I'd lost my mom. But for the first time, I realized what it was like to be on the other end, what it was like to have no idea what to say to console a friend.

Jack looked at my hand on his. Then he slowly rotated his hand so that my fingertips rested upon his palm. Another slight move and our fingertips were gently touching now. It was such a simple thing, so chaste a connection, and yet my breath caught in my throat.

"My dad's burden was too heavy for him to carry," he said softly. "I understand how he felt. I've lived with guilt of my own for so long." He cut a glance toward the demon's mark on his wrist, peeking out as always from underneath his watch.

"Jack, you have nothing to feel guilty about. You can't hold yourself responsible for a decision that was made before you were even born."

"In theory, I know that. I also know what it's been like to see my brothers lose both their parents, to see them endure a hurricane of unflattering gossip both from witch-kind and the Sightless, to see them come to terms with the fact that in a few months' time, I most likely won't be in their lives anymore. This mark I bear, simple symbol that it is, has wreaked so much havoc in our lives and caused so much chaos.

"I've done my best to shield them from as much of it as possible. After our grandfather was found, once we'd taken a leave from St. Andrew's to grieve and be among our clansmen, I insisted they return to school while I further investigated the matter. I didn't want them caught up in whatever darkness I stumbled upon, and I certainly didn't want to attract evil to them because of this mark. Sometimes I wonder if I shouldn't just speed up the process and offer myself to the demon now, if their lives wouldn't be better for it. No more looking over their shoulders for demons. No more tragedy."

"And no more *you*. Do you really think they'd trade in all their troubles if the cost was your life?"

"My point is they shouldn't have to make the decision in the first place. Had it not been for me, all of them would've had the normal lives they deserved to have."

"You don't know that. You don't know if another difficulty altogether would've reared its head, forcing your dad straight to that crossroads demon again. I also don't get the impression your brothers hold your curse against you. From what little I've seen, they'd do anything for you. People would kill for that kind of loyalty. Myself included. I look at the relationship you have with your brothers, and it makes me think of how much I miss that."

His brandy-colored eyes settled on mine. Our fingertips were still touching, and at some point while speaking, I must've stepped closer to him because I was near enough to smell that foresty scent of his.

"You're talking about your mother," he said.

I felt the familiar pinch at my heart. I glanced away, watching the rain fall. "She was my best friend, my world. When she was taken from me, it took me a while to figure out how to even continue living. I'm still trying to figure it out. She was just such a big part of my identity. When you lose that, it's disorienting. Though I'm sure I don't have to tell you that."

He gently curled his fingers, squeezing mine. Warmth spread up my arms and to my chest and neck. "No, I know the feeling all too well."

"I know you're the eldest brother and that you probably feel an obligation to protect the others from every possible harm. But they want to protect you too, Jack. That's what family is all about. That's why they're here at your side. Connor especially. He looked so worried when you were casting runes back in the forest."

Jack exhaled a long breath, eyes trained on the road in the distance. "Yes, that."

"Were things supposed to go that way?" A chill ran down my back as I recalled the brief spark of fear that had coursed through me amidst all that lightning.

"Definitely not. My brothers think it's because the Old Moon deadline is approaching, that it's somehow making my magic stronger. But it's the least of my worries honestly. Right now, my priority is helping my grandfather's soul before it's too late."

I squeezed his hand, nodding. "Then we'll go see your mom first thing tomorrow morning. Where does she live?"

"She lives in a place called Serenity Falls."

"Is that a town nearby?"

"It's not a town," Jack said.

"What is it then?"

There was a long pause, and then he answered. "It's an asylum."

20

"They used to lobotomize people here, you know."

Both Jack and Connor gave Lucas a disapproving look at the volunteered information.

"What? It's true." Lucas shrugged, shuffling his cards. "Don't worry, Scarlet Ibis. We won't let them get to you with their ice picks."

"Funny," I said as my stomach churned.

The exterior of Serenity Falls Asylum—or Serenity Falls Mental Health Institute, as it was now called in an obvious effort to move away from whatever reputation it'd had during the lobotomy era—had been welcoming enough. Though it was yet another overcast day in Ireland, the sun was doing its best to perforate the clouds, painting everything with a slight gild of pale gold. Outside, men and women in scrubs had been patiently walking alongside their wards, others merely supervising as residents played badminton or croquet or tilled the soil of large vegetable patches.

Inside, the building was bright and airy, though the place had that antiseptic smell to it hospitals were notorious for. In a common room to the right, residents played checkers, read books or newspapers, or watched the black-and-white movie currently playing on a large TV.

A scratchy record played, its slow, dreamy music filtering out of speakers affixed to the walls down each stretching corridor. In these corridors, there were more residents casually walking along, engaged in conversation with each other. Others simply sat in chairs stationed by the floor-to-ceiling windows, gazing at the views beyond in quiet reflection.

We walked down one of these corridors now, led by a nurse whose curly, blonde hair was pinned up in a neat chignon under her cap. "I was wondering if you'd be coming by for your usual visit," she said to Jack with a dazzling smile, her lipstick apple red. They were a few paces ahead of the rest of us.

"I bet you were," Lucas murmured with a smirk, springing his cards from one hand to another.

Heat stabbed my chest. I crossed my arms and focused on the tiles. They were so polished they glowed under the fluorescent lights.

"How's she doing today?" Jack asked.

The nurse let go of a sigh. "I'm afraid she isn't much improved from your last visit."

Jack glanced to Connor. In the parking lot, he'd suggested his brothers hang back.

"No way in hell," Connor had said.

"It might be for the best. We're not going to get very far with her if your anger's suffocating all the energy in the room."

"I'm liable to side with Jack on that front," Lucas said. "In fact, tell me why we haven't just ditched Connor on the side of the road at this point?"

Before they could get into it again, Jack had dropped the matter and ushered us all inside.

Up ahead, a woman with thinning hair was shuffling back

and forth in the hallway, wringing her hands and murmuring to herself. As we passed her, she didn't make eye contact, as if she wasn't even aware we were there. She only kept muttering. Counting, I realized. She was counting to six over and over again.

Some doors were open, revealing rooms that looked like bare college dorms. White walls, white bedsheets, white floors, and little to no furniture. All of the windows had grates over them.

In one room, a young man sat on his bed, crying into his knees as he hugged his arms around his legs. A male nurse sat across from him, quietly speaking to him. The young man started moaning, clamping his hands to the sides of his head. "No, no, no," he whined. In a room a few doors down, a man was arguing with someone who wasn't there. "I told you I didn't want to see them again," he said, jutting a finger toward his invisible opponent's chest.

This was the section of Serenity Falls where Alison Connelly dwelled. It wasn't lost on me how far out of sight she and her neighbors were tucked away.

The nurse finally stopped at a room and pushed open the door. I kept to the rear as we entered. The sun had at long last managed to break through the clouds, and its golden light spilled into the room, staining the tiles yellow. The space was like all the others I'd seen. Minimally furnished with no personal effects. The air inside was warm, heavy, and stale.

It was the figure by the window that most drew my attention, though. There, a woman who looked like she weighed no more than a hundred pounds sat in a wheelchair, slightly hunched over. She was small and frail, as if she were withering away. Graying brown hair that had lost its shine hung limply to her mid-back, one errant strand caressing the pale skin of her cheek. She wore the same outfit all the patients did, a light blue ensemble resembling pajamas. Over this outfit she donned a ratty, pink robe.

"Alison, love," the nurse said, striding into the room and flipping the light on. "I have some visitors for you today. Jack is here again, and he's brought your other boys with him. Isn't that nice?"

Alison didn't look up, didn't do so much as acknowledge the woman's words. As I furthered into the room, I saw why. Her eyes were practically dead. She stared toward the window, but it was with an unfocused gaze.

Her lips were dry and chapped, and she looked like she hadn't slept in days. But the oddest thing was the way her body was positioned. She held her left arm high above her head in a frozen posture, palm facing the ceiling as if she were expecting alms from heaven. She was barely breathing, and her body was as rigid as a marble statue.

The nurse's warm smile never left her face. Of course not. This was nothing new to her. "I'll leave you to it then," she said, patting Jack's arm before she showed herself out and closed the door behind her.

Jack wasted no time in bridging the distance between him and his mother. He placed a delicate hand to Alison's shoulder. "Mam, can you hear me?"

No response. No movement. Her eyes remained vacant, and the arm remained uplifted.

My mouth and throat became a desert, and any words I might've offered completely vacated my mind. The lack of response from Alison didn't seem to bother Jack. Connor, on the other hand, looked like a tea kettle about to burst its top. His arms were crossed tightly, his face reddening as he stared at his mother with a withering look that could've leveled buildings. His resentment, whether it was over her abandonment or over her letting things get to this point, practically electrified the air.

Fearing another brotherly quarrel was hemorrhaging, I found my voice, though I couldn't keep it from cracking slightly. "Is she...?" Aware? *Alive*?

"It's called posturing," Jack explained. "She'll maintain a position like this for hours. She generally doesn't respond to any stimuli, and she's mostly mute. Sometimes she may mutter things, but it tends to be...it tends to not make any sense. But it's normal for her condition."

Connor scoffed. "It's anything but normal."

Jack ignored him. "The doctors haven't been able to explain it or cure it. When she was first admitted, she was already mostly disengaged with the outside world, but she hadn't been the slightest bit catatonic like this. This is something that's developed within the past year."

"Why would The Wise Ones tell us to come here?" I asked, keeping my tone gentle. "If she's unable to speak, how could we possibly get any answers from her?"

"Actually," Jack said. "I've been thinking about that all night, and I think I have an idea. But there's a catch."

"What is it?"

"It's going to be incredibly dangerous."

21

"It's called a transference spell."

As Jack spoke, Rory pulled crystals and candles out of the backpack he'd brought into Serenity Falls, setting the objects on a table by the window.

"It's powerful magic that allows you to cast your subconscious into the mind of another person."

"So where does the dangerous part come in?" I asked, goosebumps sleeving my arms. With what looked to be a piece of charcoal, Rory began drawing a large, elaborate circle on the floor. A sigil, Lucas explained. It looked like something out of a medieval alchemy book. There were symbols at the circle's cardinal points, a string of runes along its edges, and Irish words filling up the body.

"Typically, you'll find yourself in the person's memories," Jack said. "You might happen upon their dreams and their hopes as well. But it's not unusual to also stumble upon their fears and nightmares. And for many people, the fears in their mind can be just as terrifying as the monsters in the real world. There's also the risk of becoming lost in someone's mind. The entire experience feels very real, in the same way that a dream feels real when you're in the midst of having one. The longer you stay, the more your sense of self begins to deteriorate, until you believe the thought world you transferred into is your actual reality. If you've made your home in a happy memory, drawn in by its allure, it might not sound like a bad thing. But if it's a fear or nightmare that's drawn you in..."

"Then you're stuck in a living hell," Connor finished, "with no chance of returning to your own body, given that you've lost yourself in the other person's mind."

I blew out my cheeks with a breath. "Wonderful."

"There's one more thing," Jack said. There was a look on his face akin to guilt. "My brothers and I can't be the ones to transfer."

"What?" Connor and I said it at the same time. He flung a scornful look at me like a dart, as if I had no place taking the words right out of his mouth.

"It's too risky," Jack said. "There's no guessing what memories we'll walk into the moment we step into our mother's mind, but whatever they are, we'll be too emotionally attached to them, too affected by them. Which means we run a greater risk of losing ourselves either because we'll want to stay or because the darkness of the memories will pull us under easily. It would be best for someone with no attachment whatsoever to our past to do it."

"Have you gone mad?" Connor asked him. "You're pinning all your hopes on her? She doesn't even know what she's doing."

I bristled, but the truth was Connor was probably right, which only made me bristle more.

"All you have to do," Jack said to me, "is find our mother and engage her. The spell's magic will allow you to break the memory's 'fourth wall,' so to speak, so you won't just be an observer. You'll be able to interact with her. When you do, tell her who you are and why you're there."

"Will she have the information I need if I'm interacting with a past version of her, though?"

"When we relive our memories in our minds, we do so as our present-day selves with our present-day knowledge. Once you break the illusion of the memory for her, she'll have the same awareness she does right now, even if the memory itself occurred decades ago. Does that make sense?"

"I think so."

Connor shook his head, muttering something under his breath.

I resisted the urge to narrow my eyes at him. "Will this change your mom's memories in any way, my poking through them?"

He shook his head. "No, the memories will revert to their original 'script' after you leave, as if you were never there. Oh, and one more thing. There's really no rhyme or reason behind how the spell works as far as interacting with the person. In some memories, the person will note your presence easily and engage you, and in others, it'll be as if you're completely invisible. Don't let the latter discourage you. Just move on to the next memory and try again."

I nodded, doing my best to remember everything he was telling me.

I must've looked overwhelmed because Jack's eyes softened. "I don't mean to put this burden on you. But it's the only chance we have at getting any answers from her. If you'd rather not, though..."

Then he'd volunteer. Even if the risk of him becoming trapped in Alison's mind was greater than it would be for me. I looked at Alison, hunched over in her wheelchair. The Wise Ones had sent us here for a reason. There was clearly a secret locked in Alison's mind, one that could very well help me get my dad's soul back and help Jack give his grandfather peace. Not to mention free all the other souls the sluagh had stolen.

Alison was a stranger to me. A literal trip down memory lane wouldn't affect me the way it might Jack and his brothers because I'd have no emotional attachment to them. How hard could it be to see whatever images played behind those lifeless eyes? And besides that, as Lucas was apt to remind me, maybe I really was the Scarlet Ibis alluded to in the Seer's message. Maybe this was the part I was ultimately supposed to play in this strange turn of events. This was my purpose. No one else but me could do it.

The trill of my pulse tapped against my wrist like the rapid-fire percussion of a woodpecker's beak, but I straightened and met Jack's eyes. "I'll do it."

Within minutes, Rory had finished his sigil. Lines intersected the circle at various points, creating triangles and diamonds, and amongst these, Rory had added even smaller circles and crescents as well. The design was beautiful, if not a little terrifying. When the time came for me to step inside the sigil, I very much felt like the sacrificial lamb being led to the slaughter. Along the circle's boundary, flames trembled atop the black candles Rory had set out.

"Why black?" I'd asked him when he lit them all at once with the snap of a finger.

"It helps you delve deeper into the unconscious." He moved some auburn hair out of his eyes, thinking. "And if anything evil tries to come through, it won't be able to pass the boundaries of the candles, so at least the rest of us will be safe."

My smile was thin. We'd really have to work on Rory's people skills when this was all said and done. My stomach seethed, and I was glad I hadn't bothered partaking of our inn's continental breakfast this morning.

"You'll be fine," Jack assured me, giving his youngest brother a disapproving look. Rory only shrugged, as if he wasn't sure what was so wrong about what he'd said. "Remember, whatever you see is only a figment of our mother's mind. It's not real. Don't let any dark memories or fears or nightmares pull you under. Hold on to your sense of self as tightly as you can, and don't forget why you're there. And if at any time you want to leave, all you have to do is close your eyes and envision this room. That typically transfers you back instantly."

Typically? I didn't like the sound of that. Nonetheless, I nodded and slowly laid down across the circle's center, folding my hands over my stomach, my fingers clutching a lock of Alison's hair. One by one, four heads peered down at me as the brothers took up their spots at each cardinal point.

"Ready?" Jack asked.

Not really. I slowed my breathing to calm my palpitating heart. *Remember why you're doing this.* My dad needed me. This was the only lead I had right now in getting back his soul. There was no way I could back down, not even in the face of the unknown. I closed my eyes and nodded.

Jack began to chant in Irish.

"*Isteach san aigne, trí spiorad agus croí.*"

He'd told me earlier what the words meant: *into the mind, by spirit and heart.*

Within seconds, his brothers joined in. Their voices were hard, somber, and yet the words still managed to sound lyrical in their melodious accents. If I wasn't about to be whisked away into someone's subconscious, I might've found the spell enchanting.

"*Isteach san aigne, trí spiorad agus croí.*"

They spoke the chant over and over again. My body warmed.

The boys' Irish words wove around my bones in silken tapestries, dancing in my blood, making my heart beat faster. I was suddenly lighter, as if the laws of gravity had ceased to exist in the room, and there was a crackle of electricity all around me, my fingertips buzzing. I waited for something more, some grand light at the end of a tunnel to lead me into Alison's mind or a breathtaking demonstration of wind and rain such as what Jack had done back in the forest.

But nothing came. After a few moments, I noticed the brothers had gone quiet too.

My stomach sank. The spell hadn't worked. Connor had been right. I was the wrong person for the job.

I opened my eyes to ask what had happened.

Then I gasped.

Alison Connelly's room had entirely vanished.

22

I was somewhere else entirely, the brothers and their mother nowhere to be seen. I sat straight up in a rush, ignoring the brief lightheadedness that overcame me, and threw my hands down to steady myself.

My fingers met cool blades of grass. The sky was like I hadn't yet seen it in Ireland, a robin's egg blue with bloated clouds meandering by, as soft and tattered as pulled cotton balls, almost close enough to the earth for me to touch. It was spring. The air was scented with lilacs and daisies and snapdragons, their blooms a spread of rainbow colors in a valley downhill.

Then a scream pierced the serenity. A heart-wrenching, soul-crushing scream that stabbed my heart like a knife. Behind me stood the back of a two-story house. The scream had come from inside.

I entered the house through a back door, creeping into a yellow-tiled kitchen where the sink faucet was still running, the water cascading over a bowl of fruit. The fridge was wallpapered with family pictures of boys with gaps in their teeth holding up sports trophies, of trips to the beach complete with sand castles and a blow-up ball, of a man setting up camping equipment with his sons. On the stove, scrambled eggs were sizzling and browning, filling the air with a burnt aroma, a plate of French toast abandoned on the counter nearby.

I furthered into the house until I found my way to the sitting room, where a woman was on her knees by the open front door, a slice of sunlight striping the ratty carpet. Beyond the threshold, a solemn police officer stood outside.

The woman sobbed into her hands. "No, no, no," she moaned. "It has to be a mistake. He would never do such a thing."

Something moved in the corner of my eye. I looked to my right, where four boys in their pajamas were standing on the staircase, watching on. The oldest one, a pre-teen, descended a few steps, his eyes pained and world-weary, as if he'd already seen too much of the world at such a young age.

This had to be the day Alison and her sons had learned of Redmond's death.

Jack made it all the way to his mother and rested a comforting hand on her shoulder, but she just continued sobbing, oblivious to his presence, her cries getting louder and louder.

I grabbed my throat and tried to soothe the painful knot growing there. Watching Alison was like watching a reflection of myself. I'd known that raw grief not too long ago. I'd cried those gut-twisting sobs before, the ones that left your entire upper body sore and your mind utterly exhausted. While friends of mine threw birthday parties or went on dates or posted pictures on social media of their enviable summer vacations, I'd sequestered myself in the bedroom I shared with Natalie, wondering at the point of life when the pain of loss was so paralyzing. For the first week or two, the ache in my chest was so sharp I was sure I was dying of a broken heart.

At the thought, I could practically feel Alison's own pain

intensifying. Her grief was so suffocating, so overwhelming. I could scarcely breathe. My knees wobbled, and I leaned against a wall.

I couldn't take my eyes off her, crumbled as she was on the floor, or off this younger version of Jack, who at such a tender age was already assuming his new role as man of the house. At what point had he begun blaming himself for his father's decision? At what point had he decided he'd do everything in his power to spare his brothers from further tragedy?

The filaments of Alison's pain stretched across the room, grabbing at me like so many hands, stoking my own sadness. Little by little, they worked at the dams holding back my ocean of grief until the barricade gave way completely and all my emotions about my mom's death washed over me like a tidal wave. Anger, despair, emptiness, lostness. I thought, not for the first time, about all the things my mom would never get to see: my graduation, my wedding, any children I might have. I thought of all the things left unsaid, all the plans left unfinished, all the conversations we'd never get to have.

My vision blurred and I rested more of my weight against the wall. It wasn't fair. I didn't know how I was expected to live out the rest of my life without her. She'd been my rock, my comfort, my everything. Why did she have to leave me? I closed my eyes, tears racing down my face, and eased myself into everything I felt, into that insurmountable pain that bellowed in Alison's heart and my own like thunder.

But...wait.

Wait.

My eyes snapped open. *Don't let any dark memories or fears or nightmares pull you under.* Jack had said that. I blinked several times, as if waking from a dream, slowly breaking the surface of the dark waters into which I'd been sinking. I quickly wiped away my tears.

I took in a sharp breath of air and remembered myself. This wasn't real. It was only a memory from the past. I'd let Alison's emotions hook into me and pull me down deep, and it'd been a lot easier than I'd anticipated.

I needed to get out of here.

I backed away, nearly stumbling over myself, and ran as fast as I could out the back door...and into another scene entirely.

It was nighttime now. Behind me, the house had disappeared. There was nothing but stretching landscapes in every direction. And singing. Singing and music. I faced the direction of the sounds and found a lively group of young adults who looked to be in their twenties.

They were gathered around a snapping bonfire, the orange flames waving in the cool breeze and setting their happy faces aglow. One of them strummed a guitar. Another banged a tambourine against her palm. They sang cheerfully, laughing and leaning against each other, swaying to the rhythm.

This time, the people in the memory noticed my presence. One of the women looked my way and smiled broadly. It was Alison. A younger Alison. Her hair tumbled down her back in lush waves, a crown of flowers upon her head. Beside her, a handsome man was glowing as he took her in, nothing but love in his eyes. Redmond. This was from a time before Jack and his brothers, before a bargain and a curse would haunt them for the rest of their lives. A simpler time, an easier time, a more joyous time.

Alison extended a hand toward me, inviting me to join the group. I sat upon the scratchy bark of a log with the others, the bonfire warm against my face. The group continued singing. Some of the songs were in English, others in Irish. I didn't know any of the words, but I smiled as I watched them, their happiness and peace warming my heart.

It was such a stark contrast to Alison's present-day life that I couldn't stop marveling at her radiant beauty. At one point, Redmond took her hand, pressing a gentle kiss to her knuckles. Alison beamed, and their eyes were only on each other, as if they were the only two people in the world.

I hated to think I'd have to pull her aside to ask why The Wise Ones had sent us here. It would be cruel to tear her away from such a joyful moment, but I had no other choice. When the guitarist suddenly struck up a fast-paced melody that was wholly Irish and half the group leapt to their feet to dance, I decided I'd give Alison this final song before breaking the illusion of the memory.

As I waited, I settled into the moment, clapping along with the others as to not feel out of place. At first, I was only playing a part, but it only took a few minutes for the group's contagious bliss to affect my heart. It was impossible not to feel happy around them. The guitarist's song made me think of sunshine and fireworks and racing through the woods.

I missed this kind of communion. It made me think of the friends I used to sit with at lunch, the way we used to admire our crushes from afar, how we'd heartily discuss the latest storylines in our favorite TV shows, stepping on each other's sentences, the inside jokes we'd toss back and forth until we were laughing so hard tears spilled out of our eyes. I grinned, reflecting on it.

Sitting around this bonfire kindled the happiness from those memories, feeding it until I had a wildfire in my chest licking at my bones, sending sparks through my veins. I felt energized. I felt ignited. I felt...*alive*. I clapped harder, laughed more. Everything was so beautiful. Everything was so perfect.

Alison, in particular, was overflowing with exuberance. I watched her, remembering I needed to speak with her about something. Something serious. What was it? I chased after the thought, trying to grip its coattails, but it was too fast for me and eventually disappeared around a corner. Maybe I'd been mistaken. This wasn't a night for serious topics anyway.

Alison spun and spun and spun in place, her hands in graceful arcs above her head, her petite body like that of a ballerina's, her hair gliding through the air. When she stopped, it was only to grab my hands and yank me to my feet. Then I was spinning too, my grip locked with Alison's as we rotated around the center of gravity that was our hands.

Everything else became a blur. There was only the music and the laughter and the heat from the bonfire. I breathed it all in. It had been a while since I'd let loose, since I'd allowed myself to feel even a glimmer of happiness. I couldn't remember why, what sadness had stopped me. But here, with Alison and her friends on this beautiful night when a thousand stars sparkled like diamonds above us, I could let go of it all, could forget it all.

Laughter escaped me, and I grinned at Alison. Our eyes locked on each other, and her cinnamon gaze was filled with love and serenity and immeasurable elation. I wanted to feel that way too. Always. Everyone here was just so happy, and I wanted more of it.

But there was a scratch at the back of my mind.

You don't belong here.

I pushed the thought away and focused on the melody of the guitar. Of course I belonged here. These were my friends. I'd known them forever. We came out to this spot every weekend to sing and dance and drink and laugh.

The music around us became faster. Someone had joined in with a hand drum. The beat awakened something primal in my muscles, and I threw my head back, releasing a squeal of delight.

You. Don't. Belong. Here.

Again, I ignored the nonsensical thought. I kept moving,

spinning with Alison, every iota of who I was set ablaze with laughter. I wanted to be as carefree as Alison and the others. I wanted the night to never end. I wanted—

YOU DON'T BELONG HERE!

The realization coursed through me like an electric shock, and I yanked away from Alison at the jolt. The force by which I'd pulled back coupled with the momentum of my spin sent me dizzily careening across the ground until I tripped over myself and fell face first onto the grass.

Ow.

I remained still for a few moments before turning over, thankful I hadn't knocked the wind out of my lungs at least. As I rested there, as my sense of identity slowly pieced itself back together again, I realized what had happened. I mentally chided myself for my foolishness. Twice now already I'd done the very thing Jack had warned me against. I'd let the memories bewitch me.

I'd gone into this thinking it would be easy. How wrong I'd been. I'd have to be smarter moving forward. I remained where I was, trying to come up with a game plan. How could I ground myself? After a few moments, I had an idea. I'd repeat a mantra every few seconds: *This is not real.* Surely that would be enough to keep me anchored in myself.

Dirt hit my face, startling me out of my thoughts. I was surrounded by four dark walls, the smell of earth invading my nostrils. No, these weren't ordinary walls. I'd fallen into some kind of hole, the soil surrounding me filled with roots and gravel and worms. Frowning, I sat up and craned my neck back to gauge how I might climb out. The view above was in the shape of a rectangle, and four boys were gathered along the edges, looking down into the hole. The Connelly boys at their current age, all dressed up in suits and ties. Jack tossed a handful of dirt into the hole. It hit the polished oak of the object that suddenly appeared beneath me.

My stomach flipped.

It was a casket, the old-fashioned, Victorian kind with a viewing window.

And behind the glass pane was Alison's lifeless face.

I scrambled back, but the hole in the ground was only big enough to swallow the casket up with barely any additional space on either side. I couldn't get away from it, and my eyes once again fell to Alison's face, the bile rising in my throat. This obviously wasn't a memory, so it had to be one of Alison's fears. Not just death, I thought, but perhaps the idea of being permanently separated from her boys.

Another handful of dirt slapped me, this time on my shoulder. I was in a grave. I was in a grave with a dead body, and I was about to be buried alive.

"Stop!" I cried out. I waved my arms at the Connellys, but their eyes were glazed over, their faces blank. They could neither see nor hear me.

When the last brother, Rory, tossed in his handful of dirt, which made a hollow thud against the casket, the boys peeled away from the grave. Machinery roared to life. That had to be the backhoe operator, who was seconds away from filling in the rest of the grave with earth.

I rushed to a wall of the grave, clawing at the cold dirt to pull myself out, my fingernails blackening. I should've been able to make it to the surface, standing as I was atop Alison's casket, but the walls of the grave only seemed to grow taller and taller, ever stretching above me until I was at the very bottom of an endless chasm and could barely see the sky anymore.

And then the dirt came rushing in.

"Stop!" I screamed. "There's someone in here! Help!"

But the dirt kept coming, gushing forth quicker than I had ever seen dirt move, like it was a flood of water.

"This is not real," I told myself as the dirt quickly rose over the sides of Alison's casket. "This is not real, this is not real." My heart said otherwise. It was pounding against my chest so fast I thought it'd burst right out of my body.

I started for another wall to attempt a second climb. I moved too quickly. I slipped across the shiny surface of the casket and crashed into its hard wood, my stomach and arms throbbing. I rolled over onto my side, cradling my elbow.

"This is not real!" I squeezed my eyes shut to envision Alison's room at Serenity Falls just as Jack had instructed. But when I opened them, I was still in the grave and more dirt charged for me without mercy.

I shielded my face with my arms as it kept coming, until it covered me entirely and filled my mouth when I parted my lips for a breath of air. But no air came—just dirt, reaching past my tongue, down my throat, filling my lungs.

I screamed. I screamed and screamed and screamed, but it was muffled and choked off by the dirt as I thrashed against it, until my thoughts dimmed and my movements stilled and there was nothing left but blackness.

23

I bolted upright with a cry, wheezing as I tried to quickly inhale lungfuls of oxygen.

Jack dropped to his knees beside me and clamped a warm hand over my mouth. He threw a glance to Lucas, who poked his head out the door, looking up and down the hallway. The younger Connelly clicked the door back shut and gave a thumbs up. No one had heard.

Jack removed his hand, though the warmth of his touch remained on and around my lips for a few moments longer. I proceeded to catch as many breaths as I could without hyperventilating.

"Scarlet, are you all right?"

I rushed to brush my hands down my arms, my legs, my face, clearing away any lingering dirt. There wasn't any, of course, which left me mystified. How could something so imaginary feel so real? Even now, my skin crawled as if I were still trapped in that grave, wriggling earthworms all around me. I plugged my fingers into my ears to ensure nothing had crawled into them. Nothing had. I puffed out air through my nostrils because I could still feel dirt there too. All clear.

"Scarlet?" Jack prompted again. "What did you see?"

I glanced to Alison, still hunched over in her wheelchair. She hadn't moved from that eerie position of hers, and her eyes were as dull as ever. And yet sealed inside her mind was a vivid world of color and song and heartache and tragedy.

"It was a blur," I replied. Not exactly a lie, considering the speed by which I'd been swept from one memory to another.

"Were you able to speak with her?"

Speak with her? I'd barely been able to keep my sanity intact. "No," I answered. My voice sounded small, in part because I could feel Connor's disapproval from here. It was a flame-tipped arrow that bit into my neck and made the skin there flush. "I'm sorry."

"It's all right. We can try again if you're up to it. Now that you know what to expect."

I pictured myself in that grave again, the dirt gushing in to block all hope of escape. What other tortures awaited me inside Alison's mind? I'd been lucky enough to wake up inside my own body this time around. Who was to say I'd luck out again? I could end up imprisoned in Alison's memories forever.

"I tried to envision the room, but it didn't work. At least not as quickly as I'd hoped it would."

"You might've been too overwrought by whatever it is you saw. Sometimes we buy into the fear because of how real it seems, even if we know somewhere in the back of our mind that it's only an illusion."

"We're wasting time," Connor snapped. "She obviously doesn't know what she's doing. I'll transfer."

"No," I said, steeling my voice. "I'll try again."

I finally brought myself to look at Jack. His eyes were as world-weary as they'd been in the first memory I'd walked into. I didn't want him to relive any other memories like it, to be reminded of his family's tragedies. He deserved to be spared this.

"I'll try again," I repeated, picking up the lock of Alison's hair and gripping it tightly.

Jack nodded, the gratitude evident in his eyes, almost as if he could guess my reasons why. "Thank you."

This time when I transferred, my first assumption was that something had gone wrong with the spell. I was in Alison's room at Serenity Falls. The same cold, white floor, the same mind-numbingly, plain, white walls, and the same low, white ceiling. Except I soon realized there was no sigil underneath my body, Alison's wheelchair was on the other side of the window, and the brothers were nowhere to be seen.

Alison was still in her catatonic state, which meant this had to be a memory from within the past year. She wasn't nearly as frail or as withered away as her present-day self, but she was still largely detached from the world around her. She was posturing again as well, with one arm stretched straight out to the side. Only her eyes moved as she took in her view of the institute's grounds. Below, a large group of residents were moving their arms in slow, flowing, hypnotic motions. Tai Chi.

Get her to talk before you forget where you are. Right. That was my new plan of attack, to jump right into action before this world of hers could beguile me.

"Alison?" I croaked.

The woman didn't acknowledge me, only kept staring out her window. The way the sun filtered in through the window's grating made it look like she had dozens of gold coins resting on her skin.

I moistened my lips and drew closer. "Alison?" No response. I leaned over slightly, nearly blocking the woman's view. "Alison? My name's Scarlet. Jack sent me here. Your son? He—"

"Alison, love," sang out a cheerful voice, "Jack's here to see you." The golden-haired nurse who'd greeted us earlier this morning strolled into the room with a sunny smile, Jack a step behind. I froze but soon realized neither of them could see me.

When the nurse left, Jack shrugged out of his St. Andrew's blazer and folded it over the back of Alison's wheelchair. Then he knelt before her, trying to catch her eyes. Alison continued watching the Tai Chi class below.

"Hello, Mam. How are you feeling today?" He tenderly moved her stretched out arm and slowly bent it at the elbow to set it on her lap. Then he took one of her hands in both his own and began to gently massage it. There was something so tender about the gesture, so pure. I thought of the days when my mom would spend hours receiving chemo in the hospital, how I'd sit beside her as we watched home decorating shows off my phone or put together scrapbook pages. It was simply a way to get her mind off the cancer, but we had ended up fitting more bonding into those afternoons than what might typically occur for others over several months. Maybe even years.

"Are you eating well? You've got to keep up your strength so that when the time comes, you're able to walk out of here on your own two feet." He moved to her other hand, kneading the muscles delicately, as if trying to wake up the dormant life underneath her skin, as if trying to wake up the magic.

"I made varsity today. Connor too. Though the jury's still out as to whether or not Coach Stewart only intends on benching him for the entire season. You know how Connor gets. Exeter still refuses to play us because of that incident.

"Lucas has entered the science and technology fair, if you can believe it. I know I didn't at first, but I was happy to hear he was taking his studies more seriously. Of course, then I learned his project concerned whether a dog and person could switch bodies, so I can only imagine what sort of prank he's got up his sleeve for the big reveal.

"And Rory's doing well. You should see how the greenhouse has come along. He's actually heading out to Japan in a few months for Easter holiday. I wasn't sure how I felt about it, since none of us have ever been that far apart from each other, but I think it'd be good for him. Maybe he'll make a friend or two."

Jack kept talking in spite of Alison's silence, unbothered by her inability to respond, accustomed to it.

But then Alison *did* respond. Her gaze still fixed on the window, her chapped lips slightly parted. "I can't hear their songs anymore." It was no more than a coarse whisper.

Jack looked up from massaging his mother's hands, his expression pained. He stood and dragged a chair over to the room's door, barricading it lest someone walk in on them. Then he returned to his mother, kneeling before her again, and he took both of her hands.

"I'll bring them to you," he said.

Slowly, the seams of the world began to bleed away, like water washing away the colors in a fresh oil painting. The room faded, everything did, until the scene changed completely. We were no longer at Serenity Falls. We were in a place that looked very much like the rooftop greenhouse at St. Andrew's.

Terracotta floors in numerous shades of red appeared beneath our feet. The air warmed, scented with fresh soil. The walls of Alison's room were replaced with hanging pothos plants, the vines of which reached several dozen feet in every direction. I stumbled back a few steps, taking it all in with utter amazement.

Then the songs came.

Beautiful, melodic, enchanting.

Birdsong.

The place was full of them—birds. Every size, every color, every species. It was a menagerie of birds. And their songs filled the air in chirps, whistles, sirens, and caws. A Zebra finch zipped down and perched atop Alison's finger, cocking its head, its tangerine cheeks giving it a cheerful appearance. After a moment, it sprung into flight again. Alison's eyes lit up. She looked at Jack in awe, as if to say, *Did you see that?*

Jack smiled at her, a warm, tender smile, nothing but affection in his eyes. He followed her through the aviary as she marveled at the birds, as she watered the plants, content to simply while away the time. She had risen from her wheelchair with such ease and now strode along with the utmost vivacity. I knew I should leave and find a new scene to explore or at the very least attempt to get Alison's attention again, but I was so taken aback by the change in her and wanted to see how the rest of the memory played out.

Just remember this isn't real, I told myself. I didn't want to lose myself again.

At one point, Alison opened a storage locker to retrieve feed for the birds. As the door swung open, a picture fluttered to the floor. Alison picked it up. In the photograph, she was surrounded on all sides by her four boys, everyone beaming happily into the camera. It had to be only a few years old. She studied it for several long, quiet moments, her brow furrowing. Jack had gone tense beside her, waiting.

"I know these people," Alison whispered. She caressed the glossy surface of the picture, her finger pausing over Jack's face. She turned to him, looking at him as if he were a puzzle she was trying to solve.

Jack held her gaze, saying nothing, wanting her to reach the answer on her own.

I saw the moment when Alison's eyes began to clear, like a

summer sky brightening when the clouds finally unveil the sun. Her features stretched into astonishment. "...Jack?"

The tension instantly melted out of Jack's body. He gently grabbed his mother's arms to hold her steady, to comfort her. "It's me, Mam."

Alison looked about her in confusion. "What happened? How are we here?"

"It's all right. You don't have to be afraid. We can stay here as long as you'd like."

Tears pooled in her eyes. I wasn't sure what had saddened her until she asked her next question. "How long have I been away this time?"

Jack hesitated to respond.

It was all Alison needed. Her tears skated down her face, their trails glimmering on her cheeks. "My sweet Jack," she said, a palm cradling his jaw. "You never give up on me, do you?"

"And I never will." He put his hand over hers, squeezing her fingers. "You're going to get better, Mam. Just stay with me a little bit longer, all right? Tell me what I need to do to help you."

Alison's body went rigid suddenly as her eyes flew past him. "We're already out of time. They're here."

Jack whirled around to follow her line of sight, but there was nothing there. "Whoever or whatever they are, I'll stop them. I'll stop this from happening again. Just tell me how."

Alison scrambled back, knocking over tin watering cans that crashed with a metallic bellow. "They're coming for me. Every time I try to surface, they're sure to pull me back under." Her eyes were already clouding over again as she shook her head unendingly. She couldn't hear Jack anymore, didn't even know he was there. "No, please. Not again. Don't keep me away from my boys!"

Jack's eyes darted all about the aviary, trying to hone in on his opponent, but he was blind to whatever was assailing his mother.

So was I. Initially. And then shadows began to materialize right before my eyes. They were bodiless, made entirely of black smoke, and even then they were still terrifying. Demons. Somehow, in my gut, I knew it's what they were. There had to be dozens of them, an infestation of the worst kind.

"No!" Alison screamed as they descended upon her, throwing her back and then funneling into her mouth, her nose, her ears. To Jack, it must've looked as if his mother were having a seizure on the ground.

"This is not real, this is not real," I chanted to myself, tapping the sides of my head as if that might wake me up. I tried once more to envision Alison's room back at Serenity Falls, urging any part of me that thought this was my actual reality to cease and desist lest I be stuck here longer than necessary.

One of the shadows noticed me in a corner, though. In the next instant, it materialized before me, solidifying into a humanoid form. It gripped my throat like a vise. I felt my face bulge from the pressure. Its eyes were like swirls of hellfire seeking to pull me into their scorching flames. The shadow demon lifted me into the air, my kicking feet dangling several inches from the floor.

This is not real, this is not real, this is not real!

I clawed at the demon's digits, tearing at skin with my nails, but the pain didn't faze the creature in the least. Its grip wouldn't yield. My mind grew foggy from lack of oxygen, my muscles tiring the more I thrashed about.

This is not real!

I screamed it through every corridor of my mind even as I felt myself shattering into a million pieces, even as my vision faded, even as I felt an abyss of nightmares swallow me whole.

24

I didn't return to Serenity Falls. Instead, I found myself racing through a forest under a full moon, breathless and sweating. Though I couldn't see them, I knew the shadow demons from the aviary were pursuing me, were closing in. I pushed myself harder, adding heat to my speed, my feet hitting the earth with an impact that made my head throb.

I tripped over an upraised tree root and slammed into the cool dirt. My chest and stomach screamed in sharp pain. Coughing out moist earth, I scrambled to my hands and knees and righted myself to my feet, sprinting through the forest once more.

In the dark, the trees were like gnarled hands grasping at the stars. As I passed them, glowing eyes peeked out of trunk cavities before winking out of sight. Small animals rushed out of my way, cutting a crackling course through the dry leaves on the ground.

That's when the young woman in the white nightgown appeared in front of me. Like me, she pelted through the woods, looking over her shoulder every few seconds at the monsters pursuing her. Alison.

Somehow, I knew this wasn't a memory. It had the same feel as my stint in Alison's grave, which meant it was either a fear or a nightmare.

I called out Alison's name again and again, but she either didn't hear me or assumed the demons were merely playing tricks on her mind. I opened my mouth to try again, but the yell died at the base of my throat when a cliff edge suddenly appeared at my feet. Thrown off balance, my arms frantically windmilled as I tried to steady myself, but my body pitched forward and I started to fall...

...and then a hand fisted the back of my shirt and yanked me away from the edge at the last second. I whirled around to face my savior, my heart throbbing.

"Alison!"

"You have to stop them." She looked crazed, eyes blood-shot and wide with terror. She gripped my arms so tight her nails dug into my skin.

"Stop who? Alison, I'm here because I need to ask you something very important. I'm a friend of Jack's. The Wise Ones—"

She wasn't listening to me. The whispers held her attention. They were low, dark, and inhuman. The way you'd expect the devils from a nightmare to sound. I couldn't make out their words. They were in a tongue unknown to me, one that was guttural and harsh so that every syllable sounded cruel and dangerous. They were all around us and growing louder, covering my arms with gooseflesh.

"You have to stop them," Alison said again.

"The shadow demons, you mean? How could I possibly stop them?"

"Please. It's the only way to help."

The demons materialized before us, a daunting legion of them. My beloved *'this is not real'* mantra wasn't going to cut it this time. Because as far as I was concerned, this was very real. All too real.

The demons drew closer, and I backed away until my heels were flush with the cliff edge.

"You can stop them," Alison said. "You must."

"But I don't know how."

"Then we're all doomed," she said. Her eyes grew faraway and glassy. As she shuffled her feet back, pebbles dislodged from the cliff edge and plunged into the darkness below. In one fluid movement, Alison stretched her arms out horizontally and fell back to join them.

Then the shadow demons lunged for me, and when I jerked away from their attack, the momentum sent me over the cliff edge, rushing after Alison.

I woke to the sound of whining hinges.

Whine, *whoosh*, whine, *whoosh.*

A swing. My eyes slowly yawned opened and I winced at the brightness of the sun, throwing up a hand to shield my face. To my left, a brown-haired boy with cognac eyes swung back and forth on a playground made of wood, his pale hands tightly gripping the swing's thick chain.

I sat up, my head spinning. I had finally managed to speak with Alison, but her words were an enigma. Stop the demons? But how? I didn't know what I'd done to 'banish' that demon at the rugby game, if I'd banished it at all.

Nearby stood the Connelly home, and arguing voices from within filled the silence. I padded over to an open window and peeked inside.

"I can't believe what you've done," Alison was saying, her face red and tear-stained.

"At least I did something," Redmond threw back.

"Endanger one son for the sake of another?"

"Would you have rather I let Connor die?"

Alison blanched, her eyes doubling in size as her body stilled all over. "How dare you ask me such a thing?"

"You dote on Jack to the exclusion of the others. You don't think the boys notice it? The firstborn witches in your line are unfathomably powerful, but that doesn't mean Jack's the only one who needs his mother's love. He was able to give Connor back to us. That's something to celebrate."

"And I'm thankful beyond words. But look at what it cost Jack. The clans will never look at him the same way again. They fear him now, Redmond."

"Let them believe what they will. Why should we care?"

"Because I know what it feels like to be ostracized by your own people from a young age, and I purposed that none of my boys should ever know that pain. But you went behind my back in this and asked Jack to do something I didn't even know was possible, something he wouldn't even know was possible had you not told him. How can I trust there won't be a second time or a third? It terrifies me more than anything else that we'll lose him sooner than later."

Redmond exhaled a long breath, the fight draining out of him. He rubbed his forehead. "I stressed the importance that he never do it again. But it was the only way, Alison. I will always do whatever it takes to protect our boys and keep our family together."

Alison's eyes were shining. She shook her head as tears raced down her cheeks. "And that's what scares me the most," she said. "I want nothing more to do with demons and dark magic, Redmond. There has to be a point when you and Maurice stop trying to change fate. Returning Connor to us is one of the greatest gifts you could've ever given me, and I will be thankful for it until my dying breath, but we mustn't expose Jack to such darkness ever again no matter what. You have to promise me that."

Redmond studied her for a long moment. "You've seen something," he said. "You've seen Jack's future."

More tears slipped down her cheeks. "Only a possible future, a new path that recently unraveled for him and one we must avoid at all costs. For should he, as powerful as he is, be exposed to magic that dark again..." She trailed off, pressing a hand to her throat.

"What is it?"

She swallowed thickly. "It'll be the end of him," she said.

Thunder roared overhead as the sky quickly swelled like a bruise, gray clouds rushing in to block the sun's golden rays. Within seconds, the heavens instantly transformed. Night fell, the black canvas above studded with an ocean of stars. When I returned my attention to the Connelly house, Alison was alone, paging through what looked to be a family album.

This was my chance.

Moments later, I was inside, slowly making my way toward the living room and wincing at every creak the floorboards gave off. Above me, feet pounded up and down the second level, and I could just make out the muted voices of boys horsing around. I couldn't be sure, but it almost sounded as if they were playing rugby indoors.

The windows in the living room glowed in a flash of lightning. The accompanying thunder seemed to shake the very foundations of the house. Alison continued flipping through the family album, each page covered in a shiny, plastic sleeve that glistened in the lamplight.

"He finally found you," she said.

I blinked and glanced around the room. I hadn't seen anyone

before, but maybe I'd missed them. I hadn't. I was very much the only other person present.

Wind whistled as it rushed past the windows, making them tremble in their frames. I furrowed my brow. No, not wind... what was that? I honed in on it, taking another step forward. My heart shuddered. It was black smoke. Thick tapestries of black smoke wrapping around the house like colossal serpents.

The shadow demons.

"They're called Wraiths," Alison said. She had turned in the couch and was looking in my direction.

I looked over my shoulder, but no one was there. She was addressing *me*. I hadn't expected to acquire an audience with her so easily once given the chance, so it took me a moment to move past my surprise. "Why are they here?" I asked, realizing that what I'd wrongly assumed was a memory was instead another fear or nightmare.

"They're the little-known byproduct of dark magic used against the mind."

That gave me pause, but I had little time to think about it. The black smoke was suddenly slithering into the room, filling it quickly as if the house had caught fire. "We have to get out of here!" I exclaimed. I knew she wasn't real, but I couldn't just leave Jack's mother to this nightmare's hellish end.

In a blur, one of the shadows detached from the mass and shot out at Alison, a ring of black forming around her neck in a chokehold. She coughed and thrashed against her captor, a captor that quickly evolved from mere smoke to a towering, horned creature that made my stomach fall to my knees. It was the most terrifying thing I'd ever laid eyes on.

The surrounding shadows hissed, the sound of a hundred venomous snakes whispering into my ears, making my skin crawl. The Wraiths continued populating the space around me, enclosing me and Alison in a thickening band of shadows.

Though they had no form, red eyes gleamed from various parts of the smoke as if with hunger.

I held my ground. I was mildly aware of the fact that I was trembling, but as I watched Alison struggle against her assailant, I knew I couldn't stand to find out what they'd do to her. She needed me, and I wasn't going to let them take her.

I squared my shoulders. "Let. Her. Go."

"You have no power here," the horned Wraith said, its words sounding as if they'd gone through a voice modulator of the most disturbing kind. "Leave."

I took a defiant step forward. "I'm not going anywhere. I'm not afraid of you."

"Oh, but you are. And how delicious your fear tastes."

My heart shivered, but I kept my head high. "I'm not afraid of you," I repeated, making my voice as hard as iron. This time, the horned Wraith and its kin snarled, so I said it again. "I'm not afraid of you. I'm not afraid of you. I'm not afraid of you!"

With each proclamation, warmth gathered in the pit of my stomach like a growing fire. I locked eyes with Alison, and she nodded at me inasmuch as she could. Her words from before came to mind. *You have to stop them*, she'd said. *It's the only way to help.* Without warning, the warmth in my stomach shot through my right arm so that it was like fire sleeved my skin. I looked down at my palm, fingers splayed. It was as hot as if I held a flame. The heat continued to build, refusing to be contained. I nearly cried out in pain.

Roaring at my defiance, the horned Wraith shoved Alison away and charged for me. And then I knew what I had to do. Just as it lunged at me, I threw out my hand to stop it, aiming the scorching heat its way. A hellish shriek pierced my ears as white light flooded the room. I squeezed my eyes shut as the deafening screams of the Wraiths surrounded me.

When I dared to look again, the shadow demons had

vanished, nothing but plumes of smoke rising in their wake. In front of me was a blotch of scorched hardwood floor marking where the horned Wraith had last stood.

"You see?" Alison asked, smiling softly. "You *are* one of Them."

"One of what?" But she had already disappeared, and all around me, the room shimmered and gave way to a new scene, to a familiar, yellow-tiled kitchen.

I was immediately greeted with laughter. Alison and her four sons gathered around Redmond. The man sat at the kitchen table with a lopsided cake before him covered in brightly lit candles and an excess of chocolate icing. His wife and sons were singing Happy Birthday. The room smelled like vanilla, and was filled with love and warmth. I wanted to stay longer to bask in it, but I knew I couldn't.

A noise from above pulled me upstairs. As I ascended the steps, the wall to my left continuously changed. From crayon doodles on the wall to new paint to cover those doodles to multiple frames coming and going, showing the boys as they aged.

At the top of the stairs, giggling came from a room down the hall. As I made my way for it, the walls transformed around me, taking on the bones of another house entirely. I pushed open a cracked door and discovered a gathering of young women in lavender dresses, bouncing on their heels with uncontainable excitement as they surrounded a friend of theirs.

It was Alison. She stood before a long mirror in a simple but beautiful wedding gown. There was a crown of flowers in her hair. It contained dried lavender and baby's-breath and pale roses. The bridesmaids didn't notice me standing there, but Alison smiled knowingly at my reflection in the mirror, as if she'd been expecting me.

"You're here at last." She turned away from the mirror. The

bridesmaids were gone. She held out her hand. "Come closer. There's something you're here to ask me, isn't there?"

I closed the distance between us and took her hand. It was warm, full of life. I wished Jack could hold it now, could see his mother like this, beautiful and radiant and young and happy.

I did have a question in mind. It wasn't the one I was here for, but I had to know her answer. "Would you change anything?" I asked her. "If you could do it all again, would you still marry Redmond? Would you still have a family?"

She smiled. "I would change nothing. Because that's the beauty of life. We take the mess with the magic. A life with one and not the other is only a life half-lived." She squeezed my fingers. "Now what is it you must tell me?"

I needed to tell her about The Wise Ones and ask what she knew concerning the sluagh. I opened my mouth to begin, but the words were odd-feeling on my tongue. I had the impression that there was something else I was supposed to do, something more.

And then two words came to mind. They didn't make sense. I didn't know why I felt I needed to say them, but I leaned forward and whispered them into Alison's ear nonetheless.

"*Wake up.*"

As soon as the words left my mouth, the ground trembled and the walls shuddered. I gasped and tried to pull away, but Alison's grip on my hand was unyielding.

"Thank you," was all she said before everything came crashing down upon us.

25

I threw my arms over my head to shield myself from the falling debris.

No debris came. When I opened my eyes, four faces were peering down at me. I was back in Serenity Falls.

"Oh, thank God," I breathed, sitting up. "You wouldn't believe what I—"

There was a sharp gasp from beside me, and all of us turned to find Alison gulping for breath. She blinked furiously, trying to make sense of her surroundings, thrashing back against her wheelchair. She didn't know where she was or why.

"Mam?" Jack rushed to her, taking one of her hands. I didn't know if it was the familiarity of his voice or simply the gentleness of his touch, but she slowly relaxed, the tension gradually draining out of her. The rigid muscles in her body loosened one by one, the arm that had been stretched heavenward floating down to rest upon her lap. The clouds in her eyes cleared. A healthy flush of red slowly pooled into her cheeks. Even her chocolate hair seemed to regain some of its luster.

After a few moments, her eyes switched to me as I stood. "You've unlocked me," she whispered. She looked down at her hands, at her body in its wheelchair, as if seeing it all for the first time. "I've been imprisoned for so long."

"What do you mean imprisoned?" It was Connor who asked, his brow furrowed.

"A dark enchantment," said Alison. "A curse."

"Someone did this to you?" Connor's tone was blatantly doubtful.

Jack cut a sharp look in his direction. "Who cast the curse, Mam? Did you recognize them?"

"The witch in the hood," Alison said. "A face cast in shadows."

"Whose face?"

"I don't know how much time we have," Alison said. "I feel myself fading, weakening."

"It's all right," Jack said. "We can help you regain your strength. You're safe now."

"We're far from safe. They're coming. They're coming for all of you. I've seen it all, and I've been powerless to stop it."

My heart missed a beat. "Are you talking about the sluagh? Do you know anything about them? The Wise Ones sent us here. They seem to think you know something about how to stop them."

"The sluagh aren't working of their own volition," Alison said, looking completely different from that withered woman we'd first walked in on. Years had melted away from her face. Where she sat was more a throne than a wheelchair. "Someone's controlling them."

Jack nodded. "We know. They're working for The Black Hand."

"No. Hunters play no part in this. The opponent we face is far more formidable. There is darker magic at work here. Forbidden magic."

"What are you saying?" I asked. My chest was tight. The

Black Hand had seemed a formidable enough enemy. What could possibly top them? "Who's our actual opponent?"

Alison met my eyes, her soft brown irises flooded with fear. "A Reaper."

The word was like a strike of electricity. The boys visibly recoiled from the word. Lucas and Rory even stepped back.

"What's a Reaper?" I asked, the hair on my arms rising.

Jack was the one to respond, his face noticeably pale. "Reapers are witches who slay other witches in order to reap their magic. Their Masteries specifically. Their goal is to acquire more and more power each time until they're an unstoppable force."

"And this Reaper is unimaginably powerful," Alison said. "They have great darkness at their command."

Great darkness in the form of demons? "Could this Reaper have been the one to summon the demon that burned down The Wise Ones?" I asked.

"Most likely," Jack said, raking his fingers through his hair, his face ashen. "If a Reaper's behind the stolen souls, then we're already too late."

"No," Alison said, shaking her head. "The Reaping has not yet been performed, nor is the Reaper interested in Masteries alone. They mean to use the stolen souls as a sacrifice in a dark ritual. They mean to awaken ancient evil."

The floor was tilting. I grabbed the edge of a table to steady myself.

Jack squeezed his mother's hands. "Can you see who the Reaper is? In the visions you've had, have you seen their face?"

"The witch in the hood," Alison repeated. "A face cast in shadows."

"What is she saying?" Connor asked. "That the Reaper is the same witch that cast this curse on her? Why won't she give us a name?"

Jack shook his head. "They must've placed a block on her mind to keep her from revealing their identity."

Alison seized Jack's arm as if she hadn't heard the exchange. "You must recover The Book of Fates. It alone contains the spell that can bind the Reaper and stop the ritual before it's too late. As you already know, the girl plays a role as well."

Jack's eyes slid to me and then back to his mother. "What role specifically?"

"She's one of Them, Jack. The last of her kind. If all else fails, she's our only hope. But time is running out. The ritual draws nigh."

"When will it take place?" Jack asked.

"When the Blood Moon fills the sky. The earth where the mother goddess sleeps awaits." Alison suddenly clutched her chest, her breathing becoming labored.

"Mam? Mam, are you all right?"

She was wheezing. She pitched forward, stumbling out of the wheelchair until she was on her hands and knees. Her coughs came out wet and chesty. Jack helped her to her feet, and when she opened her mouth, it was painted red. Blood dribbled down her chin, trickled out of her nose.

"Get the nurse!" Jack ordered Lucas, who scrambled out of the room. With a wave of his hand, Rory cleared the sigil from the floor and rapidly began returning the candles and crystals into his backpack.

Alison broke free from Jack's hold and tried to walk on her own, but she tripped over herself and fell into Connor's arms, Connor whose face was painted with panic. "What do I do?" he exclaimed to Jack. "What do I do?"

"Connor," Alison said, her voice small and thin. She touched a palm to his cheek weakly. Her skin had lost all its color, her facing aging rapidly. Threads of gray appeared in her hair. She was reverting back to the frail woman I'd first seen. "I pray one day you may forgive me for my neglect."

Connor's face grew sallow, his body going tight.

The door burst open and a pack of nurses rushed in to help Alison, but no sooner had they taken half a dozen steps into the room, her body went completely limp in Connor's arms.

26

Alison was stable.

Or as stable as one could hope. Unfortunately, the doctors had no explanation for what had happened to her but worried a sudden onset of stress had been the culprit. As such, they'd cleared the room, allowing only one visitor to remain at Alison's bedside while she slept. Connor, surprisingly, had volunteered, the hard lines in his face softened into an expression I hadn't yet seen from him.

The entire experience had me phoning my dad's hospital for an update, but the nurse who answered fed me the same words they always did. No improvements. Dejected, I assumed a roost in an empty nook of Serenity Falls and distracted myself from Alison's ominous and enigmatic words by going through new text messages my phone had notified me about earlier but that I hadn't had time to check yet. There were a few texts from Natalie, asking if I were dying in a ditch somewhere or if I'd been kidnapped by an axe murderer. I realized I'd never responded to her after missing our video chat date. I fired out a quick update.

Me: I'm alive! Sorry, it's been an insane couple of days. I promise I'll catch you up on everything soon. xo

I would've loved nothing more than to hear her voice right about now, but I didn't know where I'd begin with explaining everything that had happened to me in the past week. Besides that, with the time difference, it was currently 4AM in Colorado.

I was surprised to find the next message was from Liam.

Liam: Hi, Scarlet. The school told us your father had been admitted to the hospital over the weekend. Is he all right? If there's anything I can do to help (bring food to the hospital, drive you home, etc.), I'm only a call or text away. Let me know.

It touched me that even though we'd only been friends for a few days, Liam had cared enough to check in on me. I wasn't sure how the school had found out about my dad, but I assumed in a town as small as Rosalyn Bay, it probably took little effort to find a missing professor. Though I was a newcomer myself, my dad had long established himself here. There were people, students included, who cared about him. I smiled softly as I typed out my reply.

Me: Liam, thank you for the offer. That's really sweet of you. I'm okay for now, but I'll let you know if I need anything. My dad's stable at the moment. I'll keep you updated.

"Coffee?" Jack approached me, holding out a red, paper cup.

"Thank you." Even though the cup was nested inside a paperboard sleeve, the coffee's heat still seeped into my palms. I welcomed the warmth and breathed in the drink's French vanilla aromatics. After blowing on the coffee through the gap in the plastic lid, I took a slow sip. The liquid was velvety on my tongue, and I savored the rich flavor.

I waited a few moments before saying the words that had been on my mind since the transference spell. "Your mom is the Seer you went to see after your grandfather died, isn't she?"

Beside me, Jack stilled. We were seated in a lounge with floor-to-ceiling windows that overlooked one of the institute's many man-made waterfalls. This waterfall was multi-tiered and flanked on either side by lush vegetation, its white ribbons of water crashing into a koi pond below.

Jack smoothed his thumb across the dimpled sleeve of his coffee cup. "Is that one of the memories you saw? Her conveying the message to me?"

"No," I said. I told him about the aviary memory in his mother's mind. "The Seer specifically mentioned a bird in her message. I realized it was your mom the moment I saw her affinity for them. And then when she later mentioned my playing a role in all this, my suspicions were confirmed. My only question is why the secrecy? Why not tell your brothers the truth to begin with?"

"It's complicated."

"Is it?"

A male nurse passed by, making light-hearted conversation with a patient pushing along an IV pole, the wheels of which gave off a high-pitched squeak. The nurse spotted us and offered a polite nod and smile before resuming with his conversation.

"I didn't want the others to know that I could temporarily pull our mother out of her catatonia."

"Why not?"

"If you saw that memory through to its end, you must know why."

The Wraiths. Just thinking about them made the skin on my

arms dimple. "You didn't want them to see your mom's demons overcome her."

"It would break them to see her dissolve into madness like that. It's why I proposed the transference spell to begin with. That, and my mother's lucidity has always been so brief when I've tried to awaken her myself, lasting only seconds. I knew we'd hardly get anything out of her that way. She'd be overcome before I could even get the question out. Although I'm sure my brothers must've drawn the same conclusion as you at this point, about her being the Seer, in light of what she revealed about you."

I slowly drank more coffee as I listened, relishing the way the liquid warmed my throat and chest with each swallow. Like every other medical facility, Serenity Falls was freezing inside. "Connor seemed bothered by your mom's state when we first entered her room. Has it been a while since he last saw her?"

"Our grandfather feared that our mother, in her grief, might harm herself, which is why she was checked into Serenity Falls to begin with. At first, all four of us would visit her, but as her condition worsened over the years, I think it became too hard for my brothers to see her like that, to see her deteriorate before their very eyes. So one by one, they started to drop out of our weekly visits. They assumed I'd stop going as well, but I couldn't bear to leave her on her own like that. If I could bring her a little bit of peace, even if only briefly, then it was worth it."

Alison had said in one of the memories that Jack never gave up on her. She couldn't have been more right. "Your mom mentioned the Wraiths being the byproduct of dark magic."

Jack nodded. "If her catatonia was in fact the result of a curse, the Wraiths must be connected to that. Maybe they were a way to keep her locked in her mind, to keep her from surfacing. It makes sense, considering she was blocked from revealing the identity of the Reaper as well."

I started to ask why his mother of all people would be targeted, but I stopped myself, the answer coming to mind immediately. If Alison had once been the most powerful Seer of her generation as Connor had said, she would've seen the Reaper's intentions well in advance, would've been able to warn the other clans before the sluagh had begun to attack. I assumed, of course, that she hadn't doled out predictions since becoming lost in her grief years ago, but it seemed the Reaper hadn't wanted to take any chances. I tapped a finger against my coffee cup's plastic lid. "What did she mean when she said I was one of 'Them,' that I was the last of my kind?"

"I have an idea about that," he said, turning slightly toward me and holding my eyes. "Scarlet, I think you might hail from The Lost Clan, the one no one's heard from in ages. You could very well be the very last of them, in which case, it's more important than ever that you nurture your magic. That particular bloodline was once made up of extremely powerful witches, and if you're all that remains..."

Then I had an obligation to embrace my heritage, as it could very well mean the difference in the fight we now faced. My stomach curdled, though. Jack was right. I was all that remained because my dad was magically incapacitated, and there was no guarantee I'd be able to save him in time. "A bird of rare feather will arrive and lead the way," I murmured. At this point, I couldn't deny there was some kind of power in me. A power I didn't yet understand or fully know how to wield but power nonetheless. Even so, it was difficult to grasp that I was the only remaining descendant of an entire race of witches.

"How do I nurture the magic on a fast enough timeline to make a difference, though? Lucas told me witches normally spend their entire childhood and adolescence mastering their abilities."

"It's true, but that doesn't mean it's impossible for someone to come into their magic later on. I'll help you, Scarlet. We'll figure it out together."

The novelty of my name in his mouth hadn't yet worn off. I didn't think it ever would. *Together.* My chest warmed like a furnace, and the warmth spread all over my skin, as if I were basking in the afternoon sunlight of a summer day.

"There was something else I saw in your mom's memories."

"Oh?"

Part of me didn't want to bring it up. I worried it was uncharted territory. Jack felt guilty enough with everything else that was going on. But I knew it'd bother me if I didn't ask. "Your parents were having a disagreement about Connor. Your dad asked your mom if she would've rather he died."

Jack nodded slowly. He looked down at his coffee in the following silence. He hadn't taken a single sip of it since sitting down. Maybe it was more so to give his hands something to do. "When we were children, Connor sustained a severe head injury during a game of rugby. It put him in a coma he wasn't supposed to wake up from. Not even the Healers from our clans could do anything for him. The doctors had begun preparing us for the inevitable. But my father pulled me aside the day Connor's body began to shut down and told me there was a way I could save Connor, but that I'd have to be very brave. I said I'd do anything no matter what it took. He explained the demon's mark on my wrist had come with a sort of caveat. The demon would come for me either on the Old Moon during my eighteenth year or upon the fulfillment of my third and final entreaty."

"What are you saying? That the demon's mark allows you three wishes?"

"To be used as the mark's bearer sees fit. Outside of wishing the mark away, along with the usual restrictions such as being unable to change the past, take a life, or raise the dead, nothing is off limits as long as it doesn't interfere with another demon's bidding. Long story short: I summoned a demon using the mark and asked that Connor be healed and revived. He awoke within seconds. The doctors were mystified, as were our clansmen. Connor showed no lingering side effects and was up and about as if the incident had never happened. He said he'd never felt better. Of course, my father and I never told him the truth behind his recovery. I never wanted him to feel as if his being well again brought me closer to fulfilling my debt."

"I'm assuming you summoned the demon in private. How did your mom find out what you'd done then? Couldn't it have just been a miracle?"

"She realized it because of the magic's kickback. Using the mark meant using dark magic, and dark magic isn't without a price. You see, the demon hadn't healed and revived Connor by his own hands, he'd simply given me the power to do it myself. And I became sick almost immediately as that great, barely containable power began to slowly work its way out of my system afterward. Then, about two or three days later, we were visiting members of another clan. Connor, being Connor, got into it with a lad a few years older than us named Declan. Naturally, I rushed to his defense and pulled Declan off him, shoving Declan away as hard as I could to break up the fight. When I did, lingering dark magic rushed out of me beyond my control and I ended up..." He faltered.

"You ended up what?"

Jack blew out a long breath and dragged a hand across his face, as if he could rub away the memory from his mind. "I ended up setting Declan on fire."

My mouth fell open like a drawbridge. Remembering myself, I quickly snapped it shut, my teeth smacking each other in a loud *clack*.

"Fortunately, onlookers were quick to run to us and put the fire out, but Declan still sustained serious injuries, and I never forgave myself for what I did to him. From that moment on, other witches never looked at me the same way again. Though they never spoke a word of it in front of me, it was written all over their faces that they knew I'd done something dark to bring Connor back. My father made me promise I would never use the other two wishes again, no matter what."

I plucked at the edge of my coffee's paperboard sleeve, letting that sink in. I imagined it had been a horrifying sight to see fire consume a fellow witch, to realize the fire had been your own doing. Alison had said a new path had opened for Jack the moment he'd been exposed to that bout of dark magic. Could that have contributed to the overwhelming guilt Redmond had felt, the guilt that had ultimately driven him to take his own life mere years later?

"Scarlet, I know this has been a lot. I'm sorry for everything I've put you through—"

"You didn't put me through anything," I gently assured him, putting my hand on his arm. "I'm here because I want to be here. This is as much my fight as it is yours, and now we know what we're up against. A Reaper. Tell me more about what that is exactly."

Outside, the sun was back to warring with the clouds, painting the lounge in ever-shifting shadows. Jack's face was half gold and half dark as he responded. "When a Reaper has killed another witch, they perform what's called a Reaping. In the Reaping, they extract any Masteries from the soul and absorb them through dark magic. Afterward, the souls are discarded like scraps of unwanted food without receiving any sort of blessing into the afterlife, forcing them to become wandering spirits. It's a heinous practice. Reapers have no right to call themselves witches." His eyes darkened, the shadows on his face giving him a fierce look.

"That's horrible."

"It's made worse by the fact that this particular Reaper isn't casting aside the souls but using them for a sacrifice. In light of what my mother's shared about awakening ancient evil, I think it's safe to assume the sacrifice is intended for some kind of demon. As for the end result, though, it's anyone's guess. I can't fathom what a Reaper might hope to achieve with such a ritual or what the demon has promised them."

"Has something like this ever happened in recent history?"

"Not recently. But there's a well-known story among our clans about a woman named Celeste, who lived in the early 1800s. By that point, The Burning Times had already entered a decline, but that didn't mean persecution was entirely gone. Celeste's entire village had been massacred during a witch hunt. Her mother and father, as well as her sisters, had been among the fallen. She'd been spared only because she hadn't been in the village at the time. She'd gone into the woods that night to practice magic under the full moon.

"Celeste was consumed with vengeance and tried to enlist the help of other witches to exact her revenge. But understandably, they refused to become involved, knowing exposing themselves would only turn them into the hunters' next targets. Celeste eventually sought sanctuary among the Elders of her time. She devoted herself to study, swearing she would never have to run from hunters again, that she would have her revenge no matter the costs.

"Years later, she returned to the villages of those who'd refused to help her, but she didn't come as Celeste. She came as a Reaper. She'd grown in knowledge and was unimaginably powerful. People tried to stop her, but they were no match for her. It's said she could turn a man or woman into ash merely by looking at them. She's also the witch who stole the Hallowstones from the other clans, so her victims were defenseless against her. And her bloodthirst knew no bounds. She slew every witch in her path, trapping their souls inside an amulet she wore around her neck, performing a Reaping every few days to absorb her victims' Masteries."

A chill crept down my arms, and I quickly drank more coffee to chase the cold away.

"The reason Reapers crave so much power is because it takes great power to perform the high-level dark magic of which they're devoted students. Celeste, in particular, wanted to perform resurrection magic."

"You mean...?"

"Raising the dead, yes. With so many Masteries now contained within her bones, she had enough power to command one of the Forbidden Spells. However, the spell itself, which had never been used before, explained only how to bring someone back from the dead. Celeste hadn't factored in how to return her loved ones to their former glory. So when she raised her mother and father along with her sisters, they were nothing more than rotting corpses. And devoid of any memory of who Celeste even was, they ripped her body to pieces in a craze."

I shuddered.

"It's because of Celeste that any witch who loses themselves to dark magic is immediately excommunicated from the clans, stripped of their power, and sent to The Citadel, a prison for wayward witches located Elsewhere. As added insurance, especially considering not all prisoners are necessarily divested of their magic if they're serving lesser sentences, the prison's spelled, making it impossible to escape and just as impossible to break into."

"So The Book of Fates will be able to stop what the current Reaper's doing?"

"It's one of the Sacred Grimoires. They're holy texts believed to be given to witches by The Triple Goddess, Brigid, herself and contain unimaginably powerful spellcraft. A normal binding spell would be ineffective. A binding spell written by a goddess on the other hand..."

"So where's the grimoire located?"

"When conquerors invaded Celtic societies here in Ireland, they burned our grimoires and other sacred texts in an effort to wipe Ireland clean of any pagan influence. One of the clans, however, took it upon themselves to rescue these books and protect them from being forever lost. They hid the books in secret, underground libraries where they'd never be found by hunters or the Sightless. We have a contact in that very clan who I've already called. They've agreed to meet with us tonight."

Eerily, his phone rang a second later. Furrowing his brow, he retrieved the cell from his coat pocket and checked the caller ID. He blanched just slightly. "But first, it looks like I'm going to have to explain to Seamus why we aren't at Crowmarsh anymore."

27

"So we know the Reaping will take place on Samhain."

It was almost dusk, and we were in Dublin, where Jack's contact had said The Book of Fates was last seen. We'd taken up headquarters in the penthouse suite of a five-star hotel. The two-story space was massive, larger in square footage than my small, humble home back in Colorado. It was also dripping with luxury: balconies with stunning views of the busy city, bathrooms with Italian Carrara marble and waterfall shower heads, gorgeously tiled fireplaces, and the largest flat screen TV I'd ever seen in the common room.

After showering and changing into fresh clothes, I'd found the Connellys gathered around the dining table, a spread of room service before them that included pizza, hamburgers, cold sandwiches, and more.

"I wasn't sure what you might want, Scarlet Ibis" Lucas had said, speaking around a mouthful of crisps, "so I ordered liberally."

I now sat with an untouched turkey-and-cheese sandwich in front of me, struggling to find my appetite. I balled up a napkin and dabbed at the cold water trickling down from the still-wet bun atop my head. "Samhain," I repeated. "That's Halloween, right?"

"Halloween originates in part from Samhain. Samhain is one of our Greater Sabbats and is a Celtic festival that marks the end of the harvest season and the beginning of winter, or the 'darker half' of the year. It's a time when we remember our dead and celebrate the lives they led. But of particular note, it's also when the veil between this world and the Otherworld momentarily thins, making it easier to harvest power from the other side. It's the most auspicious night of the year to hold a dark ritual."

"But how can you be so sure that's when the ritual will take place?"

"Our mother said it would happen when the Blood Moon fills the sky. That's what we call October's full moon, not to be confused with the total lunar eclipse of the same name. Our designation comes from our way of life. Back in the day, the clans would spend October hunting, slaughtering, and preserving meats for the coming winter, inevitably spilling blood. This year, the Blood Moon just so happens to fall on the thirty-first of the month."

"If that's the case, we only have two weeks to stop the Reaper."

"Which is why we need to act quickly."

Pressure built in my chest. It was bad enough when my dad's soul had been in danger of becoming an eternal prisoner of the sluagh. But learning he was instead meant to be a sacrifice in some deranged ritual involving demons? That was a new level of terrifying. "So we know when the ritual will take place. What about where?"

"Our mother gave us a clue about that as well. She said, 'The earth where the mother goddess sleeps awaits.'"

"The Hill of Uisneach," Connor said.

Jack nodded. "Ireland's sacred center. It's one of the country's most treasured and mysterious historical sites. It was an ancient ceremonial site, a place of worship, a seat of the High Kings throughout the years, and the place where the first Beltane fire was lit. But more importantly for our purposes, it's also where Ireland's matron goddess Ériu, after whom the country is named, was laid to rest according to legend, making the site holy ground. Ériu's resting place is said to mark a hidden gateway to the Otherworld. With the veil between the natural world and the supernatural world thinning on Samhain, there's no better place for the Reaper to hold their ritual. Being so close to a doorway to the Otherworld would amplify their magic immeasurably."

"So why are we still talking about it?" Connor asked. "Let's get the book and end this."

I glanced at him, still growing accustomed to his blossoming determination when he'd been so reluctant about everything since the beginning. Seeing Alison had shaken him, and she hadn't yet awakened by the time we'd left either. Jack and his brothers had to feel helpless, but if the witch who'd cursed Alison was the same witch running amok as the Reaper, then they knew their best chance at helping their mother was to recover The Book of Fates and bind the Reaper.

"You know we have to wait," Jack said.

"For your contact, you mean?" I asked.

"Part of protecting the secret libraries from hunters and the Sightless entailed casting glamour spells to keep them hidden. The spells can only be undone by a member of the O'Manacháin clan, so we'll need to be escorted by our contact." Jack tapped a finger against the shiny lacquer finish of the table, weighing something in his mind. Finally, he cleared his throat and quickly said, "Zoe will be here within the hour."

"Wait, what?" Connor straightened, a storm sparking in his dark eyes. "*That's* the contact you reached out to?"

Jack sighed. "I had no other choice, Connor. We have few allies among the O'Manacháin clan. Choosing her made the most sense."

Connor muttered a curse, pinching the bridge of his nose. "I swear to the gods..."

I looked between him and Jack. "What am I missing?"

Lucas was all grins, his playing cards organizing themselves into a three-level house beside his plate of pizza. "Let's just say Connor has a very colorful history with one of the daughters of O'Manacháin."

Jack went on, not giving his brothers the opportunity to start another argument. "Zoe will lead us to wherever the library's located, undo the spell, and then help us in locating the book. Provided it's even there at all. Let's hope it is."

"What about Seamus?" I asked. "Shouldn't we wait for him to get here?"

Seamus had still been Elsewhere when he'd called, but even from there, he'd been able to check on Crowmarsh's wards. Upon discovering they were down, he'd assumed the worst, so hearing Jack's voice on the other end of his phone call had primarily been a relief, though it definitely hadn't stopped him from immediately segueing into disciplinarian mode.

Jack could barely get a word in, but finally he'd found a large enough gap in his uncle's telling-off to mention Alison surfacing from her catatonia and her message about The Book of Fates. Seamus, awestruck no doubt, had gone silent at that for a long moment. Subdued, he and Jack had then spoken further, the conversation ending with Seamus agreeing to meet up with us in Dublin to help search for the book.

"When he called, The Council was still deliberating the matter of the sluagh and The Black Hand," Jack said. "They're notoriously slow in their deliberations, preferring to avoid confrontations with hunters or the Sightless whenever possible. Now that we know it's a Reaper we're up against, though, it'll hopefully change the tone of those deliberations and expedite the decision process. Even so, it may be a day or two more before he's here. Possibly even longer. Unfortunately, we don't have the luxury of time. Every second that passes is a second that brings us closer to Samhain and the Reaper's ritual. It's best we get a head start by beginning our search for the book now."

An hour later, a knock pulled us all to the front door, where we gathered around Jack as he opened it. On the other side of the threshold stood a girl my age with flawless, olive skin and curly, black hair tied back in a long ponytail. She was dressed head to toe in black, her form-fitting pants accentuating her hourglass figure, her thumbs hooked into the pockets of a vintage, faux-leather jacket. With metallic nails and an ouroboros ring on one index finger, she looked like a girl who'd just climbed off a Harley Davidson. A wing of mascara on each eyelid gave her a feline look, and she smirked at the boys.

"Hello, lads," she practically purred. "Are you ready for an adventure?"

Zoraida "Zoe" Rivera was vivacious. She was only two or three inches taller than me, but she might as well have been the size of a skyscraper with her larger-than-life personality. As we made our way through the compact streets of Dublin, threading through crowds like fine-point needles, she carried herself with an enviable swagger I'd never been able to master.

I lost count of the number of times she turned heads. Men would look up from their pints of Guinness with mustaches made of foam, hungrily admiring her sauntering figure until she was out of view. I wanted to believe it was some kind of spell, but I knew it wasn't. She was stunning, plain and simple. But she was beautiful in the way a deadly storm is beautiful, in the way the pink flowers of the poisonous Amaryllis are beautiful. For all the coquettish smirks she flashed at admirers with those pomegranate lips, Zoe was a modern-day femme fatale.

My eyes fell to the black backpack she carried, filled to the brim with weapons, and then to the blade strapped to her thigh holster, cloaked with magic so the Sightless were blind to it.

"Hunters," she'd explained back in the penthouse.

"They're here in Dublin?" I croaked. I'd been hoping we wouldn't have to deal with their kind at all ever since learning they weren't behind the sluagh attacks.

"Of course they are. They scour big cities like this whenever a Sabbat approaches in hopes of netting themselves a few witches. And Samhain is the holiest Sabbat of them all. So they're out in droves." She cocked a gun with a smirk, a dangerous gleam in her eyes. "But fortunately for you lot, I don't scare easily."

As it happened, we made it to the side street where Jack had parked the SUV without incident. Zoe assumed the shotgun seat to provide directions—and to snap off Jack's choice in music—leaving me in one of the backseats with Connor. He'd cleaned up rather well in the hour before Zoe's arrival. My guess was he'd paid a visit to one of the shops on the hotel's main level because his blond locks were styled with hair product and he was even wearing cologne, the fragrance a mix of vetiver and pine needles.

Zoe had casually greeted him upon entering the penthouse, almost as if it were an afterthought, and he'd returned the salutation with enough nonchalance to suggest there was clearly unfinished business between them. I tried to picture him and Zoe as a couple or as whatever they'd been, and imagined two combustible personalities that must've been fireworks on the best of days and wildfires on the worst.

When we pulled up to an empty field thirty minutes outside of Dublin and filed out the SUV with flashlights, I blinked at the endless miles of pastures and grazing cows, the scent in the air a combination of wet grass and manure.

"Is this the right place?" I asked.

"O ye of little faith," Zoe said, a smirk tucked into the corner of her heart-shaped mouth as she strode through the damp, tall grass as if strutting down a runway, her ponytail swaying from side to side.

We walked for nearly half an hour before we happened upon the ruins of an abbey, its towering, sandstone walls like a carcass in a barren wasteland. In the light of the waxing moon, it was breathtaking and haunting all at once. I aimed the beacon of my flashlight at the impressive architecture, marveling at the Gothic arches and clustered columns. With no roof and no windows, what remained of the abbey looked like old, tired bones sprouting from the earth, covered in moss and vines.

Zoe stepped up to a column, passing a hand over its façade. As she did, symbols appeared, glowing in a soft, blue light. Small sigils, I realized. She pressed her palm to the sigils and closed her eyes as she whispered an incantation I couldn't make out. The light from the sigils quickly branched out like veins, coursing through the length of the column and then spreading all across the ruins until the entire structure was aglow in a latticework of blue.

"Here we go," Lucas said beside me, rubbing his hands together eagerly.

The abbey shimmered, as if it were a reflection in a

disturbed pool of water. And then, amidst the ripples, it began to materialize into something more. I took a step back, my eyes widening as my jaw went slack.

Breathtaking stained glass filled the gaping cavities under arches or between the traceries of rose windows. They depicted apostles and saints in striking, bright colors that gleamed like jewels against our flashlights. Grime and overgrowth dissolved and fell away. In their place, the sandstone walls shed centuries' worth of aging, becoming like new again. Tile by tile, a roof patched itself together atop the ruins, and a lone steeple rose above it all, piercing the sky like a bayonet as a massive bell filled its center. The bell swung left to right, and the clapper within struck the metal with fervor, each loud bong a wistful tune that reverberated in my chest and held my heart closely, as if by the hands of angels.

The bell continued tolling, and as it did, the abbey's exterior walls rebuilt themselves brick by brick. What had taken years—decades even—was completed by magic in mere seconds in a spectacle I would've never believed had I not witnessed it firsthand. Even the surrounding air was heavy, vibrating around us as if charged with an otherworldly energy. Finally, the walls drew themselves together, fully enclosing the abbey, and two massive doors fashioned from oak filled the arched entrance before us.

The bell sang out one more time, and then there was nothing but silence afterward. Still, I stood there staring, as if expecting the abbey to metamorphose again like a chrysalis into a butterfly.

"There are sites like this hidden all over the world right under people's noses," Jack said, seeing my awed expression. "They're disguised as ruins or abandoned lots, and yet they house our most prized treasures."

"That's nothing," Zoe tossed over her shoulder as she

pushed open the doors of the abbey and led us inside. "You should see what Stonehenge really looks like."

Stepping into the abbey was like stepping into another era. There were black chandeliers and floor candelabras everywhere, their decorative scrolling covered in dripping wax. They each held a fleet of ivory candles, the flames of which came to life in our presence, trembling atop their wicks. The abbey was cavernous inside, the vaulted ceiling nearly touching the heavens, its ribbing giving the sense you were trapped inside the belly of a beast. Even though night had fallen, the imagery in the stained glass windows still glowed in the candlelight with ethereal beauty, painting quivering, kaleidoscope-colored shadows onto the stone floor.

I thought about the generations of people who had once called this abbey their place of worship, the pilgrims who'd walked down this very nave, the devoted who'd knelt before shrines to say a prayer and light a candle. The history surrounded me like a warm blanket, the age of the abbey sinking deep into my bones.

"It's unbelievable," I said, taking it all in. I turned in place, the beacon of my flashlight striping the walls and wooden pews. "But where are all the books?"

"Right this way," Zoe said as she made for a shadowy stairwell that descended into darkness. "I just hope you're not afraid of the dead."

28

The dead in this case referred to the abbey's catacombs.

We progressed through a cold, stretching corridor that smelled of earth, flanked on either side by stone tombs set within recesses. Recumbent effigies were carved upon their tops, depicting each tomb's occupant in a state of eternal rest. Some of the stone men laid with their arms crossed in an X over their chest. Others gripped a broadsword. A few maintained a posture of prayer, hands pressed together above their hearts. They all wore crowns.

"Welcome to the Hall of Kings," Zoe said, her tone solemn.

Torch-shaped sconces attached to the rock wall and spaced out every few feet roared to life as Zoe passed, their spitting flames bright and hot. I kept waiting for the tombs to stop appearing, but there was an endless parade of them. Eventually, I started to compare their extravagant designs. Most were decorated with the typical foliage and scrolling. The most popular symbol, however, was something I hadn't expected.

"Harps?"

"Harps have always been revered in Celtic culture," Jack said beside me. "It was said the All-Father had a magical harp that could call forth the four seasons. Its melodies were the favored music of the gods in their celebrations. In the hands of a druid, the harp became an enchanted weapon. He could use it to induce sleep in his listeners or provoke great joy or sorrow. Centuries later, the harp was still a staple of Irish heritage. So much so that it started to represent resistance to the British Crown in the sixteenth century. Queen Elizabeth was so threatened she ordered all harps burned and all harpists executed in an attempt to gain control of Ireland."

"They wanted to strip us of our identity," Zoe added. "Under penalty of death, the Irish were forbidden to speak their own language, own their own land, or receive an education."

"But we held fast to our culture," Jack said, "and the harp came to represent the spirit of the country. Today, it's the national symbol of Ireland. It's even on the back of our coins and features prominently on our passports."

"Not to mention it's stamped on every pint of Guinness you'll ever have," Lucas chimed in with a grin.

"Are these catacombs protected by the glamour spell as well?" I asked. "Wouldn't people want to know about all this history, about the kings laid to rest here?"

"Unfortunately," Zoe said, "that's a risk we can't take. These are druidic kings after all. Their remains are as sacred to us as the bones of a saint might be in other places of worship. We regularly use them in higher forms of spellcraft, channeling the remaining embers of their magic. In fact, the magic contained in these tombs is part of what upholds the abbey's glamour. That said, if hunters knew we housed dead kings here, they wouldn't hesitate to find a way in to destroy every last bone."

My stomach soured at the mention of hunters, and we continued our trek through the catacombs in silence. The corridor seemed to go on forever, and the more we walked, the more claustrophobic I felt, as if the walls of the catacombs were closing in on me. The stale air was stifling, as if I were breathing in ghosts with every breath. After my experience being trapped in Alison's grave, communing with the dead wasn't high on my list of experiences I wanted to revisit. I paused for a moment, resting my hand against the jagged rocks to right my head.

"Are you all right?" Jack asked gently, cupping my elbow. In the swaying shadows of the Hall of Kings, Jack's face was a study in contrast. He looked as beautiful as ever, like a painting by one of art's Old Masters. The concern in his warm gaze made my skin flush. It felt a lot like sinking into a bowl of warm honey.

"Just a little spooked, I guess."

Jack nodded to his brothers to continue past him and then looked back to me. He still held my elbow, and his thumb softly moved back and forth over the thin fabric of my cardigan. In an effort to soothe me, I supposed, but it only worked my pulse into a frenzy. He was so close I could look at nothing else, my head tilting back slightly to take in his beautiful eyes.

"Do you need some fresh air?" he asked softly. "I'll walk back outside with you if you want."

My insides wobbled slightly. I glanced in the direction the others had gone. They were already turning a corner in these labyrinthine catacombs, but fortunately, Zoe's torches hadn't gone out in her absence.

When I looked back to Jack, the flicker of shadows on his face was so mesmerizing I couldn't respond at first. I was acutely aware of so many things at once. His fingers gently cradling my elbow and the way my skin woke up to his touch. The set of his lips; how they were perfect and thin like a longbow. His steady gaze studying me, holding me; how he knitted his brow with worry. I was surrounded by a host of dead kings, but even if they had risen from the grave, I wouldn't have noticed, and with Jack shielding me from them, I wouldn't have been afraid.

"Scarlet?"

I blinked, my face blushing furiously. I instantly looked away. My only consolation was the hope my red cheeks weren't too noticeable in the dimness of the catacombs. Shaking my head, I straightened. "I'm all right," I said. "We should catch up with the others."

The others were waiting at a second set of doors, these as tall and as old-looking as the ones at the abbey's entrance. *Finally*, I thought with relief, *the end of the catacombs.* Zoe placed her hand upon one door, using a whispered set of Irish words as a key. Hidden gears whined and shifted and clicked, and then a large, metal bolt on the other side slid free in a sound like a sword blade dragged across stone.

The doors swung open as a drop gate just beyond them slowly lifted to offer us an unobstructed view of the space beyond. Candles flared to life atop more chandeliers and sconces, instantly flooding the room with soft, dancing light. In the immediate vicinity, there were about half a dozen rustic tables with bench seating. Beyond them were endless rows of bookshelves, reaching so far back the light couldn't penetrate the furthest end of the room.

The books came in all shapes and sizes. There were manuscripts bound with leather cords, ancient tomes with covers made of animal hides, books small enough to fit into my back pocket, and others as tall as my upper half. To my left, there was an entire section dedicated to scrolls, which were stored in pigeon hole cabinets. Clustered together as they were, their centers looked like hundreds of eyes staring ominously into the distance. Glass table cases protected scraps of yellow parchment from the elements, and dusty volumes that had to be hundreds of pages long reclined in wooden book holders, opened at the center.

I breathed in the smell of old pages, letting it fill my lungs.

While I hadn't been overly fond of the walk through the Hall of Kings, I had to admit it'd been well worth it for the opportunity to be inside a secret library filled with magical books.

"So where's The Book of Fates?" I asked.

"And therein lies our problem," Zoe said. "Most of these books know how to behave themselves, but grimoires as powerful as The Book of Fates can be ornery little things. They're pure magic, and as such, they can do as they please. So it doesn't matter where they were last set. They almost always relocate themselves. And they never use the same hiding place twice. I think they do it just to make our lives more difficult. Here, let me show you."

She led us to one of the glass table cases, this one bearing medieval latches and locks. She gestured to the vacant space inside. At the bottom of a red, velvet cloth, a tag read, 'The Book of Fates.' I assumed this is where it was returned whenever a witch finished studying it.

"It just left?" I asked. I almost asked how, given the measures that had been taken to secure it, but then I remembered: magic. Right.

"Like I said, ornery little things. But at least we know it's somewhere in here. There aren't any records of it being loaned out since its last return."

In light of the enormity of the library, it wasn't exactly solace. There had to be thousands of books here. Possibly even tens of thousands. I hadn't thought our search would be so 'needle in a haystack.'

"Let's start looking through everything then," Jack said, undeterred.

Lucas swept a gaze over the library's vast inventory. "Everything?"

"At least we don't have to scour every druidic library across

Ireland. Besides, there are four of us. It'll cut down our search time considerably."

"Six of us," I amended. "Right?"

"Wrong," said Zoe. "Only a member of a clan can read that clan's spell books. To anyone else, the pages would appear to be something else entirely." She pulled a heavy hardback off a shelf and dropped it into my arms. "See for yourself."

My arms sank past my waistline under the book's weight. I hefted the tome onto a table and opened the cover, waving away flecks of dust. The pages were brittle, and I turned them delicately until I came to the title page. "An Exhaustive History of Eighteenth-Century European Thought?" I continued turning the pages. Sure enough, they were filled with nothing but unending blocks of text.

"That's what you see," Zoe said. "But if you were a son or daughter of the O'Manacháin clan, you'd see a spell on every page like I do. The glamour serves to protect the knowledge contained within the pages. That way, should a book turn up in someone's private library, or in a museum, used book store, Sotheby's auction, and so on and so forth, our secrets stay with us."

"But I thought The Book of Fates was given to all witches by Brigid?"

"As the story goes, Brigid appeared in a dream to seven Elders during the height of The Burning Times. They each transcribed her wisdom into what would later be known as the Sacred Grimoires, each for one of the remaining druidic clans. It was around this time that the Elders went on to form The Council, to give hope to our people. The Book of Fates happens to be the Sacred Grimoire that belongs to the Connellys' clan, hence why their mother directed them to it."

"But how do the books know whether or not you're a member of the right clan?"

"Through blood spells," Zoe said. "A witch can bind a grimoire with his or her blood, so that only witches who share their bloodline are able to see the spells. If you're not of that bloodline, the glamour automatically kicks in. Those of us who have to fulfill loan requests from other clans usually have nothing to go by except what a grimoire's cover looks like, as it's all we can see."

I handed the O'Manacháin book back to her. She took it and slid it back into the gap on the shelf. Her ouroboros ring glistened in the candlelight. The serpent's eyes were made from green gems, and I was reminded of all the red-eyed demons I'd encountered thus far—both in the real world and in Alison's mental prison. I rubbed my arms to keep the goosebumps at bay.

"Are all grimoires loaned out only by request? Can a witch not visit a library themselves to check out a book?"

"They're more than welcome to, but the perimeters of this and every library are spelled. No book can leave this place unless it's in the hands of a Guardian, which is what those of us who maintain these libraries are called. Usually, we simply hand-deliver any book that's requested, no matter how far away the witch lives."

"What happens if a non-Guardian tries to carry a book out?"

"They're struck dead on the spot," she answered, her shoulders bouncing up in a quick, carefree shrug.

My insides spun. "Good to know."

She twisted the ouroboros ring around her finger. "It may sound like a bit much, but it's for the common good. A witch who's trying to steal a grimoire without anyone knowing is typically up to no good. The irony, of course, is that not even these precautions are enough to stop the most determined of witches.

"Some decades ago, there was a traitor who could possess the bodies of other witches. She used the ability to mentally hijack Guardians and spirit away a number of grimoires in a single night. The boundary spell allowed it because it just senses a Guardian's flesh, not what's going on in the inside. Fortunately, she was caught before she could make use of the grimoires and sentenced to The Citadel, where she lived out the rest of her life in exile and without magic."

"Wow."

"I know what you're thinking. Not even a slap on the wrist first? But we witches live in a dangerous world. You've only been a part of it for a few days, but by Jack's account, it sounds like you've been through a lot already. I, for one, live by a strict code. Once someone's lost my trust, they can never win it back. It's the only way I know to survive."

For the next few hours, the Connellys went through book after book, spreading out to the four corners of the library. It was a tedious task. First, they had to leaf through the first few pages of every volume to determine if it was even a grimoire from their own clan. If it was, they then had to conduct a more thorough read-through to determine whether or not the grimoire was The Book of Fates in particular. Apparently it was too much to ask that every single spell book have a helpful title page, and Zoe couldn't remember if The Book of Fates was one such grimoire, much less what it looked like exactly.

"It's been years since I've come to this particular location," she said with a shrug.

Despite what Zoe had said, I tried my hand at opening a few books, willing them to reveal their secrets to me regardless of my bloodline. But sure enough, the pages I handled would hold tight to their glamour, protecting the spells hidden on their surface. I came across books about art history, books about the reigns of legendary kings, and books about traditional Irish cuisine, the description of Irish stew and soda bread making my stomach growl, but not a single word I read was about magic. Zoe knew of no libraries containing preserved grimoires or other texts from The Lost Clan, so by process of elimination, it seemed a telling indication that Jack had been right about my heritage. If I was a witch and couldn't read any of the remaining six clans' grimoires, I had to be descended from the mysterious seventh.

Feeling useless, I took to wandering around the library, running my fingers along the leather spines, occasionally swatting away a cobweb overhead. Save for the sound of turning pages, and the occasional muttered curse tumbling out of Connor's mouth, the library was as silent as a mausoleum.

Upon one wall of the library, there was a colorful mosaic. It was three times my height and stretched several dozen feet wide. It depicted a garden scene. At the center was a giant tree made entirely of elaborate, complicated Celtic knots, its branches stretching to the very edges of the mosaic. Its leaves were a vibrant green, and it bore bright, shiny fruit. All around the tree were animals of every species, a colorful assortment of flowers, and a flowing river. Where each animal's heart would've been, there was a triskele instead. The triple spiral also appeared in the currents of the river and on every last flower bud.

"Beautiful, isn't it?" Zoe stepped up beside me.

"Is it supposed to be The Garden of Eden?" I asked.

"It's our own origin story. That's the Tree of Life. The legend is that the first of our people sprung from its seeds. Our most important rituals are held before it."

"You mean it actually exists?"

"Of course. It's located Elsewhere." She crossed her arms, leaning a shoulder against the mosaic. There was a sharp glint in her eyes that made my heart skip a beat. I hadn't been sure how Zoe would receive me when we first met, if she'd be as distrusting as Seamus and Connor had initially been. Or as Connor still was honestly. It looked like I was about to find out.

"Listen," she said. "I want to be real clear about something. I've known the Connellys for years. I care a lot about them. Whatever happens with this Reaper, they're still going to be pariahs when it's all said and done, so you need to make a decision about where you stand now."

"Where I stand?"

"Meaning, are you just using Jack and his brothers because you have something at stake here? Or are you going to stay by their side even after you save your father?"

I opened my mouth, but I was too taken aback to produce any words.

"I know," Zoe said. "Blunt. But sometimes you have to be. Because I don't put my neck on the line for people who aren't fully committed. If you intend on leaving the Connellys high and dry once you've gotten what you want, then I'd appreciate it if you let me know up front, girl to girl. No hard feelings. I'd understand. I wouldn't respect the decision, of course, but I'd understand."

"It sounds like you've been through something like this before."

"Oh, I have. Want to know what's the fastest way to clear a room in witching society? Show up with a Connelly at your side. Want to see a witch break out in hives? Drop the name Jack Connelly into polite conversation. My family would be raging if they knew I was even here."

"I don't understand," I said. "Why?"

"The majority of the clans fear Jack. No single witch has ever had as much power as him, and with all the tragedies and misfortunes his family's faced in recent years—Redmond,

Alison, Neala, Bree—some say it's only a matter of time before he lands on the darker side of magic."

My heart missed a beat. "They think he'll start practicing dark magic?"

"Scarlet," she said, her face growing serious. "Some people believe he already does."

29

The streets of Dublin were packed tight with hordes of people, making any sort of forward-motion quite the feat. I'd learned the city was the stomping ground for one festival after another throughout the year. Tonight, music was everywhere. The foot-tapping, spirit-lifting kind that made it nearly impossible to stand still.

To my right, a ring of people had formed around a group of musicians playing on the fiddle, flute, and drums. Pre-teen girls in ringleted wigs and bright, boldly-patterned dresses commanded the attention of their onlookers, performing traditional Irish step dance on wooden boards in a percussive battle that made my pulse spike. Their legs moved so quickly their perfectly synchronized kicks were a blur. As the music raced to a crescendo, the girls picked up even more speed, jumping in circles and fast-changing formations that had their audience roaring with delight in a thunderous applause.

Jack and I continued forward, squeezing through slivers of space between the crowds. As we progressed through the city, the gaiety of the people never once dimmed. In pubs, friends toasted to each other, knocking their pints of Guinness together in a resounding clink. The mouthwatering smell of each establishment's food wafted out into the streets, filling the air with the sweetness of scones and the peppery spiciness of sausages. Live music played from both indoor and outdoor venues, rivaling with street performers who showed off everything from breakdancing and bagpipes to magic tricks and unicycling.

It was almost enough to make me forget why we'd ventured into the city to begin with, but when we finally broke away from the masses and regrouped at a lamppost, the reality of our situation was inescapable. We'd been in Dublin for days, and while we'd continued our search for The Book of Fates, we had little to show for it. At this point, Jack was willing to take creative measures, so we'd visited a small apothecary on the edge of the city, just the two of us, so that he could pick up ingredients for a locator spell. Zoe had already advised such a spell wouldn't work for a grimoire as powerful as The Book of Fates, but the general consensus was there was no harm in at least giving it a try.

As I thought about it, a red pennant flag caught my attention. It flapped against the lamppost in a gust of wind. 'Bram Stoker Festival,' its white lettering read. Jack followed my line of sight.

"He was born here in Dublin," he said. "And he went to Trinity College. The city holds a multi-day festival in his honor every year at the end of October, complete with ghost tours, costume parties, and a parade overrun with vampires, zombies, and goblins."

We continued walking. The crowds eventually thinned out, the streets becoming quieter until there were only pockets of people here and there, the lively music from earlier a distant melody I could barely hear. At one point, Jack pulled his phone from his pocket, checking the screen.

"Is Seamus still coming today?" I asked.

"I texted him earlier to check, but he hasn't replied yet. He might still be busy with The Council, especially if they've decided on a course of action. As one of their former students, it would make sense for them to insist he stay close. The clans respect Seamus, so if The Council plans on rallying the others, Seamus would be the perfect spokesman."

"You seem worried, though."

He glanced at me, his smile tired. He led us away from the clamor of the city onto the green lawns of a secret garden hidden in the very center of Dublin. 'Iveagh Gardens,' a plaque announced.

"Is it that obvious?" He pocketed his hands, letting go of a long sigh. "I'd just rather have Seamus here in Dublin with us. As the eldest of my brothers, I'm used to leading the way all the time, to having the answers to the hard questions. But in this, I feel more lost than ever. I don't know what our next course of action would possibly be if we don't find The Book of Fates. At least if Seamus were here, he could provide some sort of guidance."

"It sounds like you're very close to him."

"I am," Jack said as we passed a beautiful water cascade and continued on down a tree-lined promenade, gravel and dry leaves crunching under our footfalls. "We were always close to him as children. He was the uncle who indulged us with the birthday toys we'd asked for all year long, who took time out to coach the youth rugby team Connor and I were a part of when we were younger, who whisked us away from home when things were strained between our parents and mentored us in our magic for hours. Nevermind the way he stepped up once our mother was admitted to Serenity Falls. Raising four boys all under the age of thirteen certainly hadn't been a part of his life plan, but he never once complained. For the past six years, he's been like a father to us. I don't know how any of us could ever repay him."

In the moonlight, the trees cast long, skeletal shadows onto the lawn. Our own shadows moved across the portrait of pitch-black branches in a slow progression, like passing ships. There wasn't a soul in sight, transforming the gardens into an intimate, peaceful sanctuary.

"That's the beauty of family," I said. "When people make sacrifices like that, it's not with the expectation of being paid back one day. They just do it out of love. Everything your uncle's ever done for you and everything he does now is because he loves you and your brothers. I understood that the moment I first met him back in Crowmarsh, when he wanted nothing more than to protect you."

We eventually found our way to a fountain. At its center was a stone angel standing atop a cluster of large rocks, holding a plate atop its head. From the plate, water sprung, falling in a gentle shower all around the angel.

"What about your family?" Jack asked softly. "Was it only you and your mother in Colorado?"

At the mention of my mom, my heart quaked. I wondered if there would ever be a day when the memory of her wouldn't hurt so much. "She was an only child, but her parents lived in Colorado same as us. Less than two hours away, in fact. Unfortunately, they were extremely conservative, so when my mom returned from Ireland pregnant and unmarried, they were scandalized. So much so that they refused to continue paying for her tuition and kicked her out of the house.

"She had no choice but to drop out of college and work full-time to support the both of us. But she did what she had to do, sometimes working as many as three jobs at a time to keep a roof over our heads and food in our stomachs. Up until I was five years old, she went by her parents' house a few times a year in an effort to reconcile with them. She wanted them to know their granddaughter. But I guess they had no interest in that. They never answered the door, as if we were complete strangers to them."

Jack angled his body toward me. "Scarlet, I'm so sorry."

I shrugged, playing with a loose thread of my cardigan. "In the end, the joke's on them. I guess they wanted to punish my mom for making such a big 'mistake,' but she rose above it all. Once I started school, she returned to college. She went on to graduate from law school and became an attorney for nonprofits. There wasn't a lot of money in it, but she loved advocating on behalf of disadvantaged people who had the odds stacked against them and helping them to overcome their obstacles. It was her way of giving back. She believed that was the ultimate religion, to just love people. To defend those who couldn't defend themselves and help the less fortunate.

"Of course, in a rare show of compassion, my grandparents ended up coming to my mom's funeral, but I could tell they were relieved to learn I'd be going to live with my dad, thus relieving them of any responsibilities toward me. Not that I would've wanted anything to do with them anyway. My mom had spent so many years trying to reconcile with them when she was alive, but it was only when she was gone that they..." My throat unexpectedly pinched, a wave of emotion coming over me.

"Hey," Jack said, gently taking my arm and slowly turning me more fully toward him. I hadn't realized how close we were standing, the small sliver of space between us sweltering as our eyes met across the short distance. The thump of my heart was like the increasing beat of a bass drum. The place where his fingers closed around the sleeve of my cardigan burned like a brand. I thought I might drown in that spellbinding gaze of his. I simply couldn't look away. And as I looked at my miniature self reflected back to me in each iris, I realized Jack's despair matched my own, and yet even in the midst of what he'd lost, he cared about my loss as well. Truly, genuinely cared.

Before I knew what I was doing, I took the small step that bridged the gap separating us and slipped my arms around his neck, burying my face into the warm place where his shoulder met his neck. His strong arms instantly closed around me, holding me in place in a protective way that made a heat wave rush through me from head to toe. The hard planes of his body made me think of the marble statues Michelangelo had once carved, and I leaned against him further, as if doing so would take all my worries away.

I didn't cry as the wave of grief ran its course. I closed my eyes before the tears could slip down my face, but my heart was sore, bruised. God, how I missed her. It was in unpredictable moments like this when the loss felt so deep, in conversations when I had to speak of her in the past tense, when I reflected on the lives she'd changed in her work and how that work had been so cruelly cut short, when I thought of all the things she'd never gotten to do, all the places she'd never gotten to see.

I breathed in Jack's foresty scent, letting it clear my mind and soothe the heartache. It felt nice to be held, to be comforted, to *connect* with someone. After my loss, I'd distanced myself from almost everyone in my life save for Natalie and her family, putting walls around my heart to guard against the pain. And hadn't I done the same thing upon arriving in Ireland, insisting I wouldn't get attached to anyone, that I'd leave at the first opportunity? I'd thought I was doing myself a favor, but standing here with Jack, who so tenderly stroked my back, who knew my pain all too well and wasn't afraid to brave it with me, was more a balm to my soul than anything else had ever been.

I finally opened my eyes—and then my breath caught in my throat.

Pulling back from Jack, I stared in shock at the vibrant

scenery surrounding us. I knew these maples well, recognized the large growths of spike moss draped over their ancient branches. I'd seen these fallen trees before, knew the fog that crept toward us like an aimless spirit.

"This is the Hall of Mosses Trail," I whispered. I'd hiked it when visiting the Hoh Rain Forest in Olympic National Park. "But how...?" I turned to Jack, realization dawning on me. "You're doing this. It's the same thing you did when you brought your mom to the aviary. Are we really here?"

"No, it's only an illusion unfortunately."

I strayed to a Sitka spruce, pressed my hand against its thin, scaly bark. "But it feels so real."

"It's fashioned from your own memories," Jack said. "As we were standing here, you inadvertently pushed a memory to me. Several actually. I thought this one might bring you comfort. It seemed to be one of the more cherished ones."

I didn't know how I'd telegraphed a memory to him, but I was glad for it all the same. "My mom and I hiked this trail for my sixteenth birthday," I said. I swallowed thickly but smiled, savoring the atmosphere, illusion or not.

I looked back to him, touched. These past days, I hadn't been able to get Zoe's words out of my mind, the ones about Jack practicing dark magic. I didn't believe what the other clans did, of course. Jack himself had told me his brothers believed his growing power was merely the result of the nearing Old Moon. How anyone could believe Jack would willingly give himself over to the darkness was beyond me. He was gentle, kind. The depth of the love he possessed for his family wasn't something you came by often, nor was the way he cared for his friends. *Myself included*, I thought, the realization sending a warm flutter through me. It upset me that anyone could see Jack as anything but good.

"This is incredible. You have no idea how much it means to

me." I craned my neck back, admiring the height of the Sitka spruce, which sprouted hundreds of feet into the air. From somewhere far off, an owl hooted into the dark. "I can't even begin to imagine what other miracles you're able to work."

He smiled gently. After a moment, he closed the distance between us and extended his hand to me. "Would you like to find out?"

30

The moment I took his hand, there was a rush of wind all around us. The ground underneath our feet transformed from the soft earth of the Hoh Rain Forest to the hard, unrelenting cement of...the top of a building! I stumbled back in shock, but Jack gripped my arms, holding me steady.

I stared in wonder at the gorgeous city skyline before me. From here, I could see the numerous bridges that crossed over Dublin's River Liffey, the inky water aglow with orbs of yellow as it reflected lampposts and building lights on its shimmering surface. Double-decker tour buses and taxis zipped up and down the avenues flanking the river, the symphony of honking mingling with the general din of pedestrians, restaurant patrons, and the stirring live music that made my heart dance.

This was the city where my parents had met, where they'd fallen in love. If I looked hard enough, I could almost make out the gothic towers of Trinity College in the distance. 'Trinners.' My mom had said that's what the students and locals called it. What pubs had she and my dad haunted when they were first courting? What cobblestone streets had they walked hand-in-hand, and which shops had they slipped into, giggling like couples do, their eyes only for each other? It occurred to me, standing there on top of that building, that I was under the same stars that had watched my parents' love story unfold over seventeen years ago. I gazed up at them now, feeling connected to the past like never before.

When I returned my attention to Jack, there must've been something in my eyes that said, 'show me more,' because he smiled again and looked heavenward. Almost immediately, there was the first pitter-patter of raindrops, and then all at once, a torrential downpour assaulted the city. Below, umbrellas popped open one by one like swiftly blooming flowers while those unprepared for the rain raced inside stores or took shelter under awnings.

Within seconds, I was soaking wet, but I didn't care, could barely sense the cold. Jack's magic energized me, and I laughed, tilting my head back and raising my arms to embrace the rain. "This is amazing," I called out to him over the roar of the storm.

He raised his hand in a gesture like 'stop,' and suddenly the air was filled with thousands upon thousands of glimmering crystals frozen in midair. No, not crystals, I realized with astonishment. The raindrops! They were suspended mid-descent, hanging all around us like glass ornaments. I touched one, and it gently floated away, wobbling but maintaining its form.

And that's when I noticed how silent the city had become. I dared another look below and my heart shot up my throat. *Everything* was frozen. The traffic had come to a complete standstill, a throng of pedestrians paused halfway down a crosswalk. On the outdoor terraces of restaurants, diners sat with spoonfuls of food halfway to their mouths, and a street performer two blocks down was motionless in the middle of spinning atop his head. The resulting silence was eerie, as if we existed inside a vacuum, the only two people in the world.

"Does the magic only exclude who you choose?" I asked.

"I've never been able to keep more than one other person in the present with me, and I can only sustain magic of this magnitude for seconds at best. It's also usually a few days before I can summon it again."

"Is that normal?"

"With newly emerged Masteries, yes. It takes time to command the magic expertly. Sometimes years."

With a flick of his fingers, the world below us was unfrozen, and people resumed their activities without the slightest clue that something had momentarily interrupted their evening. The rain continued falling as well, but Jack eventually had it ease, perhaps not wishing to ruin anyone's night.

"Shall we?" He offered his hand again, and I took it. As before, blasts of wind blew up against us from all sides, and then we were back in Iveagh Gardens. I would've expected to be nauseous, but it was a lot like stepping out of one room and into another.

So among his many abilities, Jack was a Wayfarer just as Lucas was. He could create incredible illusions, he could stop time... And I knew that was only scratching the surface. There was a wealth of power inside of him. There had to be for entire clans to fear him.

In the shadows of the gardens, I shivered, but it wasn't out of fear. I was still dripping wet from Jack's impromptu rainstorm. I twisted my hair over my shoulder and strained water out of the locks. There wasn't much I could do about my clothes, though.

"Here," Jack said, stepping closer to me as he bracketed his hands onto my arms. What happened next was a lot like a sun rising inside me. Heat developed deep in my core and then surged through every muscle, bone, and ligament. It was as if I'd been sitting in front of a fireplace for hours, and when Jack finally pulled his hands away, I was surprised to find my clothes and hair were completely dry.

"With all the rainstorms we've been through, you're only now pulling out that party trick?" I teased, flashing him a smile. After what he'd just shown me, the night felt enchanted, and I was more than a little enraptured. Jack had told me about kickbacks, but I wondered if there was such a thing as being high off magic as well.

An easy smile touched his lips, and he pocketed his hands. "Something tells me you would've run away screaming had I done that back when we'd found you on the side of the road."

"Probably true."

"Only after you'd assaulted me with that rock, of course." There was a playful glint in his eyes that left me momentarily breathless. I had only ever seen Jack as the serious eldest brother among the Connellys. Witnessing another side of him, a lighter, relaxed side, only added to the magic of the night.

I nudged him with my shoulder as I strayed to the fountain. "I really need to learn some magic of my own," I said.

"I still intend on helping you with that. You said what happened at the rugby game was the first time you'd done anything like that, right? Have you exuded any magic since, even if only on a small scale?"

I shook my head. "No, that was the only—actually, wait. I'm not sure if it counts, but when I was in your mom's mind, I was able to conjure magic against the Wraiths. It was a lot like what I'd done before." I briefly described the scenario, mentioning the blast of white light and the heat that had emanated from my palm as well.

Jack listened, nodding along, his brow furrowed. "It could very well be your Mastery finally emerging, though I don't know what such a Mastery would be called. As I mentioned before, I've never known a witch who could banish demons with the mere flick of a hand. Those of us with stronger magic can cause them to briefly dematerialize, but even then, the magic's only effective against lower, weaker demons. Creatures like the Wraiths and others would typically be immune."

I looked back to the fountain. There was a quickening in my chest, a budding excitement. "If it is my Mastery, and it's beginning to surface, does that mean I'll be able to call upon the four Quarters now?"

Jack's eyes went distant for a few heartbeats, the way they did when he was mulling over something in his mind. "Typically, that comes long before the Mastery. It's strange that those abilities haven't emerged yet. But let's try something." He knelt before the fountain. He gestured for me to do the same, so I lowered myself one knee at a time, the gravel digging sharply into the knees of my jeans.

"Dip your hand into the water." He waited for me to do so before proceeding. "Now concentrate on feeling the water. Really feeling it."

My hand had made contact with water every day for the past seventeen years, so it wasn't exactly a novelty. Nonetheless, I closed my eyes and tried to experience the water in a new way. I focused on the coolness of the liquid, the way it sleeved my hand up to my wrist like a delicate glove. I wriggled my fingers, noting the rhythm of the water, the way it gave way to my movements.

"Now what?" I asked.

"Water is one of the four Quarters. As a witch, it's a power you have the privilege of calling upon. That doesn't mean you're the master over it, though. Druids venerated nature and lived in balance with it. When you summon the Quarters, you do so with respect, acknowledging the divinity in them just as they acknowledge the divinity in you. A good way to maintain that humility is to thank the Quarter you mean to summon *before* you begin working with it."

I remembered what Lucas had told me about young witches

spending time in nature to begin that holy communion that would eventually rouse their magic. With his words in mind, I'd tried to connect with one of The Wise Ones without much success. Maybe this time would be different. *Thank you*, I mentally said to the water in a reverent hush. *Thank you for all you do, for all you provide.* To ensure I wasn't merely paying the water lip service, I purposed to feel the words in my heart, allowing them to glow in my chest like stars.

"Now imagine yourself reaching out to the water with threads of magic. Then picture a single drop separating from the rest. See it break the surface and rise into the air."

A single drop didn't seem so difficult. I knitted my brow and pictured the fountain clearly in my mind, recreating every detail from the textured feathers of the angel's wings to the number of rocks it stood upon. I honed in on the pool of water itself, initially seeing it as one unified body. A perfect, peaceful unit. I magnified my focus, thinking about all the miniscule drops that made up the pool, and then I selected just one, capturing it in my field of vision and then reaching out to it with those threads of magic. I saw them as wisps of gentle mist as they gathered around the drop, holding onto it. The drop tried to slip from my grip, but I kept grabbing for it, furrowing my brow harder. It was a fine line juggling respect for the water at the same time that I firmly directed it to do this one thing for me. I willed the drop to detach from the others, practically wrenching it free, and then I pictured it ascending up, up, up—

"Scarlet, stop."

A trickle of warmth slipped from my nose, and a moment later, a coppery taste reached my lips. I rushed to wipe the blood away with the back of my hand, my cheeks flushing. "What happened?" I asked, unable to keep the panic out of my voice. I gripped the ledge of the fountain's wall, a slight wave of dizziness hitting me.

"You overexerted yourself. Don't worry. It's normal when you're first coming into your magic. Let yourself rest for a few moments."

"Overexerted myself? I barely did anything."

"You were focusing for over fifteen minutes."

"Over fifteen minutes?" How was that even possible? It'd felt more like fifteen seconds. I sat back on my heels and sank against the fountain wall slightly until the lightheadedness passed. "I didn't think it'd be that hard."

"Magic is a living thing," Jack said. "Think of it as taming a wild animal. It takes time to coax it into emerging. It takes time to win its trust. Even then, you still have to train it, grow with it. It's a process."

The dizzy spell at last subsided. "I want to try again."

"Of course. But this time, let's do something differently. You'll focus on the same task, separating a single drop of water from the rest, but I want you to hold my hand as you try."

As his fingers slipped into the spaces between mine, my stomach somersaulted. It was such a little thing, I knew, but I relished the warmth of his skin, that slight buzz of electricity that radiated off its surface.

He nodded at me, encouraging me to proceed just as a strange sensation began filling my hand, as if I were leeching warmth from him. He was giving me some sort of magical jump-start, I realized. My heart picked up speed. The sensation coursed through me, racing up my arm and igniting points all over my body that soon went off like fireworks one by one. It was energizing, electrifying. A weightlessness came over me, as if I were filled with helium and could float into the air at any minute. I could've burst from the happiness that built up in my chest.

"Remember," came Jack's voice. "When we call upon the four Quarters, we do so with respect. Earth, air, fire, water—

they're all living things. Magic is alive in them the same way that it's alive in you. So you have to almost merge with the Quarter you're summoning. You have to get so lost in it that its magic and your magic come together as one."

With renewed vigor, I concentrated on the water encasing my free hand. I moved my fingers through it as before, in a motion like plucking the strings of a harp. The water was satiny against my skin, so tranquil and at peace. *There's magic in this water*, I thought. And with Jack's help, there was now magic crackling inside me. I pushed out those threads of magic once again, embracing the water. If I needed to become one with it, I could do that. I drew close to it at the same time I drew it closer to me.

Thank you, I said. *For your power, for your magic.* Gently, I mentally eased myself into the water. I let myself dissolve into its essence until I couldn't even feel my body anymore. Instead, I was every drop that made up the fountain's pool, and I floated in the basin, buoyant and free. There was only the water now, flooding through every party of me until I was filled with it, until I couldn't tell where one of us ended and the other began. We were one and the same now. Equals. It was one of the most amazing things I'd ever felt.

Finally, I held a single drop in my mind and beckoned it away from the others. *Will you come away with me?* I felt the drop's initial resistance to my request, felt it pulling back to join its brothers and sisters, but I mentally cupped my hands around it, gently, kindly, and whispered to it. *I won't hurt you. You'll return to the others. But will you help me in this one thing first?*

The drop hesitated, testing the truth behind my words. I could feel Jack's magic glowing around me like an aura, and I pushed some of that magic to the drop to ease it. Its resistance receded. It became compliant, slowly spinning before me, ready to do as I asked. *Thank you.* I guided it through the pool, past the fountain's surface, and watched it in my mind's eye as it rose into the air like a perfect, transparent marble. It gleamed in the moonlight.

"Scarlet."

I opened my eyes, ready to see what I'd accomplished. My jaw fell open.

I hadn't called forth one drop as planned. I'd called forth the entire pool.

I bolted to my feet. The water rose up in glorious, arching waves like flames of blue, tall enough to dwarf the angel at the fountain's center, held in place only by magic. My concentration broke, and the water immediately came crashing back down into the basin with a loud splash, sloshing over the sides to wet our feet. The surface trembled as the water sought to calm itself.

I faced Jack, exhilaration bursting in my chest. The last embers of his magic were still smoldering inside me, falling all around my bones like volcanic ash. "How…?"

He smiled. "I channeled my magic into you. Sometimes, when young witches haven't yet come into their powers, a mentor will do it to help wake up those first sparks of magic. It won't be enough for you to summon the four Quarters on your own just yet, not without channeling power from another witch or a charmed object, but I felt your magic, Scarlet. It's there. I've roused it from its sleep. It just needs a little bit more nurturing since it's been dormant for so long. But with regular practice, it'll eventually come. It helps that you already had an appreciation for nature in your heart."

I hardly knew what to say. I was still a little bit in raptures as Jack's magic continued to swirl around in my body, my stomach flipping as if I rode a rollercoaster. For a few moments, all I could do was stare at him, my face flushed, my skin warming with gratitude and wonder.

"If I'd never met you," I said, "my magic would've stayed

dormant for the rest of my life." I shook my head, the reality almost incomprehensible. It wasn't just that Jack had stirred my magic from its deep slumber. He'd changed my whole world, introducing me to a reality I would've never imagined existed. "I don't know how I could ever thank you enough."

"Scarlet," he said in response, my name almost a whisper. He tucked a stray lock of hair behind my ear, his fingers moving ever so delicately, as if not to startle me, as if to ensure the gesture was okay. He met my eyes. "You don't have to thank me for anything."

"Well, well, well. Isn't that sweet?"

Jack and I spun toward the gravelly male voice and were greeted by the sight of a dozen onlookers spaced out around the area, all wearing sinister, black trench coats. My heart slammed against my chest when I noticed they were each holding a metal police truncheon by a hand gloved in black. One terrible word instantly shot to mind.

Hunters.

Jack's face became hard, a dangerous gleam in his eyes. He moved me behind him. "She has nothing to do with this."

"Is that right?" The man was barrel-chested, his bald head overrun with tribal tattoos. "Because we just witnessed the girl accomplish quite the magic trick." He threw out an arm toward the ground, and his truncheon elongated with a snap. A spark of electricity sizzled at its end.

"You have no idea who you're dealing with," Jack said, his voice firm, threatening. It was a tone I hadn't yet heard from him.

"Oh, but we do. We know all about you, Jack Connelly. They say you're the most powerful witch alive." His smile was cruel, his dark eyes wells of poison. "I think it's about time we do something about that, don't you?"

Thunder rumbled above us. Lightning struck out like the

forked tongue of a snake, answering Jack's summons as it speared the earth just yards from the hunter's feet. A warning.

The man was undeterred, taking another step forward with a menacing glint in his gaze.

Jack quickly twisted toward me and made to grab for my hand so that he could wayfare us to safety, but the man was quicker, his truncheon already extended our way. Electricity rushed out of the weapon in a river of brilliant white and came right for us.

31

I woke up in a cell.

My head was pounding, and it whirled like a spinning top as I tried to sit up. Nausea hit me quick, and I twisted to the side to empty my stomach onto the rock-hewn ground. Every muscle in my body was sore, as if I'd just run a marathon. It hurt to do so much as blink.

Cold dread flew through me then as I remembered why I was here. I'd blacked out from the hunter's electric shock, but not before that angry current had pummeled me in a way that had felt like my insides were on fire. Heart racing, I took note of my immediate surroundings, guided only by the flickering light from the wall sconces just outside my cell.

Jack was nowhere in sight. My stomach flopped. Where was he? Was he okay? Was he still...*alive*? Bile rose in my throat as I thought about what the hunters might be capable of. These were the very people who'd killed Bree, an innocent three-year-old girl, who'd killed many of the witches laid to rest in Crowmarsh's cemetery. I needed to get out of here. I needed to find Jack before it was too late.

The bars of my cell were thick and made of iron. I curled my hands around them to test their strength—only to immediately yank my hands back with a yelp. The bars were scorching hot, and my palms pulsated with fiery pain from the contact.

The steady click of heels filled the silence, and I quickly drew back to a corner. A parade of yellow flames marched through the darkness. I could just make out the figures of the torch bearers and the outlines of their trench coats. There were half a dozen of them. They each set their torch in wall-mounted holders surrounding an expansive, circular space just beyond my cell. Under the glow of one torch, a man lifted a giant light switch that looked like something out of *Frankenstein*, the gears whining in protest, and overhead bulbs flickered once, twice, and then came to life in a loud buzz, flooding the area below with light.

My pulse stopped.

My heart, my breathing, my ability to think—all of it. Everything stopped.

Jack.

He was strapped to an upright, cruciform structure made of wood, ribbons of dry blood trailing from his nose, mouth, and ears. He was pale, the black shadows under his eyes emphasized against his pallid, sweat-drenched face. His hair was wet with perspiration as well, plastered against his forehead.

"Wake him," a woman said, her tone bored. She wore knee-high boots with heels long enough to be lethal, and her white blonde hair fell in a shiny sheet down to her waist.

The bald man from Iveagh Gardens held something under Jack's nose. Jack jerked against the board and then blinked several times, as if pushing through the fog in his brain. When his eyes cleared and landed on the woman before him, his body went rigid.

Her smile was cold, wicked. "Hello, Jack. It's nice to see you again." She clasped her hands behind her and approached him. *Click, click, click.* Her heels were like the talons of a menacing predator nearing its victim. "My colleagues tell me you aren't being very cooperative with us. They thought you might benefit from a personal visit from me. I was happy to oblige. We do, after all, have history."

The long, slender fingers of her ungloved hand ghosted over an assortment of instruments laid out on a table. I caught the gleam of silver off a blade and had to press a hand over my mouth to keep from getting sick again.

"I know what you're thinking, of course. You're thinking it makes no difference who stands opposite you. Even now, you intend on clinging to some lofty ideal of heroism. But let me share a secret with you, darling." She drew to his side and ran a fingertip down the length of his jawline. "Your disobliging behavior won't make you a hero. Only a fool. A fool who will suffer unnecessarily if he continues to test us."

She walked a few paces away from him. *Click, click, click.* She turned back to him in one swift motion and held out her arms, gesturing to the other hunters. "But we are civil people, Jack. Which is why I'm offering you this promise. Tell me where your brothers are, tell me now, and you have my word the four of you will meet a quick end. Deny me this information, and when we catch your brothers—and believe me this, we *will* catch them— their final hours will be absolutely horrific. What my colleagues have done to you will be nothing compared to what they'll do to your brothers. And you will be responsible for it all."

Jack struggled against his restraints—worn, leather straps across his chest, arms, and legs, and iron manacles at his wrists and ankles.

"You know better than that," the woman said. "Every piece of iron in this room is spelled to suppress your magic. Ironic, I know. To fight magic with magic. But it was the parting gift of a repentant witch centuries ago. She saw the errors of her sinister ways and cast the spell in exchange for mercy. You'd do well to learn from her example. So come now. Open your eyes to the light, dear boy. Your end has come. Make penance before it's too late. Where are your brothers?"

Jack stared back at her, jaw set and eyes defiant.

The woman let go of a sigh. "Such a shame." She nodded to one of the others and a man no less than seven feet tall stomped forward, holding the same truncheon the hunters had wielded at Iveagh Gardens. *No!* The truncheon's spark of electricity cackled and glowed so bright I had to momentarily shield my eyes.

For the next few seconds, seconds that stretched for an eternity, Jack's yells filled the space, echoing off the walls, filling my ears until I was drowning in his pain as if it were my own. I forced myself not to look away, if only because I thought the anger and terror and sickness overcoming me might finally call forth my magic. But no magic came. The spelled bars of my cell rendered me completely useless. There was nothing I could do for Jack but watch in absolute horror until the hunter finally stepped back and lowered his weapon.

Jack sagged against his restraints, fresh blood running from his nose, his complexion so pale it was practically alabaster. My heart was stuck in my throat. I could barely breathe around it.

"I can't imagine that was in any way a delight," the woman said, examining her nails. She clasped her hands behind her back again and sighed. "And I'd really rather not result to such tactics, but you're forcing our hand. Can't you see that? We're here to help you, not hurt you."

Click, click, click. She was inches away from him now. She tutted at his condition. "You know what we're capable of. Don't make this any harder than it needs to be. Spare yourself and your brothers. Tell me, darling. Where are they?"

The muscles in Jack's jaw moved. He seemed to be working against the daze inflicted by the electrical currents. He moistened his lips and then parted them as if to speak.

The woman's eyes glowed hungrily. She drew closer. "Yes, that's it. Go on. Tell me."

Jack forced three words through his clenched teeth. "Go...to hell."

The woman's eyes narrowed into poisonous slits, a vein twitching in her neck. "Fool," she hissed before turning on her heels and storming toward my cell. *Click, click, click.* "I wonder. Would this petty insolence of yours persist if *her* fate hung in the balance?"

There was the briefest flash of alarm in Jack's eyes when he saw me. "This doesn't concern her."

"Such a pretty girl," the woman said, ignoring Jack as she studied me. "Weak, though. She wouldn't last very long opposite the Chamber Master. I can already picture the colorful afflictions he'd subject her to." She turned back to Jack. "This is your final opportunity. I won't extend my mercy again. Loud and clear, tell me where your brothers are."

Jack's eyes switched to me, a conflict warring in them. He was clearly tortured, and in the end, only apologetic, guilt-ridden. I gave my head a quick shake. There was nothing to be sorry for. I would never ask him to betray his own blood for me. I knew he could never bring himself to commit such an act. And besides, I didn't trust the woman to keep her word anyway. Mercy? The word was surely foreign to her.

"So be it," the woman said at Jack's silence, turning on her heels. She nodded to the others. "You know what to do with him. When he regains consciousness, deliver him and the girl to the Chamber. It's time they meet their end." She stormed out of the room, disappearing from sight. *Click, click, click.*

The hunter with the truncheon stepped forward again.

"No!" I cried out at the same time Jack's yells returned. "Stop it! Please!" But my voice was overpowered by Jack's, and the hunter paid me no mind.

"Jack, you have to wake up."

I stroked his damp hair, combing it away from his face. I tried to ignore the pinch in my throat, but Jack wasn't stirring. By looks alone, anyone would've guessed him dead, but the faintest of pulses rapped against his skin, slow and faltering. Dried blood stained the corners of his mouth. He'd most likely bitten the inside of his cheeks when enduring the onslaught of electricity at the hunter's hands. They hadn't bothered to give him a mouth guard. Not that that surprised me. We were their prisoners, not their guests.

"Jack," I said again, leaning close to his ear. "Please wake up."

When they'd finished with him, the hunters had undone Jack's restraints, not even bothering to keep his body from sagging to the floor like a puppet cut from its strings. They'd dragged him to the cell by the back of his shirt and had tossed him inside like an animal. Once I was sure they were gone, I'd rushed to him, turning him onto his back to try and revive him. That had been at least half an hour ago.

"Jack, please." My voice broke on the last word.

I took his cold hand, closed my eyes, and tried to picture a current of magic racing out of his body and into mine, something powerful enough to spirit us away from this place. But the iron bars of the cell wouldn't give. Magic didn't exist so long as they stood.

There was no way to call for help either. The hunters had apparently taken our phones away, though being that we were presumably underground, my guess was I wouldn't have caught a cell signal anyway. My frustration festered in the pit of my stomach and then bubbled up my throat as I cried out in anger. I was powerless. Totally and completely powerless. I hadn't been able to stop the hunters from torturing Jack, and I could do nothing now to free us from this prison and from whatever awaited us in the 'Chamber.'

"Jack." I gently shook him. He was so cold. They'd taken his black coat from him, and he had nothing but a thin shirt underneath to keep him warm. I used the damp parts of the fabric to clean away the blood from his face, but in the absence of the crimson marks, his face looked even sicklier. I shrugged out of my cardigan and set it over him like a blanket.

We were going to die here. The realization hit me in such a powerful blow I thought an invisible hunter had struck me with his truncheon. The others wouldn't know what became of us, and if they didn't continue the quest to stop the Reaper, there would be no one left to save my dad's soul or the souls of all those witches.

This was the end for us. And if what I'd already witnessed was any indication, it was going to be a brutal end. The staggering truth of it left me momentarily paralyzed. I almost gave in to the defeat. I almost curled up right there on the floor to await my doom.

But I couldn't give up. I refused to. I took Jack's hand again, kneading the muscles gently the same way he'd once done for Alison. *Please help me*, I urged his magic. *Please fight against the spelled iron and come through.*

I waited and waited and waited, but there was nothing on the other end of my call. Nothing but silence.

I sank back onto my heels, holding Jack's hand on my lap.

And then my eyes fell upon the demon's mark.

I froze.

Outside of wishing the mark away...nothing is off limits...

My heart started hammering against my chest.

Jack had only used one wish, meaning there were still two left. He'd made a promise to his father, but all things considered, surely Redmond Connelly would've insisted on using up another wish if it meant saving Jack's life. And perhaps if I was the one making the wish, it'd spare Jack from being exposed to the dark magic, thus keeping him off whatever path Alison had seen in her visions.

I rubbed my thumb over the mark, feeling the bumps of the raised skin. I didn't know the first thing about summoning a demon, whether or not there was an incantation I was supposed to utter or gold coins I was supposed to offer up like Jack had done with the fear gorta. I didn't even know if this would work, seeing as how the mark belonged to Jack, not me, so what business did I have using up a wish?

Still, I closed my hand over the demon's mark and let my eyelids fall shut. *Please come*, I whispered in my mind. And then I tried every other invocation I could think of.

Awaken.

Come forth.

Arise.

I summon you.

I evoke you.

I beg you.

Please.

I pictured some red-eyed, horned beast in a forsaken land of the Otherworld hearing my call. I imagined it materializing in this cell, ready to do the bidding of the mark's bearer, no obstacle, not even spelled, iron bars, too great for its powers.

Then I opened my eyes.

But I was only met with the same darkness as before, Jack and I the only occupants in the dank cell. It hadn't worked.

Despair flooded my chest, and I could've wept.

And then a low, smooth voice from behind me suddenly spoke.

"You have a lot of nerve summoning me..."

32

"You're not Jack."

I didn't process the demon's words at first. I was too busy wrapping my mind around the fact that he didn't look like a demon at all. That is, of course, if you excused the wisps of black smoke floating off his person as if he'd been singed.

His hair, dark as midnight, was disheveled under a lopsided crown. He wore a patterned, medieval tunic with a lace-up front and black trousers that disappeared into oversized boots. A gold chain of office was draped over his shoulders, outfitted with blue emeralds and pearls and rubies. All so very human. But the eyes gave him away. At first, I mistook them for brown, but then he shifted ever so slightly, and in the flickering firelight, I realized they were actually a deep garnet.

They were also currently glaring at me. At a loss for words, I moved out of the way so I no longer blocked his view of Jack.

The demon seemed to not understand what he was looking at initially. Then he muttered a foreign word I assumed was meant to be a curse. "As if this night couldn't have gone any more spectacularly." He strode over to Jack and nudged his body with the tip of a boot. As he passed me, I caught the distinct scent of burning leaves. "You can never seem to keep yourself out of trouble, can you?"

"Can you help him?" I asked. "Us, I mean. There are hunters—"

"Let me stop you right there, little witch. The mark only functions in a certain capacity, and once you're outside of its rules—"

"I get it. Jack's technically the only one who can summon you. But can't you make an exception in this case?"

"I could," the demon said, "but I won't. I've had about as much family drama as I can stomach for one evening. Now if you'll excuse me..." The ribbons of smoke reappeared, slowly wreathing around the edges of his form.

"Wait! If you had no intention of helping, then why did you come at all?"

He shrugged, adjusting the cuffs of his tunic. "Clearly a momentary lapse of judgment on my behalf. I felt the summons, and I foolishly answered."

"I don't get it," I said. "Jack's bound to you, isn't he? Wouldn't his welfare matter to you?" And then I realized my error. If Jack died now, the demon would get to collect his debt sooner than expected. Why would he ever want to intervene considering what he had to gain?

"Bound to *me*? On the contrary. He's bound to the Dark Lord. I'm merely an associate who handles the more mundane tasks of each bargain. Wish-granting and the like."

"And yet you're deliberately denying this wish. If Jack was conscious, he'd want you to save us. You know that. It's bad enough he has to surrender his life to this 'Dark Lord' in three months. The least you can do is abide by the terms of the bargain and fulfill one of his remaining wishes. It *is* the right thing to do."

That drew a quick laugh out of him. "I'm a demon. I don't

exactly live by a robust moral code." But the edge of his mouth twitched up in the slightest smirk, and the smoke receded just a bit. "Which lion's den have you fallen into exactly?"

"They're called The Black Hand."

"Yes, I assumed as much. But who is the leader? That will tell me a fair bit about whatever particular sect you're at odds with presently."

"I didn't catch her name. I can describe her, though, if that helps. She's tall and thin with waist-length, white blonde hair."

Something flashed in the demon's garnet eyes. He studied me, considering something. "Tell me, how badly do you wish to save your precious Jack? I may be willing to provide my assistance in an arrangement separate from his mark and its mandates, but it'll come at a price."

My pulse thundered in my veins. A demon's bargain, like the one Redmond had once made, the one that had eventually destroyed his family. "What exactly is the price? And before you say it'll cost me my firstborn, I'll go ahead and tell you that's off the table."

The smirk deepened, his garnet eyes glittering like jewels. "Not to worry. Firstborns aren't really my thing. I'll only ask a favor of you."

"What kind of favor?"

He shrugged. "That's yet to be determined. But whenever I come to you—be it tomorrow, next month, next year, or twenty years from now—you must oblige me. Should you deny me, it'll cost you."

"And are you going to tell me what that cost is?"

He waved a hand dismissively. "Oh, merely the eternal damnation of your soul. So on and so forth. You know, the usual fine print in matters such as these."

Because *that* was a fair exchange. A chill raced down my spine. I looked at Jack's unmoving figure, the paleness of his skin, but I already knew what my answer would be. This was our only hope. There was no other way to escape the hunters. "Just to be clear, I won't kill anyone for you. Nor will I marry a demon or spawn the anti-Christ."

"Bless Hollywood and their portrayal of my kind. Now then, are those your only stipulations?"

I wracked my mind for any obvious loopholes. "And by help us, I mean help us get out of here. *Alive.*"

"Of course," he said. "You have my word. Do we have an agreement then?"

A small part of my rational mind urged me to back out of the deal before I struck a bargain I'd later regret, but it was either this or whatever gruesome death the hunters had prepared for us. "We have an agreement. Now let's go."

"Not so fast." With a snap of his fingers, his appearance instantly changed in a plume of smoke. His crown disappeared and his ebony hair was slicked back in a perfect shine. His face, which had been slightly flushed, regained its complexion, and replacing the medieval clothes was a sophisticated black suit with shiny dress shoes. In his hand, a saw-toothed dagger appeared, its polished ivory handle made from an animal's jawbone. I recognized it at once.

"You're the same demon that attacked Jack at the rugby game."

He scoffed at that. "Please. My approaches are a bit more decorous than that. We all bear these weapons. As for the demon who paid you and Jack a visit, he was merely a fellow associate. A sycophant really, one trying to curry favor with the Dark Lord."

I didn't like the glint off the blade and took a step back, uncertain what his intentions were. The cell suddenly seemed three times smaller now that I was sharing it with a demon. "Did that associate possess an Xavier student then? I thought he had, but when I banished him, he completely disappeared."

"That was simply a form he fashioned for his purposes. We can possess humans, yes, but more often than not, we prefer a custom, hand-made fit."

"So is this one of your custom ensembles?"

"Oh, no. Some of us are just this handsome." He glided to me, the smoke dancing around his figure. I retreated until my back was pressed against the rock-hewn wall. When he was close enough for me to touch, I could smell the lingering wine off his thin lips.

"Enough stalling," he said. "You'll need to drink my blood."

I pushed past him and put several strides between us. "Excuse me? What on earth do I need to drink your blood for?"

"It'll strengthen you against the hunters."

I stared at him blankly.

He examined his nails, using the point of the knife to clean their undersides. "Come now, little witch. You didn't think I'd fight your battle for you, did you? That's not how this works."

"You gave me your word. You said you'd help us get out of here."

"Yes, but I never specified how, now did I?"

"What are you saying? You actually want me to face them? Look at what they did to Jack. He still hasn't gained consciousness."

"He's perfectly fine," the demon said. "His magic's keeping him under for the time being to let his body heal. He'll wake up eventually. It'll take more than a beating from a rag-tag bunch of hunters to bring down a witch of his caliber."

"I don't get it," I said. "Why can't you just whisk us away and be done with it?"

"As it happens, I have a nasty score to settle with this particular lot of hunters after my last contretemps with them. I'll ensure your escape, but we might as well have a bit of fun with our predicament, don't you think?"

"You've got to be kidding me," I said. "Fun is the last thing I'm interested in having right now. If you want revenge, why don't you attack them yourself on your own time?"

"A fair question," he said, clasping his hands behind his back and strolling the length of the cell as if on a Sunday walk in the park. "Members of The Black Hand have defenses against my kind. You think you witches have it bad. You should see what they do to us. Spelled iron is nothing opposite my power, but the amulets they wear can capture a corporeal demon and keep him imprisoned for ages. So I have to rely on puppets like you to get a dig in now and then."

That's all I was to him then. A puppet. My temples were pulsating. I raked my fingers through my hair, my eyes stuck on Jack's motionless figure. "What will happen when I drink your blood? And this time, don't leave any of the fine print out, thanks."

The flickering shadows danced across the sharp planes of his face. "Within minutes, the dark magic will spread through your system and be at your command. My powers will be your powers, to wield as you wish. It's only temporary, but you'll have enough time to leave quite the impression."

I hesitated.

"Oh, dear. Don't tell me you're one of those holier-than-thou witches who wouldn't touch dark magic with a six-foot pole. Or did you think dark magic only meant practicing forbidden spellcraft? It encompasses many things, not the least of which is communing with demons."

Jack had already told me using the mark meant calling upon dark magic. I just hadn't thought it involved drinking demon blood too. Is that what Jack had done to heal and revive Connor?

"Will something happen to me?" I asked.

"You mean will you become a red-eyed, raging monster who eats little children at every meal and picks her teeth with the bones of her enemies? Sorry to disappoint. It isn't nearly as grave as you're making it out to be. The dark magic will fade away in a few days' time. Those cautionary tales your people feed impressionable minds are about witches who continually abused dark magic. In doing so, they became its slave."

I hesitated, doubt crawling all over my skin like hundreds of tiny insects. I hated that I had to take a demon's word for it. What if he was lying? What if this was all some cruel trick to somehow forever bind me to him? My eyes dropped to his dagger.

"Is this what's bothering you? Say no more." The weapon vanished and in its place was a champagne flute filled with a near-black liquid. "Some prefer to drink straight from the source, but I can appreciate those with a bit more class. But tick-tock, little witch. We really are wasting valuable time."

"I have a name, you know. It's Scarlet." I instantly regretted sharing it. I didn't want to be on a first-name basis with a demon.

"Kai," he replied, giving a mock bow as he smirked.

Footsteps echoed from far off, and my stomach turned over. "They're coming."

Kai extended the champagne flute to me with an arched brow. I wanted to wipe the amusement clean off his face.

I snatched the glass from him, his blood sloshing from side to side.

I drank.

33

I didn't put up a fight as they strapped me to a cruciform in the Chamber, though the iron cuffs burned against my wrists and ankles. The room was aptly named. It was a torture chamber straight out of the Middle Ages, one that made my heart stutter in my chest.

Black manacles hung from the walls, joined by sinister-looking collars with nails facing inward. There was a wooden table with rollers on either end to stretch a person's limbs, a coffin-sized iron tomb with spikes on the interior, and more cages than I could count. Nevermind the tools and instruments laid out with care on a table beside me, each one sharp and frightening.

Click, click, click.

Even with a demon at my disposal, the familiar sound filled me with paralyzing dread, as if lethal venom were slowly spreading through me. I hadn't liked the plan Kai had shared as I drank his blood.

"Are the theatrics really necessary?" I'd asked before insisting yet again that he forget about his revenge and simply take us away from this place, my lips warm from his blood. I'd practically retched when the first drops rushed onto my tongue, only to be surprised by the sweet taste of it, and far more surprised when I easily downed the entire drink within seconds.

"I'm doing you a favor, little witch," Kai replied, already fading into his wisps of smoke. "Do you want to elude them, or do you want to strike fear into their tiny, black hearts?"

What I wanted was for me and Jack to be alive when it was all said and done, but before I could argue further, he'd vanished with the empty, blood-stained champagne flute, and moments later, the hunters were already unlocking the cell, leaving me to simply wipe the blood from my mouth.

"It occurred to me," the blonde woman said, stopping inches from me, "that perhaps you might have better sense than our beloved Jack here."

Jack and I mirrored each other on opposite ends of the Chamber. He hadn't yet roused, and his head was lolling to the side in an eerie way.

"The Chamber Master can be such an animal," she went on. "I assure you you don't want to endure what he's prepared for you and Jack this evening. Between you and me, I never watch when things progress to this gruesome point. I only oversee each detainee's Purge."

"What's the Purge?" I asked. The word alone sounded horrifying. My throat felt swollen as it left my mouth.

"You poor thing. Has no one ever told you?" She tutted. "Probably for the best. It only means there isn't nearly as much wickedness in you. The less time you've spent among witches, the better."

"Why do you hate us so much?"

"Oh, it's nothing personal, darling," she said. "This conflict between my people and your kind has been in place for ages. But we're only doing the sacred work we've been called to do. You see, you and those like you are the offspring of a most unholy union, one fashioned between man and the devil eons ago. Where do you think those abilities of yours come from? It's the byproduct of great evil. Yours is an unnatural and dangerous bloodline that must be eradicated before you contaminate all of humanity. Otherwise, we face a future where every man, woman, and child carries a drop of the devil's blood in their veins."

Had the circumstances not been quite as grave, I might've laughed. Jack had called the members of The Black Hand zealots. He'd been much too kind. "You can't honestly believe that."

She secured the straps holding me in place, the edges of the leather rough against my arms. "I suppose in your stories, we're the monsters. But tell me this: would a monster concern itself with the salvation of your soul? Call us what you will, but at the end of the day, we're doing you a great kindness. When someone like you goes through the Purge, you're delivered of your tainted blood. Every corrupt drop is drained from your body to free you from its evil. And when the end draws near, we administer the last rites that absolve you of your wickedness, commending your redeemed soul into the life beyond."

The room started spinning. The food in my stomach from hours ago churned unpredictably. *Kai*, I said in my mind, panicked. *Please tell me you're there.*

I must say, I haven't seen Mary-Anne in years. I'm almost relieved to know she hasn't changed in the slightest. Still as sociopathic as ever.

"Now do you understand?" Mary-Anne asked, securing another strap. "Our methods may seem cruel, but I'm of the mind the end justifies the means. This isn't to say I relish your suffering, of course, which is why I want to offer you the opportunity to spare yourself from the ministrations of the Chamber Master. All you need do is tell me where Jack's brothers are. I'll release you from your restraints at once and ensure your Purge is completely painless. You'll be fast asleep before it even begins."

Her euphemisms were almost as disturbing as the reality they were meant to sugarcoat. "Do you really think I'd betray them?"

She scoffed. "Such displays of virtue. They won't inoculate you against the pain that otherwise awaits you. This is your final chance, girl, and I'd advise you choose wisely."

I met her gaze full on. "I've already made my choice," I said.

Her glacial eyes were hard as diamonds as they impaled me. I almost felt frostbite developing on my bones. "Send for the Chamber Master," she ordered someone I couldn't see.

That was my cue. *Here goes nothing.* "Actually, you don't want to do that."

She lifted her eyebrows at my tone. "You're hardly in any position to say so." But her eyes switched to my side, following something as it ascended and wreathed all around me. Kai's inky black wisps of smoke. They coiled around my arms, around my neck, twisting like charmed snakes as I beckoned them. His blood awoke at my summons just as he said it would. It burned inside me, as if I'd swallowed fire, and the magic sparked to life like flint against steel.

Mary-Anne checked to ensure the iron cuffs were still around my wrists and ankles. They were. She stepped back. "What is this?"

My hair started to rise as if charged by static, and then it blew in a phantom breeze all across my face. I kept my eyes pinned on Mary-Anne all the while, filling them with poison. Kai's magic thrummed in my veins, strengthening more and more with every passing second. It was different from Jack's magic. Where Jack's had been light and buoyant and uplifting, Kai's was dark and heavy and grounding. There was an inescapable darkness expanding in my chest like a swelling storm cloud.

And the storm raged. I didn't know if it was Kai's influence or my own, but Mary-Anne filled my vision, and all I could think about were the scores of witches she and her fanatics had tortured in rooms like this all over the world. Their prejudice had cut short countless lives, had erased entire bloodlines from the face of the earth. The anger—no, the rage—cut me deep, leaving behind a searing wound that was like a flame in my chest.

And that's when I realized this wasn't Kai's influence at all. Zoe had said I needed to make a decision about where I stood. But I already knew where I stood. From the moment Jack and I had first exchanged words, I'd become a part of this world. I was a witch in the same way the Connellys were witches, and the people The Black Hand had hunted for centuries were *my* people. My family. A family that had been persecuted in ways that were unforgivable.

Mary-Anne reached for one of the nearby torture instruments, but before her fingers could touch the metal, the devices flipped into the air and levitated several feet above us. They formed a ring over the woman's head and slowly pointed down toward her. Mary-Anne frowned and backed up further.

"I need reinforcements *now*," she called out, and within moments, hunters rushed into the Chamber. They didn't stand a chance. One by one, I threw them across the room with Kai's magic, where the manacles, suddenly animated, closed around their wrists and restrained them. I hurled others into cages that sat with doors wide open like hungry mouths, doors that promptly snapped shut once a hunter was inside.

Kai's magic was an untamed tempest at my fingertips. It was so easy to lash out, unrestricted by the spelled iron, to fling the magic about like deadly knives and watch the blades sink into their targets with astounding accuracy. When my own magic had yet to awaken, it felt wildly satisfying to suddenly have so much power under my control. It slaked a thirst I didn't know I possessed. Above, the lights flickered, and all manner of contraptions and tools clanked against the floors and walls in a deafening chorus, the demon blood in me pulsing along with the rhythm like a second heart.

Mary-Anne's ice blue eyes were double their size as she watched it all. "This is impossible."

"Not really," I said. "You just messed with the wrong witch."

Gritting her teeth, she whipped the truncheon hanging from her belt loop free, but I knocked her onto her back before she could attack me. Then I willed the truncheon away, and it flew across the room, slamming into the wall with enough force to crack in half like a pencil. Mary-Anne blanched.

"Now you're going to listen to what I have to say," I said. "We witches don't need your absolution. We don't need you to Purge us of whatever wickedness you think we have. We never asked for these powers, but for whatever reason, we were born with them. And we'll keep being born with them generation after generation. You think you can silence us, but you can't. You think you can wipe us from existence, but we'll survive. We're not going anywhere. So let me make one thing clear. If you ever come for the Connellys or any other witch again, you're going to deal with me, and I promise you I'll make your life a living nightmare."

Mary-Anne actually growled. Bared her teeth and growled. She threw something at me, lightning-quick. I didn't have enough time to deflect the knife as it raced straight for me. I twisted my head away at the last second, the edge of the blade blazing across my cheek in a streak of heat before it pierced the cruciform. In a blur of color, Mary-Anne shot to her feet, and charged at me as she pulled a second knife free from a hidden holster. *Click, click—*

A burst of smoke and fire and ash exploded before me, burning my eyes so badly I had to squeeze them shut.

When I dared to look again, my face still warm from the fire, Mary-Anne had vanished, as had every last hunter in the room.

A moment later, Kai materialized before me. His wisps of smoke trailed down my arms and stretched across the space between us, returning to him. The power he'd granted me left me in a rush, like air blasting out of a quickly deflating balloon.

He slow-clapped, a twisted smile stretching across his lips. "Brava, little witch. Brava. I have to say, if anyone has a flair for the theatrics, it's most certainly you. I think we make quite the dynamic team. What do you think?"

"You didn't kill them, did you?" My breath sawed in and out of my lungs. The assumption, of course, was that Kai had been the one to banish the hunters. It's what I wanted to believe. I hadn't meant to do that, but what if I'd lost control in that split-second? What if I'd done something horrific?

Kai started to undo the straps holding me down. He quirked an eyebrow. "They were about to gruesomely torture you before draining every last drop of blood from your body, and you're concerned about whether or not they met a most deserved end?"

"Kai."

He met my pleading gaze. His garnet eyes were dancing. "I simply banished them to the farthest reaches of Siberia. I hear it's rather lovely this time of year. Single-digit temperatures and all."

I let go of a sigh of relief. Yes, it might've been a 'most deserved end,' but I wouldn't have been able to live with myself had I stooped to their level in so grim a way.

"Had I not intervened, she would've cut you up rather nicely, you know."

"I thought demons didn't have robust moral codes."

The corner of his mouth twitched up at that. "I suppose some of us can surprise you. Easy!"

I sagged against him once I was free of my restraints, my legs giving out. My entire body felt heavy, my movements slow as if I were moving through water. "What's wrong with me?"

"You're experiencing your kickback," Kai said, holding me up. "Demon blood is one of the most potent sources of dark magic a witch can use. Once the power runs its course, there's a nasty withdrawal period to contend with. I apologize. Did I not mention that?"

My head hurt too much to properly glare at him. The world was a carousel around me. Jack had told me about the dreaded kickback, of course, but I hadn't known just how quickly it would come or to what extent.

"Look at you, though," Kai went on. "Scarred in all your wonder. I have to admit, I'm impressed."

Thin streaks of blood leisurely trailed down my face from the cut on my cheek, but I was too nauseous to care, and there wasn't enough fight left in me to object when Kai traced a fingertip along my jawline to collect a few beads of crimson. He stuck his finger into his mouth and slowly tasted my blood.

Almost immediately, there was a spark in his eyes, and something changed in his expression. He looked at me, taken aback.

"What?" I asked. "A-Positive not your usual poison of choice?"

Something unreadable danced in his gaze like a flame. "My word," he whispered, rapt. "You have no idea what you are, do you?"

Everything was dimming, my thoughts slipping away from me fast. "Kai," I moaned. "Please just take us home."

My eyes were already closed when he responded, but I still heard his voice, coming to me as if from a dream.

"As you wish, little witch."

34

"You summoned a demon, didn't you?"

I was face-to-face with a toilet bowl, clinging to its cold, porcelain frame as if for dear life. My pajama pants were hardly a suitable fortification against the hard tiles of the bathroom, and I sank back onto my heels before I keeled over. Connor was leaning a shoulder against the doorway, arms crossed. It was four in the morning, but I guessed in the wake of all the excitement we'd endured recently, no one was getting any sleep.

"If you're going to lecture me," I said, my throat sore, "could you at least wait until I'm not seeing double?"

It had been a few hours since Kai had magically ferried me and Jack to the door of our hotel room. I wasn't sure how he knew where we were staying. Maybe he'd plucked it out of my thoughts. I hadn't been in any condition to prod.

"Until we meet again, little witch," he'd said before knocking on the door three times and vanishing into his wisps of smoke.

"I'm not here to lecture you," Connor said. He pulled a few tissues from a plastic box beside the sink and handed them to me.

I used them to dab at the corners of my mouth and flushed

the toilet. The water spun on its way down, making a pattern like a lollipop swirl—one part clear, one part black. I looked away, not relishing the reminder I'd upchucked what essentially looked like petroleum.

"I'm not in any position to," Connor went on, "considering I wouldn't be standing here if Jack hadn't once summoned a demon for me."

I paused mid-dab. "You know about that?"

"*You* know about that?" After a moment, he shook his head. "I guess I shouldn't be surprised. Jack seems to tell you just about everything."

"He only kept it from you to protect you, Connor. He didn't want you to feel guilty."

"I know," he said. "Typical Jack. But I knew something was off from the beginning. The tension in our home, Jack suddenly being sick the way you now are. Nevermind his inadvertently setting Declan O'Neill on fire. Though, for the record, the bloody langer deserved it."

"So you've known all along?"

"Jack was uncharacteristically cagey after my 'miraculous' recovery, and after the Declan incident, I overheard my parents arguing about dark magic, dropping my name and Jack's in the mix. I looked for answers in a few grimoires and history texts, and though I was young, it wasn't hard to put two and two together. I never confronted Jack about it. I knew he was embarrassed about using dark magic, so if it made him feel better to keep it a secret, then I was willing to play along."

I couldn't help but wonder if Connor's previous resentment toward Alison had just as much to do about what she'd said that day as it did her later abandonment. Though she'd been grateful to have Connor back, it was clear she'd lamented what it'd cost Jack. I knew her words could've easily been interpreted as her wishing Redmond had just let fate run its course. "Your mom loves you all very much, you know. Having been in her mind, I can say that without hesitation."

Connor considered it, the glare of the bathroom light reflecting off his glasses. "I never doubted her love for us. Though I sometimes caught her looking at Jack back then as if he were already lost to us, and I couldn't help but feel like she would've rather I died than have Jack use the demon's mark."

"Connor—"

He held up a hand. "I'm not fishing for sympathy, Monroe." He sniffed the air and grimaced. "You smell a mess, by the way."

Rolling my eyes, I balled up the tissues and tossed them toward a neighboring waste bin. The ball floated halfway there and then plopped onto the tiles. "Question: I'm not going to have to worry about accidentally setting people on fire, am I?"

Connor leaned over to pinch the tissues between two fingers and deposited them into the trash. "You haven't fully come into your magic, so no. There's nothing for the demon blood to amplify. You'll most likely just feel sick until it leaves your system." He studied me further. "Listen. I know I've given you somewhat of a hard time since we met."

"Somewhat?"

Now he rolled his eyes. "Anyway, I appreciate what you did for Jack."

It was about as much of an apology as Connor would probably ever utter. I nodded. "He would've done the same for me, for any of us."

Connor sighed and adjusted his glasses on the bridge of his nose. "I guess that's two wishes down. We only have to make sure there's no reason to call upon a third."

"Actually, Kai—that was the demon's name—said I couldn't use the mark. So I struck a bargain of my own with him instead. Apparently I'll owe him a favor at some point in my life."

A soft curse fell from Connor's mouth, and he passed his fingers through his hair.

His reaction made me feel sick again, and I turned toward the toilet, waiting for another spell to come over me. Fortunately, for the time being, it looked like I was in the clear. "Truth be told, I would've done it again if I had to. Anything to get away from that psychopath Mary-Anne."

"Mary-Anne?" Connor's spine stiffened.

"You know her then? She said she and Jack had history."

"Mary-Anne is one of the most ruthless hunters around. She can trace her lineage all the way back to the very first members of The Black Hand, something she takes considerable pride in. With as many abilities as he has, she's had an obsession with Jack ever since she first learned about him. Capturing a witch like that would be the ultimate notch in her belt. She's gone after him plenty of times, but he's always outsmarted her."

A trickle of warmth slid down the side of my face. The small gash from Mary-Anne's knife was bleeding again. I pulled myself to my feet and stumbled to the sink, frowning at my pallid reflection in the bathroom mirror. I hadn't caught a wink of sleep since arriving at the hotel, and it showed in the dark shadows under each eye.

I peeled off the old bandage, cleaned the wound with warm water and lemon-scented liquid soap, and stuck on a new Band-Aid. Since it was courtesy of Zoe's supply, it was black with tiny skulls and crossbones. Once that was done, I reapplied ointment on the burns on my palms, wrists, and ankles from The Black Hand's spelled iron. It was a special, magical blend also from Zoe's supply, and I was relieved by how quickly it soothed the pain and made the red marks on my skin fade away.

"How's Jack doing?" I asked Connor's reflection. Jack had finally regained consciousness within minutes of us returning to the hotel room, but he'd still been in something of a daze, his face burning from a fever.

"Scarlet?" he'd said, panicking as he sat up on the couch in the common room.

I moved into his line of sight. "I'm here, Jack. It's okay."

"The hunters—"

"They're gone," I said. "We're safe."

His eyes slid to the wound on my cheek, and there was pain in his eyes. The guilt of not being able to protect someone. The sight had been a weight on my chest.

"He's sleeping it off," Connor said. "The sooner we find The Book of Fates, the better. We need to get out of this city. It's bad enough you crossed paths with The Black Hand, but we also have the sluagh to contend with. We sighted them earlier tonight, around the time the two of you went missing. I initially thought they were the reason for your delay. They've finally caught up to our scent."

I had almost forgotten about the sluagh. How many enemies was that now? Getting rid of the hunters—at least Mary-Anne's small group of them—had seemed like a minor victory. Remembering they were the least of our worries, though, was woefully sobering.

Suddenly, there came a pounding at the front door. Three thunderous knocks that bellowed out like a battering ram. I jumped, my pulse galloping. Kai had taken care of all the hunters, hadn't he? What if he hadn't? I realized with growing dread that I might've underestimated their numbers. There could've been countless others out in the city at the time of our escape, and somehow, they'd tracked us.

Connor strode to the front door, grabbing a gun on his way there. The Connellys hadn't yet had any reason to use any of the weapons they'd packed on this trip...until now. His steps became as light as a cat's as he neared the door, and he inched forward slowly.

Boom, boom, boom! The knocks were angry, violent. There wouldn't be a third round of them. The hunters on the other end would surely storm their way in within seconds. My eyes darted around the penthouse, quickly assessing the best hiding places, the best furnishings to use in self-defense.

Connor pressed his back against the door and then quickly turned and dared a look through the peephole. He stayed there longer than I would've expected him to, but nothing surprised me more than when he swung the door wide open.

"Zoe?"

My shoulders fell with relief, and I sagged against a wall.

Zoe, who was staying a floor below us, stood out in the carpeted hallway, her chest rising and falling rapidly. Her eyes were large and wild.

"What is it?" Connor asked, stepping back so she could come in.

Either she didn't hear him or she was too stunned to move. She held up her phone, looking between us. "Something's happened," she said. "The Council of Elders has been found dead."

35

Our search for The Book of Fates became a frantic one in the passing days.

Samhain was now only a week away. Jack's locator spell (he'd acquired new ingredients on his own this time, disappearing in a blast of wind before any of us could protest) hadn't worked, just as Zoe had predicted. Granted, the surge of power from his magic had caused every last candle in the library to flare tall and bright, and the room had shaken violently until cracks ran down its floor and walls. But when the spell was said and done, we were still as empty-handed as we'd been at the start.

I was beginning to wonder if The Book of Fates was in the library at all, a library that had turned into quite a madhouse in the wake of our desperate hunt. The brothers had foregone all library etiquette, tearing books off the shelves in haste and letting them fall to the floor if they weren't of their clan. Only Rory bothered to leave his part of the library just as he'd found it, calling to mind how immaculately organized he'd kept the greenhouse back at St. Andrew's.

"Here's a thought," Connor had announced one evening when everyone's frustration was steadily mounting, speaking to no one in particular, his feet surrounded by a growing mountain of books. "Why not catalogue these grimoires by clan, not by their subject matter or what year they were written or whatever bloody system these Guardians have in place?"

Zoe crossed her arms, eyes simmering. "Oh, we've inconvenienced you, have we? Gods forbid that you, Connor, be in any way inconvenienced by something. That's typically the point when you make yourself scarce, isn't it?"

"Is that what you think?" Connor slammed a book shut with a thud, a plume of dust shooting upward. He tossed the book to the pile around him. "Well, we can't all be the spitting image of perfection like your Patrick Doherty, now can we?"

Before things escalated, I hurried over. "Guys, now isn't really the time—"

"Stay out of it," they both shot at me in unison, their glares never once leaving each other.

Blinking, I stepped back and walked away just as they resumed their bickering. Lucas appeared beside me and tugged on my hair before draping an arm over my shoulders with a grin. "Ah, don't take it personal, Scarlet Ibis. You get used to it after a while. I, personally, was starting to worry that one wasn't eating the head off the other yet."

Back at the hotel later that night, I let myself stew in a hot shower for longer than usual. The scalding water relaxed the muscles in my neck and shoulders, and breathing in the steam helped clear my mind. I hadn't recovered my cell from the hunters, so earlier I'd used the hotel phone to check in on my dad. The news wasn't good.

"We've been trying to contact you to update you on his condition," the nurse on the other end had said. I listened, my heart like a block of concrete in my chest as she told me my dad had taken a turn for the worse in the past forty-eight hours, with more than one organ system beginning to slow down.

"The doctors aren't hopeful, I'm afraid. Now is the time to be calling family and friends." Which was hospital talk for 'the end is coming; make sure everyone's had a chance to say goodbye.'

I couldn't sleep after my shower, though I couldn't tell if the nausea was from the hospital phone call or from me coming off the tail-end of drinking Kai's blood. I wondered around the penthouse suite only to discover insomnia had visited us all. Lucas was shoveling crisps into his mouth as he watched one of those late night talk shows that hosted celebrities and musical performances. Rory was sketching at the dining room table, and Connor was nowhere to be seen. Assuming he was back on speaking terms with Zoe, he'd most likely joined her for one of her nightly sluagh and hunter patrols. Ever since the news about The Council, not to mention our run-in with The Black Hand, she'd made it a point to do reconnaissance several times a day, especially while we were in the underground library.

"It gives me something to do," she'd said

"You're not afraid of them?" I asked. The girl had nerves of steel to brave Dublin on her own in the wake of The Black Hand's attack. Even if Connor sometimes accompanied her, I wouldn't have risked it either way with all the dangers lying in wait for us in every shadowy corner.

"If I let myself be afraid of them," she said, filling a revolver with silver rounds, "then they've already won."

I found Jack on the hotel balcony, once again listening to Maurice's voicemails, except the phone in his hands wasn't his own. It belonged to one of his brothers, I assumed, and he'd simply used it to dial into his message inbox. Despite the hour, he was still in the clothes he'd worn earlier. It was weird to see him without his black coat, though, as if he wasn't quite complete now that it was gone.

He turned to me as I joined him at the railing. In the halo of the street lamps below, you could just make out the gentle mist of rain that descended upon Dublin, but we were protected under the balcony's awning, the raindrops playing a soft beat against its stretched cloth. As they'd done ever since our confrontation with The Black Hand, Jack's eyes flew immediately to the cut on my cheek. The wound no longer stung, but that hadn't kept the guilt from shadowing Jack's face every time he saw it. I wanted to tell him he couldn't continue holding himself responsible, but I already knew by now that Jack carried the weight of the world on his shoulders and probably always would.

"Have you been able to get in contact with Seamus yet?" I asked. The night Zoe had told us about The Council, we'd immediately woken up Jack, whose first response had been to call his uncle, who'd still been Elsewhere at the time. But every last call only rang and rang and rang before ultimately going to voicemail. Seamus's body hadn't been found among the Elders, so the hope was he'd already left by the time the Reaper had arrived. Because that was the one thing we had no doubt about: the Reaper's obvious involvement. Six powerful witches slain with a dark ritual just on the horizon? Their blood was most assuredly on the wayward witch's hands.

Jack leaned against the railing, a sigh sliding out of his throat in a long, smooth breath. "I can't help but fear the worst. Even if he managed to evade the Reaper's attack on The Council, there were plenty of dangers waiting for him here. Hunters, the sluagh. Something has to have happened. Otherwise, he'd be here with us right now."

I wanted to believe Seamus was perfectly safe, perhaps only hiding out somewhere until it was safe enough for him to emerge. The last thing the Connellys needed was to lose yet another important figure in their lives. We stared out at the busy city in silence for a while, both of us lost in our own thoughts.

"I saw you on the hotel phone earlier," Jack said eventually, facing me again. "Your expression completely changed. Was it the hospital you were speaking with? Is your father all right?"

I was tempted to lie. Not because I wanted to withhold anything from Jack but because I wanted to pretend, even if just for a moment, that I was living in another reality. A reality without the magic and the monsters and the mayhem. A reality where I was just an ordinary girl with an ordinary guy, and my ordinary father was waiting for me at home, completely healthy and safe. In the end, I went with the bitter, inescapable truth, relaying everything the nurse had told me.

"Oh, Scarlet," he said, my name in his brogue like a gentle caress. "I'm sorrier than you know."

"Yeah," was all I could say back. My throat tightened, and I nearly choked on the word.

"Come here," Jack said softly, opening his arms to me.

Though he'd only held me once before, his embrace was familiar, as if I'd known it all my life. This time, as I leaned against him, a tear did escape me, rolling slowly down my cheek. I was surprised by the show of emotion, but then, I had just nearly been killed by an extremist group mere days ago. I had just made a bargain with a demon I wasn't sure I could entirely trust. And the one thing that could bind the Reaper and help my dad continued to elude us, leaving everyone's morale at an all-time low. Throw in a spell of insomnia, and it was any wonder I wasn't outright bawling. I'd known people to have bigger outbursts just from missing a meal.

I didn't think Jack had noticed the tear, but his thumb slid across my skin, collecting the drop before it could continue its descent. "We still have time," he said, speaking into my hair in a way that sent shivers through me.

I closed my eyes and kept my arms looped around his middle, not wanting to let go, my head at rest against his firm chest. I thought I could fall asleep like this, be lulled into slumber by the metronome that was his steady heartbeat.

"I hope one day you can forgive me," he said then.

I pulled back and opened my mouth to ask what he meant, but of course. His attention had returned to Mary-Anne's cut.

"Not just about this," he said, smoothing his thumb over the Band-Aid, feather-light. "But for what you had to do to free us." In the distance, a siren wailed, making Jack's words sound even more ominous.

Was that what most bothered him? The favor hanging over my head and the demon who pulled the strings? I put my hand over his, trapping his fingers against my cheek. "What's done is done," I said softly. "And if I had to do it again, I would've made the same choice. There was no way I would've let the hunters take your life. Besides, we still have a Reaper to stop, and I'm not giving up yet."

36

Samhain was in six days, and we still hadn't found The Book of Fates.

"I'm completely knackered," Lucas said, collapsing into a chair beside me in the library. "I could sleep for a hundred years right about now."

I had my face in my hands, but I sat up at his arrival. It was becoming a struggle to keep my eyes open. Actually, it'd been a struggle for the past three hours. I reached for the coffee cup beside me. The liquid had cooled considerably, but I was hoping the caffeine inside would still do its trick. I was simply glad the nausea from Kai's blood had finally left me for good this morning. "What time is it?"

"Half two," he said, which I'd learned meant it was thirty minutes past the hour. I guessed that meant Samhain was actually in five days then. "And I'm pretty sure a few of the books I just went through were ones I've already looked at. Meaning I'm clearly going mad."

The words didn't mean anything to me at first, but then I stiffened. "Wait. Do you think the ordinary grimoires are rearranging themselves the way Zoe said the really powerful ones do?"

Lucas balanced his chair back on its rear legs, considering it as he took out a deck of cards and began shuffling it. "I wasn't thinking that at all actually, but now I am. Bollocks. I've been on a carousel of books for over a week now. What a nightmare."

My stomach sank. If the books in here were playing musical chairs every time we left, then it was no wonder we were hardly making any progress with our search. And if only a few titles were pulling the wool over the boys' eyes each day, it'd make sense they wouldn't notice it until later in the game. Especially if they were as mentally exhausted as I imagined them to be. Nevermind the possibility that grimoires from one brother's section could be relocating to another brother's section, meaning the boys wouldn't even know it if someone had already gone through a book.

I rubbed my temples, feeling a migraine coming on. I'd never been a glass-half-empty type, but I could feel the time slipping away from us as if I were watching the sand rush down in a giant hourglass.

Zoe stomped past, muttering under her breath. It was time for another patrol, but it looked like she well intended on going at it alone.

"Trouble in paradise?" Lucas called after her with a grin.

With a quick flick of her wrist, she sent his chair toppling over.

He yelped and landed hard on the stone floor, his cards flying into the air and settling all around him like fallen leaves. He started to move but decided against it, making himself comfortable on the ground. "I think I've earned myself some sleep anyway."

As always, Zoe armed herself liberally and then slung her black backpack over a shoulder. When I'd first seen its contents what seemed like ages ago, my stomach had soured at the crossbow and knives inside. A femme fatale for sure. While I'd initially thought her insane for surveying the city for threats on her own, I was coming to admire the sheer audacity of it all. Not to mention the selflessness. The idea was that Zoe would lure any threats away from Dublin to protect the Connellys while they continued their search. A true ally when so many had turned their backs on Jack and his brothers.

"Stay safe," I offered as she made for the catacombs.

That feline smirk danced on her lips. "Gods forbid." And then she was gone.

Leaving Lucas to catch his sleep, I wandered through the library for a time, begrudgingly picking up after the boys if only because it pained me to see books scattered all over the ground like storm debris. I didn't know if I was shelving them properly, but considering the possibility some of the books were rearranging themselves anyway, I didn't think it mattered.

Eventually, I found my way to the Tree of Life mosaic. I'd paid homage to it every day we'd been here, something about it calling to me, as if it had tied an invisible string to my heart and gave a gentle tug whenever I was near, reeling me in. Jack had told me the seven main limbs of the tree each represented one of the druidic lines that had survived The Burning Times.

"The limb in the center represents my own clan," he said. "The Ó Conghalaigh clan. Connelly is one of the many anglifications of the name. We're the largest of the seven, made up of more septs, or branches, than we can possibly count or keep track of. Though it's fair to say a good portion of those families would prefer we not keep track of them at all."

Because it was safer that way, was the unspoken reason.

Remembering Jack's words, I ran my hand across the mosaic's smooth tiles, an ache in my heart. My experience with The Black Hand came unbidden to my mind, making me feel sick. I couldn't get past Mary-Anne's vile words, the way she'd spoken so calmly about practices that were the stuff of nightmares. More specifically, I couldn't get past what she and the others represented. Generations of senseless hate that had resulted in the loss of innocent lives again and again and again. Including the disappearance of what was likely my own clan, The Lost Clan. It was hard to believe an entire people had been decimated by other human beings. Something like that, death and destruction, wasn't human at all.

A lump formed in my throat, and I bowed my head slightly, paying respects to the dead. I understood more than ever now why some witches chose to live among the Sightless, hiding their identity, keeping their descendants in the dark. I understood why entire branches of a clan would forever cut off ties, parting ways with their heritage and magic. What other way was there to avoid persecution?

I heard Zoe return and peeked around a bookshelf just as she was setting her backpack onto a table. It hadn't been more than an hour since she'd left, so if she was back this early, it meant the city had been quiet as far as threats went. Much to her chagrin, I was sure.

I looked back to the mosaic. These people had been terrorized for far too long. I stopped. No, not *these* people—*my* people. The truth of it had struck me while I'd faced Mary-Anne. I was no longer on the outside looking in. This was my heritage, who I was and always would be. I might've known nothing about this world for the past seventeen years, but the veil had finally been lifted, and I had no intention of turning my back on it, even at times when it felt like too much to bear. As Zoe had said, if I shrank back in fear, then I was letting the hunters win. And not just the hunters, but the Reaper, the monsters, all of it.

I wouldn't let that happen. I owed it to those who hadn't been able to embrace their true selves. A sense of pride flared up in me like a steady flame. I couldn't change history. I couldn't save those who'd already been lost. But I could make a small difference by embracing who I was and working toward a world where witches no longer had to live in fear.

I pressed my fingertips to each of the tree's main limbs. It was my way of connecting to the members of each clan, of promising myself to a cause that was probably too big for someone who hadn't yet fully come into her magic, but one that was still worthwhile, one I couldn't walk away from even if I wanted to.

When I reached the center limb, the one representing the Connellys' clan, I felt the bump of an uneven tile. Furrowing my brow, I looked closer, tracing arounds its edges. Yes, there it was. One palm-sized tile didn't lay quite as flat as the ones beside it. The grout around it wasn't as aged either, as if it'd been a later installment. A repair most likely. I knocked on it. I expected to feel the solidness of a wall directly behind it. Instead, there was a hollow echo.

My heart started racing.

The tile was covering a cavity.

"Jack!" I called out. "I think I've found something."

Within seconds, the others were gathered around me, and I summarized my findings. Jack hammered the side of his fist against the tile, but it wouldn't give.

"I've got a better idea," Connor said. "Step back." He took out his gun and shot at the spot three times in quick succession. Plaster and tile shards exploded on impact, and I was only glad I'd shielded my face in time.

Jack waved away the dust and dove into the cavity with his hand. When he frowned, my stomach sank. I'd misled them. The cavity was empty. He pulled back, scraping dirt and dead leaves out of the nook.

"Connor, give me your phone," he said. He turned on its

flashlight and aimed the beacon into the cavity, leaning down to inspect its depths. He reached in a second time, pushing his arm through up to his shoulder, and then pushing harder. When he stilled, disbelief flooding his eyes, it was all I could do to remember to inhale and exhale.

Jack pulled his arm back out, and this time his fingers were gripping a rolled-up, leather-bound journal. It had to be hundreds of years old.

"Bloody hell," Lucas breathed.

We crowded around Jack as he, with trembling hands, unfurled the journal, untied its strap, and opened the book. I couldn't make anything of its contents, of course. All that stared up at me were various censuses and inventories of some kind. But the brothers had stilled to the point where they dared not even breathe, their eyes pinned on the pages as Jack turned them. I didn't know if the journal was what we were looking for. I'd expected something vastly different—a hefty, hardcover tome with hundreds of pages, for instance. But there was no denying the energy surrounding us in the air like the static before a lightning strike. Whatever the journal was, it was armed to the teeth with magic.

"This is it," Jack finally whispered, his face a portrait of awe. The words seemed to be more so for him than the rest of us, as if he needed to assure himself of the authenticity of what he held and assuage any remaining doubts. I couldn't blame him. As much as I'd wanted to find The Book of Fates, I'd had my doubts now and then about whether we would. I was sure we all had. I glanced to the now empty cavity, wondering how the journal had found its way there to begin with. Then I remembered it'd been powerful enough to undo the latches and locks on its display case. Burrowing itself into the heart of a mosaic was nothing compared to that.

"Is the spell to bind the Reaper in there?" I asked. My legs were fast becoming jelly. I didn't know if it was because of the magic coming off the book or simply the adrenaline of the moment, but my pulse was hammering against the inside of my wrist in a high-octane beat.

Jack continued turning the pages, his eyes quickly scanning over the text. He stopped three-quarters of the way through. "I recognize these sigils. This has to be what our mother was referring to." He shook his head, running his fingertips across the page. "The language is extremely dated, though. Much of it's written in Old Irish. Some words I'm not familiar with. I'll need to grab a few texts from the library at Crowmarsh to help me translate most of the passages."

"Then let's get out of here," Connor said.

We gathered our things in a rush, the excitement going off in us like firecrackers, and charged for the catacombs, stopping just short of the library's boundary. Here, Jack extended the book to Zoe, the only one among us who could safely carry The Book of Fates out. On previous days, whenever Jack or the others had asked Zoe to carry out a grimoire for them, she'd always pass the threshold first. It was a safety measure to prevent confusing the boundary spell.

Zoe drew closer to the boundary. Despite the backpack of weapons she carried, I noted the hesitation in the set of her shoulders. Connor apparently noticed it too.

"You've carried out a Sacred Grimoire before, haven't you?" he asked.

"Not exactly."

He started. "What? Are you even sure you can do it then? We should call in someone who's done it before. You know these hold more power than a typical grimoire."

"There's only one way to find out." She took a step forward.

Connor grabbed the crook of her arm and pulled her back slightly. "Have you gone mad?"

She shrugged out of his hold and looked to Jack. "I'll pass over first," she said. "Wait a few seconds before following after."

"Zoe!" Connor called out, but she hurried forward before he could stop her again.

We watched breathlessly as she stepped toward the boundary, not a sound leaving our mouths. I braced myself for the worst, almost turning my eyes away. Zoe was a level of brave I could only hope to one day achieve. My chest was tight with every step she took, my muscles coiled up in anticipation of some fatal, magical blow from above.

Three more steps, two more steps, one...

I tensed, praying her Guardian status would shield her from the boundary spell's rules like it was supposed to.

She cleared the threshold.

I let go of the breath I'd been holding. Connor raked his fingers through his hair, muttering a curse. The tightness left Jack's body in a rush; Lucas's and Rory's too.

We started forward to join Zoe. I was ready to throw my arms around the girl in a hug. But we hadn't taken more than two steps before the library's drop gate suddenly came crashing down in a loud clamor, barring our exit.

A soft, unfamiliar, and strangely sad smile crept over Zoe's lips as she slowly turned toward us. "I'm really sorry about this, lads," she said.

And then her features shimmered like ripples in a pool as she shapeshifted into someone else.

Seamus.

37

Jack was the first to speak. "Uncle Seamus? What are you...?"

Silence consumed us, swallowed us whole as the pieces slowly shifted into place. All we could do was stare at Seamus, trying to make sense of what had just occurred. Upon the Connellys' faces sat a variety of expressions, confusion and surprise among them. But they all ultimately reached a unanimous reaction to their uncle's sudden presence: dawning realization, and then dread.

My stomach dropped as if I were free-falling. There was a tingling sensation from my shoulders to my fingertips as the adrenaline sent a staggering jolt through me. Zoe's words came back to me about the boundary spell only noting a witch's body but not what was on the inside. Meaning witches who could possess other witches weren't the only danger. Shapeshifters were too.

"No," Jack said, shaking his head, as if doing so would erase the image before him.

"I really wish you lads had stayed at Crowmarsh," Seamus said, heaving a sigh. He looked down at The Book of Fates, running a thumb across its worn, leather face. "But I suppose something useful came out of this adventure."

He couldn't use the book himself, of course, as he didn't have Connelly blood in his veins. But he could stop it from being used.

Against him.

"You're the Reaper," I said, my voice just above a whisper.

"I'm afraid so." Surprisingly, he genuinely sounded apologetic, as if he hadn't chosen the role for himself, as if he'd been burdened with it.

"No," Jack said again.

Seamus offered a sad smile. "You always did think the best of people, Jack. It's perhaps your greatest strength and greatest weakness all at once." The flames from the wall sconces spasmed, painting Seamus with sharp angles that gave a cruel edge to his features, making him look a little less human.

"No," Jack repeated. I could see the way his denial wrestled with the reality right in front of him. He didn't want to believe it, couldn't. "Someone's forcing your hand. Who?"

"I suppose you could say love is forcing me."

"Love? That's rich." Connor gripped the bars of the drop gate, fuming. "What did you do with Zoe? I swear to the gods, if you've—"

"Relax, Connor. Zoe is perfectly fine, fast asleep in the abbey above. I've been watching you lot for days, trying to determine the best way to intervene in your quest. Zoe's patrols provided an ideal opportunity. I couldn't have imagined you'd end up finding The Book of Fates today of all days, though. It must be a sure sign I've taken the right path."

"What path? Seamus, this isn't who you are," Jack said. "You would never turn against your own kind. The clans admire you. They look up to you. We all do. I can't accept that you would become a Reaper. What's really going on? Tell us so we can help you."

Seamus sighed. "When Neala and Bree were taken from me, Jack, it shattered me. Utterly shattered me. I'd never felt so lost in my life. As you well know, I became a ghost of myself, a recluse. I no longer saw a point to life, and I'm not sure what I might've done had your grandfather not intervened and suggest I oversee Crowmarsh. He was rarely there, preferring to stay in Rosalyn Bay to be close to you and your brothers now that you were all at St. Andrew's. The estate's upkeep kept me busy, but it was nothing more than a routine, my body simply going through the motions in a vain attempt to distract me from my loss. I needed something more."

"That's why you went to study with The Council of Elders," Jack said.

"Indeed. I studied every grimoire I could get my hands on. Unlike the books here, those Elsewhere aren't bound by blood spells. Knowledge is freely shared between the clans. And though the Forbidden Spells are kept under lock and key after what happened with Celeste, I curried favor with the Elders, eventually earning their trust. I was allowed to study not only those spells but other texts most witches don't even know exist, including summoning sigils for some of the most powerful demons alive."

A chill crept down my spine, spread to my arms and neck. It was as if the library had suddenly turned into an ice chest.

"The simple sigils witches are taught in their adolescence accomplish the most basic of tasks, and the ones meant to summon creatures from the Otherworld call forth only the lowliest of demons, demons unable to disturb the balance between life and death. But the demons I learned about Elsewhere...they're the monsters of our nightmares, their power unfathomable. And they're able to do far more than a simple demon's mark allows."

I glanced to the brand on Jack's wrist, remembering the restrictions with which it came.

"One demon in particular caught my attention," Seamus went on. "A Soul-Eater. With every soul it's fed, especially the soul of a practitioner of magic, its power magnifies, equipping it with incredible abilities, not the least of which is the ability to resurrect the dead. And unlike Celeste's rudimentary spell, the dead return just as they once were in waking life because of the demon's great power. It was the perfect solution."

"You intend on bringing back Neala and Bree," I said, realizing why the Elders were secretive about such texts. If witches knew they could easily revive family and friends by calling forth mighty demons, the world would be overrun with the beasts. We'd all be consumed.

"But at what cost?" Jack shook his head. "Seamus, you know Neala would do anything to return to you, but not at a price this high. She wouldn't want the blood of innocent witches on her hands."

"But you went after your own kind anyway," Connor said, his knuckles turning white from his grip on the bars.

Seamus let go of another breath. I couldn't tell if it was from shame or mere exasperation from his nephews' inquisition. "It was the only way to make the Soul-Eater as strong as I needed it to be. It was easy enough to puppet the sluagh. Each time they brought me a new soul, my demon ties allowed me to grant one of their flock access to the Otherworld, where they were finally freed from their eternal obligations."

"And The Wise Ones?" Rory asked, his voice as soft as velvet even as his face was carved with betrayal.

I couldn't tell in the shifting shadows, but I was sure Seamus almost grimaced for a moment. "An unfortunate case of collateral damage. They'd been silent for so long, refusing to cooperate in any sort of rune casting or other divination magic for decades, but if there was anyone they'd speak to, it'd be Jack. I couldn't risk what they might reveal to him and how it might disrupt the plan I had in place, a plan that would help me win the clans to my cause. You see, I knew that if witch-kind believed hunters were behind the sluagh attacks, it would enrage them like nothing else, would transform generations' worth of hiding into focused and concentrated anger. Anger directed at The Black Hand."

Connor scoffed. "And you think anyone would follow you in your cause once they discovered the truth?"

"Hence the necessity of the Reaping," Seamus said. "While it was my hope no one would learn about my involvement in waking the Soul-Eater, I couldn't leave myself at risk. So long as the souls were being sacrificed, I decided it best I Reap their Masteries as well. The increase in power and abilities would be a way to protect myself from any opposition, yes, but also a way to carry on the legacies of those who'd fallen."

"Well, aren't you a bloody saint?"

Seamus's face instantly became stern. "We can no longer afford to see morality as black and white, Connor. Do you think I relished committing such egregious acts against my own? Gods, no. But I understood I had to sacrifice the few in order to save the many. Don't you see? The Soul-Eater will be bound to me once I wake it from its slumber. It will devour the souls of those to whom I direct it, making it the perfect weapon against our enemies."

The realization struck me like a blow to the stomach. "You're going to use it against hunters."

"Precisely. We'll at long last be able to overcome them with the Soul-Eater at my beck and call. Witches will no longer have to live in fear, will no longer be hunted down like animals. Is that not worth the sacrifice of a handful of our own if it means the salvation of our entire race? Would not any man in my position do as I've done? This is the answer to all our prayers. We'll finally have our vengeance against hunters everywhere. The Black Hand will at long last be destroyed, along with all those who ever stood back and watched us burn."

A painful lump formed in my throat at those last words. "You don't mean the Sightless, do you?"

"What have they ever done for us? Their petty superstitions and dogmas have largely contributed to the persecution we've suffered over the centuries. No, we'll create a new society from the ashes, where witches rule like kings and queens, where the Sightless are in the minority and forced to serve their betters. Those who resist..." He shrugged.

I thought of Natalie and her family back in Colorado, who were completely oblivious to a world filled with witches and demons. Even so, I knew they would never treat me differently if they ever learned the truth of my heritage. And what about Liam? He'd said himself he didn't like the way the townspeople of Rosalyn Bay treated the Connellys. Seamus wanted to punish innocent people like this, despite their never harming a single witch?

"And what happens once all the souls of your enemies have been consumed, the hunters and the Sightless alike?" I asked. "Witches will be the only ones left. What's to stop the Soul-Eater from turning on you and all those you mean to protect?"

"The beast will have served its purpose by then, at which point I'll return it to its slumber. Until then, I'll use it to witchkind's advantage. It's time we step into the roles we were always meant to assume in this world. It's a future I've seen in my dreams many a time. It's one I now intend on working toward."

A future he'd seen. Something occurred to me suddenly.

"Alison implied the Reaper was the same person who'd cast the curse on her."

Jack's head whipped in Seamus's direction. "You didn't."

Seamus didn't respond at first, as if weighing his words. "It was for her own safety."

Connor's grip on the drop gate tightened so much I thought he might actually crush the bars to dust. "You son of a b—"

"Her own safety?" Jack asked, incredulous.

"I knew she'd awakened from her state, hence my call while you were still at Serenity Falls. I love Alison very much, but once I chose my path, she was able to foresee its end, and I worried its severity would be enough to rouse her from her long-standing grief. I needed to silence her, but I would never harm my sister, so I made it so that she couldn't relay a message to those on the outside by placing a block on the truth, and I locked her inside her mind, at peace within her happiest memories."

"Happiest memories?" I said. "More like nightmares. Her mind's overrun with Wraiths." I knew Jack didn't want his brothers to know about that part, but Seamus needed to realize the hell he'd put Alison in. Nevermind the fact he'd rendered her catatonic.

Seamus frowned at that, knitting his brow. "No, that's impossible. I cast the spell myself."

"Then the dark magic you worked on her mind had an unexpected kickback."

"What about Grandda?" Jack asked then.

Seamus held his eyes for a long, tense moment before heaving a heavy sigh. "He was a great man, Jack, and he did a lot for me after I lost Neala and Bree. But he'd learned of my dealings in dark magic. Bless his soul, he swore to never speak a single word of it to The Council if I but sever my ties with the practice. I couldn't do that, nor could I let him go to the Elders. They would only take my powers away and force me into exile, thus preventing me from ever being able to save my wife and daughter. So I did what I had to do and sent the sluagh after him."

The truth hit Jack like a wave. He staggered back, shaking his head, unable to accept it.

"And when you realized we were looking for The Book of Fates," Connor said, "the one thing that could stop you, you slaughtered The Council before they could learn about it and try to help."

Seamus looked pained. "I assure you it was never my intention to bring harm to The Council. I had hoped to reason with them, to rally them against the hunters. But they have never advocated violence and wished to devise ways to simply protect our people further, to better hide them the way they've always done. When I learned you lot had found a way to stop the Reaping, I couldn't risk their learning of it and getting involved to ensure the success of your plan. They wouldn't dare lift a finger against The Black Hand, fearing the repercussions, but a wayward witch practicing dark magic? That they have no problem contending with. As such, I needed to remove them from the equation. I know I must look something of a monster to you lads. But is there anything you wouldn't do to save your own family?"

"I thought we were your family too," Jack said, as if from a daze.

Seamus frowned. "You are, of course. Which is why I wished to keep you out of the fray just as I wished the same for your mother. And so I beg you all to end your journey here. The road ahead is fraught with danger. There will be witches who resist what I'm trying to do, who will come against me, but when I absorb all the Masteries during the Reaping, I'll become the most powerful witch of us all, more powerful than even Jack. Unstoppable. The others will have no choice but to fall in line as

I lead the charge against the hunters and the Sightless. But my hope is they'll come to understand, that they'll learn to make peace with what had to be sacrificed to finally know freedom."

"You can't expect us to just sit back and watch while you sacrifice innocent souls to some demon," I said. "Especially when my dad's one of them, when Maurice is one of them."

Seamus studied me for a few moments. "I have to admit, I was concerned when you crossed paths with my nephews. Alison saw you coming, warned me you'd stand in my path. I feared everything I'd worked for would be destroyed. If anyone could stop me, it would've been you. But as you stood before me at Crowmarsh, answering my questions about your experience with magic, or lack thereof, it was clear you posed no threat whatsoever, that you had no idea what you even were."

Kai's words suddenly came to me. *You have no idea what you are, do you?* I hadn't given the statement much thought, but now it throbbed between my temples. "What are you talking about?"

"Isn't it obvious?"

"Clearly it's not," Connor spat. "So why don't you spell it out for us?"

"She's one of the god-touched."

Jack and his brothers fell deadly silent, and one by one they turned to me, staring at me in utter disbelief.

"A Daughter of Brigid?" Jack intoned, as if speaking the words of a prayer.

I had to grab the bars of the drop gate tighter to keep myself standing. "*What*?" Seamus had to be mistaken, or maybe I'd simply misheard. Brigid's hand-selected elite were warrior witches according to Jack.

"Why do you think you felt compelled to rush to Jack's defense at the rugby game? He was a witch in harm's way, and as is your solemn calling, you were driven to protect him at all costs. Nevermind the Echo that appeared to you at the menhirs, showing you your destiny. You, Scarlet, are the bird of rare feather Jack couldn't help but go on about, the one who was meant to arrive and lead the way. There hasn't been a Daughter since The Burning Times until you were chosen by the goddess. A rarity indeed.

"I tried to convince Jack the message meant nothing, of course, that your arrival was merely a coincidence. But Jack, tireless believer that he is, wouldn't drop the matter. So my only other option was to keep you all imprisoned in Crowmarsh while I expedited my plans by going to The Council sooner than later."

I shook my head, unable to process the words. "That's im—"

"Impossible? I assure you it's not. Though why the goddess would choose you, an ordinary girl who hasn't yet fully come into her magic, is anyone's guess. All the more indication to me that the path I've carved for our people is what's meant for us right now. In light of that, I can't have the five of you trying to interfere with my plans again. You'll remain here until after I've performed the Reaping, at which point we can discuss the roles you'll play at my side moving forward. For now, I'll appoint a demon to tend to your needs over the coming days."

Connor's glare was filled with vitriol. "One demon isn't going to hold us back."

"Oh, I think otherwise," Seamus said. "You see, I've prepared for every eventuality. That said, Lucas, I'm very sorry about this."

"Sorry about wh—?"

He didn't get to finish his sentence. Seamus produced the crossbow from Zoe's backpack and launched an arrow straight into Lucas's chest.

38

Jack rushed to his fallen brother, dropping to his knees at Lucas's side. "Lucas!"

Lucas fell into a coughing fit, clawing at the front of his shirt. The sight of the arrow protruding from his chest made my stomach turn over. Retreating footsteps echoed down the catacombs. Seamus had already fled the scene.

Jack angled his brother's head up as the younger continued coughing. Lucas's face grew chalk white within seconds, and before Jack could get another word out, his eyes rolled to the back of his head. He was out cold.

"Lucas!"

Rory was beside Jack. His long, deft fingers made quick but gentle work of tearing Lucas's shirt from the point of entry outward to get a better look. "It's not a fatal wound," he said. "But..." He furrowed his brow, examining a clear, slimy residue on his fingertips that he'd collected from Lucas's wound. It was speckled with black. He sniffed it.

"But what?" Jack prompted.

"Seamus put something on the arrowhead. I'm not sure what it is. I've never seen anything like it."

Connor was striding back and forth, cursing under his breath. "So he goes on about not wanting to harm us, and then he attempts to kill our brother right before our eyes?"

"If he meant to kill Lucas," I said, "why not aim for his heart?" Not that I in any way wanted to defend Seamus, but he could've easily taken us all out in an instant if he'd really wanted to.

"He obviously missed."

"No," Jack said after a moment of thought. "His aim was deliberate. Whatever the arrowhead was treated with, it was only meant to incapacitate Lucas, presumably for the full length of our stay here."

"What makes you say that?" Connor asked

"Because, as far as Seamus knows, Lucas is the only Wayfarer among us."

There was a long pause as we all let that settle in. "And therefore he's the only one who could've gotten us out of here," I finished. "Seamus doesn't know about you?"

"That particular Mastery emerged while he was studying with The Council. By the time he returned, so many others had emerged that it fell to the bottom of the pile in terms of significance. I don't think I ever mentioned it to him. We have to get Lucas to a Healer as soon as possible."

"Is there one nearby?"

"There's one in Rosalyn Bay, but we'll have to drive there. I can only wayfare with one other person at a time."

"Can't you just bring us one by one then?" I asked.

"Crossing that much of a distance, basically the entire width of the country, would exude too much magic, as would the multiple trips back and forth. I would only attract demons. And they're the last thing we need to deal with right now. Rory, let's err on the side of caution. Go ahead and bind yourself to Lucas in case he unexpectedly takes a turn for the worse. Afterward,

I'll bring us all above level to the abbey one at a time so we can get Zoe. Then we'll head to Rosalyn Bay."

It was a four-hour journey from Dublin to Rosalyn Bay. By the time we arrived, the golden arch of the sun was just starting to peek over the horizon, endless fields glowing in soft hues of yellow. It had been a tense drive, and for once, Jack didn't have the radio on, so instead of riding to the crooning of Jerry Lee Lewis and Chuck Berry, we were contained in a vacuum of silence, each of us no doubt still reeling from Seamus's betrayal.

I kept playing his words over and over again in my mind. *You were chosen by the goddess.* I still wanted to believe there'd been a mistake, but what reason would Seamus have to lie? Alison had foreseen it, Jack and I had crossed paths just as we were meant to, and trying to protect him against the demon at the rugby game had called forth a spark of my magic. But even if it were all true, what exactly was I supposed to do? How could I possibly stop someone like Seamus?

I glanced over my shoulder. Rory sat beside a still unconscious Lucas in the furthest row. In front of them, Connor and Zoe sat angled away from each other. I tried not to stare too much at Connor's slightly sore nose. When he'd cast the spell to awaken Zoe from her magically induced sleep, she'd punched him square in the face, thinking she was still being held captive by Seamus.

I was surprised when Jack guided the SUV onto St. Andrew's property, parking behind the school's chapel. The campus was still in the throes of early morning, its students not yet having stirred to begin a new school day. Even if there'd been boys out and about in their uniforms, though, I knew the place still would've felt foreign to me. Too much had happened since my last time here. I'd changed. It was like trying to squeeze a foot into a wrong size shoe.

Rory and I followed Jack into the chapel. The place was heavy with the aroma of incense. We passed rows of stained glass windows, which branded jewel-toned prisms onto my arms, and made our way down the nave and past the altar until we reached a room in the back. Jack opened the door without knocking, and we filed in behind him.

We found Father Nolan inside, polishing gold communion bread plates. He started when he noticed us. "Jack! Mother above, you put the heart crossways in me." He pressed a palm to his chest to steady his breathing. "Where have you lads been? I feared the worst. I've tried to get in touch with you repeatedly."

"I'm sorry, Father. The past days have been something of a whirlwind to say the least. I'll tell you all about it, but first, we need some kind of antidote for Lucas." He produced a cloth from his pocket and unfolded it to reveal the arrowhead. It was a simple bullet point shape, ending in a slight dome. Its shape had made it easy to pull it out of Lucas's chest, as opposed to the damage a wide broadhead would've done. "It's coated with some strange substance."

Father Nolan took the arrowhead, holding it an inch from his glasses to better examine it. "Demon venom," he replied almost immediately. He handed it back to Jack and strode to a space on the floor covered by a thick, Oriental rug. He rolled up the rug, motes of dust ascending into the air. There was a trap door beneath. He heaved the door open by an iron handle, its tired hinges whining in a screech that was like nails on a chalkboard. Then he nodded to us. "Let's get to it, shall we?"

We descended into a windowless cellar that smelled like herbs and spices. The stone walls were lined with dozens upon dozens of shelves, each one boasting glass bottles, jars, and vials of every shape and size. Their yellowing labels bore spidery, ancient script that was barely legible, but for the most part, it was easy to get a general idea of what was inside. Some were filled with seeds, some with leaves, some with grounds. And then there were odder things, things that made my stomach sour. Small bones, for instance. And preserved specimens like frogs in one case and what seemed to be rat tails in another.

Pressing my hand to my mouth, I pulled my eyes away from the sight. In a corner, planters filled with herbs were set under lightbulbs. There was a weathered table at the center of the room with candles upon it, their stands dripping with wax. With a snap of Father Nolan's fingers, the candle wicks roared to life with dancing flames.

I blinked. "You're a...?" I couldn't get the word out. For some reason, I was afraid of offending him, given that he was a man of the cloth. I'd simply assumed his knowledge of demons hailed from his line of work.

He only smiled in that warm, grandfatherly way of his. "I am, yes. And healing is my Mastery."

"But you're a priest," I said, my eyes dropping to his clerical collar.

"I don't believe the two have to be mutually exclusive," he said. "These days, a witch can practice the Ancient Path and still follow whatever religion they choose—or no religion at all! You'd be surprised by how eclectic a witch's personal practice can be, and by how interwoven several belief systems truly are. The early churches in Ireland, for instance, adopted many Celtic customs and symbols into their traditions. I'm of the mind we'd do better by each other if we focused more on what unites us as opposed to what divides us."

He grabbed a mortar and pestle, setting it upon the table beside a black-handled knife with Ogham runes carved into its hilt.

"An athamé," Jack said beside me. "It's a double-edged dagger used in ceremonies and spellcraft."

Father Nolan went about the room, collecting bottles from the shelves and calling out herbs to Rory, who gently tore off leaves from the miniature garden across the way. As they did this, Jack explained everything that had happened since his initial return to St. Andrew's, from the demon's visit at the rugby game to Seamus's shocking act of treason against them. At the mention of my being a Daughter of Brigid, the priest paused, his eyes nearly doubling in size as he took me in.

"I should've guessed it sooner," Jack had said. "It was right in front of us all this time. I wrongly assumed the Echo was simply showing Scarlet that she was a witch like us, and I thought her rarity was a nod to The Lost Clan. I hadn't even considered the possibility of her being a Daughter, as there hasn't been one chosen in ages."

By the time Jack was finished, Father Nolan was already combining all the ingredients into the mortar and crushing them, adding liquid from a flask until the mixture became a thick, sticky poultice. The smell of mint and freshly cut grass wafted through the air.

Father Nolan then took the athamé, easily slicing the blade across his palm. I winced, but the elderly man didn't seem the slightest bit bothered by the wound. He clenched his fist over the mortar and allowed several drops of his blood to splatter onto the wet healing paste. "The blood of a Healer is the final ingredient," he explained to me before tying a cloth around his hand. "Rory, continue mixing that for me, won't you? Just a few stirs and then you can take it out to Lucas straightaway. That should rouse him in no time, though it'll take a few days for the venom to fully leave his system."

"Thank you, Father," Jack said, watching as Rory finished with the mixture and hurried back upstairs to tend to Lucas.

"Of course, Jack. You know I'm always here for you lads. I can hardly believe what's become of your uncle. It doesn't seem like Seamus at all."

"There's something I still don't understand," I said. "If Seamus is taking the Mastery from each soul for himself, why would the Soul-Eater still be interested in the soul? Wouldn't it be magic-less at that point?"

Jack shook his head. "A witch's entire soul is made up of magic. Your Mastery is only one part of your soul, much in the way your organs are each only one part of your human body. As long as the Soul-Eater has magic-filled souls to consume, it wouldn't care less that Seamus has already taken out the Masteries."

"You must stop Seamus from himself, Jack," Father Nolan said.

"How can I? The Book of Fates is gone now."

"Nevermind The Book of Fates. There's yet hope when a Daughter of Brigid is at your side." Father Nolan turned to me, his eyes filled with reverence as if he couldn't believe such an entity stood before him in the flesh, as if I were a saint materialized from one of his very prayers.

My face heated. "I'm not sure how much help I can be. I'm not exactly warrior material."

"Nonsense," Father Nolan said. "What makes you think the first Daughter was chosen because she was battle-ready? The goddess came to her because of her heart, her courage, her desire to not see her clan fall into the hands of its enemies. The annals of history called her mighty, fierce. But at the end of the day, she was an ordinary girl just like you. The only difference is that when the goddess called her forth, she willingly accepted the summons. You may not have come into your magic yet, but with a Hallowstone in your hand, the trademark weapon of a Daughter, you would be quite the force to contend with."

"But no one knows what became of the Hallowstones," I said. "And I thought some witches nowadays wrote them off as the stuff of legends anyway."

"Oh, I assure you they were never mere legend," Father Nolan said.

"How can you be so sure?"

He smiled, a twinkle in his eyes. "Because I happen to have one in my possession."

39

Rosalyn Bay's coast was eerily vacant. I blamed the sky, which, despite showcasing a gorgeous sunrise earlier, was now quickly becoming the color of gunpowder, stamping out all traces of light so that it looked like evening. Fishing vessels bobbled from side to side in the jerky waters, and seagulls circled the air in lazy hoops, letting out angry squawks at the lack of fishing crews and fresh catches. The familiar briny smell of salt water filled the air, and the ocean waves pounded against the shores with dangerous, white claws in an unrelenting assault. I thought about Liam, who probably would've loved to surf in this weather.

Father Nolan, Jack, and I ascended the red-and-white striped lighthouse atop the bluff at the far end of the beach. It was hard to believe I'd been in this very spot recently, hoping to catch a glimpse of migrating humpback whales. Now I was hoping to happen upon something entirely different.

"Although there are those who would have the clans believe the stones were never more than legend," Father Nolan said, who, despite his age, easily made do with the lighthouse's steep, interior steps which coiled round and round like a snail shell, "it's only because the stones have been swathed in secrecy for centuries now. After what happened with Celeste, who'd stolen the Hallowstones from each clan so that no one could stand against her, the Elders came together and decided it best no witch should ever become that powerful again. This was the reason they established their temple Elsewhere, hiding away the Forbidden Spells along with other texts that could become dangerous in the hands of the wrong witch."

I thought about the summoning sigils Seamus had found. The Elders probably would've never expected their most prized pupil to go dark, to turn on them.

"The Hallowstones were never lost, however. The Elders had simply recovered them in secret. And given their great power, it was decided the Hallowstones should be sealed away until such a time as they were needed again. So the Elders clandestinely appointed a trusted individual from each clan to become a Keeper, someone who would guard their given stone with their life. The Keepers spread to different parts of the world, and as time passed, their descendants took up the role, and their descendants after them, and so on up through the present day."

We finally made it to the top of the lighthouse. The door to the observation deck had been left open, and fierce, icy winds tore into the circular room with a shriek. My hair whipped all about my face, and I secured it back into a tight ponytail as Jack closed the door.

"Do you know where the other six stones are?" Jack asked.

The priest shook his head. "Every Keeper maintains the secrecy of his stone's location, even against other Keepers. It's the only way we can protect the stones from evil. And when The Lost Clan disappeared, their Hallowstone disappeared with them unfortunately."

He strode to the center of the room, where the large block of stone sat with the plaque embedded into its face, the one I'd touched during my last visit. "If you're no longer able to bind Seamus before he performs the Reaping, then you have no choice but to fight him. Scarlet, if you would." He gestured for me to stand before the menhir fragment. "The Keepers each bound their stone by magic so that only a Daughter of Brigid could call it forth and wield it. Meaning, as the only known Daughter among all the clans, you're the only one in existence who can summon any of the Hallowstones."

The words were a weight on my chest, the pressure building in me like the humidity before a storm. Even though I didn't know how I could possibly tip the scale against Seamus, I couldn't help the feverish warmth that rushed over me in budding anticipation. My skin was sleeved with gooseflesh, and my stomach shivered in a sensation like looking down from great, dizzying heights.

The only one in existence. A bird of rare feather indeed. I'd thought the only part I was meant to play was navigating Alison's memories. I could've never anticipated a destiny of this measure. But if this was the role destined for me, then I already knew I would embrace it. There was no turning back now.

"How do I summon it?" I asked.

"This particular Hallowstone is buried deep in the center of the menhir before us." He directed me to hold my hands over the menhir and concentrate on the power nested inside like a pulsating heart. It wasn't lost on me that I'd sensed an unmistakable energy buzzing from the block the last time I was here. Was I sensing the Hallowstone even then, my magic yearning for the weapon I was meant to wield?

Outside, the wind howled, distant thunder beginning to rumble. The crash and hiss of the ocean waves clamored for attention, as if not wishing to be outdone by the skies. In response, the old bones of the lighthouse shuddered against the storm winds.

"Not to worry," Father Nolan said with a smile, rapping his knuckles against the walls of the room. "This lighthouse has withstood centuries' worth of storms. It'll most assuredly weather another."

I closed my eyes tight and focused on the menhir, my hands splayed out inches from its face, just above the triskele carved there. I didn't know what the Hallowstone looked like, only that it'd been a part of a star once, one that had presumably solidified into a usable weapon when plucked from the heavens by Brigid. I pictured an orb of light nesting inside the menhir, a core of white that glowed brighter and brighter as if I were slowly turning a dimmer dial.

Come to me, I whispered to the Hallowstone. I imagined threads of magic extending from my fingertips to the menhir. I saw those threads pierce the rocky flesh of the menhir and dive into its depths like sharp needles, burrowing deep, deep, deep until they found the Hallowstone at the center. They quickly wove themselves into a net around the Hallowstone and pulled.

The Hallowstone resisted.

Come on, come on, come on, I urged. I pulled harder with the threads of energy, my face scrunching up with concentration.

The Hallowstone didn't budge.

I tried to charm it, persuade it, demand it to help. It didn't respond to me at all. I barely felt a pulse of life from it, or a flicker of acknowledgement.

Bordering on frustration, the threads transformed into talons, and I clawed at the rock around the Hallowstone to free it by force like harvesting a pearl from an oyster. The Hallowstone's resistance intensified and met me measure for measure, steeling itself against my charge.

"Scarlet, stop."

Jack's voice yanked me out of my mind, startling me as if I'd been suddenly woken from a dream. I blinked furiously, my head swimming as the room came back into focus. I staggered back, but Jack was there to catch me before I could sink boneless to the ground. His grip was firm on my elbows, and I leaned against his solid form, surprised by my exhaustion.

A warm drop slid over my upper lip. I touched it, and when I pulled back my hand, there was blood on my fingertips. I'd overexerted myself again.

"Maybe if she channeled power from me," Jack offered, looking to Father Nolan.

The priest shook his head solemnly. "I'm afraid it won't work. The Hallowstone would sense the magic is coming from another. She must do it herself."

"It fought me," I said, trying to right myself even as the dizziness made my head feel like a boat on stormy waters. "Why would it do that? I thought you said I was the only one who could call it forth."

"It's testing you," Father Nolan said. "The Allhallow was one of the most powerful weapons ever given to a witch by a god. The Hallowstone must ensure you're worthy of it. You must show it your true mettle."

I was still lightheaded, but I stepped forward for a second attempt. The Hallowstone wanted me to prove I was strong enough? I would do just that. This time, I thought about the Echo I'd seen during the school field trip. The image of a warrior witch filled my mind, and I channeled her ferocity. I summoned those talons again, and I raked at the menhir like an animal. *You're mine to wield,* I told the Hallowstone, *and I'm not leaving here without you.* I clawed and clawed and clawed, but it was as if the Hallowstone receded with every inch of progress I made, burrowing itself deeper into the menhir. I would've lost myself to the hunt completely had it not been for the strong hands that grabbed my shoulders and pulled me back.

I recovered quicker than last time, though the headache still throbbed at my temples. I swiped at the space under my nose with the hem of my cardigan sleeve, already knowing there'd be fresh blood there. I'd approached the Hallowstone like an animal, and now I probably looked like one too.

"Is there something specific she's supposed to do to unlock the spell?" Jack asked Father Nolan, his arm still around me.

"She must only lay bare the truth of who she is."

"But I'm doing that," I said. "It's not working. It keeps struggling against me." It wasn't until I uttered the words that I noticed the irritation burgeoning in my chest. What did it mean that the Hallowstone wouldn't emerge for me? What if Alison had been wrong? What if all we were doing here was wasting our time?

"Scarlet," Father Nolan said, taking my hands in his own. His palms were wrinkled and leathery and warm. "You were born for this. You are strong enough. You must simply believe that you are."

I looked to Jack, who nodded. "There's a reason you came to Rosalyn Bay, Scarlet. From the first moment our worlds collided, I knew there was something different about you, something extraordinary. You've proven that every step of the way since. If there's anyone who can change the tides now, it would be you. Reach down into the deepest parts of who you are, and trust in your magic."

His words glowed in my chest like a flame in the dark, flooding my ribcage with warmth. I looked back to the menhir. When I approached it this time, I did so slowly, admiring it for the simple fact it had stood the test of time. It hailed from an age long ago, a simpler time before the persecution of its people. It was like a mirror into that world, connecting me with the past.

I placed my hands against its jagged exterior, my fingers resting upon the spirals of the triskele. Then I closed my eyes and steadied my breathing, directing my thoughts to the structure and pinning them in place, ignoring the wailing winds and pounding thunder from outside. *Focus.* I breathed in, I breathed out. In, out, in, out. With every inhale, I imagined myself breathing in the magic of the menhir. With every exhale, I rid myself of doubts and cleared my mind. In that moment, I remembered something Jack had said at Iveagh Gardens about the four Quarters.

As a witch, it's a power you have the privilege of calling upon. That doesn't mean you're the master over it, though. Druids venerated nature and lived in balance with it. When you summon the Quarters, you do so with respect, acknowledging the divinity in them just as they acknowledge the divinity in you.

My heart fell. What a fool I'd been. In my quest to claim the Hallowstone as my own, through all my demands for it to come forth, I'd completely forsaken humility. I'd thought to lord it over the Hallowstone, and it had resisted me, perhaps alarmed by my pride. Father Nolan had said the first Daughter had been chosen because of her heart, not because of any sense of entitlement, not because of a thirst for power.

I quelled the tempest of shame that spiked within me and bowed my head, my hands still on the menhir.

Forgive me, I supplicated.

And then I unwound my soul before the Hallowstone. I showed it what I'd lost in Colorado, those last days when I'd sat beside my mom's hospital bed as she steadily lost her battle, the friends and home I'd left behind. I showed it my arrival in Rosalyn Bay, how I'd felt so foreign, so disconnected, so out of place. I showed it my desire to leave, and then the unlikely afternoon when I'd happened upon Jack and the demon, changing everything. I showed it all that had transpired since then, and what we stood to lose if I was unable to fulfill my purpose.

So you see? I need you. We need you. Then directing my thoughts to Brigid, I spoke to the goddess herself. *I don't know your reasoning, but if you believe me worthy, then I'll humbly answer the summons. I'll be your warrior. I'll be your chosen vessel in the fight that awaits us.*

A Daughter of Brigid. My heart beat faster, a heat wave consuming me, the last of my doubt disintegrating into ash as my eagerness and determination built. I saw myself then, as the most recent in a long line of god-touched soldiers imbued with the strength of the goddess. I was meant to take my place among them. I was meant to take up the mantle and continue the sacred lineage.

It didn't matter if I was hardly qualified, and it didn't matter that I hadn't yet fully come into my magic. All that mattered was whether or not I was willing to fight the battle ahead.

I was.

Thank you for choosing me. I'm here now, and I'm ready.

My palms heated up as if I held them before the roaring flames of a bonfire. Something danced in my chest, expanding like a blooming flower. The heat intensified, surging to my neck, my face, the top of my head.

Thank you for choosing me, I said again. *Thank you, thank you, thank you.*

The heat was an inferno between my ribs. I might've thought I'd caught on fire, but the burning didn't hurt. If anything, the sensation was euphoric. There was a rush through me from head to toe, as if a dam had burst open, letting through a flood of magic, and I was caught in the rapids. But I wasn't drowning in them. I was riding them, and the power crested, shooting from my heart, down my arms, out my fingertips.

Crack.

The sound was a low, guttural baritone, the sound of rocks grating against each other. My eyes snapped open as another crack filled the air, and then another and another and another. The menhir was covered in fissures like a veined living thing, and out of each crevice, radiant light glowed and poured out. The cracks continued racing all across the menhir's surface until it was fragmented into dozens of smaller pieces, the light becoming even brighter, like glimmers of a high noon sun.

The menhir trembled, rumbled. The entire room shook with it. I took a step back, but my eyes were riveted to the menhir. Without warning, it exploded, the jagged pieces shooting outward and then pausing in their trajectory and spinning in place. A brilliant light shot up from the center of the menhir like a beacon, the room aglow with white. Amidst all the misshapen menhir chunks, one stone rose within the beam of brightness, flinging prisms of glimmering light against the walls as it slowly rotated.

The Hallowstone.

When it was at eye level, I held out a hand, my breath caught in my throat, my lungs clenched in anticipation. The Hallowstone floated to me. It hovered above my open hand for a heartbeat. Maybe two. Then it gently came to rest upon my palm, entrusting itself to me. When it made contact with my skin, the heat inside me spun like a cyclone before detonating in a starburst of magic that sent tingles up and down my arms.

The Hallowstone was as hot as if it'd sat in the sun all day. I marveled at it. It wasn't perfectly spherical or polished as I'd imagined. It had edges and facets and a cluster of crystal points on one end. It was slightly cloudy in some parts, the way a block of ice would be, with fractures and fissures, and though it looked completely harmless, I could sense the great energy radiating from its core. A soft light pulsed from within the Hallowstone in time with my heart.

"My word," Father Nolan breathed, coming close to me.

"You did it," Jack said from my other side, his voice hushed, as if the lighthouse had been transformed into a temple. "I knew you could."

I couldn't stop looking at the Hallowstone. I could hardly believe I was now holding one of witch-kind's holiest relics. *Thank you*, I sang to Brigid, to the Hallowstone. *Thank you.*

"This will stop the Reaping?" I asked Father Nolan, finally finding my voice.

"It would be enough to stop just about any force of evil," the priest said, nodding. Like me, he found himself incapable of peeling his eyes away from the Hallowstone. "But you must consecrate and charge it first so that its magic fully awakens, at which point it'll become bound to you. From then on, it'll be an unconquerable weapon in your hands and remain that way so long as you remain worthy of it."

I smoothed my thumb across one of the Hallowstone's facets. Its power already radiated through me, a pulse in the center of my palm beating a steady rhythm in response to that power. If this is how it acted when its magic was still asleep, I couldn't begin to imagine what it'd be like when its magic was stirred.

I met Jack's eyes. "Whatever we need to do, I'm ready."

He held my gaze for a long moment before nodding. "Then it's time we perform the most important ritual of our lives."

40

At night, the menhirs of Rosalyn Bay were especially terrifying, an army of unmoving stone giants watching our every move. It had been three days since Father Nolan had led us to the Hallowstone. During that time, the star fragment had been buried in the earth here to cleanse it of its past energies.

"Magical objects are like sponges," Jack had said. "They tend to absorb the various bits of energy surrounding them. Before you can work with them, you have to wipe the slate clean, so to speak, and attune the object with your own energy and goals."

Once we'd excavated the Hallowstone, we took it to the ocean, washing it in the salt water to purify it. Afterward, Jack had passed the Hallowstone back and forth through the smoke trailing upward from a smudging stick, the aroma of burnt herbs and flowers heady. Now we were back at the menhirs, where we would consecrate the Hallowstone and charge it. Seeing as how it was the spot where the very first Daughter had been selected by Brigid, the Connellys decided there was no better place to call upon the goddess for her help. I watched the others set up for the ritual, apprehension coiling up in me like a ball of yarn.

Rory drew one of his sigils upon a large, wooden board we'd

brought with us. The sigil was filled with symbols I'd never seen before along with those I had: Ogham runes, phases of the moon, and triple spirals. In fact, triple spirals were everywhere. Father Nolan had said the triskele was representative of Brigid as The Triple Goddess. And to think, I'd drawn the symbol all my life, never once guessing its significance. Had something in me known all along who I truly was, who I was meant to become?

As Rory drew, Lucas set out countless white candles along the edges of the sigil, moving slowly and occasionally wiping away beads of sweat from his pale face with the back of his wrist. Father Nolan's antidote had revived him, but he hadn't yet made a full recovery. The surest indication of his still being ill was in his silence. Gone were the jokes and teasing, the egging Connor on. I hadn't seen him take out his playing cards once these past days, and I was starting to miss his nickname for me. Scarlet Ibis.

A bird of rare feather will arrive and lead the way.

Another knot in my stomach pulled tight. I approached Jack, who was arranging tools upon an altar which would be situated at the sigil's center once Rory was done. Before him were bowls of flower petals and herbs, a gold chalice with incredible detailing, vials like the ones I'd seen in Father Nolan's underground cellar, and an athamé as well. My heart trembled as I considered how the dagger would be used tonight.

"We're almost ready," Jack said once I was close enough. In the moonlight, he looked every bit a phantom, the circles under his eyes darker than usual. No doubt the result of Seamus's betrayal. I couldn't imagine the heartbreak it had caused in Jack. He'd withdrawn into himself these past days, disappearing once or twice without a word, his mind surely a storm of thoughts. If there was one thing I knew, though, it was that he, as always, was blaming himself for it all. Each time I tried to talk to him about it, I didn't get very far, until the morning we went to wash the Hallowstone in the ocean.

"What happened with Seamus isn't your fault," I'd said to him as we lagged behind the others.

Jack buried his hands into the deep pockets of the coat he'd recovered from his dorm room at St. Andrew's. It was the identical twin to the one he'd lost to the hunters. He looked complete with it. "We should've been there for him more. This isn't who Seamus is. He's a good man, Scarlet. He filled a void in our lives at a time when we'd lost so much. His grief over losing Neala and Bree undid him in ways I hadn't realized."

"I know how much he means to you," I said, trekking across the grooves in the sand, the ocean tide's rise and fall like the gentle rhythms of a lullaby. "But taking away other people's loved ones just to resurrect his own? And intending to use them as a sacrifice to stir a demon he'll wield as a weapon against hunters and the Sightless alike?"

"Unforgivable," Jack said, tipping his head back slightly to stare at the stars still glimmering in the sapphire and blush, predawn skies. "His desire for revenge made him lose his way, and he let his anger consume him. He's done evil things, yes. Terrible things. Monstrous things. But does that make him irredeemable?"

Didn't it? Connor had easily made his mind up about Seamus. Zoe as well. For them, a trust once betrayed was apparently never gained again. I couldn't say I disagreed with them. The things people were willing to do gave you a good indication of their character. The Black Hand, for instance, committed unspeakable acts against witches. That definitely made them irredeemable in my eyes. Of course, with that line of thought, Seamus's plan to destroy every last one of them should've been something I easily bought into. It's just that hunting them down the way they did us—*killing* them the way they did us—made us no better than them. Was that really the story we wanted to write for ourselves, the one we wanted to pass on to future generations of witches? That to defeat our enemy, we became just like them?

Then again, I knew the situation with Seamus wasn't black and white for Jack. It never could be. Because though Seamus had betrayed his people and spilled innocent blood, he was also the man who'd taken Jack and his brothers in, who'd tried to be a father to them, who'd tried to protect them even from his own maniacal plan. How did one go about reconciling two completely different versions of the same person? I could see why Jack was conflicted. I stopped and turned to face him. "I know it'll be hard for you to confront Seamus when the time comes. Right now, I wish more than anything that the Reaper could've been anyone else."

"I appreciate that," Jack said, his eyes still trained on the stars. He let go of a breath that was so long, it was as if he'd emptied his entire body of air. "When we face him on Samhain, I won't hesitate to stop him, despite how difficult I know it'll be. It's only that this whole situation shows it's easier to lose ourselves to the darker side of magic than most of us think. We want to believe ourselves immune. We want to believe we would never do wrong. But who knows what we'd be capable of if our mind was no longer our own?"

I thought about the surge of power I'd felt when facing off against Mary-Anne and the other hunters, how for the briefest moment, yes, I'd wanted to strike fear in them, to hurt them just a little bit. How far would I have gone had Kai not intervened and sent the hunters away, especially when Mary-Anne had been so intent on ending me? Shuddering, I pushed the image to the side, and we'd spoken no more of it since then.

Now, as the boys finished preparing for the ritual, I couldn't help but wonder what it would feel like to have a goddess, not a demon, imbue me with her strength.

"Will I still be myself?" I asked Jack at the altar.

He understood my meaning immediately. "Absolutely," he said, putting down the chalice and focusing his full attention on me. "Brigid isn't going to possess you and deprive you of your free will. You'll still be in full control. She's only lending you her power, her divinity. You'll channel energy from her, much like what you've already done with me. Think of yourself as a conduit through which she's able to work." He placed a hand on my arm. "There's no reason to be afraid."

"Surprisingly, I'm not as afraid as I thought I'd be at this point. More like restless to get the ritual over and done with." I knew a lot of that had to do with yesterday's visit to the hospital where my dad was being treated. Despite what I'd last been told about his condition, I still hadn't been prepared to see his gaunt frame, his pallid complexion, or the graying hair that had previously been as brown as mine. He was like a withered shell of a person, and that shell wasn't going to last much longer without its soul. The doctors expected the end any day now.

I looked over the altar, the sigil beyond, the candles outlining it. "Will all this be enough to summon her?" I hadn't been raised on a religious upbringing. I'd joined Natalie's family for mass a handful of times, but I didn't know very much about how deities normally communed with their parishioners. A part of me was still trying to accept that a pantheon of gods existed at all somewhere out there.

"You're her chosen warrior," Jack said. "Even if she finds me unworthy to do so much as cast the circle that summons her, there's no reason she wouldn't appear to one of her own."

I wanted to ask why he'd ever think himself unworthy of a god's attention, but twigs snapped underfoot to my left, signaling somebody's arrival. Two somebodies. Connor and Zoe.

They'd patrolled the immediate vicinity to ensure we were in the clear where it concerned the sluagh and The Black Hand. We couldn't afford to have a ritual as important as this one be interrupted.

"We're good," Connor said, nodding to Jack.

By this point, Rory had finally finished his masterpiece of a sigil and was standing back, admiring his handiwork. With a snap of his fingers, Lucas illuminated the dozens of candles he'd set out, and the flames threw dancing shadows against the giant menhirs.

"Then let's begin," said Jack.

41

The six of us stood inside the sigil, spread out in a circle, the heels of our bare feet flush with the ebony edges drawn with charcoal. The warmth from the flickering candles seeped into my bones, and I welcomed their hot glow against my skin. In the dark, our faces, lit up as they were in the candlelight, seemed to float apart from our bodies. We all wore long, black robes, the hems of which were embroidered with gold triple spirals.

Jack's solemn voice cut into the silence like a knife.

> *"Darksome night and shining moon,*
> *East, then South, then West, then North;*
> *Hearken to the Witches' Rune--*
> *Here come we to call ye forth!*
> *Earth and water, air and fire,*
> *Wand and pentacle and sword,*
> *Work ye unto our desire,*
> *Hearken ye unto our word!"*

He nodded to Lucas, who lifted his palms skyward and intoned, "Hail to the East, Powers of Air. I do summon, stir, and call you up to witness our rites and guard this Circle." A rush of wind surged across the circle. The candle flames snapped, dancing wildly.

Connor followed after, mirroring his brother. "Hail to the South, Powers of Fire. I do summon, stir, and call you up to witness our rites and guard this Circle." The flames doubled in size, brightening like comet tails. The space instantly became several degrees hotter, as if we were in a sauna.

"Hail to the West, Powers of Water," came Jack's voice, eyes fastened to the night sky. "I do summon, stir, and call you up to witness our rites and guard this Circle." Instantly, thunder bellowed like the rumbling stomach of a hungry beast, and a downpour of rain charged down to earth, but an invisible barrier snapped into place above us and kept us dry.

Rory called upon the final Quarter. "Hail to the North, Powers of Earth. I do summon, stir, and call you up to witness our rites and guard this Circle." Leaves the color of cherries and apricots rattled on neighboring trees and then took flight in the wind, dancing around us like a living ribbon as the ground trembled slightly beneath the wooden board we stood upon.

I felt the exact moment when the circle was infused with magic. It was invigorating, bliss-filled. Invisible threads of magic reached out to me from the sigil's center, wrapping around me, pulling at me. I felt connected to the sigil but connected to the boys as well, to Zoe, as if we were all threads in a piece of string art.

"The circle is cast," Jack said. "The ritual is begun."

My heart struck against my ribs in hard, resounding beats that reverberated throughout my body. Though I'd seen the boys practice magic before, this was different somehow, perhaps because it was more ceremonial in nature. I couldn't take my eyes off Jack, who looked every bit a high priest in his black robe, his airs somber.

He approached the center of the sigil, where he'd set the altar. The Hallowstone waited for him there. He sprinkled the flower petals and herbs upon the table, creating a bed upon which he set the Hallowstone. Then he tipped one of the vials against his fingertip until a drop had emerged. He pressed the drop to the Hallowstone. He repeated this for the rest of the bottles, anointing the star fragment. Finally, he took the Hallowstone in his hands and lifted it above his head, as if presenting it to the gods.

> *"Cords and censer, scourge and knife,*
> *Powers of the witch's blade--*
> *Waken all ye into life,*
> *Come ye as the charm is made!*
> *Goddess, whom we humbly serve*
> *Grant ye now thy truth and light*
> *Lend your pow'r unto our work*
> *Grant our will by holy rite!"*

The thunder roared, lightning flashing like spears of bright light. The rain fell even harder now, thick sheets of water blinding us to our surroundings, but still the magic of the circle the boys had cast protected us from the elements.

Jack set the Hallowstone back upon its bed of herbs and flowers and looked across the circle at me. He nodded. My time had come.

Swallowing, I forced myself forward, the ends of my robe trailing against the wooden board in a hush. When I reached Jack, he gently took my right hand, turning it over so my palm faced the sky. Magic hummed from his fingertips like an electric current. Without meaning to, I opened myself up to his magic, drawing in what he sent me, and his energy fizzled throughout my hand like champagne bubbles.

Jack brushed his thumb across the center of my palm, and when I looked up, his hypnotic eyes bored into me, searching. "Are you sure about this?" His voice was a whisper, reserving the question for my ears only.

"I'm not afraid," I assured him, closing my fingers over his thumb for a brief moment. "I'm ready."

Jack held my eyes for a few seconds longer, as if giving me the opportunity to withdraw from the ritual if I still wished to. When he saw I had no intention of doing so, he reached for his athamé. It was quite possibly the most beautiful knife I'd ever seen. Its ornate hilt was made up of scrollwork, Celtic knots, and a carving of a dancing goddess. The crossguard of the hilt was in the shape of curling horns. As Jack handled the dagger, its long, silver blade glistened in the firelight.

He'd told me what would need to occur in order to consecrate and charge the Hallowstone. I pushed iron into my veins, willing myself not to flinch as he swiftly cut the blade across my palm. I hissed against the sting of the wound, a small river of red spilling out. Jack closed my fingers over my palm, encouraging me to make a fist over the chalice. Blood trickled down and pitter-pattered into the cup, which bore a triple moon insignia with a triskele in the center. When the chalice had collected enough drops of my blood, Jack quickly tied a cloth around my hand to staunch the flow.

He lifted the chalice above his head, his lips moving slightly as he once again petitioned the goddess. I watched breathlessly as he slowly tilted the chalice and let the blood fall upon the Hallowstone, staining it crimson.

Almost at once, the world around me bled away, and I was instantly transported to a place of muted colors. It was like being trapped inside a Polaroid picture that hadn't yet fully developed. The edges of this place were blurred, hazy at the seams like a dream. Apart from a breeze that tugged at the hems of my robe, the storm at large had stopped, and the complete absence of noise was jarring. As was the fact that though the menhirs remained, Jack, his brothers, and Zoe had completely vanished into thin air.

"Welcome, sister."

My heart went wild. I spun around, and the breath flew out of my lungs.

Before me was the warrior witch from the Echo I'd seen, the very first Daughter of Brigid. She looked exactly as she had in the vision. Stripes of war paint cut across her cheeks, and as she approached me, her necklace of animal teeth rattled against her breastplate. Up close, I realized how right Father Nolan had been. She couldn't be more than a few years older than me, though her eyes were brimming with the type of wisdom that made it seem like she'd existed since the beginning of time. She smiled at me, inclining her head in a surprising show of respect. She was there and not there at the same time, her bluish form transparent enough for me to see through.

"Welcome, sister." Another apparition joined us. She was older, her hair tied back in thick braids. She clasped her wrinkled hands before her heart and bowed her head to me.

"Welcome, sister."

"Welcome, sister."

"Welcome, sister."

I turned and turned and turned, and all around me, the spirits of women appeared until I was surrounded by a throng of them. They were all ages, all nationalities, from every imaginable time period, and the energy they exuded suffused my body until I was humming with their vibrancy, until I felt practically weightless.

Scenes began playing in the air above their heads. Echoes. Scores of them. Each showing the gathered women in the throes of battle, of persecution—conflicts that had spanned seemingly from the very dawn of humanity. There were inquisitions and trials, hunts and invasions, public executions and whole villages engulfed in flames. And in every instance, there was a Daughter, standing her ground, facing off against her oppressors, protecting her people—sometimes to victory and other times to her dying breath. There were women charging into battle astride heavy-muscled horses, Hallowstone in hand, the clash of swords ringing all around them. There were women rescuing imprisoned witches, leading them through dark and dank underground tunnels by the light of their star fragment. There were women arguing for their brethren in old-time courtrooms, women fending off attackers in small villages, and yes, women holding their heads high at the gallows as well.

I took it all in, my lungs clenching tight, warm tears gathering in the corners of my eyes. What I'd known of these dark periods in history came from brief textbook units in school and from what Jack had told me at Crowmarsh. To see it for myself, to have these moments in time stretch across the ages to reach me...it unraveled me piece by piece.

There has always been a need for my warriors, a voice spoke from inside my head.

A powerful brightness shone from behind me, and when I turned, I nearly staggered back from shock. Though I had never seen a rendering of her, I knew who she was instantly, something in my blood coming to life in her presence.

Brigid.

I fell to my knees in reverence, and though I bowed my head, I quickly lifted my eyes again, not wishing to look away from her. Because she was breathtaking, radiant. The beauty of the heavens personified. She was the first snowfall of winter, silent fields blanketed with endless white. She was spring in full bloom, butterflies and bees dancing from flower to flower in rainbow-colored gardens. She was every stained-glass window in churches the world over, every masterpiece painting hanging in museums, every love sonnet and shooting star and sunset.

In the back of my mind, I knew she hadn't really come down to earth. Jack had said she could only walk among us on her feast day. No, I'd been whisked away to some sort of place in between, a place where I could interact with the spirits of my sisters, a place where I could commune with gods.

A cloud of mist surrounded Brigid as she approached me. As she glided to me rather, every movement so effortless, so graceful. Though the colors of the world around her were subdued, everything about her was bright and vibrant and alive. She wore a gown of the deepest green, which complemented the glittering emeralds in her gold circlet. Her thick locks of hair trailed down her back in a river of vivid red. When I blinked, there were suddenly three versions of her, all identical save for what they held in their hands: one a harp, one a bouquet of flowers, and one a sword. The Triple Goddess of inspiration, healing, and smithcraft. I blinked again, and there was only the original Brigid before me now.

She regarded me tenderly, as a mother would a child. Though I was only now meeting her, I felt as if I'd known her my whole life, as if we'd always been connected. Her voice entered my mind again, warm and soothing. She held my eyes as she 'spoke,' her lips never moving. *Now, more than ever, the need for my warriors has grown. Long have my people called out to me, and tonight, I shall at long last answer. Thus I summon you forth, my Daughter. Will you heed the call?*

My heart beat double-time, pounding against my chest, but I knew what my answer would be. I'd known it before she'd even asked. "I will," I said, making my voice heard above the sudden gusts of wind.

Wisps of hair blew across Brigid's face, but she remained as still as ever, seeing only me. *And do you swear to always be worthy of the honor I bestow upon you on this most sacred of nights, to uphold the values and virtues befitting a Daughter, to always be a beacon of light even in the darkest of hours?*

"I swear it."

And do you vow to unfalteringly defend those who've been entrusted into your care, to put their lives before your own, to fearlessly protect the last and the least—even to your dying breath?

"I vow it."

The current of power surrounding me from the other Daughters intensified, the hairs on my arms rising. Brigid drew closer, pressing two fingertips to my forehead. The skin beneath burned under her touch, as if she were branding me.

Then, my precious child, she said, *with your dear sisters serving as witness, and under the watchful gaze of the stars in the glorious heavens, I claim you as my own.* Instantly, heat surged through my body until it felt like I might explode. *Go forth now, my warrior. Go forth and defend your people.*

In a blast of light, Brigid and the Daughters of old were gone. I was back with the others within our circle, kneeling before the altar. The striking color of the world had returned, as had the raging storm beyond our magical barrier. Everyone's eyes were on me, watching, waiting.

There was a strange sensation in my arms, a build-up of pressure. I turned them over, palms facing up, and gasped. A line of runes topped by a triskele trailed down each arm from my wrist to the inside of my elbow, glowing in a soft blue light before dimming out like the stars at dawn. I ran my fingertips over the skin, but there wasn't the slightest trace of the runes left behind.

"You've been Marked," Jack whispered, coming around to help me to my feet. "Brigid has officially claimed you as a Daughter." He reached back to grab the Hallowstone and extended it to me.

When I grabbed it, the pulsing light at the center was brighter than ever. Its energy shot out into my hand, intermingled with my own magic, bound itself to it.

"So what happens now?" Zoe asked.

Brigid's words stirred up in my chest, and I tightened my fingers around the Hallowstone. I looked at each of the others in turn, my eyes coming to rest on Jack last. "Now," I said, "we fight."

42

Hours before the start of Samhain, we sat around the dining table of a quaint, Georgian-style bed-and-breakfast in County Westmeath, the hosting couple having already left us for the day. As Samhain was a day of remembrance for witches, we'd lit candles for the dead. Now we sat in the glow of those candles, counting down the minutes until we confronted Seamus.

"The moon will reach the highest point in the sky at midnight," Jack had said earlier, "at which point, Samhain officially begins. Seamus will time the height of the ritual so that it coincides with the moment the veil between the natural world and the supernatural world begins to thin, meaning we'll have to stop him before then. Even the slightest delay can turn the tides in his favor."

Ideally, we would've stopped Seamus well in advance of midnight, but there was no way to know his present location, only where he planned to be. My eyes fell on the Hallowstone, set on the table in front of me. Ever since it'd bound itself to me during the ritual, I could feel its consciousness nested in my chest, as if it were a living thing. We were connected now, its pulse of light forever beating in time with my heart. I pushed threads of magic out toward it and wrapped them around it. The Hallowstone glowed brighter in response, acknowledging me, welcoming the embrace.

We'd made an experiment of it earlier to test the strength of the bond and strengthen it even further, with the boys hiding the Hallowstone in different parts of the bed-and-breakfast. I'd broadcast a signal to the Hallowstone, tuning in to its presence until I felt a tug. Then I'd follow the tug all the way to the Hallowstone's location. It was slow-coming at first, but as I became more and more familiar with the way the Hallowstone felt, I could find it within seconds.

I only hoped it would truly be enough to stop Seamus. I nudged my dinner—takeaway from a nearby fast food joint—to the side, my stomach too constricted to digest anything.

Lucas, sitting beside me, seemed to be of the same mind. He stared absently at the glossy bun of his burger, looking as if it were more likely to make him nauseous than sate his hunger. I worried he was not yet well enough to face Seamus tonight. He was still pale, his golden hair slightly damp and plastered to his forehead. I knew Father Nolan's antidote was working because Lucas at least wasn't sleeping as much as he had been lately, having now regained his strength, but he wasn't at one hundred percent either.

"Lucas, are you okay?" I asked softly, lowering my voice so the others wouldn't hear, though they were preoccupied enough with bringing up a map on Connor's phone.

Lucas blinked out of his daydream and looked over at me. He forced a smile that didn't reach his eyes. "Course."

"You know, I'm sure Jack and the others would understand if you wanted to sit this one out."

"What, and let them have all the fun?" He tried for another smile, but it was weak.

Nonetheless, I smiled back and put my hand atop his. "We'll be glad to have you there."

"Here it is," Jack said then, enlarging the map on Connor's phone and setting it on the table for everyone to see.

"Are we still absolutely sure The Hill of Uisneach is the place?" I asked.

"It has to be Uisneach," Jack said. "It's what makes the most sense. Ériu, the matron goddess, lies under the Cat Stone there. That's what we call the boulder on the southwest side of the hill."

"So named because some people believe it resembles the shape of a sitting cat," Zoe said. "I personally don't see it."

"It's also known as *Ail na Míreann,* Stone of the Divisions," Jack went on. "So named because it once marked the dividing point between the provinces of ancient Ireland. These days, however, it's most famous for marking Ériu's resting place, which in turns marks the hidden gateway to the Otherworld. Once the veil thins, Seamus will have more energy at his fingertips than any of us can imagine with such proximity to the Otherworld."

"Which is why I still think we need to contact the other clans and ask for their support," Zoe said. Today, she was wearing fingerless, leather gloves with silver studs on the knuckles. When she bracketed her hands on the back of a chair, the studs were more pronounced, and I couldn't help but picture her plowing them into the side of Seamus's face.

Jack shook his head. "No."

"No?" It was Connor who spoke. "She's right, Jack. Considering how far gone he is, we won't be able to reason with Seamus. And we can't place all our hopes on a Hallowstone that hasn't been wielded in centuries. We need reinforcements."

"At what expense? If we involve the other clans, they'll stop at nothing to bring Seamus down. Even if it means ending him."

"And?"

"Why should we care?" Zoe's grip tightened. Her dark eyes were the color of coal, and theirs was a blistering look. "There's blood on his hands, Jack. Nevermind the fact he drugged me with magic. Or that he sent an arrow into Lucas. That pretty much exempts him from any sympathy on our behalf, don't you think?"

"He's our uncle," Jack stressed to Connor. "Our blood."

"Who betrayed us."

Jack only shook his head again. "We take care of this like family business, no other clans involved."

The Hill of Uisneach, which rose six hundred feet above the earth, was located on a private cattle farm only open to visitors accompanied by a knowledgeable guide, though today's afternoon tour had been the last of the season. Meaning we'd have the hill to ourselves, though I hadn't yet decided if that was a good thing. Initially, I hadn't known how Seamus could perform such a ritual at a site like this, which from this height commanded views of several counties far and wide. Surely someone would see us. But Jack had explained Seamus would most certainly cloak the site with magic tonight, so that any onlookers gazing upon the hill from their window wouldn't see the slightest disturbance.

The surrounding landscapes were plunged into utter darkness, but we had the pearly light of the Blood Moon (moments away from becoming full) to guide us as we exited the SUV, every last one of us armed with an assortment of menacing weapons. Four doors slammed shut in succession, and we faced the hill before us.

I touched the pocket containing the Hallowstone to assure

myself it was there. I also had a long knife strapped to my waist much like the one Zoe carried, but I'd never used a weapon like that before, and my hope was I wouldn't have to now. Jack seemed to be of the mind he could reason with Seamus, and while I had my doubts, I hoped for his sake he was right.

When we finally reached the summit of the hill, clearing all obstructions so that we had a full view of the ritual about to take place, a terror I'd never known before struck my heart at the sight waiting for us.

43

There were torches everywhere, standing tall and ominous. They were positioned in a ring around the area, so that from above, it must've looked like a fiery eye was glaring up at the heavens. Each flame popped as it danced in the wind, its yellow center almost blinding. Seamus stood at the middle of the ring before an altar, his expression betraying nothing as we approached. He'd positioned the altar in front of what had to be the Cat Stone Zoe and Jack had mentioned. It was enormous, easily weighing more than two dozen tons I imagined.

But that wasn't what chilled me. I switched my gaze back to the sight that most struck dread in my heart: the large, burly men assembled behind Seamus. There were more than a dozen of them. They donned floor-length, black robes with hoods, hands clasped before them as they stood as still as statues. It wouldn't have been so terrifying a sight were it not for the masks. Each man wore the face of a deer skull, antlers protruding from the top like the gnarled branches of a tree in winter. The gaping eye sockets were as black as the night, making it impossible to see a flicker of life in the eyes of the men.

"The Unredeemed," Zoe whispered, her face visibly paling.

"What are they?" I asked breathlessly. I couldn't help but wonder if we'd made a mistake by not involving the other clans.

"The undead," Jack answered. "They're witches who lost themselves to dark magic. They never received a proper burial on hallowed ground, nor did they receive their last rites. So they're cursed to do the bidding of all dark magic practitioners until the end of time."

We continued approaching, entering the ring of torches before stopping a respectable distance from Seamus's altar. A yellowing human skull sat at the altar's center. Beside it, an athamé with red staining its blade and the body of a dead black bird, its frozen legs clawing at the air. Its feathers were damp, as was the wood of the altar beneath it. A fresh kill. A gust of wind blew against our faces, carrying the metallic scent of the blood to us.

My stomach flipped, and I forced my eyes away to a massive black cauldron beside the altar. A fire roared underneath it so that the turbulent water inside gurgled and spilled over, the flames hissing in response. The cauldron itself was elaborately designed with intricate drawings and gold embellishments. For a long moment, all I could do was stare—at the cauldron, that altar, those men.

Seamus was the one to break the silence. "You lads have become far more obstinate than I'd like."

"Yeah? And you've become far more murderous than we'd prefer," Connor threw back, earning a look of reproach from Jack.

"Is that the Cauldron of Rebirth?" Zoe asked, striding forward a few paces, disbelief on her face.

"One of the Four Great Treasures," Seamus said. "It was once used to resurrect fallen warriors on the battlefields of old.

Tonight, it will serve a far greater purpose in a sacrifice that will change everything for witch-kind."

Zoe tightened her fists. "The Cauldron of Rebirth was hidden away Elsewhere by The Council of Elders to ensure witches as gone in the head as you are never got their hands on it. Is that one of the reasons you slaughtered them?"

"The Council wished to reduce the Cauldron of Rebirth to no more than a relic from the past. Why should tools of such unfathomable power be kept from witch-kind? It's this senseless thinking that's forced us to live as an oppressed people for far too long. We can summon the deadliest of sea storms. We can call upon wind and fire to ravage entire villages. And yet we play the part of the hunted and we hide ourselves from our persecutors, as if our powers are something to be ashamed of, something we must apologize for."

"For our own protection," Jack said. "The mandates to practice magic in secret are meant to preserve our bloodlines."

"Those mandates stem from nothing but fear. We are the apex predator opposite the Sightless, the hunters. Why act otherwise? Why concede our power to The Black Hand, to people who have sought to exterminate us for so long?"

"Then why not try to broker peace with them?" I asked. "There have to be hunters who've grown disillusioned with The Black Hand's philosophies over time. Or what about the next generation of hunters, people our age who are born into The Black Hand and aren't sure they agree with their parents' beliefs? What if we could make change happen from within?"

"You don't think we've already attempted such a thing? Countless witches have sought to make peace with The Black Hand over the centuries, to show its members how our people could live in harmony with each other. Do you know what became of those witches? Examples were made out of them by wolves in sheep's clothing. The hunters never desired peace, but they filled our ears with honeyed words to lure us in. And then they butchered us. I was there for one such incident. I barely escaped with my life."

"You never told us about that," Jack said.

"It was long before your time, when I was a naïve youth who thought I could change the way hunters viewed us. But how can you establish peace with a people who don't even believe you're worthy of it? The Black Hand thinks us the children of their devil, sub-human and innately evil. The time has come for those beliefs, and the ones who hold them, to become extinct."

My eyes darted across Seamus's altar, jumping from object to object as he spoke. Jack had said Celeste had kept her stolen souls in a special amulet she wore around her neck. Seamus didn't wear any such necklace, but I couldn't see anything on the altar either that might serve as a vessel for a host of spirits.

"Looking for something?" Seamus asked. "You won't find them here. But I'm happy to show you where they've been kept. The moment is drawing nigh in any case." He raised his palm through the air, as if lifting an invisible object for all to see. Once his hand was above his head, he quickly closed it in a tight fist. "Behold!"

Not a second later, the ground trembled, as if we stood on the back of a giant beast beginning to stir. I lost my footing and almost toppled over, but Jack grabbed my elbow and held me firmly, and I widened my stance for better balance. Outside the ring of torches, stone structures punctured the earth from below, rising higher and higher to double, triple, quadruple our heights. Menhirs. There were at least two dozen of them. The towering giants formed a large circle around us like stone, warrior angels angled toward their prey. When the menhirs reached their full height, the ground became still once more, the only sound on the summit the snapping of the torches and the cauldron's bubbling water.

"Every time the sluagh delivered a new soul, I locked it into one of these menhirs, thereby keeping it safe until the time of the Reaping and sacrifice."

I stared at the closest menhir, trying to find my breath. My chest flared up with heat as I thought about my dad's soul being contained in a stone prison all this time. Ever since Brigid had Marked me, I hadn't felt any differently besides a deepened determination to stop Seamus, but right now, I was almost sure the wrath of the goddess was sparking in the pit of my stomach.

I fixed a heated look on Seamus, the muscles in my body taut. "We're not going to let you complete this ritual. To get to any of these souls, you're going to have to go through us first."

"I thought you might feel that way," Seamus said, completely unfazed. "Lucas? Take care of them, will you?"

And then before any of us could process his words, Lucas suddenly drew his gun, turned to Jack, and pressed the barrel against his brother's head.

44

"What the hell are you doing?" Connor exclaimed at Lucas. He started for his brother, but Lucas threw up a hand and a burst of air pummeled Connor, sending him flying back a number of yards. He landed with a hard thud that made me wince.

"Have you lost your bloody mind?" Zoe drew her own gun and pointed it at Lucas.

"Actually," said Seamus, "he has. I'm afraid Lucas isn't quite himself at the moment."

For a string of seconds, no one said anything, his words settling in. Then realization dawned on us. "The demon venom," Jack said at the same time I thought it, remembering the treated arrowhead. A chill coursed through me.

"The venom was meant to hamper his magic and keep the lot of you contained in the library, but the nature of demon venom is that so long as it's within someone's body, they're no more than a marionette under a puppet master's strings. I can give Lucas any order, and he will obey it. He need only hear my voice. Should you have miraculously found your way here, it was my final insurance against any attempts at interfering with the ritual."

"But Father Nolan gave us the antidote," I said.

"And surely he mentioned it would be days before the venom fully left Lucas's body?"

My eyes swung to Lucas as my stomach sank. I hadn't thought twice about his uncharacteristic behavior. None of us had. I'd assumed he was merely weathering the side effects of the toxin much in the way I had with Kai's blood.

Jack turned to Lucas slowly, the barrel sliding from his temple to the center of his forehead, his hands raised to show he bore no weapons. "Lucas, come on. It's me. Jack. You don't have to do this."

Lucas's face remained devoid of expression. He only stared back at Jack, gun still aimed, ready to pull the trigger if it was demanded of him. In the firelight, there was movement in his eyes. Dancing flecks of red that hadn't been there just minutes ago. The same red I had seen in the eyes of the sluagh, the Wraiths, the demon at the rugby game, and in Kai's eyes.

"There's no sense trying to reason with him," Seamus said. "You're only speaking to his shadow self."

"His shadow self?" I asked.

"Yes, we all have one, that dark aspect of ourselves we refuse to identify with, that contains all the parts of ourselves we try to suppress and hide from others. But Jack knows all about that, doesn't he?"

Connor was making his way back to the group from his fall, an incendiary look in his eyes. "What's that supposed to mean?"

"He hasn't told you?"

The flames of the torches all around us cackled, as if in mockery. Though there was a chill in the night air, their fires bathed us in warmth. My skin was flush with their heat. Grass and dry leaves rustled in the breeze, but I paid no mind to their music, too caught up with Seamus's words, too stunned by the striking resemblance they bore to something the demon at the rugby game had said to Jack. *That's it, isn't it? They don't know. You haven't told them what you've done.*

"Well," Seamus continued, "I suppose he'd prefer not to tell you, wouldn't he?"

"Prefer not to tell us what?" The *T* in the last word left Connor's mouth with a snap of his tongue like a twig cracked in two. "What is he talking about, Jack?"

"Would you care to do the honors, Jack, or should I?"

The soaring menhirs cast a patchwork of shadows across the space. One shadow split Jack into two perfect halves, one bathed in light, the other in darkness. He was still facing Lucas, but Seamus's question had leeched the color from his face, and a train of thoughts flitted across the surface of his eyes, as if he faced a firing squad and could only be absolved if he figured out the right sequence of words.

Seamus took Jack's silence as his cue and stepped around the altar, coming closer to us. "I'm afraid your brother's losing the fight to his own shadow self," he said. "More and more every day. He's put on an admirable show for you and the others. He hasn't wanted any of you to worry. But the truth is the darkness within him is rising."

"Like hell it is." Connor marched forward, drew a gun, and stuck it in his uncle's face, his anger rolling off him in waves, as if he were about to spontaneously combust. There was practically an earthquake rumbling under his skin. "Don't think I won't pull this trigger just because we're blood."

"Connor, please. I'm not the enemy here. If you don't believe me, why don't you ask Jack himself? The truth of the matter is his demon's mark allowed him three requests. The moment he exhausted all three, the cost would be the immediate collection of his debt, as opposed to having until the Old Moon of his eighteenth year to pay it."

"I know all about that," Connor snapped, "but he's only used up one wish." I saw the surprise on Jack's face, though he dared not move so long as Lucas's gun was trained on him.

Seamus let go of a long sigh. For the briefest moment, he was their uncle again, the sadness in his eyes genuine. He didn't want what he said next to be any truer than the rest of us did. "And then he used up two more in his recent quest to learn what had become of Maurice, summoning demons and asking favors of them to help solve the mystery, thus sealing his fate."

Your time's up whether you like it or not, the demon at the rugby game had said. And then Kai's words came back to me too. *The mark only functions in a certain capacity, and once you're outside of its rules...* I had assumed he'd been referring to my ineligibility to make a request, seeing as how I wasn't the mark's bearer, but Kai had been hinting to something else altogether: the fact that the mark was no longer valid. Because all of its wishes had already been used. Dread pooled in my stomach as my veins became like ice.

"Why do you think a demon would come for him in broad daylight?" Seamus asked. "It was there to bring Jack to his new home."

"No," Connor said, shaking his head, but as I studied Jack's face, I knew it to be true. It was in the resigned set of his jaw, in the guilt consuming his eyes, in the dark patches under them— the same patches that had graced my own face when I was detoxifying from Kai's blood.

"Think about it, Connor," Seamus went on. "After Maurice's death, Jack insisted you and the others return to St. Andrew's, didn't he? He wished to investigate the matter further on his own. Didn't you ever wonder why? Perhaps you thought he needed space to grieve, but it wasn't just that. More than anything, he didn't wish for any of you to know it once he started using dark magic."

They think he'll start practicing dark magic? I'd asked Zoe.

Scarlet, she'd said. *Some people believe he already does.*

But the dark circles under my eyes had faded away after a day, two at most. Jack's had never left. Which meant..."You're still practicing." His losing control when casting runes at the sacred grove of The Wise Ones, his blowing out an entire block of street lamps when separating Connor and Lucas at the inn...possibly even the way his power had cracked the walls of the library outside of Dublin. It'd had nothing to do with the approaching Old Moon. It'd been the kickback from dark magic. Indeed, Jack had only ever said that his *brothers* believed his coming deadline was the cause of the increase in his power, not that he believed it himself. I considered all the times he'd mysteriously disappeared throughout our journey too. Had he gone off to do something he didn't want any of us knowing about?

Jack's body remained still against Lucas's gun, but his eyes switched to me, and the maelstrom of emotions in them nearly left me breathless. Shame, despair...and was that fear? He worried I'd judge him, condemn him.

It's only that this whole situation shows it's easier to lose ourselves to the darker side of magic than most of us think. We want to believe ourselves immune. We want to believe we would never do wrong. But who knows what we'd be capable of if our mind was no longer our own?

Jack's own words.

He had been speaking of himself the entire time.

"The darker side of magic is unimaginably alluring," Seamus said. "Once you've had a single, addicting taste of it, it can take everything in you to break away. And so few ever succeed. Jack was only able to withstand his first encounter with it because Alison and Redmond policed his entire childhood, ensuring he never stepped onto that path. Maurice took up the role later on. But it would seem losing the old man was the final tipping point. I knew about Jack the moment the third and final entreaty was satisfied. It's all the demons of the Otherworld could talk about."

The rustling leaves were louder in my ears. I tried to ignore them again, but this time, something crawled over the toe of my shoe, forcing me to look down. It took me a moment to make out exactly what I was seeing. I blinked, furrowing my brow. Were those…? Yes, they were. Roots.

My heart sped up, and I threw a quick glance in Rory's direction. As I expected, he was directing them, sending them toward Lucas. He briefly met my eyes, and I nodded in understanding. We'd have only seconds to act once Lucas was restrained. I was the closest one to him and Jack, so I'd have to be the one to make the move. And I'd have to do so fast.

As the roots steadily made their way to where Lucas stood, keeping to the shadows, I focused on distracting Seamus. "If anyone's to blame for what happened, it's you. If it wasn't for your desire to wake the Soul-Eater, Maurice would still be alive today. Jack would've never had to do what he did to get answers."

The roots were seconds away from Lucas. My heart pounded so hard I feared someone would hear it. I tried to control the throbbing beat at my temples.

"In theory, yes," Seamus said. "But we must all take responsibility for our actions at one point or another. Jack had a choice. And this is the path he chose."

"That's all you have to say about it?" Connor asked, incensed.

The roots encircled Lucas's feet like a wide-mouthed lasso, coiling once, twice, three times. It was now or never. I looked at Rory and nodded again. I was ready. I faced back ahead, and a heartbeat later, the roots suddenly tightened like a sprung trap, squeezing Lucas's ankles together. Startled, Lucas tried to jerk away, but he easily lost his balance, and seeing my chance, I threw myself at him in a tackle.

The gun fired, loud and angry and deafening. The sound

swallowed my heart whole, but I had no time to see who, if anyone, we'd struck. Lucas and I crashed to the ground hard. I quickly clawed at his shirt as he tried to get away, forcing him back down and scrambling to straddle his back so that I could restrain his hands.

But he was stronger. He roughly turned over, throwing me off him and onto the ground, large, jagged rocks digging hard into my spine like broken pieces of glass. He came on top of me, his fingers closing in around my throat and tightening. The makeshift root bindings on his ankles hardly slowed him down at all.

His hair fell across those red-stained eyes, his cheeks smudged with earth. There was nothing but soulless fury carved into his features. It was hard to reconcile the image with that of the boy who'd performed card tricks for me, the mischief in his eyes sparkling like so many stars. I thrashed against his weight, trying to buck him off as I felt my windpipe close, but he was immovable. I clawed at his arms, pounded my fists against his elbows. The pressure from his fingers only intensified.

And then suddenly a blur struck the side of Lucas's head, the impact so hard I heard it when his teeth smacked together. Lucas slumped to the ground, unconscious. Jack stood behind him, one of the large rocks in his hand.

"Enough of this." Seamus looked to the sky, where the wind set the clouds adrift, undressing the full moon. "It's time we begin." He faced The Unredeemed, who hadn't moved a single muscle since we'd arrived. "You know what to do," he told them.

Then the men did move. They drew back the hoods of their robes and unmasked themselves. They weren't men at all. They were fearsome, devilish, monstrous things, creatures straight out of a nightmare. And they were coming right for us.

45

The Unredeemed couldn't have been more aptly named. It was as if they'd been born out of darkness, born out of the very pits of hell. Each one had the face of a goblin, with wrinkled gray skin, devilish eyes redder than blood, and a salivating mouth filled with dagger-sharp teeth.

"I thought you said they were witches," I called out to Jack in a panic.

"They are," Jack said. "Or at least they were. This is what's left of them."

Our eyes met, and the air between us was filled with so many unspoken things, not the least of which was Seamus's revelation about Jack. There were questions I needed to ask him. Why was he still practicing dark magic and to what extent? Kai had said dark magic encompassed many things: some summoned demons to do their bidding like Seamus had done, others drank demon blood as I had, and still others simply practiced forbidden spellcraft. What was Jack's poison of choice? And did he regret the decision now that he faced The Unredeemed, the very witches who'd lost themselves to dark magic, their spirits becoming these malformed creatures who knew no rest? More importantly, could he still be saved from the grips of dark magic?

My questions would have to wait. The Unredeemed were nearly upon us, forming a wall between us and Seamus as they drew weapons that made up a deadly variety: axes, scythes, and flails among them. The flails were particularly daunting, considering the spikes on each metal ball were the size of half my arm. They backed us out of the ring of torches and further still, until Seamus was several yards out of reach.

Then, without warning, one of them lunged for me, bringing its axe down in an arc so quick the wind whistled against the blade. Jack shoved me out of the way hard, barely clearing the blade himself. And with that, the battle roared to life.

Despite their husky build, The Unredeemed moved with stunning dexterity and speed. They were a blur of shadows as they rushed at us, metal clanging against metal and flesh smashing into flesh in a terrifying orchestra. I scrambled to my feet and rushed over to Lucas, slowly turning him over. His eyes were closed, and I didn't dare open them, fearing the red that might still be lurking there. Though there was no way to know for sure if he was still under Seamus's influence, I couldn't just leave him here. He'd get trampled over or crushed in the fray.

I grabbed him from under the shoulders and hauled him out of harm's way, surprised by the weight of him despite his lithe frame. My muscles strained as I dragged him step by step. I deposited him by a tree and made quick work of untying his shoelaces, which I used to restrain his hands behind his back. Hopefully, when he regained consciousness, he was our Lucas again, but I had to err on the side of caution for now.

With Lucas taken care of, I quickly surveyed the scene before me, trying to decide where I was most needed. Jack faced off with an especially large opponent, hurling orbs of striking blue light at it. At first, I thought he was employing some sort of

Mastery, but then lightning cracked powerfully overhead, a white harpoon cleaving the sky in two. He was calling upon the Quarters. He shot the lightning-filled orbs at The Unredeemed, and they exploded against the creature on impact, throwing it yards back and setting its flesh on fire. The Unredeemed let out an ear-splitting screech, the stench of burning flesh nauseating.

I assumed that would be the end of the creature. It wasn't. It roared as it righted itself, but it didn't immediately charge for Jack again. I thought perhaps it was hesitant, or that at the very least it was appraising Jack as a worthy opponent it had grossly underestimated.

I was wrong.

The Unredeemed rolled its head along its neck and rotated one shoulder after another before puffing out its chest. A moment later, a hand pressed against the skin of the creature's abdomen—from the *inside*. A second hand joined beside the first. Both pushed out further and further, stretching the skin like thinning dough until the flesh ruptured, bile spilling everywhere. From the cavity in the abdomen, a new creature crawled out, all spindly limbs and wicked eyes and hungry teeth, its gray flesh slimy. And then a second creature emerged, and a third, and a fourth. Until The Unredeemed had produced seven copies of itself in total. When the last creature crawled out, the gap in the original's chest sealed up as if the wound had never existed to begin with.

My stomach twisted itself into knots. They could multiply themselves. We'd already been outnumbered. Now we'd be even more so.

Dizzy, I checked to see how the others were holding up. Rory did his best to restrain his opponents with tree roots, but the roots could only snake across the ground so quickly, and even when they bound their targets, The Unredeemed easily broke free of their restraints. Zoe and Connor worked together to fend off half a dozen Unredeemed at once, their movements like poetry in motion. Zoe had disarmed one of the creatures of its spear, and she twirled it dangerously fast, impaling one Unredeemed after another. She tossed the spear easily to Connor, exchanging it for the dagger he threw back to her, and neither missed a step as they swung into their next attack, dodged a punch or swipe, and then went in for the kill. But just as had happened to Jack, The Unredeemed they faced only multiplied until what had begun as a ragtag assembly of creatures now quickly escalated into an army of dozens.

The only way to end this was to strike a blow at the source.

I honed in on Seamus.

He stood behind the altar, loudly chanting. The words didn't sound like Irish. It was a language far more ancient than that, something that sounded like it had been around since before the beginning of mankind. Something that sounded unfathomably evil. A demon tongue? I shuddered at the thought. Though I didn't understand what he was saying, the words pulled at my stomach, ran icy fingers down my spine.

The cauldron started to glow, the boiling water inside gurgling more violently. Slowly, a wisp of red light rose from the cauldron. Like a snake, it weaved through the air until it attached itself to one of the menhirs. Another wisp followed soon after, forming a tight thread between the cauldron and a second menhir. The same happened with a third.

It was beginning.

My heart accelerated as I removed the Hallowstone from my pocket. Gripping it tightly, I rushed headlong into the battle, my eyes focused only on Seamus as I charged through the commotion of snarling creatures, weaving through gaps like a thread in a loom, my free hand itching for the knife Zoe had given me should I need to quickly free it from its holster at my waist. When I was halfway to Seamus, I sped even faster, half carried by adrenaline alone, the only sound in my ears the pounding of my feet against the hard-packed earth. I was so close. I was almost there...

"Scarlet, watch out!"

Before I could react, a force rammed into me from the side, the impact so brutal my entire skeleton rattled within its skin. I went sailing through the air, and when I met the ground, a burst of light filled my vision as the breath flew out of my lungs in a throbbing rush. Blades of grass crunched underneath approaching footfalls as my attacker drew closer. My head was spinning, my vision nothing but black spots and wobbly landscapes. I desperately patted the ground around me for the fallen Hallowstone, ignoring the roaring pain in my ribs. *No.* Where was it?

A hand fisted my hair at the skull and roughly jerked me to my feet. I cried out in pain, but the sound died in the back of my throat when I found myself face to face with one of The Unredeemed. They were even uglier up close. This one had few teeth left in its slimy, rancid-smelling gums. The ones it did have, though dangerously sharp, were decaying and covered in plaque, gnats darting from one to the other. The Unredeemed brought its face in close to my neck, inhaling the smell of me and drawing its rough tongue along my skin. I squirmed against it, stretching my fingers for the knife at my waist.

"I'm going to swallow you bone by tasty bone," the creature snarled.

"Swallow this." I tightened my grip on the knife's hilt, yanked it free, and jammed the blade into the creature's neck.

It shrieked, flinging me to the ground. I scrabbled away, falling twice as I tried to get to my feet, ignoring the fiery sprain in my ankle. Gritting my teeth, I pushed forward. My gaze swung back and forth across the ground as I scanned the earth for a glimpse of the Hallowstone.

"No, no, no." Where had it gone? I reached out for it with my magic, but a growl from behind stopped me. I looked over my shoulder. The creature I'd stabbed had gathered its bearings and was striding my way. With no weapon at my disposal, I had no other choice but to abandon the Hallowstone for now and run toward Jack and the others, where there was safety in numbers.

Chaos met me everywhere. Moments ago, I'd had a clear opening to Seamus. Now there were dozens of Unredeemed where there hadn't been any before. They were multiplying faster than we could keep up. I spotted a dropped gun a yard away from me and snatched it up, pulling the trigger at a creature who was coming hard at Zoe. I wasn't prepared for the recoil, my arms jerking back slightly from the pressure. But once I knew what to expect, I moved my feet farther apart to ground myself and fired a volley of bullets at every Unredeemed near me, the vibration of the discharges making my bones hum, each deafening pop of gunfire pounding against my eardrums. One particular Unredeemed started racing toward me. I shot at it, dispatching one bullet after another. Its head and torso jerked back with each impact, but it continued forward nonetheless, teeth bared and vying for my flesh. That is until Connor struck it hard from the side, bringing it down.

"Bullets won't do anything," Zoe called out to me. She jumped back as an Unredeemed swiped out at her with an axe, and then she swung an axe of her own at its arm in response. The limb came clean off. "Not these at least. And cutting off a head or limb hardly fazes them. They just grow it back. Only iron to the heart can kill them. But it has to be the heart of the original."

I surveyed the growing army of Unredeemed. Every last one looked identical. "How can you tell which ones are the originals?"

"You can't," she said. She pulled a spear from the blood-soaked, limb-ridden ground and tossed it to me. "You just have to kill everything that comes your way and hope you get lucky at some point." The formerly one-armed Unredeemed, who'd already sprouted a replacement limb, came for her again, and she blocked its attack with a grunt, throwing a powerful kick against its chest.

I shifted the spear in my hands, pocketing the gun, and faced the mayhem before me. For the briefest seconds, I closed my eyes and channeled the moment when Brigid had come to me, when I'd been surrounded by my sisters. I recalled the flow of energy that had coursed through my body, the way my skin had burned under Brigid's touch. *The god-touched.* She'd chosen me. I was here for a reason. And I'd make it count.

I tightened my grip on the wooden handle of the spear and bulldozed my way into the fight. The stench of blood and sweat was everywhere, and my ankle still screamed in pain from my earlier fall, but I was operating under one unilateral focus: kill or be killed. My strategy was to attack from behind. I sank the blade of my spear into one creature's shoulder-blade. It snarled and turned toward me with an open, hungry mouth...which I filled with three bullets from my gun. It was enough to knock the creature down for a brief count.

I freed my spear and went on to the next Unredeemed. This one was fighting against Jack, whose face was covered in fresh, bleeding cuts, his hair in disarray as it fell over his eyes. I stabbed one of the creature's calves as it leaned over Jack's fallen figure. It roared and spun toward me before I could free my spear, swinging a club embedded with spikes. I almost didn't duck in time.

The club came for me again. I dropped flat to the ground to avoid getting my head bashed in. As I clambered to my feet, The Unredeemed made for a third attempt, lifting the club high above its head to smash me right where I crouched. There was no time to react. All I could do was stare as the spikes sped toward my face. I was going to die.

Except the club froze mid-attack. As did the creature wielding it.

Everything froze.

My heart galloped as I tried to make sense of what was happening. Was it Brigid's doing? But then the creature's head rolled cleanly off its shoulders and its body slumped to the ground. Jack stood behind it, my spear in his hands. He forced its point into the creature's heart. Out of breath, he took my hand and pulled me to my feet. All around us, the others were paused in varying scenes of combat, like action figures on a collector's shelf.

"I can't hold it for much longer," Jack said. "Are you okay?"

I nodded, too breathless to properly respond. Jack handed my spear back to me. Then he swiped a weapon from the ground and beheaded three more Unredeemed, his magic losing hold just as the third one's head hit the earth. The battle resumed.

I forced myself through the sea of creatures, cutting, ducking, slicing, dodging. I tried to get a visual on Seamus and the ritual, but I couldn't tell up from down or left from right. It was like being at the center of a disturbed hornet's nest, absolute anarchy surrounding me. My greatest fear became that we'd be too late, that we wouldn't stop the ritual in time.

No. We *had* to. Failure wasn't an option. *Help me, Brigid.* I summoned all my adrenaline, all my resolve, all my anger, pulling it from the pit of my stomach and pushing it through my body in a hot rush. There was something else kindling too, deep in my chest, the same sensation I'd felt when I'd told Seamus we wouldn't back down without a fight. Surely it was the goddess, stirring something up in me, empowering me with her strength. And indeed, the moment her name filled my mind, I couldn't feel the pain in my ankle anymore. The fear vanished. The exhaustion in my muscles faded. I felt as if I could take on the world.

Riding the high, I zeroed in on my next kill and sped forward, only to come up short when my wrist caught on something. Or rather something caught hold of me. An Unredeemed sneered at me cruelly, its grip like a vise on my wrist. It applied more pressure, and I cried out in pain. It could easily snap my wrist like a twig if it desired.

The Unredeemed yanked me against its chest and snarled in my face. I glared at it, baring my own teeth. Then I tipped my head back and rammed it full-force against the creature's face, ignoring the pain that blossomed throughout my skull. The creature staggered back, blood gushing from its nose, staining its filthy teeth. Before it could retaliate, I plunged the blade of the spear into its heart. It eyes sparked once. Then the life slowly drained out of them. It sagged forward and crashed to its knees, and when it did, seven other creatures instantly dropped too.

An original! Finally!

Something savage and wild in my heart made me reach down to dip two fingers in the creature's blood. I smeared it across my face on both cheeks, making parallel stripes like the war paint the first Daughter had worn. Emboldened, I went after more of the creatures, stabbing them from behind to pierce their hearts as well. Some fell without further fanfare. Others fell and brought down their replicants with them.

The others were succeeding in finishing off The Unredeemed too. Lifeless bodies were strewn around Rory, who'd come into possession of a flail and used it in close combat against two opponents. Zoe and Connor had taken out an impressive number of the creatures, their movements lightning-quick and yet so eloquent, like a dance they'd performed many times before. Connor shoved a knife into a creature's heart, and it, along with its carbon copies, slumped to the ground.

Five Unredeemed were ganging up on Jack, though. I pressed forward, swinging wildly at the creatures approaching him. I kicked at the back of one creature's knees, and the second it fell forward, I forced the spear into its back until the iron point emerged from its chest, dripping blood. I heard bodies drop to the floor a moment later. Another original.

With so many bodies fallen, I finally had a line of sight to Seamus and the ritual. My heart screeched to a violent halt. Seamus had both hands lifted to the skies. He was yelling an incantation to be heard over Jack's lightning and thunder and wind.

I raced for the altar, but before I reached the menhirs and the ring of torches, I slammed hard into an invisible wall, pain shooting down my face. I stumbled back, my breath caught in my throat.

No! Seamus had lifted a ward around his ritual. I pounded my fists against the force field, screaming. "Let my dad go!"

But Seamus was deaf to my pleas. He continued petitioning the skies as if absorbing the powers of heaven itself. I slammed my fists against the ward again and again as if one more hit might be the one to shatter Seamus's defenses. Jack was beside me a moment later, his palms against the ward as he muttered something under his breath, but not even his magic could bring down the force field.

I was so consumed by the obstacle of the ward that I didn't notice it at first when the ground began to tremble. It shook far more aggressively than it had when the menhirs had emerged from the earth. While I'd never been in an earthquake before, it was precisely how I'd imagined one to be. It was impossible to stay upright. I fell back, and Jack crashed down next to me.

"What's going on?" I asked.

Before he could respond, the earth began to tear in two, a jagged line carving down the center of the hill's summit before it split open like a hungry mouth. The gap slowly widened further and further, the ground still shuddering in spasms. The remaining Unredeemed fell into the crack, screaming all the way down as flames lashed out at them.

I started to redirect my attention to Seamus, but then I noticed the stricken look on Jack's face. "Jack, what is it?"

He met my eyes, and the terror in his gaze froze me. He only said two words. Two terrifying, horrifying words.

"They're here."

46

They were demons. Actual demons this time. The fire-and-brimstone kind.

And there were hordes of them. They crawled out from between the cracks that were quickly splitting the summit into so many fractions, like ants chaotically zigzagging out of a fallen kingdom. If The Unredeemed were the byproducts of dark magic unchecked, then these creatures were the ones who'd spun that dark magic into existence to begin with.

Their skin was an oily black, and though humanoid, they moved on all fours, spines curved against taut skin like a column of giant knuckles. Bat-like wings stretched out along their arms, the flesh so thin you could see the web of veins, and there was a hungry look in their red eyes that made my heart hiccup. They were everywhere, an infestation, and wave after wave of them kept emerging from the cracks in unending throes, as if the earth was bleeding them out.

I needed the Hallowstone!

My eyes scanned the tumultuous landscape as I broadcasted a pulse of magic to the star fragment, letting it know I was searching for it. Its consciousness burned in my chest, acknowledging the summons. Immediately, there was a tug in my stomach, and I turned in the direction it'd come from, my gaze swinging back and forth anxiously.

There!

An approaching demon had moved its leg at just the right moment, allowing me to catch a flicker of light on the ground. But as the earth we stood on continued to split and shift, the Hallowstone was racing down an incline, heading straight for a crevice that led to the unknowable abyss beneath us.

I bolted for it. Jaws snapped at me in passing, and talons clawed at my arms, drawing blood. I kept running. I dodged lunges; I disentangled myself from gangly arms. Nothing was going to stop me. Not even the earth's tremors as the summit ripped itself apart, throwing me off balance more than once. But I sprung back to my feet each time and kept going. I leapt over a crevice that was already three feet wide and growing and charged for the Hallowstone. It was nearing the jagged edge of a fissure. I had only seconds now. I pumped my legs harder and dove to the ground for it—and caught it!

"Where do you think you're going?"

I quickly shoved the Hallowstone into the front pocket of my jeans before turning around to face the hideous demon. The thunder was raging above us, and lightning filled the sky from horizon to horizon, brilliant and bright and devastating, like glorious bayonets shooting down from the heavens. The summit was a sea of black, overrun with demons.

The creature before me grabbed my arm and dragged me along, carefully navigating the gaping clefts in the earth lest we fall in to our deaths. Once we neared the ring of torches, it shoved me to the ground, where I joined Jack and the others, who were already kneeling before Seamus's ward, demons surrounding them. Lucas had finally come to and was still restrained, but the dazed look in his eyes told me he was still trying to piece together what had happened between our arrival at Uisneach and now.

Everyone else was focused on Seamus, and when I turned my attention to him, I saw why. The Reaping had begun. All of the menhirs were now attached to the cauldron by those red threads of light. From above, the ritual must've looked like a giant wheel with glowing spokes. My eyes jumped from one menhir to another, as if I could somehow determine which one contained my dad's soul.

Then my breath caught. A form made entirely of light began to slowly emerge from one of the menhirs, taking the shape of a person at rest like the recumbent effigies in the Hall of Kings. My eyes widened, and my heart throbbed. It was a soul. It slid across the thread of light leading to the cauldron, and as it did, flashes from its life played above it. There was a wedding, the birth of a child, a house fire, holidays with loved ones. Significant moments that had impacted this person's life, that had been permanently engraved on their very soul.

Seamus stood at the end of the thread of light with a scythe, symbols like Jack's demon's mark engraved on its blade. When the soul approached him and paused, he carved open its chest with the point of the scythe. He held out a hand, speaking words in that evil tongue. After a few moments, small orbs of blue light tentatively rose from the cavity like a cluster of will-o-wisps. The soul's Mastery.

The Mastery seemed to hesitate, perhaps sensing Seamus's impure intentions. It tried to dive back into the soul of its witch, but Seamus barked a command at it, and black fibers of his dark magic materialized, pulling at the Mastery until it was stretched so tight I was sure the Mastery would snap in two. The dark magic intensified, wrapping itself around the Mastery like a leech, choking it out. The Mastery dimmed, losing its strength, and then it blinked out in the dark magic's grip as it was swallowed whole and absorbed by Seamus. The first Reaping complete, the soul continued down the thread of light until it reached the cauldron, where it dissolved and poured its essence into the bubbling water.

My stomach lurched.

A second soul emerged from the next menhir. This one was clearly a young man. When flashes from his life played, I saw birthdays, rugby games and trophy ceremonies, parties with friends, a kiss with a girl on a rooftop. His life had fewer flashbacks given his age, and it wasn't long before Seamus butchered him for his Mastery. As before, the Mastery tried to resist, but the dark magic was too strong, eventually overcoming it. Afterward, the young man's soul joined the boiling stew in the cauldron meant for the Soul-Eater.

My heart pounded a wild rhythm between my ribs. A quick glance assured me the demons closest to me were preoccupied with the ritual, their beady eyes trained on Seamus like dogs watching a master's every movement. Slowly, I pulled the Hallowstone from my pocket. Once it was free, I cupped both hands over it, tucking them between my knees as I sat back on my heels.

Three more souls went through the Reaping. I wanted to watch the scenes from their life. I wanted to honor them in that way. But I needed to focus on the Hallowstone. I needed to focus on channeling Brigid's power if I wanted any chance of ensuring Seamus didn't take any more victims. I closed my eyes and allowed the sensation of the Hallowstone's pulsating life to bleed into my palms, warming them. Our magic intertwined, weaving together, drawing closer.

I reminded it of the vows I'd taken as I'd knelt before Brigid, surrounded by all the Daughters who'd ever come before me. It was my turn to continue their legacy. I'd been born for this very moment, destined to defend these witches with my life. *It's time,*

I told the Hallowstone, embracing the energy radiating from its center, my heart welling with gratitude as I opened myself to its power, to the strength with which the goddess would equip me. I'd felt a glimmer of it earlier, but now I was ready to let it completely consume me.

Something pierced the inside of my arms, as if someone were using a fountain pen to engrave words upon my skin, its tip burning. My eyes snapped open. The runes Brigid had given me —they were glowing! I rushed to cross my arms before any of the demons could notice, tightening my fingers around the Hallowstone. Heat was pouring into me from the top of my head. It raced down my veins, as hot as fire.

My body instantly felt several sizes too small for me, as if in my true state, I was taller than mountains. My pulse spiked, my adrenaline becoming a fast-paced battle march. The Hallowstone grew hotter too, so hot I was afraid I'd drop it. Brigid's power overtook every part of me: my muscles, my bones, my lungs. It hummed just under my skin, igniting the magic in every cell of who I was. It was like a phoenix awakening within my ribcage, my chest transforming into a forge to keep its fires raging. It startled me at first, but when I hesitated, the heat reduced, so I made the choice not to be afraid. Whatever this was, I would feel it fully, embrace it fully, be it fully. When I made that decision, the heat returned, sweeping over me. I was a living inferno, flames wholly engulfing me to create something new out of the ashes.

I felt more alive than I'd ever felt before.

Alive and strong. Strong enough to end this now.

Beside me, Jack tensed, which is how I knew Seamus had finally come upon Maurice's soul.

"Seamus, stop!" Jack darted to his feet in a single bound and made for the ward, but demons were upon him at once, restraining him. He struggled against them, shoving them away, but more came until he was pinned to the earth.

The images from Maurice's life played as his soul journeyed across the thread of light. Like the others, there were the typical scenes: family gatherings, a wedding, the birth of his children. There were battles from war as well, lone pilgrimages to sacred sites, and many, many interactions with the Connelly boys, Jack most especially. Jack aged right before my eyes, from a little boy hiking through the forest with his grandfather as he learned about the holy connectivity between a witch and nature to the young man he was today, poring over books with Maurice as they tried to find any method by which they could break his curse.

"I'm sorry, Jack," Seamus said. "I truly am." His face was aglow in the milky light of the moon, and though his features were tortured with regret, there was a gleam of power in his eyes. He'd already consumed so many Masteries. There was no chance he'd decline the invitation to feast on more.

As the other souls had done, Maurice's soul paused before entering the cauldron, and Seamus approached it with his scythe.

I bolted to my feet. "Stop it now!"

The demons around me stirred, as if woken from a dream. I wasn't approaching the ward, so though they drew closer, they didn't move to restrain me, wrongly assuming I was no threat. I kept my arms pressed to my sides, hiding the glowing runes as I cut a venomous look to Seamus.

Seamus had the audacity to offer a tender smile. "What I've told you about yourself has bolstered your confidence, I see. Unfortunately, it won't be enough."

"Won't it?" I twisted my arms so that the runes faced him.

He furrowed his brow, perhaps confused over what he was seeing. But a second later, his face paled. More so when he saw the Hallowstone in my hand. "Where did you get that? You haven't even fully come into your powers. Something as powerful as that would've never given itself over to an ordinary girl."

"But I'm not an ordinary girl, remember?" My smile was ice. "I'm a Daughter of Brigid." I thrust the Hallowstone into the air, high above my head, and it burst with brightness like the beacon atop a lighthouse.

Seamus's eyes went wide. "Stop her!" he roared at his underlings.

The demons hesitated for a moment, but then they came rushing for me. A blur of claws and wings and fangs was the last thing I saw before a terrible, blinding brightness exploded from my hands and cancelled out everything.

47

Just as the demons pounced upon me, the blast of white light shot out from the Hallowstone in every direction, catapulting the creatures yards away. I stood at the center of a crater, the earth charred at my feet in a perfect ring. Brigid's power was a wildfire in my veins, the runes down my arms glowing brighter than ever. I felt charged, like a walking explosive ready to detonate upon my enemies.

A new wave of demons surrounded me, studying me warily for any chinks in my newfound powers. They snarled and snapped their jaws and flapped their wings in agitation. I smiled at them, sickly sweet, my gesture dripping with venom.

"Don't just stand there, you imbeciles!" Seamus bellowed at the demons. "Take her down!"

They stormed for me in a stampede. When one demon sprang from its haunches and lunged for my face, I threw up a hand to shield myself. A force fired out from my palm, easily blasting the creature into smoke and cinders. I glanced down at my hand, which crackled with energy, strings of blue currents snapping along my skin. If banishing demons was indeed my Mastery, then Brigid's power only enhanced it.

The demons rushed me again and again and again, and each time, I flung out my hands, sending a tidal wave of magic at them that incinerated them on the spot and sent them back to where they came from. Jack and the others had recovered their weapons and were fighting against the demons to hold back as many as possible. Someone had undone Lucas's bindings, and he fought too—on our side this time. But the demons doubled their efforts, tripled them, and finally they broke through the line of defense until a chaotic horde of them barreled straight for me.

I went down, a dog pile of the Otherworld's most gruesome creatures piling on top of me. I struggled under their mass, gritting my teeth at the burning scratches against my face and arms. The weight of them pressed the air out of my lungs, driving my body further into the earth. I clutched the Hallowstone in my hand in a death grip. I focused on it, concentrating on our synchronized heartbeats, and I called forth its energy. I let the magic fill my body until I couldn't contain it anymore, and then I screamed, light emanating from my entire body as a burst of power exploded from me. It blasted the demons high into the sky, as if they'd been shot from a canon.

Seamus stared at me in shock. I came for him next. I held out my hands and sent one shock wave of magic after another against his ward. It crackled under my attacks, a spider web of red lights flickering across its domed shape, momentarily making the ward visible. But the force field quickly reinforced itself and remained in place. I sent another blast against it. And another, and another. The same thing happened.

I gnashed my teeth and fired a volley of blasts in rapid-fire succession. This time, the ward popped and snapped louder than before, its structure trembling as it sputtered like a bad signal. But as before, it steeled itself, refusing to budge. I stormed to the ward and slapped my hands against the force field, the Hallowstone trapped between one palm and the wall of energy. I sent all the magic I could harvest from the Hallowstone into the structure. The ward glowed white hot and started to tremble, but Seamus released his own dark magic, and the clouds of black rushed across the inside walls of the dome, fortifying them. The ward held its ground.

Seamus moved quickly, grabbing his scythe and using it to cut a design in the earth right beside the Cat Stone. A demon's mark. But not just any mark—the very one Jack bore on his wrist. With a flick of his hand, he set the mark ablaze. My chest bellowed with the thunder of my pounding heart as I realized with dread what he was doing.

"You can try to stop the Reaping," Seamus said, "or you can try to save Jack. You won't have time for both."

The marked ground rumbled and stirred as something beneath it came to life. Between one breath and the next, countless ebony claws pushed through the earth, rising skyward. No, not claws. Branches. More branches than I could count. The crown of the tree was massive, and I took several steps back, craning my neck as it reached higher and higher, piercing the dome of the force field. The tree was dead, a gruesome thing with twisted limbs and bark as black as night. Rivulets of dark, thick liquid trailed down its surface, reminding me of Kai's blood.

"You would do this to your own nephew?"

"You've left me no other choice. I won't be stopped, not even by a Daughter of Brigid. Jack has chosen his path. There's nothing any of us can do for him. Perhaps when the Soul-Eater grows in power, I may be able to arrange for Jack's release, but as for now, he must satisfy his debt. That's unfortunately the way of bargains with demons."

At the sight of the tree, the demons around me screamed and fled, like roaches at the break of light. Some vanished into puffs of smoke. Others shot away into the night on their wings. Others drove themselves into the ground, burrowing deep out of reach. Their fear made my heart stutter.

When the tree had stopped rising, it towered over me, the stars seeming to sit on its crown. The veins on its bark glowed red. There was a symbol carved onto the trunk's center, the twin to Jack's mark. The symbol smoldered, and as it did, a doorway in the tree formed, opening inward.

That's when the voices came. They started off as whispers on the whistling wind, a hundred haunting intonations speaking at once. But then there were cries, screams, shouts. They all came from the tree's doorway. The voices of the dead, of the damned. They were here to welcome Jack into their fold, to welcome him into the forsaken lands of the Otherworld.

I spun to Jack to warn him. He stood at a distance from me, struggling against a pack of demons that hadn't yet fled. Before I could open my mouth and call out his name, an invisible force knocked him off his feet, flipped him onto his stomach, and began to drag him toward the tree's doorway. More and more demons became aware of the unsightly thing, and just as the others had done, they bolted, wishing nothing to do with whatever darkness lurked on the other side of the tree's portal.

"Connor!" I screamed.

Connor had been chasing after a fleeing demon but came to a halt at my voice. When he saw what was happening to Jack, he sped for his brother, but before he could come within a few yards of Jack, something blew him back in a blast of air. Zoe made an attempt next. Then Rory and Lucas and Connor again. None of them could get anywhere near Jack. When I tried, the invisible force shielding Jack from us struck a blow against my stomach, and I flew into the air, landing hard on the dirt, winded.

Meanwhile, Seamus had resumed the Reaping, absorbing

two more Masteries. I noticed he'd sent Maurice's soul back into a menhir, though. Perhaps the old man's Mastery had put up too much of a fight, leaving Seamus no choice but to save it for last when he'd be far stronger. My eyes switched back and forth between Seamus and Jack, who clawed at the earth in an attempt to slow his capture. It wouldn't be long before he reached the ward, at which point Seamus's dark magic would no doubt permit Jack to slip through, and once Jack was sealed inside the dome, there'd be nothing we could do to save him.

Which is why we had to bring down the ward at all costs. It was the only way to both help Jack and stop the ritual. "The force field has to have some kind of weakness," I told Connor as he helped me to my feet, the others gathering around me.

Connor drew his gun and discharged an unending round of bullets at the ward, but they were like mere pebbles against a barricade of steel. Once we were close enough, we tried slamming weapons against its walls, and I once again delivered powerful blasts of magic into the dome. Nothing! The ward was bullet-proof in every possible way. Seamus had sealed himself in like a prisoner inside an impenetrable fortress.

Wait.

My mind snagged on that thought.

A prisoner...

My eyes shot to the nearest menhir still caging a soul. They had emerged from deep within the earth, which meant their bases were still embedded in the earth. We couldn't attack Seamus from the outside, but what if we could attack from underneath?

My pulse kicking at my throat, I instantly dropped to my knees and pressed my hands against the cool ground, keeping two fingers on the Hallowstone. Brigid's power purred at the center of my chest, amplifying my magic, the runes down my arms still glowing. I focused on that power, felt it expand until it'd gone from a steady candle flame to a burning pyre, the flames raging. Channeling the Hallowstone, channeling Brigid's strength, I pushed threads of magic past my body into the earth.

My mind became radio silent as I focused, imagining myself dissolving into the dirt beneath me, picturing the essence of my magic intertwining with the magic of the earth just as Jack had taught me at Iveagh Gardens. How many times had I combed my fingers through earth just like this when gardening back home? I had always felt a connection to nature, had always felt most at peace when working with it, even when there seemed to be no purpose to my pursuits.

Now I knew what that purpose was.

I released all of who I was into the ground until I couldn't feel my body anymore. Instead, I joined with the earth in holy communion, becoming one with it, our magic coming together. I felt the coldness of its soil, the age of its bones, the quiet hum of its existence. Its secrets danced along the edges of my soul, and I opened myself up to it, inviting it to tell me more. I pushed past its roots, its insects, its burrowing animals, going deeper still, into a profounder darkness no light had ever permeated.

I pushed further. *Thank you*, I told the earth, remembering this was a partnership, that there was a sacred balance to maintain. The earth welcomed me, guiding me to what I sought, like an elder taking the hand of a child and showing them the way.

And then at last I felt the icy base of the first menhir. I caressed it, and a pang of sadness struck me. The soul within was pleading for release. With my magic, I touched the next menhir and the next and the one after that, until I had grasped onto each one that was still occupied.

The power in my chest intensified. My arms were tingling as currents of magic coursed through them in an ecstatic surge. I kept my mind focused on the menhirs. Seamus couldn't have these souls. I wouldn't allow it. Tonight, they would know freedom and rest, and they would know it at my hands.

The power built and built until it reached a rapturous crescendo that would not be contained. Overwhelmed by the sheer magnitude of the magic, I yelled and let it rush out of me all at once. Instantly, the first menhir exploded in a powerful, deafening burst, as if by dynamite. The blast threw chunks of stone flying into the air like shrapnel on a battlefield. But it sent something else flying too—a translucent, glowing entity shot from the debris and sped into the sky like a shooting star. The soul that had been trapped within!

One after another, the menhirs exploded from the power I sent charging into the earth, releasing beautiful, radiant souls that fled into the night to seek their eternal rest, to seek whatever paradise awaited them. One of them, I prayed, would make its way to my dad's body in the hospital.

"No!" Seamus fumed over his ritual going to tatters. His lips moved quickly, magic fizzling out along the walls of the domed ward. A double ward, I realized. He must've locked himself in so that no one could forcefully remove him from the ritual area. With the force field now down, he charged for me, red-faced and wild-eyed. Before I could stand to defend myself, he tackled me down. My head smacked the ground hard, the back of my skull bursting with pain. He closed one hand around my throat, squeezing so hard I was sure he'd crush my neck.

He unsheathed a knife with his other hand, raised it over me, and brought it down in a quick, violent strike. I crossed my arms over my face to shield myself, and when I did, the knife struck an invisible barrier emanating from me. Seamus tried to bring the blade down upon me again and again, but he only kept meeting the wall of magic protecting me.

Connor ripped Seamus off me, flinging him across the summit with a blast of air. "Are you all right?" he asked.

Coughing, I scrambled back to my hands and knees and focused on the last of the occupied menhirs. Reigniting my magic, I dispatched a massive pulse of energy toward the stone giants through the earth. Not a second later, they all exploded at once in a dazzling display of brightness, the sound overpowering the very thunder in the skies. I focused on the cauldron next, remembering the souls lying in wait there. It trembled at the feel of my power, and then it too exploded, water gushing up as if from a geyser, the souls trapped within reforming and zipping away into the night. Though I couldn't return their Masteries to them, I said a blessing for them in my mind so that they could find their peace in the afterlife.

Finally, I turned toward that nightmarish tree and aimed my palms in its direction. The wind howled all around me, clawing at my hair, and lightning stabbed the fragmented ground of the summit in spears of stunning white. Jack was nearly at the tree's doorway, still struggling against the force reeling him in.

I reached down into the deepest parts of me, where my magic was an infinite well, where Brigid's power pulsated so that I felt its steady beat in every iota of my being. I threw all of it—everything I was—into the force rushing out of my palms and barreling across the distance to the tree. The magic was luminous and powerful as it left my hands. My entire body was shaking from head to toe, and blood slowly trickled from my nose. I was overexerting myself. The power was too much for my body. But I couldn't stop. Not now.

I stood my ground. I released every last bit of magic, every remaining fraction of power I could find within my bones, within my heart, within my soul. The Hallowstone was on the ground beneath my foot, and I channeled its power as well, receiving everything it could give me. Its life force intermingled with my own, becoming a hurricane inside me that only grew fiercer when combined with Brigid's strength.

I kept my eyes pinned on the tree, on the way it shuddered and began to crack under the weight of my assault. Still, the darkness on the other end resisted, fighting back. I clenched my teeth and delivered a storm of magic upon it, beating the tree with wave after wave of immeasurable energy. *I don't know who you are*, I told the darkness, *but you're not getting Jack Connelly tonight. Not on my watch. Not ever.*

The tree whined and groaned and shuddered. The darkness attempted one final defense, rising up like a ferocious tsunami. I wasn't afraid. I lashed out like a dragoness with the blinding hot fire at my fingertips. I raged against it, meeting it measure for measure with the might of a goddess radiating from my core, cowing it into submission, forcing it back, until suddenly, the darkness cracked under my unrelenting charge and the tree exploded in a sound louder than the earth ripping in two, bursting open in a surge of power so great it threw me onto my back.

I shielded my eyes against the sting of brightness. There was a rush of air, as if the tree were exhaling a breath it'd been holding for a thousand years, and riding on that gust of wind were dozens upon dozens of grayish blurs, racing out of the flaming cavity in the tree where I'd sent all my power in an endless stream.

"You fool!" Seamus cried out from a distance. "You broke open the portal! The damned are escaping!"

But my mind was elsewhere. Pocketing the Hallowstone, I raced with the others to Jack, who laid motionless two or three yards away from the smoldering carcass of the tree. Connor flipped him over. There was blood coming out of his ears, his nose, his mouth. He was paler than I'd ever seen him, those shadows under his eyes at their darkest.

"Oh, gods," Zoe said, slapping a hand over her lips.

"Jack?" I felt for a pulse at his neck. There was none. I

checked his wrist. Also nothing. Pushing my panic aside, I pressed my ear against his chest, but I couldn't detect even the faintest thump of a heartbeat, nor was his chest rising and falling the way that it should. He was so still. So devastatingly still. Like the way he'd been when the hunters had thrown him into our cell. Rory knelt on the other side of him, perhaps trying to find something in Jack to bind to, but the lines of concentration on his face told me he was coming up empty-handed.

"No," I said, my voice breaking on the word. "No, no, no. Jack, please." I pressed my palms to his chest, but they were no longer hot the way they'd been only seconds ago. They didn't crackle with magic, and the runes on my arms were already dimming. I didn't want to think of what it meant, that I'd used up all my magic to free the souls and destroy the portal to the Otherworld.

There was an immense emptiness inside me, my magic no more than wisps, like the smoke from a snuffed out candle. I was dizzy and spent, more than I'd ever been in my life. But I kept my hands on Jack's chest and reached into his soul the way I'd reached deep into the earth. I was a huntress in the vast wilderness of his being, searching for any last embers of his magic.

Come on, come on, come on...

A spark! I hurried to kindle it, gently stoking its flames before it died out.

Jack, it's me, I whispered to him. *Take my hand. It's not your time yet.*

The spark trembled in the darkness, but I cupped my hands around it and poured an overflow of love into it. Then I remembered something. At Iveagh Gardens, Jack had said I'd somehow pushed a memory to him. I pushed a flood of them to him now. I reminded him of his mother, waiting at Serenity Falls, who'd still need him in the days ahead. I reminded him of his brothers. He thought they were better off without him, without his curse hanging over their heads, but he was wrong. He was their foundation, the sun around which they orbited. I sent him the happy memories from Alison's mind too, his family celebrating Redmond's birthday in a yellow-tiled kitchen filled with love, and I sent him the images I'd seen from Maurice's life, of Jack and his grandfather growing closer over the years as they talked magic and myths.

And I sent him a memory of the two of us as well, hands clasped tight before a garden fountain, his magic awakening mine from its dormancy. He had promised to help me nurture my powers. I didn't want to do it without him.

Please come back to us, to me. We still need you, Jack...

I pushed all of this into his consciousness, holding on to every bit of faith that someone still remained on the other end to receive it. But it was as if I were only delivering missives into a great unknown, every memory seemingly swallowed by the black hole that had replaced Jack's essence. It was cold in the absence of his being, and that spark of magic started to die out. I sent the last glowing coals of my own magic to it, urging it to waken, to ignite.

Jack, please come back...

Nothing but silence answered.

But then—a cough!

My eyes flew open just as Jack coughed a second time. He rolled over onto his side and coughed more. Then his eyes focused on me.

"You called me from out of the darkness," he said, his tone filled with awe.

I threw my arms around his neck in a tight embrace. He curled an arm around me, and I closed my eyes, tears striping my face. It had gone still and quiet all around us, the torch fires now nothing but smoke, the earth no longer trembling, the menhirs and cauldron all in ruins. The tree from the Otherworld stood broken and lifeless, entities no longer escaping from its depths.

But the sky was a brilliant display of dazzling light, covered by what had to be a thousand stars. Stars that now swam in an ocean flooded with the spirits of the damned.

48

The storm cleared. The lightning, the thunder, the tumultuous winds—they were all gone. The earth shuddered once and then slowly stitched itself back together, each of us grabbing hold of each other lest we fall through one of the crevices in the ground. As the leaves in the neighboring trees settled, the broken menhir fragments and the tree from the Otherworld flickered with magic. A second later, they dissolved into nothing, leaving the summit as we'd first found it, the remaining untouched standing stones sinking back into the earth.

For a moment, all we could do was stare at each other, catching our breath, taking inventory of our injuries. We were all battered and bruised, covered in blood and dirt and painted in the ethereal glow of the full moon, its pale face like a pearl stuck in the sky.

It was Lucas who spoke first. "Well, that was a bloody nightmare." He pressed a hand to his head and grimaced, as if weathering a migraine. I was hesitant about him being unbound, but the glints of red had faded from his eyes. As far as I could tell, he was back to being the Lucas I knew. I could only hope it stayed that way.

"Hello, lads."

We all startled at the sudden intrusion of a new voice. I spun around, ready to attack, my hand flying to the pocket into which I'd tucked the Hallowstone. The person standing before us, though, wasn't the slightest bit intimidating. He also wasn't entirely corporeal.

Maurice.

I recognized him at once from the oil painting at Crowmarsh. The dignified air about him was unmistakable. He was taller than his grandsons and wiry thin, and he wore a tasteful three-piece suit. He called to mind a distinguished, early nineteenth-century gentleman. Except he was made of a translucent, blue light, his spirit shimmering brightly.

"Grandda," Jack whispered.

The lines at the corners of Maurice's eyes crinkled as he smiled at his grandson. There was so much warmth in that smile, so much love. "Thank you, Jack," the man said. "Because of you, I may now enter the rest that awaits me in the Land of Youth."

"I didn't do it on my own," Jack said. "Connor, Lucas, and Rory were with me every step of the way. And we had the help of friends both old and new." His eyes found me. In that brief moment, they weren't haunted. There was nothing but the utmost thankfulness in them. It made my heart feel double its size.

"Aye, that you did," Maurice said. As the Daughters of Brigid had done, he bowed his head to me, half in gratitude and half in respect. I didn't think I'd ever get accustomed to such shows of reverence, but I nodded back, paying my own thanks. Maurice had played such a significant role in Jack's life, and I was grateful for that.

A gentle pillar of light descended from the night skies then, soft and luminous. Maurice regarded it with a bittersweet smile. "The time has come."

"Grandda, wait. Surely there's a way for you to stay. This isn't supposed to be how it ends."

"I don't fear death, Jack. I don't wish to leave you, but we must all take this journey at some point. And though I had hoped my own journey would yet be far off, the gods have deemed it otherwise. So I step forward to make my last pilgrimage, thankful for the life I leave behind and for the love I now take with me."

"What about the curse?" Connor asked. "You were going to help Jack break it."

Maurice nodded. "It's the reason I've come to you now. I was permitted this final audience to convey a message to you and present you with a gift. The Lost Clan is the key, Jack. My last night on this earth, I discovered a story in a text I'd borrowed from The Council's vast library. It indicated that long ago, The Lost Clan had broken such a curse once. It could be no more than a myth, but I don't believe it is. As you well know, after all, there is truth in all the legends."

"But I thought no one's heard from The Lost Clan in ages," I said.

"Leading most to assume they were lost to persecution," Maurice replied. "And yet your very existence may prove otherwise."

I came up short at that. In the back of my mind, I'd always known that if Jack was right about me hailing from The Lost Clan (which seemed to be likely since I couldn't read any other clan's grimoires in the library Zoe had led us to), then it meant there was still a line of descent in existence. I'd just imagined it to be a very limited bloodline, especially since no one had come forward laying claim to The Lost Clan in decades. What other conclusion could be drawn except that my dad and I were the last ones?

"Find The Lost Clan," Maurice said. "And you will discover how it is they broke the curse." He extended a hand to Seamus's altar, and in a shimmer of magic, an ancient book appeared upon its surface. The text Maurice had spoken of. His parting gift, courtesy of the gods. "My hope is it leads you to the answers you need."

The beacon of light beside him brightened and pulsed. Maurice looked at each of his grandsons in turn for a long moment, and I could see the pain in his eyes, the regret that his time with them had been cut short. As he stood there, his spirit slowly began to dissolve in a passing breeze, carrying him into the light.

"I go now to join our kinsmen," he said, his face as radiant as the sun. "And we will prepare a place for you in the Land of Youth, my grandsons. One day, you will join us there. But not yet, lads. Not yet."

And we watched as the breeze gently caressed him and carried him upward, finally taking him home.

"What are we going to do with this one?" Zoe asked, nudging Seamus with the toe of her boot.

Seamus laid on his side, cradling an arm. It was bent at an unnatural angle, an injury most likely acquired when Connor had flung him across the summit in a blast of air. The man's face was contorted with both fury and despair. I almost felt bad for him, remembering he'd only wished to be reunited with his wife and daughter. But his glare was filled with fire, as if he wished to skewer us alive.

"You've all made a terrible mistake tonight," he pushed out

through gritted teeth. "You've let the hunters win. You've passed on great power that was ours for the taking. When witch-kind is eventually decimated by its enemies, the blood will be on your hands. You'll be—"

Zoe flicked her hand, and Seamus's lips sealed shut. He groaned against the invisible restraint, struggling to part his lips, but the magic wouldn't allow it. His glare became all the more heated.

"He needs to answer for his crimes against witch-kind," Zoe said. "In the coming days, after we've all had time to grieve our dead, each clan will designate a new Elder to sit on The Council."

"They'll condemn him to die," Jack said. "There won't even be a trial. The clans will demand his blood."

Zoe arched a perfect eyebrow. "And?"

"I'm with her on this," Connor said. "As far as I'm concerned, he's nothing to us anymore. He lost the privilege of calling us family the moment he cursed our mother. And killing Maurice in cold blood? He doesn't deserve your mercy, Jack. Why are you so bent on giving it?"

"What he did—it wasn't Seamus. Not truly. The dark magic corrupted him, but if we could help him find his way back to himself, there might still be hope. We can take him to Crowmarsh. We can place him under house arrest."

"Are you mad?" Zoe asked. "Absolutely not. I wouldn't trust the situation even if The Council were to strip his powers away. Who knows what creatures from Underneath are still bound to him, still ready to do his bidding? He deserves death for what he's done."

"And if we served him such a sentence," Jack said, "how would that make us the better witches? At what point does the bloodshed end?"

Connor dragged a hand down his face, muttering curses. "This is hardly the time to be a bloody pacifist, Jack."

"And if it was my fate you were deciding? Would you so quickly rush to the chopping block then?"

"It's not you."

"But if it was, Connor? If I were the one who'd gone dark, and you had to decide between sparing me and dragging me before a jury that would surely demand my death, would you so easily forget who I'd once been to you?"

Connor met his eyes, a fierceness in his expression. "Never," he said. "But you haven't gone dark."

Jack shook his head sadly. "I was dark the moment I was born with this mark." The words silenced us, sucking away any response in a dizzying vacuum. My eyes dropped to the brand on Jack's wrist. The identical copy Seamus had carved into the ground was no longer aflame, but it would be forever imprinted in my mind. My questions about Jack and the dark magic raced to the forefront. I wanted to know—no, I *needed* to know—what it all meant.

"What about The Citadel?" Jack asked Zoe, bringing us all back to the more urgent subject at hand. "Since it's located Elsewhere, no demons would be able to reach Seamus. And the prison's bound by magic, so his powers will be useless there, meaning we won't have to wait for a new Council to form to strip him of his magic."

Zoe scoffed and crossed her arms. Despite the cuts and bruises, not to mention the twigs and leaves in her hair, she still looked like an enemy's worst nightmare. The silver studs on her gloves glistened in the moonlight. "The Citadel won't protect him from those who want retribution. Besides, no one's sentenced there without first standing before the Elders."

"Not necessarily. You have connections in The Citadel, don't you? You could easily bring Seamus in under the radar and put him in isolation. No one would be the wiser."

"You've completely lost it, haven't you?"

Jack sighed. "Zoe, please. We're the only ones who know the sluagh were working for a Reaper, and we're the only ones who know the identity of that Reaper. For the time being, I need that information to stay with us. I need the chance to get through to Seamus before we have to lose yet another family member."

Zoe worked her jaw, clearly not a fan of the idea. She looked from Seamus to Connor and then back to Jack, a barrage of thoughts flying across her dark eyes. She tipped her chin up, her face as hard as stone. "I take him to The Citadel now. If you're able to salvage whatever humanity you think is left in him, we can discuss our next steps then. If you fail, and he has no interest in giving up dark magic, then The Citadel will be his home until the day he dies. I won't endanger any more of our kin. Family or not, right now, he's a threat to all of us, and that's the best I can do."

Jack took a long, hard look at Seamus. If the man felt any concern for his fate, he certainly didn't show it. He only glared at the ground, Zoe's magic still muzzling his lips. Finally, Jack let out a long breath and nodded. "Take him."

49

The hospital had that same antiseptic smell all hospitals did, the one I'd become overly familiar with this year. I strode through the freezing corridors flanked by the Connellys, humming vending machines on either side of me as I took stock of the ascending room numbers. Before we'd even left Uisneach, one of my dad's nurses had called me at Lucas's number, which I'd provided during my last call, with the news I'd feared I'd never hear: my dad had awakened. He had finally, finally awakened.

Halloween decorations overran the hospital, smiling paper Jack-O-Lanterns taped to the walls amidst stretchy, cotton spider webs. There were nurses everywhere. They bustled to and fro in their squeaky shoes, armed with clipboards and outfitted in colorful scrubs that featured skeletons, black cats, or ghosts. It was nearly four in the morning, but I wasn't surprised by the commotion. Hospitals knew no sleep.

"Can I help you?" a stout woman asked as we passed a nurses station. She adjusted her glasses, appraising us more thoroughly. She was probably trying to decide whether our haggard appearances were a part of our costumes for the day, a sort of zombie chic perhaps. Fortunately, I'd cleaned the blood from my face on the ride here. The others had done the same.

"That's all right," I answered. "We know the way." Had it really been just days ago that I was here? My nerves were a jumble of tangled wires as I finally came upon my dad's room. Heart pounding, I rushed the rest of the way and gently pushed open the door.

My dad was sitting up in bed, thin and weary. My lungs tightened at the sight, and I closed the distance separating us between one breath and the next. His hair and beard were a lot grayer than when I'd last seen him. There were a few more lines on his pale face as well. But he was alive. He was so blessedly alive.

"Scarlet?" His voice sounded more like a croak.

"Hey, dad," I said, my voice cracking slightly. I gripped the bed rail and swallowed the painful lump in my throat as I willed the tears in my eyes not to fall.

I'd been in this very position months ago. I hadn't been able to save that parent. But this time had been different. The powers that be were giving me a second chance with my dad, and I didn't intend on wasting it.

Colors flashed against his face and against the wall over his bed. I looked across the room. The TV was on, though muted, and a world news anchor relayed details about a bombing in what looked to be Eastern Europe. Footage played of a crumbling building and throngs of terrified people barreling for safety. Knowing my dad wasn't fond of televised news, a nurse had to have turned the TV on for him, perhaps forgetting to set the remote within his reach. I scanned the immediate area and found it on his nightstand, on the other side of a water pitcher. I quickly snatched it up and powered the broadcast off. The last thing he needed was to be barraged with more stress.

"How are you feeling?" I asked. My focus strayed to the heart monitor beside his bed with its mountain peaks in primary colors, each one measuring a different aspect of his health. Everything looked normal as far as I could tell.

He frowned. "Ask me again in a week." He looked past me. "Scarlet, why are the Connelly boys standing in the doorway?"

I turned. Sure enough, all four of them watched on from the threshold, as if they were each personally invested in my dad's recuperation. I couldn't help but smile a little, feeling just as connected to them in that moment as I had when we'd cast the circle to invoke Brigid. I returned my attention to my dad. "It's a long story," I said. "Do you remember anything about how you ended up here?"

"I've tried to, but it's all a blank. The last thing I recall is grading papers in my office. After that, my memory blacks out. How long have I been here? Do the doctors know what might've happened?"

My heart skipped a beat. I exchanged a look with Jack, who seemed just as surprised. He remembered absolutely *nothing*? Not the sluagh, not his time inside the menhir, not even the ritual and finding his way back? I supposed it wasn't exactly the worst news. Maybe it was better he didn't remember a thing.

"You haven't been here too long," I said, not wanting to agitate him. I rested a hand upon his arm. His skin was cold. I reached for the bed cover, pulling it up to his chest. "You should rest for the time being. On the phone, the nurse had said they might be able to discharge you before the week's out if you continue to do well. Then you can finally come home."

"Home," he breathed, taking my hand and squeezing it. "I think that sounds just perfect."

Days later, I found myself at Crowmarsh on an overcast

Saturday afternoon. The hospital had finally greenlighted my dad's discharge, and though I wished nothing more than to stay home with him on his first day back, today was an important day for the Connellys, and I couldn't bear to miss it.

I trekked across Crowmarsh's family cemetery, a bouquet of asphodel flowers in hand, their sweet fragrance filling every breath I inhaled. All around me, the trees sang out in a gentle clatter as the cool autumn breeze combed through their canopies, leaves of gold and orange and red fluttering everywhere. Those that already carpeted the earth crunched under my ankle boots as I furthered along.

I reached Neala and Bree's headstones and paused. We'd never know what would've happened had Seamus succeeded with the Reaping, whether or not he would've really been able to bring them back as their true selves and not as the grotesque things from Celeste's story. I decided perhaps they were glad for that, though. They were no doubt at peace in the Land of Youth, now joined by Maurice and many others.

I supposed that was the way of it for everyone. The dead at rest had already found their peace. It was the living who struggled with their absence. I wasn't so different. So preoccupied with what I'd lost back in Colorado, I'd forgotten what I'd gained here in Rosalyn Bay: a father who'd taken me in without question and who loved me. Yes, it would take time for my heart to heal, but while the ache of my mom's passing would always be with me, I knew she would want me to let go of the past, to begin a new chapter and a new life. For the first time since arriving in Ireland, I thought maybe that wasn't so impossible after all.

I pulled out two flowers from my bouquet and placed one on Neala's resting place and the second on Bree's. Then I continued on my way. I found the Connellys right where they said they'd be, waiting underneath the feathery gold leaves of a weeping willow, the tree so breathtaking in its loveliness I could hardly believe it was real at all.

"Scarlet Ibis," Lucas greeted, strolling over to me with a deck of cards in one hand and giving my hair an affectionate tug. "You look deadly, love." That usual glint of mischief had returned to his eyes—minus the red flecks thankfully. We'd all watched him closely these past days, and all signs pointed toward him finally being free and clear of the demon venom. It was an enormous relief, as was the trademark click of his playing cards as he presently sprung them from hand to hand.

I blushed at his compliment but smiled. "I hope you all haven't been waiting long." Every last one of them donned a black suit and tie, and though I'd seen them in their St. Andrew's blazers on a handful of occasions, I still couldn't get over how impossibly beautiful they were, their faces so otherworldly at times.

"You're just in time," Jack said.

I joined the rest of them before the shiny marble headstone. It was the one they'd commissioned for Maurice's resting place. It had arrived yesterday, allowing them to finally mark his grave. For the next hour, we stood vigil and memorialized Maurice Connelly, the boys sharing their fondest stories and memories of their grandfather. Though I had no anecdotes of my own, I was happy to be here with them, to be included in this intimate moment.

When Jack encouraged me to say some words, I rested the asphodel flowers upon Maurice's grave. "Though I never met Maurice when he was alive," I said, "he came to life for me whenever Jack spoke of him, if only because I could feel Jack's immense love and respect for him. I know Maurice would be proud that he lives on through his grandsons. He clearly cared for all of you very much. And if there's one thing I've learned these past months, it's that love like that never dies. We carry it with us wherever we go. Always."

After the memorial service, I drifted off with the others to give Jack space as he remained at Maurice's grave. Lucas offered to wayfare me back to Rosalyn Bay so I wouldn't have to take a taxi again, but I decided to stay a little bit longer, worried as I was for Jack. At one point, I saw him produce his new cell phone from his pocket and press it against his ear. I had no doubt he was listening to those old voicemails from Maurice, and the sight bruised my heart.

"He'll need some time." Connor sidled up beside me at the tree I was taking cover behind. He looked particularly sharp with the addition of his glasses, his blond hair smoothed back. The scowl that had so regularly adorned his face when we were first getting to know each other, however, was no longer present.

I turned toward him, smoothing out the skirt of my black dress, grateful for the warmth of my cable-knit tights. Even with a pea-coat on, November's chill still had a way of burrowing deep into my bones. "How has he been?" I asked. "Have you spoken with him about...?"

"He hasn't been very forthcoming about the dark magic, no. Jack's thinking is 'what's done is done, so what's the point in belaboring the issue?' Asking for help—especially from us—has never been his strong suit."

I wanted to remind him that Jack probably only felt he was protecting his brothers by hiding that aspect of himself, but Connor certainly already knew that. It's what Jack always did. "Do you think it's come to that? Him needing help, I mean. He isn't still practicing dark magic even now, is he?" After all, there was no reason to. Maurice's soul was at rest. Thinking on it, I briefly wondered if the Connelly patriarch knew about the lengths Jack had gone to for his sake. Most likely not. He would've made mention of it at Uisneach, would've insisted Jack break away from such darkness.

Connor pocketed his hands and cast a long look at Jack, as if he could determine the answer by doing so. He shook his head. "He says he isn't still practicing."

"But you don't believe him."

Connor frowned. I thought my question had irked him. Then I realized it was his answer that did. "I don't. The essence of his magic is still blue the way it should be. A Reaper's magic would be red, as you probably saw at Uisneach, and when you're as far gone as Seamus was, your magic will be as black as night. But something still just keeps bothering me about it all. Between you and me, I have half a mind to discover the truth for myself."

I was about to ask how, but I stopped myself. Of course. Connor's Mastery. The fact that he hadn't already used his magic on Jack was an exercise in self-control. Perhaps brotherly love too. He respected Jack too much to invade his privacy. But if doing so was the only way to help Jack, then so be it. We could only hope there wasn't a block in Jack's mind like the one that had been in Alison's, safeguarding his secrets. Although I supposed we could always fall back on another transference spell, provided there was a way to actually pick the memories we landed in.

"Let me know what you find out," I said. The guilt in going behind Jack's back was overwhelming, as was the fear of what we'd learn. But I'd seen what dark magic could do to a person, how it'd turned Seamus against his own blood. I didn't want Jack to lose himself to that kind of darkness.

He nodded once. "I will."

"On that note, is everything still all right as far as Seamus being contained in The Citadel?"

"Think of it as the Alcatraz of the magical world, except no one's ever escaped. Trust me, he's not going anywhere any time soon. And as far as those who were lost over the course of this ordeal, the clans still believe the sluagh were acting of their own volition. Seamus only got so far as telling The Council alone his lie about the hunters being involved."

My shoulders relaxed. Ever since Samhain, my nights had been restless, my mind plagued with nightmares of Seamus stealing the souls of people I loved and performing the Reaping once again with me being powerless to stop it. Knowing he didn't have the slightest chance of escaping The Citadel eased a great deal of anxiety. And knowing Jack didn't have to worry about the clans coming for his uncle lifted a weight as well, even if I was still conflicted over Seamus's temporary reprieve.

"What about your mom? Has there been any progress?" Alison Connelly still hadn't awoken from her mysterious, magical sleep. Stranger still, she'd aged considerably, so that a complete stranger would've assumed she was an elderly woman in her final years.

Connor exhaled a long breath. "Her state must somehow be related to the curse, or a side effect of coming out of it against the original caster's wishes, but I don't know where to begin in undoing her condition. We recovered The Book of Fates from Seamus, but I haven't found anything in there that might help."

A breeze passed and more autumn leaves showered down upon us. I plucked one from my shoulder, pinching its stem and spinning it back and forth as I thought about Alison surrounded by those Wraiths. I could only hope they didn't continue to haunt her as she slept.

"How's your father, by the way? He still doesn't remember anything?"

My stomach sank slightly. "I don't know what to do. Should I tell him the truth? Not just about the Reaping but about us being witches as well?"

"I'm not sure," Connor said. "Truthfully, it may be best to wait for the time being and give him a chance to gather his bearings. But we'll figure it out in time."

We. Because I was no longer apart from them, a stranger on the outside looking in. We were in this together. They were my friends, and I was theirs.

50

"There's still so much I have to learn about magic."

It had been a week since Maurice Connelly's memorial service, and Jack and I stood at the top of the lighthouse where we'd recovered the Hallowstone, our cheeks reddening against the biting winds. Incredibly, people were surfing in spite of the chill, Liam among them. I watched him ride a colossal wave and couldn't help but smile a little.

I'd returned to St. Andrew's earlier this week, though not with my dad unfortunately, who would be out for the rest of the term. And though Liam and I hadn't known each other very long, he'd once again been so kind and thoughtful, asking if I was okay, if there was anything my dad needed, and to let him know if I ever wanted to take my mind off the matter.

"I could teach you to surf," he'd offered.

I'd laughed softly. "How about I just cheer you on from the sidelines?" Not for the first time, I'd fought the urge to divulge everything to him about what I'd been through with the Connellys, feeling like I might burst at the seams if I kept the secrets any longer. I hadn't told Natalie either, despite the fact I had a new phone now and made it a point to never miss our catch-up dates.

I wasn't sure what held me back. Maybe I was still processing it all. How exactly did you tell your friends that a Celtic goddess had selected you to wage war against a wayward witch and his merry band of demons? I ran my fingers down the inside of one arm, missing the glow of Brigid's runes, though I could still feel their energy pulsing under my skin. For the time being, the Hallowstone was at Crowmarsh, where I thought it'd be safer among the boys' grimoires and other magical objects.

"You'll learn everything you need to know in time," Jack assured me. "Taking it slowly day by day like we've been doing is the best course of action. That way, you don't overexert yourself."

We were still working on my ability to call upon the four Quarters. Without holding the Hallowstone or channeling Jack, it didn't come as quickly or as easily to me yet as it did for the boys, but I was making progress. Somewhat. "Have you been able to learn anything about The Lost Clan from the book Maurice gave you?"

Jack stared at the spread of ocean, its choppy waters as gray as steel. In a rare cameo, the setting sun had broken free of the clouds that normally cloaked it, and the sky glowed softly like a paper lantern. The shadows from Jack's lashes striped his cheeks, accenting the patches still under his eyes. They'd faded in intensity these past days, leading me to hope it meant he'd put the dark magic behind him, but there was obviously no way to know for sure.

"Unfortunately not," he said, "nor does the story he referred to shed very much light on the matter. I may have to go Elsewhere to study the books in The Council's library for myself. There have to be clues somewhere. Of course, at the moment, we have a more pressing issue."

I sighed, understanding him immediately. "The broken portal." The one I'd blasted open, allowing the Otherworld's damned to escape. It was another reason why I urgently wanted to master my magic. I clearly needed to learn how to control it.

"Our new guests haven't made themselves known yet, but I can feel their presence almost everywhere I go in town. The people here aren't safe until we send all those spirits back to where they came from."

"Wonderful," I said. It wasn't exactly the first impression I'd wanted to make on the town.

"You can't blame yourself," Jack said. "You didn't know the consequences. None of us did. But what you did, the power you exuded…it was incredible. In fact, I don't know that I've properly thanked you yet."

A wave crashed against the cliffs along the coast, seagulls gliding just above the white foam. The structure of the lighthouse moaned and creaked against the wind, and I gripped the observation deck's railing tighter, praying it'd stay standing the way Father Nolan had said it would. "Of course you have," I said. "What more could you possibly need to thank me for?"

The edge of his mouth quirked up in a rare, brief smile. "For saving my life for starters? And not even for the first time. Or the second. You've put me to massive shame, you know."

I nudged him with a smile of my own. "I'm sure you'll survive," I teased.

Amusement glimmered in his eyes, but it faded almost as quickly as it'd come, his expression growing serious. "In all truth, we couldn't have done any of this without you, Scarlet."

I'd heard my name in his mouth plenty of times since this whole journey had begun, but this time, there was something about the way he said it, something about the gentleness of his tone and the cadence of his accent, that made me shiver. We were standing so close, only inches apart, our breaths leaving us in soft plumes of white. In the distance, the bells on the fishing boats sang and the seabirds called out to each other in a rise and fall that seemed to match the way the ocean tide rushed forward only to retreat.

"You were the only one who could've stopped the Reaping," he continued softly. "By means I could've never imagined, you ultimately did lead the way for us, just as it'd been predicted you would."

A gust of wind blew a strand of hair across my face. Without hesitation, Jack reached out and tenderly tucked it behind my ear, his fingers finding their way back to the scar on my cheek from Mary-Anne's blade. It almost matched the one on the inside of my palm from the Hallowstone ritual. My battle scars, I supposed.

Where his fingertips touched my skin, it felt like points of fire on my face, even more so as he cupped my face, smoothing his thumb back and forth across my cheekbone as if he wished to erase my scar. Then his other hand joined the first, cradling my other cheekbone, and my pulse thudded against my neck in a quick staccato.

A moment later, he leaned in and pressed a soft, lingering kiss to the top of my head, like a pilgrim kissing the marbled feet of a saint in a most holy temple. I could've had a fever and still my skin wouldn't have been as flushed as it was in that moment. I closed my eyes, savoring his closeness, feeling as if I might altogether dissolve.

When he pulled back just slightly, he smiled softly at me in a way that was starting to become familiar. Without thinking, I closed the remaining distance between us, looping my arms around his middle and pressing the side of my face against his solid chest. Almost immediately, his arms closed in around me, and I relaxed against him, wanting to melt into him. I breathed him in and was reminded of ancient trees and timeless magic.

"Could you have ever imagined," he asked, tightening his arms around me, "what you'd eventually learn about yourself once you arrived in Ireland?"

"Not in a million years," I answered as I looked out at the ocean. "Sometimes, when I look in the mirror, I realize I truly don't know who or what I really am."

"I do," he said softly, speaking into my hair in a way that made my stomach pull. "You're a warrior, Scarlet. A fearless, strong, and tenacious warrior. And on the days when you doubt it, just come to me, be it day or night. And I'll be here to remind you of exactly who you are."

We spent the rest of the afternoon perched atop the lighthouse, watching the tides and the miniature townspeople below until the setting sun finally pulled a swath of brilliant colors across the sky, setting the ocean on fire so that it blazed in beautiful shades of orange, red, and gold.

The following afternoon, after running errands in town, I found the day's paper on the frayed welcome mat of my dad's house, beads of rainwater clinging to its plastic sleeve. I grabbed it and pushed through the front door to the warmth inside, depositing the paper onto a growing pile of its siblings, all left unopened by my dad. I had to pause a moment to let my eyes adjust to the darkness inside. It had been like this since my dad's return, all the blinds on every window drawn tight, reducing the house to nothing more than a shadowy cave. Bright lights exacerbated the migraines from which he'd begun to suffer.

I set the tote bag of groceries I'd purchased in town on the kitchen counter, wrinkling my nose against the stale air. Hadn't I left the windows open before leaving? I opened a few now and then followed the sounds of the TV into the living room, where I found my dad seated before another relay of news. Footage of a mudslide and shelters overflowing with misplaced people filled the screen.

"Dad?" He made no response, so I slowly moved around the recliner. "Dad?"

He blinked a few times before looking up at me, as if I'd startled him out of a nap. His face was even more aged than it'd been in the hospital. I tried to tell myself it was only because he hadn't shaved once since being discharged, that the unkempt hair made him seem more worn down than he actually was.

"Dad, hey. Are you all right?"

"What?"

"Are you all right?"

He blinked again, looking around the living room to orient himself as the fog from his nap gradually faded. I reached for the remote where it sat beside his untouched breakfast: a cup of tea I'd brewed for him now gone cold and two slices of toast spread with his favorite apricot jam. I longed for the day when he'd regain his appetite. It would help to fill out his gaunt face.

"Are you going somewhere?"

"I just came back actually," I said, powering off the news. *I've been gone for hours*, I wanted to add. That, and: *What's going on with you? Where does your mind wander to half the time? Talk to me so I can help you.*

He still insisted he didn't remember a thing about his ordeal, but sometimes I wondered if he was really telling the truth. Did he recall the sluagh after all? Was his sanity slowly fragmenting into pieces because he was so certain he was going mad? Did he lie about what he remembered for fear those he confided in would think him mentally unsound?

Time and again, I wanted to broach the subject. This was supposed to be a fresh start for us, an opportunity for us to move forward and build a real relationship. I'd spoken about it with

Jack numerous times, but he always assured me my dad would return to his normal self once he'd had a chance to fully recuperate.

My dad heaved himself to his feet, the recliner groaning as he rose. He adjusted the folds of his robe, his go-to outerwear since his discharge. He'd stay in his pajamas from morning to night, never leaving the house. He shuffled past me in his slippers. "I think I'm going to lie down on my bed for a bit for a better rest. Will you be okay?"

I forced a smile. "Of course. I'll be fine. When you wake up, I'll make a fresh pot of tea." Though I didn't know why I bothered. I already knew he wouldn't touch it.

He slowly made his way to his room, and I followed him from a short distance, wanting to ensure he truly was all right. On the back of his bedroom door, I saw his reflection in the mirror hung there, and the shadows and lines across his lean face crushed my heart.

Dad?" I croaked. He paused, his hand on the doorknob. "Are you sure you're okay?"

I wasn't sure if he'd heard the question at first, but then slowly, very slowly, his features relaxed into as much of a tired smile as he was able to give. He looked at me through the mirror. "Of course. I just need some rest, that's all." With that, he disappeared into the room, clicking the door shut behind him so that I was alone in the hallway with only my reflection for company.

And I saw the shock on my face, saw the way I staggered back a few steps. My heart missed a beat, and all over, my body tensed muscle by muscle.

Because I was almost certain I'd seen something in my dad's eyes for the briefest moment, for a fraction of a second. There and gone again within the space between heartbeats, but there in his eyes nonetheless, something I couldn't possibly deny.

Something like a glimmer of red.

ABOUT THE AUTHOR

Lily Velez has been writing stories since she was six years old. A graduate of Rollins College and a Florida native, when she's not reading or writing, she spends most of her days wrangling up her pit bulls Noah and Luna, planning exciting travel adventures, and nursing her addiction to cheese.

You can learn more about her books and access exclusive content at www.lilyvelezbooks.com.

CPSIA information can be obtained
at www.ICGtesting.com
Printed in the USA
LVHW011453050521
686579LV00001B/85